Barbara Taylor Bradford

The Wonder of It All

HarperCollins*Publishers*

HarperCollins*Publishers* Ltd
1 London Bridge Street,
London SE1 9GF
www.harpercollins.co.uk

HarperCollins*Publishers*
Macken House, 39/40 Mayor Street Upper
Dublin 1, DO1 C9W8

First published by HarperCollins*Publishers* 2023
1

A catalogue record for this book is available from the British Library

ISBN: 978-0-00-824258-9 (HB)
ISBN: 978-0-00-824259-6 (TPB, Export, Airside, IE-only)

Set in Sabon LT Std by Palimpsest Book Production Limited, Falkirk,
Stirlingshire

Printed and bound in the UK using 100% Renewable Electricity
by CPI Group (UK) Ltd

This book is dedicated to my dear friends
Geoffrey Bradfield, Vicki Downey
and Connie and Randy Jones
with my love

CONTENTS

THE
FALCONERS

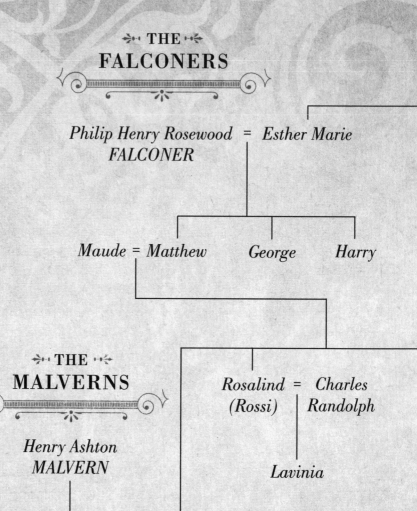

Philip Henry Rosewood = Esther Marie
FALCONER

Maude = Matthew   George   Harry

THE
MALVERNS

Rosalind = Charles
(Rossi)   Randolph

Henry Ashton
MALVERN

Lavinia

Alexis Helen = James Lionel ≠ Georgiana
MALVERN   FALCONER   WARD
d. 1900

Lionel (Leonie)
Georgiana
WARD

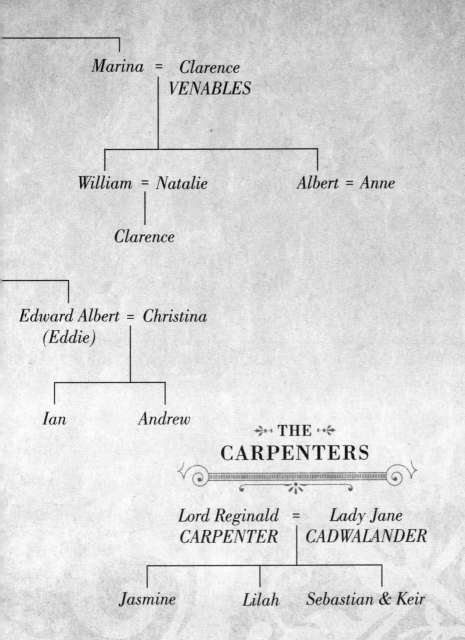

Marina = Clarence
VENABLES

William = Natalie   Albert = Anne

Clarence

Edward Albert = Christina
(Eddie)

Ian   Andrew

❧ THE ❧
CARPENTERS

Lord Reginald = Lady Jane
CARPENTER | CADWALANDER

Jasmine   Lilah   Sebastian & Keir

PART ONE

The Battle of the Somme

Picardy, France

June–July 1916

ONE

In August of 1914, when Germany declared war on France, Britain came to the aid of its ally and declared war on Germany.

At that time, David Lloyd George, the British Chancellor of the Exchequer and later Prime Minister, said, 'I felt like a man standing on a planet that had been suddenly wrenched from its orbit by a demonic hand and that I was spinning wildly into the unknown.' He was right. The storm of the Great War would be violent, merciless and destructive beyond measure.

James Falconer was in the Fourth Army, and proud of it. Tonight, 30 June 1916, he was sitting in a corner of his trench, thinking. His seat was a crate full of Fray Bentos tins of corned beef, and he smiled to himself at the very idea of this. But you made the best of it in the trenches. He knew that.

He glanced up at the sky. It was ink black, littered with stars, and there was a full moon. A beautiful night in an awful world, and eerily quiet. No sounds of bombs exploding, or guns being fired. Odd, he now thought, and stood up.

At this moment, two of his officers, Lieutenant Stead and Captain Lister, came back down the ladder and walked along their trench towards him.

'What's it like out there?' Major James Falconer asked as the two men came to a standstill in front of him and saluted.

'All quiet on the Western front, sir,' Stead said.

'Quiet as a mouse,' Lister added.

'Some *mice* indeed,' James shot back. 'I get suspicious when there are no sounds, no noises. Anyway, did you get it done?'

'We did,' Stead answered. '*Perfectly.*'

'How did you manage that?' James asked, looking pleased.

'Very carefully.' Lister grinned. 'We cut the barbed-wire fence attached to the iron stakes at one end, using our best wire cutters. Then we took a piece of chain and slotted it through parts of the freed barbed wire. Together we then pulled the chain until we had made a big enough gap to let ten soldiers through at once. Best we could do, Major.'

'You did well. Now we're all set for tomorrow morning.'

'Zero hour,' Lister murmured, and added, 'I'll be back in a minute.' He hurried off and turned left, going down another trench amongst this maze of connecting trenches. These housed more soldiers, were used as kitchens, latrines, and for checking any minor wounds and blisters on the feet. Marching in heavy boots caused problems for Falconer's lads. He sighed under his breath at the thought of the weight his soldiers had to carry when they went out to fight the enemy. Not only a large bag over one shoulder, but a water bottle, a Lee-Enfield rifle, a haversack, plus ammunition. About sixty pounds altogether. No easy feat, but they did it well and with stoicism, and fought with precision.

Stead, leaning against the side of the trench, cleared his throat, and said, 'I'll be glad when tomorrow comes and we start fighting. Get it over with, sir.'

James nodded. 'Not so sure it will be *over* quite so quickly, Lieutenant.'

Jack grimaced. 'I know.' He fell silent, then took out a packet of cigarettes and offered one to Falconer.

'Thanks, but not right now, Stead.'

A silence fell between them, and James studied the lieutenant's uniform. Comfortable to wear, and the khaki wool was ideal camouflage in the field. The four pockets on the tunic held lots of personal items, plus a soldier's pay book, and an inside pocket at the end of the tunic contained a first-aid kit.

We've got the best designed uniforms in the world, he decided, believing his own tailored khaki jacket, double-breasted, riding breeches and polished brown boots to be elegant as well as practical.

He also carried a large bag, a water bottle and a baton. His Webley revolver, the Mk VI, was in a holster on his left hip. This was a standard side arm for British troops. His rank insignia of a major was on each sleeve, and also on his steel Brodie helmet.

The sudden return of Captain Lister carrying a brown basket brought James out of his reverie. 'What's in that basket?' he asked, his surprise apparent.

'Some bread and cheese, sir, and sausage, brought up from the village by one of the women. A treat for us all. Sergeant Cox just handed it to me. She was still there, explaining what they were.'

James nodded, a smile touching his mouth. 'How very nice those village women have been to us all these weeks. I hope you thanked her, showed your gratitude on our behalf.'

'I did, Major, and in *French*,' Lister answered.

Grinning, Jack Stead murmured, 'Boasting again, Captain!'

Ignoring this comment, made in jest, Lister took the cotton

cloth off the top of the basket and showed the food to them. 'Plenty for the other lads, you know. Let's dig up a few.'

As far as James Falconer was concerned, the British Expeditionary Force, as it was in 1916, was the most remarkable military formation ever created. Especially the Fourth and Third Armies, which had already taken the field here.

When the Fourth Army had moved up from Amiens, they occupied both sides of the River Somme. A large piece of flat land on the right side of the river, an enormous field, in fact, became home to a big part of the British Army. They instantly made it their own territory and, once ensconced, James had organized the task of digging the trenches.

The Royal Engineers and the Territorials, plus seasoned Regulars, helped to build the intricate network where the soldiers lived, rested, ate, slept, and fought.

On the Somme, the trenches were well made. Food was sent up from the nearby villages; the chaplain was there to comfort those in need, and military doctors were at the ready for the wounded. And there was a great deal of camaraderie between the Tommies and their officers.

The French troops were living in their trenches nearby. The Germans, the enemy, had three lines of defence opposite the British.

By the beginning of the month, James Falconer and the other officers knew that the great attack was coming. Plans were being made; messages were coming in from General Haig, and the infantry began to drill incessantly. For the men, exhausted and ground down by over two years of war, single combat had ceased to be an option. There were only three sorts of encounter on the field of the Somme: artillery versus artillery, artillery versus infantry, and infantry versus infantry.

When he had first joined up, James had been swiftly spotted by his superiors as a leader – an intelligent, efficient and educated man. Officer material, in fact.

James became an extraordinary soldier and led his men well. He cared about them, just as they admired and cared about him and his welfare.

Deep down, James did not care whether he lived or died.

At 7.30 a.m. on the morning of 1 July 1916, Major James Falconer went up the ladder and out of his trench, accompanied by Lieutenant Jack Stead and Captain Allan Lister. These two seasoned soldiers were always close by, ready to help him in any way they could, and had been with him since 1914.

James was taken aback as he walked over to the barbed-wire fence. There were already thousands of British troops massed together, leaning forward slightly, as they all did when heading into battle. With bayonets fixed on their rifles.

His comrades were equally surprised. James reminded them that, on General Haig's advice, one hundred thousand Tommies had been assigned to Picardy, Amiens, Champagne, and the areas beyond. Many were billeted in the local villages, looked after by French civilians.

Falconer took a deep breath, then went through the barbed-wire fence they had cut open earlier, followed by the lieutenant and captain. Immediately behind them flowed the battalions in the division.

Hundreds and hundreds plunged into the fighting with their major at the head. All around James and his men, the new Lewis machine guns ratter-tattered incessantly. Cannon boomed. Tanks rolled. The air was thick with smoke from the smoke bombs thrown by the Royal Engineers into no-man's land to screen the soldiers now entering the area. The smell of cordite, blood and human waste floated around them. But all were unaware, determined as they were to win. Defeat was not a word in their vocabulary.

Many of the men were killed instantly. Two hours into the battle, James was hit in both legs by machine-gun fire. He fell, still clutching his baton. He felt the bullets hit him and the pain was intense, unbearable. He wanted to touch his legs but couldn't sit up. He groaned, and at that moment he knew he was going to die. What a way to go, he thought . . . on a foreign field because of a useless war. He closed his eyes as a wave of agony gripped him.

Half an hour later, it was Lieutenant Stead who found him and pulled him as far away from the fighting as he could. James was unconscious, his skin clammy. The lieutenant felt for a pulse and was relieved that the major had one, weak as it was. A few seconds later, Captain Allan Lister was on the scene to assist him, along with two stretcher-bearers and a stretcher.

Together, dodging through the crowds of fighting soldiers, they carried James to the Casualty Clearing Station, a large medical tent. A team of army doctors took over at once. They could give no reassurance to the lieutenant and the captain that their major would live, despite their efforts.

James's injuries were considerable. Assessed by the doctors as at risk of dying from blood loss or losing both his legs unless he was lucky, he was sent immediately to a British military field hospital in northern Picardy. After coming to, but delirious with pain, he knew little of the waiting, or the ambulance that transported him, images of the past haunting him: memories of his parents, and his beloved late wife, Alexis, playing in his mind.

James had joined the Army for two reasons: genuine love of country and king, and an enormous sorrow. Alexis had suffered several miscarriages, and had died in childbirth sixteen years earlier. The baby, a son, had also died.

At the field hospital they removed some of the bullets, before they decided that Major Falconer should be taken by a British military medical ship across the English Channel to Southampton. From there he was driven by ambulance straight to another military hospital in London for further operations on his legs. Drifting in and out of consciousness, James thought of his men, so many left dead on the field of the Somme. They had fallen in their hundreds around him, many killed instantly, but others enduring horrific wounds, trapped on the field or in no-man's land.

The moment the declaration of war was announced, James Lionel Falconer had dashed to enlist in the Army, along with many of the men who worked for him. So did thousands of other men across England, men of all ages and from all walks of life.

It seemed to James that it was an unheard of, even mystical, rush of eager patriotism that had never happened before.

Groups of men, who worked together, calling themselves 'pals', joined up and added the word 'Pals' to the names of their regiments. For example, there were the 1st Barnsley Pals (13th York and Lancaster, 31st Division) and the 10th West Yorks (Pals), which Falconer joined.

He had joined up despite being older than many, in his forties. He had been quickly promoted and, after two years of hard fighting in France, he had become a major, leading his own battalion by 1916. Now he wondered, as he lay awake sweating with the pain during the night, what had become of it, who was left to lead it.

James was moved as quickly as possible so that his wounds did not fester. Once he was settled in the London hospital, surgeons removed more of the many bullets and also the shrapnel, remnants of the bullets, embedded in his legs.

James endured the tricky operations as best as he could, always cooperating with the medical teams, thankful for their aid. But it was a strain and a huge trial for him; the pain was horrific and he knew that he might have to have a leg, or even both legs, amputated, given that the wounds were so bad. The thought that he might never ever walk again remained in the forefront of his brain. His sleep was restless from worry and the terrible memories of the war, nightmares returning night after night to haunt him.

What would his future hold now?

The other thing that his mind returned to again and again was a young woman.

His daughter.

PART TWO

Finding
Sanctuary

Kent, England

June 1917

Two

One year later, on a June afternoon in 1917, James was sitting in the garden of a military hospital in Kent, enjoying the sunshine and the rustling of the trees under a faint breeze. He was alone in the garden and, as he glanced around, he focused on the pastoral loveliness. Nowhere else like this in the whole world . . . only a garden like this in *England*. Beautiful, tranquil, peaceful, and so reassuring. *Home. His homeland*.

A few lines from a poem ran through his active mind.

If I should die, think only this of me:
That there's some corner of a foreign field
That is for ever England. There shall be
In that rich earth a richer dust concealed;
A dust whom England bore, shaped, made aware
Gave, once, her flowers to love, her ways to roam,
A body of England's, breathing English air,
Washed by the rivers, blest by suns of home.

The rest of the poem slipped away. He could not remember it exactly. Rupert Brooke got it right, James thought. What a great poet he was.

It had been many months of pain and waiting for small improvements, but he was now able to get around on a pair of crutches. And he was positive his legs would not be amputated, and that eventually he would walk normally.

The doctors had explained that he was a good healer, and he believed them. A little bit of the wear and tear of a bloody and violent war had dissipated, and he felt better as each day passed. He found it hard to believe he was now forty-seven years old.

He had been moved to a military recuperation hospital in Kent, a county he knew and loved, despite its bittersweet memories of the time he'd spent there with Alexis.

The comfort of the hospital, the constant care of the skilled doctors, and the kindness of the lovely English nurses had worked wonders for him. He felt safe at last in the Sanctuary, as someone had once called it. The name was apt, and it had stuck.

A sudden flurry of noise interrupted the quietness. Nurse Jackson came hurrying out, smiling as she almost ran towards him down the path.

James sat up straighter in the wheelchair. Before he could get a word out, she told him he had a visitor. 'A lady, Major Falconer. A Mrs Ward. Should I bring her out to the garden?'

Thunderstruck though he was, James managed to say she should bring her out, and sat back in the wheelchair, staring after Nurse Jackson as she hurried away.

Unexpectedly, a small rush of pleasure trickled through him. Georgiana Ward. After all this time. She had been very special to him years ago. And she was also the mother of his only child. At the reminder of Leonie and his neglect of her, James shrivelled inside and pushed that thought away.

Then there she was, Mrs Ward, walking down the path, accompanied by Nurse Jackson, and looking as beautiful as ever. The nurse pulled over a chair for his visitor, and promptly left, a smile on her face.

They sat staring at each other, neither of them speaking for a moment. Falconer was struck afresh by her beauty, which hadn't changed, despite the fact she was ten years older than him. The raven-black hair contained threads of silver now, but was as luxuriant and stylishly coiffed as ever, the deep blue eyes, sparkling and full of life and intelligence. He suddenly remembered their first real encounter. He had been seventeen, and she twenty-seven. Bewitched: that is what he had been then, and what he was again at this moment.

For her part, Georgiana Ward was thinking how weary and tired James looked. Always tall and slim, he seemed thinner in his pyjamas and dressing gown; gaunt, even. The fair hair of his youth was tinged with grey, but those piercingly blue eyes were the same. And focused on her now.

She spoke first. 'Hello, James. I've worried about you a lot over the past few years, when you were fighting in France. So I struck up a friendship with your sister, Rossi, and was able to keep track of you, especially once you were wounded. I needed to know you were still alive.'

In an odd way, it pleased him that she had been worried about him. He was surprised about this admission on her part. They hadn't seen each other for many years and he knew she would lay the blame for that with him. Which was only right.

He said now, with a wry smile, 'I suppose you went to her shop in Malvern Arcade and bought a shawl or two . . .' He suddenly grinned. 'That must be how you talked to Rossi.'

Mrs Ward nodded. 'You're correct, James. I've got quite a few, in fact.' She shrugged. 'They make great Christmas gifts or birthday presents. And it was worth it for peace of mind.'

'It was kind of you to be concerned about me, Georgiana. Thank you.'

'But I care about you!' she exclaimed, and could have bitten off her tongue for blurting this out. She felt herself blushing.

He stared at her, his chest suddenly tight, and he felt a desire to hold her in his arms. But he couldn't get out of the wheelchair without help. Damn and blast, he thought, and cleared his throat.

When Georgiana regained her composure, she looked at him intently, and said, 'There has always been this bond between us, James, since the first time we met. I often think how amazing it was that we just . . . well, flew at each other, fell into each other's arms.'

James nodded. 'And in a raging storm, at that.' He reached for her hand and held it in his, tightly, as if never to let it go. 'When I was celebrating my twenty-first birthday, you asked me to come to Ascot. You said you had something important to discuss. And I met my daughter Leonie. Do you remember that day?'

'Of course, I do,' she replied, her violet-blue eyes focused on his. 'Why would you doubt that?'

'Because that day you said you were part of my past, not my future . . . do you recall that?'

She merely nodded, continuing to stand in front of him.

He said, 'I have done a lot of thinking over the past year. I've changed. Leonie has been on my mind. I want to know if you are only part of my past, or perhaps you could both be part of my future? What do *you* think? Would she like to meet me?'

She looked away across the gardens, only saying, 'Let us see what happens between us, when you are better. I think it would be lovely if we could resume some kind of friendship.'

He looked at her. She was wearing a deep-blue dress that brought out the colour of her eyes. 'Sapphires!' he said. 'That's what your eyes always remind me of.'

She smiled. 'And I . . .' She broke off as Nurse Jackson came hurrying towards them, carrying a tray of tea and sandwiches.

* * *

The intensity between them was broken by the arrival of the nurse. Instead, they talked about James's time in the Army, the horrifying news from Europe and the entry of the Americans into the war. Neither wanted to break their fragile, newly restored friendship by discussing Leonie too much. But later that afternoon, just before Georgiana left the hospital, she decided to plunge in and ask James a critical question.

Looking across at him, she said, 'I have a suggestion to make, James. It occurs to me that when you finally leave here, you will still need looking after for a while. Would you consider being my guest at my house in Ascot? I have plenty of staff, and the country would be better for you than foggy, smoke-filled London. From what Rossi tells me, you live alone apart from the servants.'

He did not answer, just gazed at her with those vividly blue eyes of his, fiercely bright at this moment.

She stared back, asking herself if it was reluctance she saw reflected there. Or was it doubt?

After another long moment, he said, 'I would like to come to Ascot. Your house is beautiful. But I will need help . . . some looking after for a while. Will you hire a nurse?'

Taken aback for a second, she remained silent. Then she said in a firm voice, 'I shall look after you myself, James. You will be in my capable hands for as long as it takes. If you feel you need a nurse, we'll organize that too.'

James gave her one of his long looks. 'Then, in that case, I shall be happy to come and stay with you.' As he spoke he couldn't help wondering how it would work out. Being in close proximity might not be a field of dreams for them. Would it bring him back into his daughter's life? After years of neglecting Leonie, he had no idea. Wait and see, he told himself sternly.

* * *

He was mulling Mrs Ward's visit over the next morning, when he saw Nurse Jackson approaching, walking swiftly down the terrace. When she came to a stop, she gave him her usual big smile. She handed him an envelope. 'You have a letter, Major.'

As he took it, he smiled back at her and thanked her. She nodded, and immediately rushed off in a hurry.

After opening the envelope and glancing at the signature, he was delighted to realize that it was from his great friend Peter Keller, who had joined the Royal Navy at the onset of the war. They had not seen each other since, their periods of leave never coinciding. Peter was now home on leave in London and was planning to come and see him with Irina, his wife.

After reading the letter again, Falconer put it in his jacket pocket and leaned back in the chair, full of cheer at the thought of their visit later this week.

How strange life is, he suddenly thought, and how strange and complex we human beings are. Two old friends in one week.

Peter and he had worked together and played together. Memories of the past rushed back, took hold of him. Quite unexpectedly, he remembered the awful night when he and Peter had been jumped by a couple of thugs in a dark side street in London. They had been to dinner and were taking a shortcut when the bruisers had attacked them. How they had fought back and knocked the thugs out, in fact. James nodded to himself. They had been a good team.

Perhaps, if this infernal war ever ended, they would be a team once again.

THREE

'When do you think this bloody awful war will finally be over?' James asked, his bright blue eyes focused intently on Peter Keller.

'God knows, and he won't split,' Peter answered, shaking his head. He had arrived exactly four days after his letter, and he had come alone.

'I'm so sorry Irina couldn't make it,' he now said. 'And so is she. But she works for Commander Walton at the Admiralty, and he just couldn't let her have today off. But she will come with Natalie next week, I promise.'

'I understand,' Falconer answered, and shifted slightly in his chair, knocking his crutches over with his shoulder. 'I'd like to hear how she is, but first tell me about you, and your war.'

Immediately, Peter Keller was on his feet and picking the crutches up, placing them against the wall. The two friends were seated at one end of the communal sitting room at the Sanctuary, close to the window. It was still warm for September, but it had been drizzling all afternoon.

'It didn't surprise me when you joined the Royal Navy,' James remarked, his eyes on one of his closest friends. 'I know how much you've always loved the sea. That was apparent when you were in Hull. I suppose war on a battleship is rather different from war in the trenches, isn't it?'

'Yes. Because we are attacking with guns and cannon from a ship, not doing hand-to-hand fighting like the artillery and the cavalry. But war is lousy no matter what, whatever service you're in.'

'I know. By the way' – he raised an eyebrow – 'you're looking very dashing in your naval uniform. I bet lots of women look you over, give you a double-take, and perhaps a winning smile.'

Peter grinned. 'I don't notice. To change the subject from me, what was it like in the trenches? How did they work? More importantly, how did you all manage? You were literally living in deep ditches.'

'We learned to make the trenches work extremely well. There was one very long front trench, guarded by barbed wire. This faced the German's three lines of defence. We fought from there. But behind the front line, there were many other trenches, opening off, going back.'

'Why? What for?' Peter sounded puzzled.

'Those trenches were where we lived. Other officers and all those wonderful Tommies. Young they were, too. Their faces made my heart break almost, when they looked at me with such devotion, and *trust*. They trust us officers, look up to us. Anyway, behind the front line of attack and defence, there was . . . well, a maze of trenches. You know, like a maze in a garden made of clipped yew trees. That's the best way I can describe them. Do you understand?'

'I do indeed. I can see the maze in my mind's eye. So you slept back there when you were able to?' Peter asserted.

'Slept in them, yes, when we had a chance. One trench was a latrine, full of buckets. Another, off in a different direction, was for preparing the food we got, real food brought up by the women of the nearby villages. Another trench was for taking care of small injuries, wounds, aches and pains, and helping each other with our feet. Those army boots are great, but heavy. The lads get a lot of blisters.' James let out a sigh. 'God bless my lads, I can't help worrying about them. All the time.'

'I know what kind of man you are, James, and I'm certain you were, and are, a dedicated commander. I can imagine how you feel.'

James remained silent for a moment, then said, 'Those young lads, my soldiers, were the flower of English youth, and still are, those still at the front . . .' He paused, suddenly choked up, filled with emotion.

After a moment, staring out at the garden, he was able to continue. 'I'm afraid not many will be coming home. Sorrowfully, we'll be a country of women and old men.'

'Yes, I know,' Peter replied. 'I've talked about that with many of my sailors. We Navy lads might do a bit better, though. Millions of Englishmen have died fighting, not to mention civilians as well. However, we just won't be the same country—'

'Damned right!' James exclaimed. 'England's broke by now. I feel sure of that.'

'With all of the armies depleted, German and French, as well as ours, the war has to come to an end soon.' Peter lifted his hands and gave a shrug. 'Sooner rather than later, I believe, hope and pray.'

'I agree.' James took the cigarette Peter offered, and went on, 'I worry a lot about two of my men; very close, we were. Lieutenant Jack Stead and Captain Allan Lister. I was told later, after I was wounded, that Stead found me, and Lister came with stretcher-bearers. The two of them got me out of the fierce Battle of the Somme, and saved my life. I wish I knew where they were. Alive, I pray.'

He turned to Peter and leaned forward for his friend to light the cigarette. 'Now, let's change the subject. I want to talk about

Malvern's. My company. It's hanging on in there without us to run it – but from what I hear it's been tough going. Now that I'm home and nearly ready to leave this place, I've got to think about how to keep my business afloat amid this mess.'

'I'll come back there, once I'm out of the Navy, after the war; I promise you that, James.'

'I know, Peter. What I will have to do is get money from . . . somewhere, and work like bloody hell to revive Malvern's—'

'You'll do it!' Peter cut in. 'There's no doubt in my mind about that.'

FOUR

James Lionel Falconer had an open, easy-going personality and a great deal of natural charm. These characteristics, plus his height, his good looks, and his piercingly blue eyes made him irresistible to women.

James liked women and got on with them well, but he was not a ladies' man, and anything but a philanderer. In fact, he was very much a man's man, which was actually the way it was in this era.

It was decidedly a man's world: men dined together at restaurants and private men's clubs, went to the theatre, the varieties and the horse races. They were always together. Wives were treated kindly, lovingly, but stayed at home. Weekends were reserved for them.

James had four close male friends. There was his brother Eddie, as well as William Venables, his cosuin, with whom he had spent much of his youth in Hull; Cornelius Glendenning, the husband of Claudia Trevalian, who had been his late wife's dearest friend; and Peter Keller, of course, his closest workmate.

His thoughts were on William on this lovely September

morning. William was coming to the Sanctuary and bringing a picnic lunch. When he had told Nurse Jackson about this, she had not only been startled, but rather chuffed, liking the idea. 'Nobody's ever done that before,' she had explained yesterday, adding, 'Very nice, and a bit posh. I like that.'

James had laughed at her response, and so had she. Now he was sitting in a chair on the terrace overlooking the hospital gardens, waiting for William.

He had been at the Sanctuary for six months, and he had healed well. His doctors were hoping he would be able to leave by the end of the year. He was looking forward to that. These days he was convinced he would soon have his old life back, working, building his company back to success, enjoying a few pleasures, and most importantly, seeing old friends. Being normal, in fact.

A moment later he heard William's voice and recognized Nurse Jackson's laughter, as she led his dearest friend out onto the terrace.

William was smiling as he strode in, carrying a wicker hamper marked Fortnum & Mason. 'Here I am, James, right on time, bearing food from your favourite shop.'

'So I notice,' James answered. 'And it's great to see *you*, old chap.'

'You can put the hamper on this table, Mr Venables,' Nurse Jackson said, 'and just let me know if you need any china or utensils.'

'Thanks, Nurse Jackson,' William said. 'But I do believe the hamper has everything we'll need. A nice pot of English breakfast tea would be welcome a bit later.'

'Of course. I'll see to it whenever you want.'

'Thank you,' William said, giving her one of his biggest smiles.

Once they were alone, James settled back his chair and looked across at William, seated near the round table, his hand resting on the hamper. 'I was tickled to death when you said you'd bring lunch, but a bit surprised when the hospital allowed it, though.'

'Anything for you, Jimmy lad. You're a great war hero. And from what I hear from that nurse, you're also everyone's favourite among *all* the nurses.'

'Not so sure about all this you're saying, William. I'm just glad to have your company. I've missed you.'

'Me too. I'm sorry I couldn't get here earlier this summer. But I really was jammed with work. Now, when do you want lunch?'

As he spoke, William opened the hamper and lifted the lid. 'I've brought us a drink. Don't tell the nurse but it's a good claret. How about a glass now? There are two glasses here, and everything else we need, as well as the food.'

'You're right, I think the doctors might disapprove of booze. I have to tell you, they are very pleased with my progress. I'm learning to walk again, sometimes just with one crutch. Getting better at trotting every day.'

'You'll get back to normal,' William said in a positive tone, handing James the glass of wine. 'No doubt about *that*.'

There was a small silence and then William said in a low tone, 'I need to talk to you about the Malvern Company. But also about Georgiana Ward.'

'You sound odd. Is something wrong? She is all right, isn't she?' James sounded anxious.

'To my knowledge, yes, but I've done a lot of thinking since you told me in your letter that you're going to stay with her in Ascot. And you can't do that, you really can't.'

Falconer sat up straighter, staring at his closest friend, a look of puzzlement on his face. 'Why ever not? It's a great place for my final recuperation. And there's nothing between us again, at least not at the moment.'

'Maybe so. However, just think how it will *look*! People will think you are living together—'

'But there are lots of servants there,' James cut in, disappointed.

'So what? They don't mean anything, nothing at all. People think the *worst*, you surely know that. To the outside world, it would be something to gossip about—'

'I don't care what they say,' James replied heatedly.

'It would look as if you are *living in sin*. And you can't afford to have that sort of tittle-tattle circulating in London. You are a famous businessman, a tycoon of some repute, for God's sake, and something of an icon to many people. They look up to you. And as you start to prepare to return to the business, you need to make sure nothing could damage that.' William paused, then added, 'You must think about Malvern's, *your* company. Don't do anything that might damage it, put it at risk.'

James sat frowning at William, an expression of hurt in his eyes.

William took a deep breath and went on, in a gentler voice, 'I know you like her around, like her company, but you have to look at the situation objectively, how people will see it, how they would talk. To some extent, we're still living in the era of Queen Victoria, even though it is 1917. Old-fashioned rules live on.'

'A lot of bigots, I suppose, and hypocrites,' was James's mumbled comment. He let out a long sigh. 'I thought this bloody war might have changed things. But I suppose you're right, Will. I can just imagine the talk.' A deep sigh again. 'I give in. You are always looking out for me, have my back. I'll go to my house in South Audley Street when I leave here in December. Perhaps Georgiana can come and look after me there – and I do mean visiting, not living there. I got your message loud and clear.'

William couldn't help laughing. 'I knew what you meant, you didn't have to clarify. And I know you'll want to see her. You've been lovers, off and on, for years.'

James also laughed. 'Since I was seventeen.'

'In Hull, very sneakily. Don't forget I was there. I was a bit puzzled at first, and so were others, because she was older than you. Some think she's not a very good match for you. But she was a very beautiful woman. And your lovely wife, Alexis, was also older than you by eight years.'

'I guess I like older women, and maybe I'll figure out why one day.'

'I'd be all ears. But I think you might want to be careful about getting tangled up with her all over again. Now, lunch.' William pulled out the list of items in the hamper and then began to read it aloud. 'Pork pies with chutney, egg salad sandwiches, smoked salmon on brown bread. Pickles. Sliced tomatoes and gherkins. And finally, jam roll. How does that sound?'

'Great. My mouth's watering. I've had nothing that good since I came back to Blighty.'

'Mine, too.' William took the hamper and put it on the floor. Within minutes, he had placed all the food on plates on the table.

James had enjoyed being with William and, within minutes of his departure, he was missing his best friend. Although William had been unable to sign up to fight, owing to poor eyesight, he had done his bit for the country by keeping the family shipping business going. This meant he hadn't been able to visit James as often as he would have liked. It felt like a very long time since they'd had lunch together; his early visits to James's bedside had been brief and marred by James being in pain.

Friend of a lifetime, James thought, and family too, after all these years. James put great store in having a family. A big one, if possible. He had grown up in one, knew how important it was to be surrounded by people who loved you and cared about your welfare. It was a bitter irony that he was now alone in his own life.

There had been his Falconer grandparents, Philip and Esther, who had been in service; the latter had been the biggest influence in his life. Of course there were his parents, Matthew and Maude, who kept their little house in Camden full of love, even when money was tight; his sister Rossi and his brother Eddie, as well as his uncles, George and Harry. A loving, cosy group that was totally committed to each other.

Although only Eddie and Rossi were alive now, they were caring and close. They saw each other as much as possible. Eddie was five years younger. He had failed the military medical test because of weak lungs and so had not been in the war. Married to a lovely young woman, Christina, they had twin sons, Ian and Andrew, who were fourteen.

Eddie, always artistic and painting pictures as a child, had surprised them all when he announced he wanted to be a lawyer. James had paid for his education and Eddie had proved to be a legal eagle.

Rossi, busy sewing when growing up, had her own shop in the Malvern Arcade on Piccadilly, near Trafalgar Square. Her greatest sellers were the unique shawls she made, which had become famous. She and her husband Charles Randolph, a banker, had a daughter of eighteen, Lavinia. They had a good marriage, as did Eddie and Christina.

His thoughts went back to William. James now recalled how disappointed William had been that they were unable to join up as Pals together.

William was married to Natalie Parkinson, James's former assistant; they were a great match. Together they had produced a son, Clarence, named for William's late father. William had taken over the running of the Venableses' shipping company in Hull, but he and Natalie spent much of their time in London. William, a clever businessman, had grown the company and opened a London office. James also had come to spend most of his time in London before the war, rarely going to Hull.

He suddenly smiled to himself, thinking that he *did* have quite a large family, after all, even if some were not blood relatives. Most, actually. Even if he no longer had a wife, nor the children they had longed for, he was surrounded by a lovely bevy of marvellous people who knew they were his, and who relied on *him* for so much. And they gave back endlessly, staying close to him. As he faced life without the Army, the country still caught in this awful war, he would need them all.

PART THREE

Starting Over

Mayfair, London, England

January–December 1918

FIVE

'Goodbye!' James Falconer shook the doctors by the hand and pressed Nurse Jackson's hand particularly warmly. He was so grateful for all that the hospital – rightly, he felt, known as the Sanctuary – had done for him. But he was glad he was leaving at last. Freedom! Yes, he was free to do anything. It was January of 1918, and Major James Lionel Falconer was being fully discharged from the military hospital in Kent and also from the Army. The terrible wounds in his legs had finally healed, and he had learned to walk properly again. Although he needed to use a cane, because his left leg was weaker than his right, he was well-balanced and steady on his feet. Confident in himself again, he was longing to get rid of that cane; he promised himself that he would, one day. Just as he would go back to Malvern's and return it to its old glory.

It was Georgiana Ward who came with her motorcar to take him home to London. Now that the time had come, James was happy he had listened to William's advice and was in fact going back to his own house on South Audley Street in Mayfair, not to Georgiana's. His staff had run it efficiently during his time in the Army and the hospital. They were anxious to greet him, according to Mrs Ward.

James was quiet as they travelled, thinking about the future. He was sure the war would finally end that summer. Armies were depleted, millions of soldiers dead, and civilians killed also. The great British Empire had fallen and was no doubt up to its neck in debt. The entry of the Americans now made victory seem possible, but the world had paid a great price.

He had done a lot of thinking, alone in his hospital bed over the past year, had made a promise to himself. He would start over, take proper charge of his business empire, and mend a few fences. And then there was his daughter, his only child, borne by Georgiana. He must win her over, make up for his disgusting neglect of her. Lionel Georgiana Ward, known as Leonie.

After the first meeting with Georgiana Ward, he had written her a letter, asking about Leonie. She was twenty-eight now and a clever businesswoman, according to her mother. She was engaged to a seemingly very appropriate man by the name of Richard Rhodes. However, he was a man Mrs Ward did not like. Georgiana wanted *his* opinion of Mr Rhodes, and of their daughter, as well. Now, looking out of the window at the wintry Kent countryside, James felt impatient. He couldn't wait to meet them both.

Georgiana had told him he was in for a battle, that Leonie would not be easy to make friends with. She apparently resented him, did not want to know him on any level, and did not care that she was, in fact, heir to his enormous business empire.

His only child had told her mother she could never forgive him for the way he had abandoned her when she was in her teen years, never attempted to see her as she became a young woman. Leonie said she felt lost, almost as if she did not exist sometimes, at least to her father.

He had asked Georgiana how to approach the situation, and her answer had been a shake of her head, and a whispered, 'I've no idea.'

But later she had confided that he had to do everything in his power to make amends, to get her to come into his life willingly. That he must make Leonie *feel* she was his daughter; somehow prove that he loved her.

And he had promised Mrs Ward he would do that, no matter what it took. He was sincere about this.

The months after his return home passed swiftly. In November of 1918 the war was finally over, and peace declared. James hoped it would be a lasting one. His memories of the fighting, the dying and the chaos of the last few years never left him, however hard he tried. He plunged himself into running his business empire once again, to take his mind off the memories.

After Alexis's death, years before, he had inherited her late father's business, the Malvern Company, which he had managed for Henry Malvern since his youth. The South Audley Street house had become his too.

Now, on this November morning, he sat at the desk in the library and suddenly found himself gazing at the photograph of Alexis. How carefree and happy she looked, he thought, a slight smile settling on his lips. And very beautiful. Then the smile faltered. How she had suffered, and all because of him and his desire for her. Because of his lust for her, his need of her. And she had responded with great emotion.

Her first miscarriage had been in 1892, in the early part of their marriage. She had been thirty then. Another miscarriage when she was thirty-four. In 1900, she had died in childbirth, as had their baby, a son. He lost them both. A tragedy which haunted him.

His darling wife had died aged thirty-eight, far too young. Guilt settled on him, and he fell down into himself and his troubling thoughts. Even the business he had plunged back into running, the Malvern Company, had been set up by her father. It was where they had first met.

A moment later his head came up, and he looked at the door as Brompton, his butler, knocked and came in.

'Sorry to interrupt you, sir, but Cook would like you to look at the menu for the supper on Friday, and let her know if you approve it.'

Brompton walked to the desk and handed the menu to James. 'Thanks,' he said, read it quickly and nodded. Handing the menu back, he added that everything sounded delicious as usual. He was giving a dinner party to celebrate the end of the war.

Once alone again, James's gaze went back to the photograph of his late wife. He had been a widower for many years now. Alexis had died when he was thirty. Now he was forty-eight. And yet it seemed like only yesterday when she had been mistress of this house, running it with her usual efficiency and flair. In his head, he could hear her laughter, her lilting voice. They had assumed they would fill it with children, live a happy life together.

He had never met another woman he wanted to marry, had never fallen in love again. As the years had passed, there had been a few relationships, because he was a normal heterosexual man and needed the company and comfort of a woman. All those friendships had been fleeting and had ended eventually.

On the other hand, he had one true, good female friend, Georgiana Ward. He had come to rely on her care and kindness, after he had left the military hospital in Kent. It was to her he owed his better health – and his sanity, in a sense. When he was seventeen, she had become his mistress, and when he was twenty-one, she had introduced him to his daughter, Leonie, then two years old. What a surprise *that* had been.

Since his return, his daughter had refused to see him. If she was visiting her mother, she refused to admit him, and she never replied to any of his letters.

His mind focused on Georgiana. They hadn't seen each other for six weeks while he was away in Hull for business. She was ten years older than him, but did not look it. If anything, she appeared younger than him. And so had Alexis, who had been eight years older. He smiled to himself. Funny how he liked older women. His dearest friend, William Venables, actually his cousin, often whispered that he was always on the lookout for a delectable older woman for him.

And now James remembered that the last time William had said words to that effect, he had shot back that he already had an older woman in his life, and had then stopped short, gaping at William. His friend had been quick to answer, asking him if he was romantically involved again with Mrs Ward. James had told him the truth immediately. No, he wasn't, but he did love her in a certain way. When William pressed him further, asking in *what* way, he had not responded. He was loath to go any further.

After a short while of intense thought, James rose and stood in front of the mirror, staring at himself, weighing up his appearance. Well, he didn't look too bad for a man of forty-eight. A few lines around his eyes, but his eyes were still piercingly blue and clear. Good food and the comforts of home had smoothed away the anxiousness of war that had clouded his face for so long. And he was still six feet two and as slender as he had been at thirty.

No, not bad at all, he decided again, turning away from the mirror. She might still fancy me.

She? Well, Georgiana Ward, of course. Who else? What other woman was constantly on his mind? What other woman could he possibly want? Did he want her sexually again? He didn't know. And if he did, what if he failed her? He wanted Leonie in his life. How would getting involved again with her mother affect that? All of these questions ran through his head until William arrived to take him out to lunch. Don't confide in him, James warned himself, as they left together. And he didn't.

* * *

Brompton, the butler, opened the door, leading into the drawing room of James Falconer's South Audley Street house. He announced her name as he did.

Georgiana Ward murmured her thanks to the butler and stepped forward alone.

James stood at the far side of the room, opening a bottle of champagne. The cork popped, and he turned and smiled at her, then walked across the floor, still smiling.

Her heart tightened and she felt a rush of excitement. It was always like that when she saw him for the first time after he had been away for a while.

Six weeks in Hull, working hard, and he looked wonderful. He was tall, much taller than most men of her acquaintance. Six feet two, very slender, and extremely handsome, with those piercingly blue eyes. As he drew closer, she noticed his face was a bit fuller, and this added to his youthful aura tonight.

He grasped her arm, drew her closer, bent down and kissed her cheek, then focused on her intently. 'You look beautiful, Mrs Ward; more so than ever, I do believe.' His expression was admiring.

'And you look as if you've been on a long holiday, Mr Falconer.'

He grinned. 'I know I've put on a bit of weight. It shows in my face. It's all that Yorkshire pudding and roast beef they kept feeding me. But come, let's have a glass of bubbly and toast the peace.' He swung around and walked back to the table where the champagne stood in a silver bucket.

She followed him slowly, cringing slightly as she noticed how hard he was trying not to limp, and not doing too well. It was his pride, of course. She wished he would use the cane, but he usually tried not to when he was with her. What did it matter, that limp? He was alive, wasn't he? That's what mattered. And in good health, thank God.

As he poured the champagne into two crystal flutes, he said, 'I heard from Peter Keller today, and he has recovered from the Spanish flu. He sends you his best.'

'Thank you for telling me, James. And he's one of the lucky ones. So many people have died in this awful epidemic.'

'Only too true, I'm afraid.' He shook his head. 'I'm devastated that it took two of Peter's relatives.' James gave her the flute of champagne and touched his glass to hers, a smile replacing the serious expression on his face. 'It's so nice to see you; I've missed you, Mrs Ward.'

'Likewise,' she answered, merely smiling, not trusting herself, knowing she might blurt out something inappropriate if she wasn't careful. Since that first meeting at the Sanctuary a year before, after not seeing each other for years, they had stayed friends but no more, a careful distance between them.

'I've got something for you,' James announced, putting his flute down. 'I hope you like it.' He stepped across to a table and retrieved a package, wrapped in silver paper and tied with silver ribbon. He handed it to her.

Georgiana was both surprised and pleased that he had bought her a gift, and thanking him profusely, she opened it swiftly. Inside the box was a purple shawl, made of the lightest, softest velvet which was edged in silver. It rippled in her hands. 'Why it's just gorgeous!' she exclaimed. 'Thank you!'

He drew closer to her, took the shawl from her, placed it around her shoulders, and then stood back, appraising her intently.

'It matches your purple dress,' he said. 'And it suits you, but you cannot wear it with this . . . *gown*.' He took the shawl off her shoulders.

'But why not?' she asked, staring at him. 'You said the colours match.'

'Because this gown you're wearing is simply beautiful on you, and it's evening wear. The shawl doesn't belong.' He did not add that he wanted to feast his eyes on the alabaster white skin of her glorious shoulders, chest and breasts that the low-cut gown revealed so provocatively. It took all his self-control not to kiss her.

Turning around, he placed the shawl in the box, and added, 'You can wear it tomorrow.'

Georgiana sipped the champagne, pushing down a flare of annoyance. So he was bossy, was he? Yes, she decided, he was, and then realized she didn't care. He had captivated her years ago, and she still wanted to be with him now.

James came back and took her arm, led her towards the fireplace. 'It's coolish this evening; you know I'm always cold. Let's sit near the fire until my other guests arrive.'

'You go. I want to get my reticule. I have something for you in it.'

'Oh really!' His brow shot up, and he let go of her arm, and she went to fetch the reticule.

Once they were settled in front of the fire, she opened the bag and took out an envelope, handed it to him. 'You can read it later. You don't have to bother now.'

He thanked her, and promptly opened the envelope and read the invitation inside. He turned to face her, beaming. 'I accept. What a lovely invitation, Georgiana. I would be most happy to come for the weekend at Ascot in two weeks. Thank you.'

'Oh, I'm so glad, James. You will enjoy the countryside, and Ascot is a charming little village.'

'Is it a house party? Are you having other guests?' he asked, reaching for his flute of champagne, drinking it down in one gulp, thrilled by her note.

'Yes, although I haven't invited anyone else yet,' she explained. 'But I thought I might include a few people you know, whom we have in common.'

'Oh, quite a big weekend house party then?' he murmured quietly, his voice suddenly flat.

She caught his disappointment in his tone, just an undercurrent, but it was there, nonetheless. Clearing her throat, she said, 'Perhaps just William and Natalie?'

When he was silent, she asked, 'Or would you prefer a really,

really quiet few days ... what I mean is ... just the two of us?'

There was silence. James rose and went to fill his flute, called across to her, 'Shall I top up yours too?'

'Yes.' She stood up and went to join him at the table, offered her glass to him.

After filling it, he clinked his flute to hers. 'Here's to a lovely quiet, happy few days together at your Ascot house.'

She stared across the top of her flute at him, and added, 'Alone?'

'Of course alone. I don't want to share you.' He broke off when Brompton opened the door and ushered in William and Natalie, married to each other for some years and very much the loving couple.

James had always loved the Saturday night suppers his grandmother had given when he was growing up. Esther Falconer, who had been a housekeeper at a large house in Regent's Park, had been the biggest influence on his life. When her job allowed, on a Saturday, she had gathered 'the clan' together and given them a feast of a meal, whatever else was going on in their lives.

James had followed in her footsteps and on his return from the war he had promised himself that he would always try to hold a supper at the end of the week himself. Sometimes Fridays, sometimes Saturdays, depending on his schedule and where he was.

This week it was Friday, and now, as he glanced around his dining table in his well-appointed dining room, he smiled inwardly. He had quite a collection tonight – family and dearest friends. And it felt right for this moment that peace had been declared, to celebrate with them all. He loved this feeling of happiness and caring that floated around the group. They all belonged here together, and felt the same way he did. They *were* a family, even if some were not blood relatives. Devotion, loyalty and love combined; that's what held them together.

His only sadness was that his only child, Leonie, was not among them. Shortly before the Armistice, she had startled Mrs Ward and himself when she had eloped to Gretna Green and married Richard Rhodes. Obviously, she wanted to cut them out of her marriage and still wasn't interested in her father at all. This troubled him.

Mrs Ward had confided from the start that she had doubts about Richard. There was something odd about him, which she couldn't quite put a finger on, but it was there, she insisted. Sighing under his breath, James hoped that he could persuade Leonie one day to join the Friday dinners, be part of the family.

William's sudden laughter echoed around the room and brought James out of his reverie. Dearest William, his best friend for . . . ? Well, it seemed like for ever, and it was, in a sense – most of his life, actually.

William and Natalie were seated next to Claudia Trevalian Glendenning, who had been the best friend of James's late wife, Alexis. Since her death, Claudia had been a great friend to him, as had her husband, Cornelius Glendenning. A very caring man and the salt of the earth. He didn't know how he would have got through the past fifteen years without them. And as always, Claudia was glamorous, in a slim, pearl-grey chiffon dress in the new fashion, its V-shaped neckline trimmed with wide lace, and with a diamonds around her neck and on her ears.

Further down the table sat his brother, Eddie, and his wife, Christina, along with his sister, Rossi, next to Lord Reggie and his wife, Lady Jane. She was seated next to Charles Randolph, Rossi's husband, a banker in the City. On Charles's other side was Georgiana Ward.

James gazed at her, unable to look away.

Mrs Ward gazed back at him for a long moment, and then addressed Natalie, asking about her family in Russia, and her parents in London.

Lifting his glass, James took a sip of the red wine he preferred and often served. As he drank, he thought, what a lucky blighter I've been. I've had such a full and successful life. For a long time I thought I was unlucky. But I still have so much.

And it wasn't over yet. He must persuade Leonie to put aside her resentment of him. He must make friends with her husband. He hoped his daughter would have a child – yes, to build the family . . . The House of Falconer must live on.

Six

As he always did, James carved the leg of lamb himself, just as his grandfather had always done before him, all through his childhood.

He stood at the small square table at one end of the dining room, near the door. Brompton stood by his side, next to the stack of plates. When meat was placed on one, Brompton handed it to a maid. She, in turn, took each plate to the dinner table, where three other maids offered roasted potatoes, green beans and carrots to everyone, while the other two maids took the silver gravy boat and mint sauce and passed them around.

Rossi, in particular, loved the Friday dinners, and she looked across at her brother, and said, 'You've outdone yourself, James. I do enjoy having a Sunday lunch on a Friday evening. And the dressed crab first was just as good as Grandpapa Philip made. I bet these were his recipes.'

'Of course,' James answered, and cut into a slice of the lamb. 'I made sure to keep all his written recipes in a box, and there are some tasty dishes I've still got to have Cook make. You're in for a few more treats, Rossi, darling.'

Glancing around the table, James saw that the others were enjoying the food. It was old fashioned, very traditional, he knew that. But it always satisfied his family. And it filled him with nostalgia and memories of growing up. Rossi was right . . . it was indeed a Sunday lunch from the old days.

He looked at Georgiana, and she gave him a faint smile, then dropped her eyes, concentrated on her food. James knew that he had to have a talk with her soon, about Leonie.

He had not done so before he left for Hull, because he had been having bad dreams, nightmares really, about the war. His head filled up with the din of it all – the crashing of bodies falling, the clattering of machine guns, bombs exploding, cannon roaring. And the sorrow of it filled him until he woke up, screaming, covered in sweat, disoriented for a few minutes.

For a while, he thought he had conquered these ghastly memories. They had just gone away. And then they came back at the Sanctuary, so much so he had been taken out of the ward and put in a room alone. That way, he didn't disturb the other wounded soldiers being cared for on the main ward. Yet again, the bad dreams stopped, but they had returned. Suddenly they were flooding through him . . . he was haunted by the war. It had scarred him, changed him as a man, and he was still puzzled by why it had even had to happen. Why it had begun. A war that had probably changed nothing, yet it had killed millions . . . millions of people dead for no reason . . . unbearable to face. He wished he could move on.

James forced himself to let go of these worrying thoughts and began to chat with his guests. They were here to raise a glass to the end of the whole ghastly affair. And later, when dessert was served, he had regained his good humour. His charisma was intact, his smile beguiling.

* * *

After dinner, the ladies retreated to the drawing room and the gentlemen headed to the library. The ladies would drink tea; the men would more than likely have a cognac and perhaps smoke a good Cuban cigar. Or enjoy a Turkish cigarette.

Ushering the men into the library, James announced, 'I just received a new selection of Cubans – very good they are, too. Please, Charles and Connie, do go over to the humidor and pick out cigars for yourselves.'

The two men thanked him profusely and headed to the far end of the room where the humidor stood on a table near a large window.

James took up his usual stance in front of the fireplace. He was always cold these days, even in warm weather, and had decided this feeling had settled in his bones. Winters in the trenches had done their damage in more ways than one.

Brompton came into the library and asked James's guests if they would like a balloon of cognac, or something else instead? They all asked for the Napoleon brandy, a very fine cognac that Brompton always kept in the cellar.

Once they had their glasses in their hands, they all raised them, and Cornelius Glendenning said, 'I know we toasted the peace earlier with the ladies, but here's to the end of that horrendous war.'

'Here, here,' the others said in unison. They all came to the fireplace to touch glasses together, surrounding their host.

'And here's a second toast, my friends. To all the heroes who came back, and to the thousands of British soldiers who are buried . . . in some far corner of a foreign field,' James said solemnly.

Silence reigned. The men lifted their glasses once more and sipped their drinks. All were obviously saddened and touched by James's words.

'Well, I must say it's been quite a year, looking back,' William now said. 'The Allies slowly winning, pushing the Germans back to the Hindenburg Line after the Americans came in. Then the Kaiser's abdication, when he boarded a train into exile on the tenth of November. And then at eleven a.m. on the eleventh day of the eleventh month, the Great War was finished.'

'Yes, indeed,' Falconer agreed. 'And who could have imagined, the Armistice was concluded not in a capital city or a building of state, but in a railway carriage in the Forest of Compiègne, just outside Paris. Simply representatives of Germany, France and Britain; all the Allied Powers, in fact. That's when we really knew the fighting had stopped. It was all over, at long last.'

'And despite the terrible cost, we ended with some wins on the part of us British and our Allies,' William nodded. 'I hear Germany had to agree to relinquish all territories they had conquered, to evacuate all troops across the Rhine, and to surrender her fleet and armaments – her entire arsenal, in fact, among other things.'

'So done and dusted!' Eddie exclaimed, and they all raised their glasses in thankful relief that the Great War had finally ended.

Later on, the men rejoined the ladies, and when it was time to leave, James insisted on escorting Mrs Ward home. Her London house was only a few minutes away on Curzon Street. She protested at first, suggesting that the butler could walk with her.

But James would not hear of that, and once they were wearing top coats, he took her arm in his and led her into the street.

Although it was chilly, it was a beautiful night, with a black sky, and a bright moon floating above.

'Did you enjoy the evening, Georgiana?' James asked as they made their way along South Audley Street.

'I did, yes. Thank you for including me,' she answered. She was a little shaky inside, being so close to him, but took iron-clad control of herself.

As for James, he was enjoying being alone with her for a few minutes. Perhaps the time really had come now, for them to rekindle the spark that had always lain between them. He wanted to ask her again about trying to see Leonie, but refrained. He would send a note to her in the morning. Surely she could find a way.

SEVEN

Georgiana Ward sat in a chair in the lingerie department of Fortnum and Mason, watching Leonie selecting nightgowns. She couldn't help thinking how lovely her daughter looked today, her blonde beauty set off by a blue dress and coat.

'So, what do you think of these three, Mother?' Leonie asked, showing them to Georgiana.

'They're all nice, darling. Why don't you take all three?'

'I will, and I picked out three peignoirs as well. I tried one outer piece on, and so they'll all fit,' she explained.

For a moment, Georgiana was taken aback, thinking that Leonie was being somewhat extravagant with all this nightwear. She stood up, and said, 'I will go to the shop assistant and tell her to charge them to my account. I will ask her to have them delivered.'

Without waiting for a comment from her daughter, Georgiana went to find the assistant, making a mental note to pay more attention to this spending spree her daughter had embarked on.

Since returning from Scotland, Leonie had been buying jackets, several coats and shoes. Georgiana did not begrudge her daughter anything, but Leonie now had a husband. She did not think Richard Rhodes was a wealthy man, but he did have a good job in the City. Now he must provide for his wife. Georgiana did not approve of him, nor the sudden elopement, but *that* had happened, and therefore, it was a marriage.

Suddenly, Leonie was by her side. 'You rushed off, Mother.' She was holding all the nightwear in her arms. 'Where is the assistant?'

'She will be here momentarily.' Georgiana glanced around. 'Ah, here she is. Give her the items, Leonie, please. And then we must go.'

'But I need hats!' Leonie protested. She then handed over the nightclothes to the assistant.

'No more shopping today. That's it,' Georgiana said sternly.

Leonie knew better than to argue.

Having promised to take Leonie to Claridge's for lunch, Georgiana decided to do so. Although, for a moment or two, when they were in the store, she had thought of cancelling it.

They now sat in the restaurant, busy with other shoppers and visitors, its chandeliers gleaming and all around them people talking about the end of the war. Both women were studying the menu, and Leonie said, 'I'll have fish, the sole. What about you, Mother?'

Georgiana glanced at her over the top of the menu, and nodded. 'I'll have that, too, and I'll start with shrimp mousse.'

Leonie made a face, and said, 'Not for me. I think the pea soup will be a good choice on this cold day.'

Georgiana summoned a waiter. After they had ordered, she leaned closer to her daughter. 'You now have plenty of new clothes, and your current wardrobe is lovely, so that's the end of all this spending.'

Leonie frowned. 'But it's not a full trousseau—'

'You eloped,' Georgiana cut in. 'Women who run off to get married don't have a trousseau.'

'Oh, really,' Leonie muttered in a slightly superior tone.

Georgiana ignored the comment.

Both women were glad to return home. It was a cold and windy November Saturday and the house was warm and welcoming.

In the parlour, Georgiana found a note from James awaiting her, asking again if he might see Leonie. She read it quickly, then folded it back up.

'Who's that from?' asked Leonie, as she sat down across from her mother.

Georgiana wondered whether to tell her the truth. For some weeks now she had been debating with herself about whether or not to bring James into her conversations with Leonie. Her daughter had refused to listen to his name when Georgiana first visited him. But he wanted desperately to connect with her. Make up for his long absence from her life. Georgiana had promised to help him. Perhaps now she could begin the process and take the consequences.

'It's . . . from your father. He wants to see you.'

Leonie was gaping at her. '*My father!* I can't believe you even speak to him!' Leonie was not only astonished, but obviously very angry. She was glaring at her mother.

Georgiana held herself very still and remained calm, totally in control of the situation. She could be very tough if she had to be. It was time Leonie knew the truth.

'Of course, I speak to him, and I see a lot of him these days. Now that his business is a huge success, he doesn't work all day and all night any more.'

'Why do you *see* him? I can't believe this, and after what he did to you!'

'He didn't *do* anything to me, except love me.'

'Love you? That's a joke,' Leonie said in a sneering tone. 'He didn't love you enough to marry you, after he made you pregnant with me.'

'He did ask me to marry him—'

'I don't believe that,' Leonie cut in peremptorily. 'You're lying.'

'How dare you say that to me!' Georgiana exclaimed. She jumped up, filled with sudden fury. As she left the parlour, she said over her shoulder, 'I shall return in a moment.'

Leonie watched her leave, seething inside.

Within minutes, Georgiana returned. She was carrying a silver box. She put it down on a hassock near the fireplace. After opening it, she took out a small bundle of letters, tied with a blue ribbon. Untying this, she murmured, 'Blue for his eyes.'

Looking across at Leonie, she said in a much calmer voice, 'These eight letters are from your father. Each one is a proposal of marriage.' She took out one letter, found the page she needed, and handed it to Leonie. 'You may need the whole page, as well as the proposal. It's line four.'

Leonie, still belligerent, but also regretting her remark, had no option but to take the page and read it. It was indeed a proposal. She gave it back to her mother, silent, but looking slightly sorrowful and at a loss for words.

'Do you wish to read the other seven?' Georgiana asked.

'No, of course not. This says it all.'

Georgiana began to retie the eight envelopes together.

Leonie asked in a quieter tone, 'Why didn't you accept his proposal back then?'

'He didn't know I was pregnant. When I found out I was expecting a child, his child, I bought the house in Ascot for two reasons. I needed to live somewhere I was not known so I could be Mrs Ward, newly widowed. I also wanted to get out of smoke-filled London. I believed I should bring you up in clean air.'

'So you just left London and never told him you were carrying his child?'

'That is correct.'

'*Why?*'

'I met James Falconer when he was seventeen. I was twenty-seven. We fell for each other and had a short affair. When I discovered I was with child, I didn't want to burden him. He was just starting out in his business career. He was nineteen when you were born and doing so well at Malvern's. When he was twenty-one, he was running Henry Malvern's entire company. Brilliant at his job. Because he was twenty-one and by then well established, I invited him to come to Ascot. I told him I had something important to discuss, so—'

'Me. You were going to tell him about *me*, weren't you?' Leonie's eyes were riveted on her mother's face.

Georgiana nodded. 'I felt he had the right to know he had a child, that we had a child together.'

'And how did he react? I bet he wasn't happy to have fathered a bastard.'

'Don't ever use that word again,' Georgiana snapped.

'Well, it's true,' Leonie protested in a sneering voice.

Georgiana decided to ignore this annoying comment. 'When he saw you for the first time, you were just two years old. He knew at once you were *his* – blue eyes, blonde hair, and his sister's dimple in your chin. You ran to him, and he caught you in his arms and held you close. He held you in his lap all through lunch. He loved you then, and he loves you now. You are the spitting image of him.'

Leonie was silent, absorbing all these comments. Finally, she asked, 'So why on earth did he suddenly stop seeing me when I was thirteen? I was so hurt – *you* know that. You just said he had been through a difficult time. I never saw him ever again. I never understood his absence.'

'I should have explained it better, darling. Because I refused to marry him, he eventually married a woman he had known a long time, Alexis Malvern. Sadly, she was not physically strong. She had several miscarries, and her last pregnancy was fatal. She and the baby boy both died. James had never got over this. Grief, guilt, sorrow; all combined to block everything else out. Sad and somewhat drastic, but that was the way he was.'

'Has he changed now? Is that why, after all these years, he wants to see *me*? The discarded daughter?' she asked in a dour voice.

'I do believe he has changed. I told you all this last year: he was in the war and badly wounded. Machine-gun fire hit both his legs. He was at the Battle of the Somme in 1916, when he was felled. Two years in hospitals. There was much worry he would have to have both legs amputated. But fortunately, he had great doctors. And now he is walking well, just a slight limp. But the *war* changed him too.'

'But *why* is he asking to see me?' Leonie demanded, ignoring Georgiana's comments about his wounds and the war.

'He feels very guilty about turning away from you and he wants to make amends, apologize to you. Also, you are the heir, or rather heiress, to his fortune. He wants to have a reconciliation with you, bring you into the company to learn how to run Malvern's. To work with you so you will run it well later.'

'That'll be the day!' Leonie scoffed. 'Not interested. He can go to hell. Anyway, I have a job. I'm partner at the art gallery, and I love it.'

'I'm glad to hear that. After all, it did not come to you for nothing. If I remember correctly, it cost a lot of money to buy that partnership for you,' Georgiana pointed out.

'You're right, Mother, and I can never thank you enough for paying that huge fee.'

'I didn't pay it. Your father did.' Georgiana sat back, rather enjoying the look of total astonishment on Leonie's face. She was rendered speechless.

Before she found her voice, Georgiana decided to tell her a few more facts, information that she might not like to have. However, Georgiana wanted her to know the truth at last.

'Your father, James Falconer, has supported you since you were a child. He paid for your private school, the finishing school in Switzerland, and for all your expensive clothes as a young woman. Your holidays abroad were with me, and he paid for both of us. And so much more. You should be grateful you have such a generous man as your father, who is willing to help you to lead such a pleasant life.'

There was a continuing silence. Then Leonie said, 'But why did you let him do all that? You're a very rich woman.'

'Not any more. Not for a long time. When I first met James, I was a young widow, and I did have plenty of money left to me by my late husband. But I bought Ascot, and then you had to be schooled. My money dwindled away. They say money talks. It also walks.'

'I'm so surprised, I can hardly believe this, Mother. How did you lose your money?'

'I didn't lose it. I used it. Some of my late husband's investments lost interest; times changed. But I tried hard to manage. However, James is an insightful man, and he questioned me long and hard. I finally told him my problems. Without a word, he just stepped into the breach, so to speak. He took over the management of my accounts. He supports me – us – now, and has for years.'

'I see,' Leonie murmured. 'And how did you manage to buy this house . . .' She cut off her sentence and looked around. 'And decorate it with your usual expensive flair? Don't answer that. *He* bought it for you, didn't he? And everything in it?'

'For once, Leonie, you're absolutely correct. James Falconer has been taking care of us for years, even without seeing us. You are his only child. So naturally he wants to protect me in every way. And to have a lovely home.'

'So are you his mistress?' Leonie asked, a smirk on her lips.

'What I do is none of your business, young lady. So watch what you say. I may be indulgent with you, but my patience is growing thin. And you'd better start adjusting your attitude towards James Falconer and acknowledge that he is your father.'

Leonie was silent, shocked by all she had learned today.

EIGHT

When he was anxious, worried, or both at once, James Falconer took to the streets. He had discovered, as a seventeen-year-old boy, that walking around London, especially Mayfair and its environs, had a soothing effect.

When he was much younger, he had often gone out during the night, but he did not do that any more. Too dangerous. You never knew who you might meet in a side street on a dark night.

Now, on this cold November Saturday morning, he cut through a short street on Curzon and began to walk down Piccadilly, heading for Trafalgar Square, past Malvern's, his offices. James didn't mind the cold weather, was well wrapped up in an overcoat, scarf and hat. Anyway, it was a blue-sky morning, even sunny.

As always, there was a mass of traffic: motorcars, taxicabs, motorbuses, horse-drawn buses, carts and trucks.

All were jostling along, dodging each other, and making an alarming noise. Horses' hooves hitting stone; buses and motorcars, their horns blaring. And amid the din, he could just make out the young voices of the newspaper boys, shouting out headlines, as they lugged bags of newspapers around, looking for sales.

Despite the cold and the racket, he loved being here, pushing along with the crowds of people going about their business. In the months since his return, his pleasure had not diminished. This was London, the centre of the world, as far as he was concerned. His favourite city and the best place to be.

Being out and about helped to soothe him. He soon discovered that he was no longer anxious about the note he had sent round to Mrs Ward earlier that morning.

Leonie troubled him. Or, perhaps he should say, made him feel guilty. While he was away in Hull, he'd resolved to change things. He had the nagging desire to become Leonie's friend and would do anything to achieve this. He was well aware she detested him and considered him the enemy. He must prove otherwise.

When he reached Trafalgar Square, he went up to Nelson's Column and gazed at it for a long moment. What a tremendous man he had been. A great naval officer and a true patriot. Falconer suddenly remembered that he had come to see Nelson's Column about thirteen years ago, in 1905, when it had been hung with twenty-eight flags that spelled out the signal: 'England expects that every man will do his duty.' As he recalled, it had been the centenary of Nelson's great naval victory at Trafalgar.

Turning around, James walked back the way he had come, taking Piccadilly at a steady pace, despite his limp. He felt in full control of himself now and believed he could tackle his problems with Leonie in the proper way. He aimed to succeed.

Unexpectedly, as the crowds thinned out a little, he saw Peter Keller's wife, Irina, ahead of him. He stopped dead in his tracks and then stepped back. She was not alone. Irina was talking to a man. Not talking, actually, more like arguing. Did she need help? Should he hurry over to them?

These thoughts immediately fled as he saw the man take hold of Irina's arm. He led her to the roadside, hailing a taxicab, and helped her inside when it drew up.

James was taken aback. Who on earth was that tall, dark man? And why was Irina with him? Pulling himself together, he continued to walk on, realizing it could have been a friend or business acquaintance. Don't think the worst, he cautioned himself, as he arrived at the Malvern Arcade, which he owned. He hurried down to the far end, making for his sister's shop. He was taking Rossi to lunch at the Ritz Hotel.

The doorbell tinkled when James walked into his sister's shop. He was surprised to see Rossi behind the counter, serving a customer.

James took off his hat, raised a hand in silent greeting, and then sat down in one of the chairs.

Rossi nodded and smiled, and then made out a bill, chatting to the lady she was attending to with her usual charm.

James smiled inwardly. Very polished she was, his darling Rossi, and his dearest confidante. There wasn't anything he couldn't tell her, and he knew she was trustworthy . . . silent as the grave.

His eyes roamed around the shop, taking in the beautiful items so cleverly displayed, mostly the beautiful shawls in rainbow hues. Rosalind Falconer's shawls had become renowned over the years.

Settling back in the chair, James's thoughts settled on Irina Parkinson, now married to Peter Keller. He couldn't help wondering about the small scene he had just witnessed a few minutes ago. Now that his mind was focused on it, he did think that Irina had been arguing with him. He sighed to himself, and knew there had been nothing untoward about it. Yet it had been a confrontation, he decided, and it lingered in his mind. Should he have gone to her?

Irina was a fine woman. He knew her well, and they had been involved with each other some years ago. A love affair that had lasted a short while because Irina had gone to Russia to see her aunt Olga, who was ill. And she had been gone too long.

In his mind's eye, he saw the icon she had given him, so long ago now, but he still had it on his desk. Lovely Irina, with her soulful brown eyes and glossy dark hair. He even remembered she had worn a lilac chiffon gown one evening at a dinner they had attended.

Rossi was now walking the customer to the door, interrupting his reverie. When she closed the door, she said, 'You look cold, James. I suppose you've been wandering the streets once again.'

James laughed as he jumped up, threw his hat in the chair and hugged his sister tightly. ''Course I have. Don't you know by now that it helps me to sort things out in my mind?'

'Yes, I do,' Rossi answered. 'We all have our ways of dealing with problems.' She slipped out of his arms and went across to the counter. 'I'll just get my coat and hat, and we can be gone.'

James glanced at her. 'Where's Alice? Isn't she here today?'

'No, she has a bad cold. I told her not to come to work. I had to be here, though, because Lady Fortescue, the customer who just left, needed to collect several shawls she'd ordered. For herself and two daughters . . . Her Ladyship is having a ball tonight.'

James gave her a wide grin. 'I was wondering why you were here on a Saturday. I know Charles doesn't like you working today.'

'No, he doesn't, but he understood I had to come in to the shop for a short while. I did invite him to join us for lunch . . .' Rossi paused when she saw the crestfallen expression on her brother's face. Clearing her throat, she finished, 'But he declined. He already had a luncheon engagement with his cousin, Winifred Thomas. And fortunately, not at the Ritz.'

'Then let's be off, my beautiful one,' James said, picking up his hat. 'Let me help you with your coat?'

NINE

James was given his preferred table at the Ritz Hotel Restaurant. It faced the park, and he loved the view of the trees. Today they were without leaves, looked somewhat bereft, but he still liked the scenery in front of him, even though it was winter.

So did Rossi. Picking up the glass of pink champagne, she raised it to her brother, and said, 'Here's to you, Jimmy lad!' She often used his boyhood nickname, which usually amused him.

He laughed deeply as he touched his crystal flute to hers. 'And to you, my girl, and how glad I am it's just the two of us.'

'So am I.' Rossi sipped the champagne, then put it down and leaned across the table. 'What is it that troubles you? When we spoke yesterday, you said you needed to discuss a problem.'

James nodded. 'I do. I thought if I spoke to you about it, I might get a better understanding of it. Sometimes, hearing yourself speak out loud helps somehow. It clarifies things.'

'It does, I agree. Is this about Georgiana Ward?'

A startled look flashed across his face. 'Well, it is in a sense, but more about her daughter. *Our* daughter, actually. But *why* did you immediately think of Mrs Ward?'

'Because she was there at dinner last night. And you've been . . . *entangled* with her on and off for years and years, and I don't notice any special woman in your life. Oh yes, lots of beauties on your arm, when you need the companionship.' Rossi gave him a long, intense stare, and went on, 'I don't suppose any of them are your lovers. Just decoration for your arm.'

For a while James was flabbergasted, and just sat very still, staring back at her, momentarily rendered speechless. Finally, he sat up straighter and murmured, 'I'm not a philanderer, and you of all people know that I don't sleep around, unlike many men I know.'

'Yes, I do know that. So it's about Mrs Ward then.'

'Not really. It's about Leonie. I want to win her over, get her to understand my absence from her life. In other words, persuade her to include me—'

'That's never going to happen, James!' Rossi exclaimed, her eyes now fixed on him. 'You stopped seeing her when she was about thirteen, and she's a grown woman now. It's too late. She doesn't want to know you.'

'I don't agree,' James shot back swiftly, always fast on the draw. 'Yes, she is grown up. Twenty-eight, to be exact. You see, Rossi, I need to win her over. I have an enormous business empire, and Leonie is my heir. I want to leave it to her, but she must be trained by me, so she knows how to oversee such a huge enterprise. She can have other people to run it if she doesn't want to, but she needs to understand it.' James sat back, eyeing Rossi.

'I don't think she'd care about it, James. She wouldn't want it if you offered it to her. So don't waste your time.' Rossi announced in a tone of finality.

'I must try. Don't you understand that?'

'Well, yes, I suppose so. I do know she is a full partner in the Laughton Art Gallery, and pretty much runs it. Her two associates are . . . well, sort of silent partners. I heard that just recently,' Rossi told him.

'We've heard the same things then. So you see, she is also a businesswoman, and a clever one at that. If Leonie doesn't want the business, then I have no alternative but to sell it. All of it. The arcades, the hotels, the buildings on the docks . . .' His voice trailed off, and he slumped in the chair. The mere idea of selling this vast enterprise, which he'd spent all his life building, carefully, slowly, until he was the biggest tycoon in London, appalled him. He knew that deep in his heart he wanted to keep it and give it to his only child, estranged though she might be. A Falconer should own it. That was the way he wanted it to be.

Picking up the flute of champagne, James drank it down. Glancing around, he raised his hand to summon a waiter.

When one arrived, James asked for menus. Glancing at Rossi, he asked, 'Another champagne?'

'Thank you, yes, please.'

James nodded to the waiter. 'And two more of these, please,' he added.

Once alone, Rossi said, 'My only suggestion is to ask Mrs Ward to explain all this to Leonie, about being your heiress.'

'But I have told Georgiana, and she says she has spoken at length to Leonie, several times. I sent her a note about it only this morning, but I fear it will do no good. The girl is very stubborn.'

'Mmm mmm,' Rossi said, and then shook her head. 'You told me she'd gone and eloped with Richard Rhodes, so now she is a married woman. Could you, perhaps, engage her husband in a discussion? He might make an intervention. He might like the idea of his wife owning Malvern's.'

When James just sat silently staring out of the window, obviously in deep thought, Rossi continued, 'Isn't Rhodes a member of your club? Have you met him?'

Rousing himself, James turned to her, and said, 'Only in passing. I don't know the man, but I have the sense he may well be an opportunist.'

Rossi nodded, thanked the waiter for the flute of champagne. James did the same and lifted his glass. 'Thank you, Rossi, for listening yet again and for the suggestion about Richard Rhodes. It might work . . . for one reason.'

'Oh, and what's *that*?' Rossi raised her brow.

'Leonie is totally obsessed with him, mesmerized. Georgiana told me Leonie is madly in love with Rhodes, and won't hear a word said against him.'

'So she might well listen to him,' Rossi ventured.

'It's possible.' James gave her a wry smile. 'You know women better than I do, because you are one. So, what do *you* think?'

'Ah, James, love is blind, they say. Love does strange things to people. Love can create great happiness, or hell on earth. Love can rock the world. Politicians, famous men, religious leaders, kings . . . all have lost so much for love.' She smiled at her brother, and finished, 'I can't tell you what Leonie will do, or Richard. I don't have the slightest idea, you see.'

Silently, Rossi and James studied the menu, and then James looked at his sister, laughter in his bright blue eyes.

'I suppose you want to know what I'm ordering, before you make a decision,' he asked.

Rossi couldn't help laughing. 'True. But you always share with me. You've done it since we were little.'

'I do share, because you'd put a fork in something if I didn't. I'm having a dozen oysters, enough for two, because you're bound to want at least four, and then I'm having steak-and-kidney pie. For dessert, I'll have jam roll.'

'I think that's a big meal, my lad! Two oysters will do for me, and I'm going to have the fishcakes.' She put the menu down on the table and studied him for a long moment.

'What's wrong?' he asked, suddenly frowning. 'You're looking at me very oddly.'

'No, I'm not. And nothing's wrong. I'm just enjoying being with you, that's all. It was such a long time that you were away. You know, James, you're the finest man I know. Nobody can lift a finger to you . . . you're so fair, just and kind . . .' She cut herself off and blinked back unexpected tears. 'What I mean is: you are the best brother a woman could have, and you've always protected me. Thank you for being who you are,' she finished softly.

James was thunderstruck by this statement, but obviously pleased by her loving words. And yet slightly puzzled. Where did that leave Charlie, her husband? Was there a problem in her marriage? He didn't think so, and he did not dare ask. If she needed to confide something, she would do it in her own time, of her own volition.

The waiter arrived at the table at this moment, and asked to take their order. After he had left, James smiled at Rossi, and murmured, 'Thank you for saying those nice things, Rossi darling. I'm always here for you, whatever you might need. And I have your back permanently.'

Rossi, having regained her composure, merely smiled at him, then reached out and squeezed his hand, which was resting on the table.

James asked, 'Have you heard from Irina lately?'

She shook her head. 'No, and Peter has been so ill, of course, with the influenza. I know you said he was recovering. The last time I heard anything, he was thinking of staying in the Navy a little longer. There's a great deal to deliver still.'

'So he said to me. But that's making it a bit of a lonely life for Irina, in my opinion. I was surprised he was even considering that decision. An odd one.'

'Indeed it is. You must get lonely too, at times, James, being on your own.' Rossi looked at him, wondering why he had never remarried. It was a subject she knew was best left alone. Her brother's face was impossible to read.

Eventually, James answered her. 'I am lonely sometimes. Yes, that's true. But I've always loved my work and it's kept me busy, and is also gratifying to me in many ways. There's a huge amount to do to rebuild it now I'm back.' He smiled at Rossi. 'You don't have to worry about me, sweetheart. I can find plenty of company when I need it. But perhaps I am a little tired of being lonely.'

TEN

J ames let himself into his house on South Audley Street and
took off his hat, scarf and overcoat. He put all of them in
the cupboard before swiftly walking across the marble foyer
to the library.

He groaned as he went into the room and saw the papers
layering the desk. Remembering he had arranged them in order
of importance, he sat down in his chair. After staring at them
for a second or two, he lifted the papers on the left side and
looked at the objects on the desk, a small corner of clutter.

Then he saw it, and his face brightened as he reached for the
icon, the one Irina had given to him so long ago.

It was of the Madonna, beautifully painted in every detail and
enclosed in a very decorative gold frame. She had told him it
was very old, and Russian, and that she had found it in an
antique shop in Mayfair.

Picking it up, he stared at it for a long time, as he fell down
into himself. He remembered Irina and when he had met her.

The past was suddenly the present, right there before him. He
closed his eyes, leaning back in his chair. He saw her so vividly:

her glossy brown hair piled in curls on top of her head and her intense dark brown eyes, with thick, dark lashes. They had been in her aunt's house in Chelsea, in the exquisite drawing room full of lovely pale colours. He had always enjoyed airy, light rooms, found them soothing.

He had been staring at a table filled with similar objects, wondering what they were, when Irina had explained that they were icons. They belonged to her and her sister, Natalie. He had told Peter Keller what they were when Peter had come to join him at the table. He too was curious.

How long ago had it been since he and Peter had gone to dinner at her aunt Cheska's place? Twenty-five years ago? Perhaps.

Irina had told them later that she was half-Russian, on her mother's side.

Following that evening, only a few days later, she had come to his uncle George's flat on Half Moon Street, where he had been living. She had given him the icon that was now in his hands.

That was when their love affair had begun. They had fallen for each other that night at her aunt's house and, for some time, they were inseparable.

But another aunt, who lived in Russia, had fallen very ill, and Irina had gone to her. She was away for such a long time that neither of them felt the same when she returned. She had been lovely, and lovely to him.

Falconer opened his eyes and sat up straighter; he put the icon back in its place, smiling to himself. Eventually, Irina had married his close friend Peter, and Irina never referred to their past; nor did he.

But he couldn't help wondering what had been happening earlier today, when he had seen her in confrontation with that tall, bulky man.

William and Natalie Venables were giving a dinner party next week, and he knew he would see her then. However, he would not bring up that strange incident; he would never embarrass her, or any other woman. Still, it troubled him.

Standing up, James took off his jacket and put it on a chair. He then went back to his desk. There was a roaring fire in the grate, and he was suddenly feeling too warm.

As he settled down to work, there was a knock on the library door, and he called, 'Come in.'

It was his housekeeper, Mrs Thorpe, who stood there in the doorway. 'Excuse me, Mr Falconer. Sorry to disturb you, but I'm just off to Fortnum's. Cook needs a few things for dinner tonight.'

'Thank you for telling me, Mrs Thorpe,' James said. 'I assume Brompton got off to Wimbledon to see his mother.'

'Yes, he did, sir. He'll return by lunchtime tomorrow.'

'Yes, he told me,' James answered, smiled and nodded.

'I'll be on my way then, sir,' the housekeeper said, and closed the door.

Falconer sighed, picked up a contract for a building project on the docks and was soon deeply involved with what was called *the small print*. He never neglected that section of a contract; it held too many pitfalls. He concentrated for a good twenty minutes, making a few notations. After a moment, he stopped, his mind wandering.

Leonie. Yet again she crept into his mind. The guilt assaulted him, as it did so often these days. He should have sought her out, made friends with her.

Leonie was a married woman now. He leaned back in the chair, and thought about her husband, Richard Rhodes. He usually saw him only in passing at the club, but they had spoken once, and he remembered it well. Closing his eyes, James recalled that meeting in great detail, leaped into it, in a sense . . . lived it once more.

* * *

'Thank you, Brompton,' he said to his butler. 'I'll see you later.'

He was late, and hurried outside to his motorcar, careful not to stumble because of his limp. His leg was playing up again. Andrews, his driver, helped him into the back. Realizing his master was in a hurry, he got into the driver's seat and took off.

'We're going to your club, sir, aren't we?'

'Correct, Andrews. And I have guests waiting. I'm certain they're already at White's.'

'Not much traffic tonight, and it's not far. But I'll step on it,' Andrews replied.

'Thank you.' Leaning back against the leather, James attempted to relax, wincing as he rubbed his aching leg. He had been looking forward to having supper with William.

Andrews was soon drawing up on St James's Street, outside White's. James thanked him and alighted, limped to the front door of the club.

There was another man going inside just in front of him, and James waited impatiently a moment before pushing the door. The man had stopped suddenly, and the door hit his shoulder. The fellow swung around and glanced at James, a sour look on his face. He turned away, exclaiming, 'You bashed my shoulder in your haste. What's the big hurry? You should be more careful.'

'Look here, I'm terribly sorry,' James said. 'I didn't realize the door would hit you. I do apologize, and most sincerely. Come on, let's shake on it.'

The man turned around fully and James recognized Richard Rhodes. As always impeccably dressed in what was obviously a Savile Row suit, silk handkerchief in his breast pocket.

Falconer hadn't remembered how good-looking he was. A handsome man indeed, and more than likely irresistible to women. Leading-man good-looking, in fact, and very smart. A bit of a dandy, his clothes perfect.

After staring at James, he nodded, and a faint smile flickered. 'You're Leonie's father, James Falconer.'

'That's correct.'

'I'm pleased to meet you at last. I've long been an admirer of yours, aware of your tremendous success. England's greatest business tycoon, they say. A great achievement. Congratulations.' A wide smile spread across his face as he offered his hand.

James shook hands with Rhodes, and with a sinking feeling he realized there was something about the man he didn't like. Slick Willy, he thought. Smarmy. Out for himself, of course. And, naturally, Leonie hadn't seen those traits. She was obviously bowled over by those looks.

Clearing his throat, Falconer said, 'I must hurry on upstairs, can't keep guests waiting.'

Rhodes nodded, his smile intact.

'Perhaps we can dine together soon, with Leonie,' he suggested.

James simply nodded and headed for the staircase.

Sitting in his chair, opening his eyes, James glanced around, realizing he was in the library of his house on South Audley Street. That meeting months ago with Rhodes had been so vivid in his memory.

The sudden noise of the door knocker made him jump. Knowing Cook would not come up to open the door, he left the library and went out into the foyer.

The brass knocker banged again, and he pulled open the door, feeling irritated. As he stared at the person on his front steps, he was taken aback. Apparently so was she. Before he could say a word, she spoke.

'Goodness, James. I didn't expect you to answer the door. Isn't that Brompton's job?' Mrs Ward said, her surprise apparent.

'He's off today, Georgiana.' He noticed she was holding an envelope, and he said, 'I presume that's for me.'

'Yes, it is,' she answered.

'So give it to me.' He eyed her, thought she looked stunningly beautiful, and added swiftly, 'Better still, you can simply tell me.' Reaching out, he took hold of her arm. 'Let's not stand on the doorstep. The neighbours will be curious. Come in.'

Georgiana Ward laughed and allowed herself to be drawn into the entrance hall. James banged the door shut with his foot as he led her towards the library. 'It's very warm in there,' he went on. 'Better take off your cloak.'

He helped her to do this and hung the cloak in the cupboard. Then, he turned to her, smiling. 'Come. Let's go into the library.'

He opened the door wider and ushered her in. He then realized he was in his shirtsleeves and he exclaimed, 'Oh, I'd better put my jacket on.'

'Don't worry about that,' Georgiana said. 'Stay as you are. I don't mind.'

'Very well. Thank you.' Glancing at her, he said, 'Well, this is a nice surprise. Here we are, you and I, in a lovely cosy room, with a note you have for me. So I think we should enjoy this time together and have a drop of bubbly. What about that?'

Looking at the clock on the mantelpiece, she said, 'But it's only four o'clock.'

'Let's not worry about that; somewhere in the world it's drink time . . .' His sentence trailed off, and he walked to the door. 'Back in a minute.'

'Where are you going?' she asked.

'To get the champagne.'

She watched him leave, noticed he was limping and not trying to disguise it as he had been doing. She turned her head, looking around the library, but could not see the walking stick anywhere.

So, he was obviously endeavouring to walk without it. Oh, that pride of his did get in the way at times. But she was glad he was obviously more at ease about it now.

Georgiana settled back on the large Chesterfield sofa in front of the fire, staring into the flames, thinking about this man she had loved for so many years.

This room was her favourite because he spent most of his time in it, at that huge Georgian desk.

It displayed his great taste – the dark green walls, two covered with floor-to-ceiling shelves filled with books. The two large, tall windows with dark green velvet draperies, and the deep burgundy-leather sofa she was sitting on. It matched the red-and-green patterned Oriental rug covering the floor.

Over the fireplace there was a gilt-framed mirror, and the two side walls held Impressionist paintings. One was a Monet and the other a Cézanne. He had a good eye for art.

But most of all, she loved being in the room because it smelled of him. A mixture of cigarette smoke and his cologne. Georgiana leaned back, suddenly thinking of his huge success, the way he had gone up the ladder in business. Yes, her James was brilliant – always had been, even when he was only a boy.

'Here I am,' James said, entering the room, carrying two glass flutes in one hand and a bottle of champagne in the other, still limping a little.

As he went to put them on the table near the window, she jumped up, walked over to join him. 'Let me help you,' she said.

'It's fine. I can manage.' He stared at her after placing the items on the table, and said, 'Well, there is one thing you can do.'

'Tell me.'

He did not answer. There was a chemistry between them that had grown and grown. Slowly, he stepped closer, and then pulled her into his arms and kissed her, and passionately so. She returned his kisses, clinging to him, enjoying the feel of his body without the jacket. Although he was slender, he was very fit, with taut muscles in his arms and across his back. Her hands slid down his back, and he tightened his grip. His hands went onto her buttocks, and he drew her closer. They stood welded together, still kissing, until James knew they had to stop this at once. And so did Georgiana. She had felt his erection and knew that he was as aroused as she was.

It was James who put an end to this passionate embrace. He looked at her and shook his head. 'Just imagine this. Look what you do to me, Mrs Ward.'

'You do the same to me. Very much so, James.'

'Oh yes, I know I have a strong effect on you. I always have. You can't resist my sexual charms.'

'How very modest you are!'

He laughed. So did she. James reached out and touched her cheek. 'You have the softest complexion. It's like silk. It's the same everywhere – I remember. On your arms, thighs, and oh, your breasts.'

'James, stop it. You're behaving like a . . . a naughty boy.'

His answer was a loving smile. He drew her close to him, and she leaned against his body. He said softly, against her hair, 'I'm not a *boy* any more, my darling. I'm a man.'

Staring up at him, she thought his bright blue eyes were more vivid than ever at this moment, and she was unable to speak, held by them.

He poured the champagne, handed her a flute, and took the other one for himself. Together they went over to the Chesterfield. After clinking glasses, James said, 'I'm happy you're here because I do have a few things to discuss with you. But first, the note please.'

Eleven

Mrs Ward handed him the note. James handed it back to her. 'Read it to me,' he said, sounding slightly bossy.

Staring at him, she answered, 'Why don't I just tell you – that's quicker?'

'No, I want you to read it to me, because I love the sound of your beautiful voice, and I don't care about quicker.'

His voice had been stern, and as she continued to look at him, she saw at once that he was serious. But he was a serious man, had always been like that, even when he was seventeen. And usually very focused. Furthermore, he always got his way. Everyone kowtowed to him.

Clearing her throat, Georgiana took the note out of the envelope and began to read it.

'*My dear James,*
I have tried very hard to persuade Leonie to see you, but without success. She is stubborn. I'm so sorry. I don't know what else I can do.

*On to another matter – I need your professional advice,
about my house in Ascot. I know you will be coming to
stay in two weeks, but I wonder if you could come for the
day in the meantime and advise me on some repairs. I
would greatly appreciate your help.*
    Yours,
    Georgiana'

'Are you?' he asked, a small smile lurking around his mouth,
as he gazed at her, pushing thoughts of Leonie away.

'I don't understand what you mean?'

'Are you *mine*?' he replied.

She smiled. 'Of course. I've just told you that. How many
times do you need to hear it?'

'Every day.' He took a sip of the champagne. 'So be kind to
me; stay for supper tonight.'

Georgiana gazed at him and knew she had no alternative but
to agree. Sitting back, she said, 'I think I can probably cancel
my previous engagement.'

He grinned. 'That's wonderful, and who were you dining with?
Not another man, I hope?'

Aware that he was teasing her, she said, 'There is no other
man, as you put it. Only you. I was going to join Anne
Meredith and several other women – a ladies' evening. I won't
be missed.'

'I'd miss you if I were them,' he shot back, laughing. 'Do you
need to get in touch with her? You can use my telephone.'

'No, I'll do it when I go home to change for dinner. But thank
you.'

'Oh no, no, no! You're not leaving. You look beautiful in that
purple dress. You don't have to change. And neither will I. But
I will put my jacket on. *And you're not leaving.*'

Georgiana nodded. 'I don't need to telephone Anne. I said I'd
try to be there.'

'Then all's well that ends well,' he answered, and rose. He walked across the room to refill his flute, wanting also to hide his knowing smile. He was quite sure she had intended to stay for the evening all along. Oh, the ways of women, he thought, as he filled the glass, still smiling to himself.

When he returned and sat down next to her on the sofa, Georgiana said, 'You mentioned you needed to discuss a few things with me. Do you wish to do that now, before supper?'

'Yes, of course. I was wondering where Leonie and Richard Rhodes are planning to settle, now they are back in London.'

James noticed immediately that she was genuinely surprised by the question. She remained silent.

He continued, 'I would like to buy them a flat in Mayfair. I own a lot of buildings, you know. And you can say it's from you. A wedding gift. You don't have to tell her I paid for it.'

'They will continue to live at my house in Curzon Street, of course,' Mrs Ward announced. 'Richard Rhodes does have a flat in Chelsea, but it's not very big, so they will be more comfortable with me.'

Now it was James's turn to look surprised. He did not want to upset her, but he knew he had to prepare her. He was absolutely certain Leonie must want to be alone with her new husband, with whom she was apparently madly in love. And Rhodes would not want to live with his mother-in-law for long.

After a few seconds of reflection, James jumped in with both feet. 'I don't want to upset you, darling, but I must prepare you for the worst. A newly married couple like that will *want their own home.*'

She was silent for a long moment, then asked, 'How can you be so sure? You don't really know her these days.'

'I do, in a way. You've told me a lot about Leonie, and I've realized she's a lot *like* me, has certain traits I have.'

Again, Georgiana was silent, weighing his words. He was

undoubtedly clever, the most brilliant businessman in the country, and he did have insight into people. Also, she knew he was kind to everyone, not just her. And he wanted to protect her from any kind of hurt. A deep sigh escaped her.

Eventually, she said, 'If you are correct, then so be it. I will just have to live alone. I'll manage.'

'You don't have to live alone. You can live with me. Here, in this house. It's larger than yours. Say yes.'

'Is this a proposition or a proposal?' she asked carefully, looking at him pointedly.

He chuckled. 'Don't be daft, my darling. It's a proposal.'

Taking hold of her, drawing her closer, he stared at her intently. His face serious.

She was mesmerized by those vividly blue eyes, sparkling at this moment, and did not speak.

James said eagerly, his face now alive with happiness. 'Marry me, Georgiana, and as soon as possible.'

After a while, she said, 'I'm sorry, James. I can't, and you know that.'

'Why not?' he asked gently, not wanting to inflame her in any way, but anxious to know her reasons.

Georgiana took a deep breath, and after some thought, she said slowly, 'If I married you, I would lose Leonie. She would cut me off completely. I wouldn't exist for her.'

Her words, uttered quietly, were nonetheless hurtful. She saw the sorrow flash across his face and the pain in his eyes.

Swiftly, she explained, 'I don't love my daughter more than I love you, I promise you that. It's a different kind of love I have for her, a mother's love. I am *in love* with you. I always have been, since we first met in Hull. I love you the way a woman loves a man. I'm not really putting her first.'

'I see.' He got up, threw several logs on the fire, took the poker and moved the logs around. He returned to the sofa, picked up their crystal flutes and moved across the room again, to the table near the window. He filled the glasses with the Veuve Clicquot, and stood for a moment, settling himself down. He did not want her to see how sad he was.

Once he had placed the flutes on the table near the Chesterfield, he sat down next to her, took her hand in his.

In a steady voice, which surprised him, he said in a low tone, 'She hates me, resents me, because I let her down when she was younger. I didn't see her often, and not at all after she was thirteen. I was wrong. I know that this estrangement is my fault. I've no excuse other than that I was grief-stricken about Alexis. I felt guilty about all those miscarriages she had had. I blamed myself. But I was also selfish. I should have had the sense to keep in touch with my daughter.'

He shook his head, and she saw the hint of tears in those extraordinarily blue eyes.

'You cannot blame yourself about Alexis dying, James. You are a very sensual and sexual man, and there's nothing wrong with that. Alexis obviously wanted *you* in the same way. And you both wanted children.'

He remained silent. She continued talking, wanting to pull him out of this depressed mood. 'Is it worth trying to reach Leonie through Richard Rhodes? She *is* crazy about him, and if you could win him over, make *him* understand your behaviour, perhaps he could intervene in your favour.'

Falconer looked at her, nodding, seeing her point. 'Yes, it might work. Rhodes is a member of White's, as am I. It will be easy to start a conversation with him, at the club. We've exchanged greetings once before.'

'He's very civil, genial actually, although, as I told you, there is something about him that I don't like. Can't quite put my finger on it, though.'

'I know I found myself reacting in the same way. But he's so appropriate, so eligible. *Good* family, country gentry. *Good* school, Eton. *Good* university, Oxford. *Good* job in the City.

Good looks. And too damned *good* to be true, in my opinion.' James took a long swallow of the champagne.

So did Georgiana, and for a few seconds her mind raced. She wanted to get him back to normal, to erase that sorrowful look, to cheer him up, to give him something to look forward to. And it came to her an instant later.

She reached out, took hold of his hand, and said, 'I want to make a deal with you.'

He looked at her swiftly, and then smiled. 'You're using my jargon now, sweetheart. What kind of deal?'

'Once Leonie has had her first child, and if she hasn't changed her attitude towards you, I will marry you, James. I promise.'

He couldn't believe what he was hearing and felt a sudden flash of relief. An unexpected happiness rushed through him.

'Do you really mean that?' He looked at her with great intensity. 'You'll marry me, even if she remains obdurate in her treatment of me?' he asked.

'I do mean it.'

'Why?'

'Because she will have her husband and a child, and they will make her truly happy. And I won't feel guilty about marrying you. It will be our turn then.'

'Promise?' he said.

'I do. Cross my heart and hope to die.'

'Then let's shake on it. It's a deal.'

TWELVE

James Falconer liked Mrs Ward's new driver. His name was David Foster; he was young, energetic, and an expert with her motorcar. Furthermore, he was genial and outgoing, pleasant to have around.

On Sunday morning, they set off around ten o'clock and were driven to Ascot by Foster. James had offered to advise on some problems with the house. Both James and Georgiana were quiet, lost in their own thoughts. It was Georgiana who broke the silence in the motorcar when she said, 'You look very pensive, James. Are you troubled by something?'

He bestirred himself and looked across at her, shaking his head. 'No, not really. I was just thinking about Rhodes, and what you've told me, asking myself *why* I thought he was not quite what he appears to be that time I ran into him at White's.'

'You know I have that same feeling, and I'm just as puzzled by my reaction as you are about yours. Isn't there anyone you can ask, anyone you know who knows *him*? Could enlighten you?'

'No, I don't think so.' Straightening up in his seat, James said, 'I am having dinner with my old friend, Chief Inspector Roger Crawford, tomorrow. I'm going to mention the name to him.'

'Is he still with Scotland Yard? I thought he'd retired.'

'He did want to do so last year, but got talked out of it. Roger is there for at least another two years, running the Criminal Acts Division, which he was asked to create. He's not out in the field any more,' James explained.

Leaning forward, her eyes riveted on James, Georgiana asked in a quiet voice, 'So Richard Rhodes is a *criminal*, in your opinion?' She had a shocked expression on her face.

'Oh no, I don't think that at all! On the contrary, he's an upstanding citizen, as far as I know. He behaves like a gentleman.'

James glanced out of the car window for a moment, perplexed. Eventually, he looked across at Georgiana again. 'It's something *about* him that seems to grab me, makes me think he's not . . . *kosher*. Do you know that Jewish word?' he asked, giving her a wry smile.

Georgiana laughed lightly. 'Of course I do, I have quite a few Jewish friends, whom I met through Anne Meredith, who's Jewish herself.'

'Oh really, I didn't know that. Anyway, I will ask the chief inspector if he knows anything about Rhodes. Remember, he is with Scotland Yard and can go into numerous files, ask within the Yard, talk to the other detectives.'

'I see. Well, we have to hope Leonie is safe and sound, and happy. The latter is mandatory, to my way of thinking.'

'I agree.' James got up and moved to sit down next to her with a bit of a jerk.

'That was a dangerous move,' she said in a chastising tone. 'You could have fallen.'

'It certainly was dangerous, and I'm a dangerous man when it comes to you.' Leaning into her, he kissed her. She kissed him back, her arms wrapped around him. And they clung to each other for a long time.

Stroking her cheek, he smiled at her. 'I'm glad we're going to be alone at the house and that your butler and housekeeper are away. Perhaps we can steal a moment or two together, to continue this.'

'Larkin is there,' Georgiana pointed out swiftly, eyeing him.

'Surely the caretaker doesn't come into your house, does he?' James sounded incredulous.

'Of course not. At least not without being asked, and then he only stands near the kitchen door,' Georgiana answered.

'I'm glad to hear it.' James wrapped his arms around her and settled them comfortably for the rest of the journey to Ascot. From time to time, he closed his eyes, imagining their love-making later in the day, feeling happy, even a bit carefree. What a lucky man I am, he thought, and dozed, as Georgiana was already asleep. It was Foster who awakened them when they finally arrived at the house.

Larkin was waiting to greet them as they got out of the car, and James handed him a large wicker picnic basket. 'Would you take this to the kitchen, please, Larkin?'

'That I will, sir,' Larkin answered. He hurried off.

Georgiana was speaking to Foster, who had dismounted from the driver's seat. 'There is a picnic basket for you in the car too,' she told him. 'You can eat in the kitchen if you wish, Foster.'

'Thank you, ma'am, but I enjoy seeing Larkin and his wife; friends for years, we've been.'

He turned, took the basket, and thought to ask, 'What time shall I be ready to leave?'

'About four thirty, Foster, thank you.'

* * *

Georgiana sat in a chair in her bedroom, watching James examine the ceiling. Larkin was holding the ladder steady, and James was talking to him. 'I think this whole side of the house might be affected, Larkin. The other two bedrooms are worse than this, but this one's getting there. New roof needed, I'm sorry to say.'

'For the whole house?' Larkin sounded startled.

James began to explain that he would send one of his top roofing crews to Ascot on Tuesday, and what they would do, and he would follow their advice.

Georgiana rose, moved the fire screen, put more logs on the fire, and replaced the screen. Sitting down again, she couldn't help thinking what an incredible man James Falconer was. There was no side to him at all. He spoke to Larkin in the same way he spoke to his family, friends like Lady Jane and Lord Reggie Carpenter, and all of those he worked with.

She smiled to herself – but he did not always speak that way to her. Sometimes he sounded quite bossy, and she let him do it, never said a word. Georgiana knew he did it because he was possessive of her, and knew he could speak to her however he wished. Just as he knew he could tease her about certain things. He had been doing it for years, and enjoyed getting away with it.

Even when he first met me, she suddenly thought, when he was only seventeen . . . This startled her momentarily, when she considered all the years that had gone by. He had been a bit bossy the night of the storm.

James had had great self-assurance even then, and she understood how that originated. He came from a family well known for its high standards; it was working class but large, loving and secure. His grandparents, Philip and Esther Falconer, along with his parents, Matthew and Maude, had brought him up well. His late uncles, Harry and George, had been very caring, and instrumental in helping to shape him.

James had told her that himself, some time ago, and had been proud of their influence. He had loved his family deeply, and still did.

He had added, 'My background was modest, but my family had all the right priorities. I think I inherited my grandfather's integrity and my grandmother's ambition. She was a big influence.'

Whatever they did was obviously extraordinary, really, Georgiana now thought, but they couldn't teach him talent or drive . . . that he had been born with. Yes, of course, he was born with that brilliant mind. *That* had made him who he was today, the biggest business tycoon in England.

Unexpectedly, James was now standing next to her, smiling at her. 'Sorry to interrupt your daydreams, sweetheart, but do you know where the key is for that door in your dressing room?'

'No, I don't, James. That door was locked and without a key when I bought the house thirty years ago.'

He frowned. 'But didn't it bother you? The locked door, I mean.'

She shook her head, her expression puzzled. 'No, because behind that locked door is another guest bedroom, and the room can be entered from the main corridor. It didn't seem to matter that the door was locked.'

'I detest locked doors!' he exclaimed, making a face. 'I want every door working properly, because of fires. The possibility of a fire starting in a room scares me to death. People must be able to get out.'

Turning, he hurried across her bedroom, his face taut. Intent on his purpose, he left.

'Where are you going?'

'To get a bloody screwdriver,' he shot back, and disappeared.

Georgiana glanced around and noticed that the ladder had disappeared and so had Larkin. However, she knew James had probably sent the caretaker to look at the other guest bedrooms and the servants' rooms on the floor above.

James Falconer was far too efficient to ignore any rooms upstairs. He had told her yesterday: he was going to make sure her house was secure and comfortable in every way. *Everywhere.*

About five minutes later, she heard voices. She left her bedroom, went into the corridor, and looked inside the guest bedroom. She saw James kneeling on the floor, with a screwdriver in his right hand. Larkin was with him.

'What are you doing?' Georgiana asked from the doorway.

Without turning around, he explained, 'I'm taking the door knob off. When my crew comes next week, they will do it properly with a new lock and knob. Once I get the knob off now, I can take out the lock and put the knob on again. But it might be a bit wonky – the knob, that is.'

'Thank you, James. Thank you so much. I'm very grateful. You've made me understand the danger of a door I can't open.'

Standing up, straightening, he smiled at her. He walked over to Larkin and gave him the lock and the screwdriver.

'Thank you for assisting me, Larkin. I think you should go and eat. Foster is waiting for you, I'm sure.'

Larkin nodded. 'Thanks for letting me stay, Mr Falconer. Now I know how to handle a knob – unscrew it, I mean.' With a nod and a faint smile, as he passed Georgiana, the caretaker went downstairs.

James glanced up at the ceiling, and exclaimed, 'Thank goodness this ceiling is clean as a whistle. No leaks in here.'

Beckoning Georgiana to come into the guest bedroom, he took her arm, pushed open the formerly locked door, and said, 'Here we are, darling, in your dressing room. And now we are entering your bedroom. And oh, how easy it's going to be.' He drew her forward, a grin on his face.

She was silent as they walked towards the fireplace. He turned her to face him and stared into her eyes, dark blue like violets today. 'You *are* going to give me *that* guestroom when I come to stay in a couple of weeks, aren't you?'

'Oh, so that's what all this knob-changing is about. You want to come and go as you like, don't you, Mr Falconer?'

'I do indeed. After all, if you're not going to be Mrs James Falconer just yet, I'm not going to wait until I can get you to the altar.'

She smiled, her eyes sparkling.

He led her across to the bed. 'If you're agreeable, I'd like to consummate our union here and now.'

She nodded. 'I must lock my bedroom door, and you must go and lock the guestroom door next to the dressing room. We need our privacy.'

He nodded, and they went in different directions. James was back swiftly. He had taken off his jacket and tie in the dressing room. She had removed her short bolero and stood waiting near the bed.

As James walked towards her, he started to unbutton his shirt, his face taut with desire.

'Do you need me to help you get out of your dress, darling?' he asked softly.

'Please. There are lots of buttons in the back.'

THIRTEEN

Georgiana went into the bathroom to finish undressing. James hurriedly took off his shirt and the rest of his clothes. He turned off the bedside light as he got into the bed to wait for her.

When Georgiana emerged, she wore a blue silk robe, and she exclaimed, 'Oh, the firelight is so nice.'

'Draw the curtains, then the room will be even nicer,' James instructed. 'And take off the robe.'

Yes, Mr Bossy, she thought but did not say. She was always slightly amused by these announcements of his. After drawing the curtains, she took off the robe and slid into the bed.

James gently drew her towards him and wrapped his arms around her, holding her very close.

After they had nestled together for a few seconds, he said, 'I've longed for this moment for such a long time, I was beginning to think it wouldn't happen.'

'So did I,' Georgiana replied. 'But the war came and you were gone, and later terribly wounded.' Georgiana pressed herself close to him, and added, 'I've ached for you all these years.'

'Did you . . . touch yourself?' he whispered against her cheek.
'Yes,' she whispered back.

'Well, now *I'm* here, and I am going to love you well and truly. We will make up for lost time.' Moving slightly, he swept her hair away from her face. 'I've longed for you, too, Georgiana. Yearned to have you.'

Pushing himself up on one elbow, he leaned down and began to kiss her, and she responded ardently. Their passion grew, and she said, 'Please, James, touch me everywhere like you used to do. I want to feel your hands on me, loving me.'

Without responding, he did as she asked, murmuring, 'Your skin is like silk, but I've told you that before.'

James began to kiss her again, and when their tongues slid together, he thought this was the truest moment of intimacy and it thrilled him.

Their mutual passion soared up, and they clutched at each other frenziedly as he slid on top of her, and took her to him. Her arms went around his back, and so did her legs. He felt he was held in a silken vice. They were both sensual people, were inflamed, highly aroused, uninhibited, and now bound together as one.

Georgiana cried out and said his name over and over as she reached the pinnacle of pleasure. James did the same. He was taken to new heights by her.

Ecstasy flooded through them in the same way it always had in the past. Although they did not speak, they both knew they were made for each other, belonged together for the rest of their lives.

James had roused himself and left her side, after whispering loving words to her following their lovemaking.

She was sitting on the edge of the bed, smiling up at him, and then, as she dropped her eyes, she gasped loudly.

'Your wounds! Oh my God, your terrible wounds, James!' Georgiana exclaimed, staring at his ruined legs, unable to look away.

He glanced down and realized how truly ghastly his legs looked, and how they would appal most civilians, especially female.

Mostly he attempted to forget about them, and he did so quite frequently, because they were concealed all day and night by his trousers.

In a consoling voice, he said, 'They're not wounds now, Georgiana; they are healed. But I know I'm badly scarred.'

'They must hurt, though,' she replied, her voice trembling, tears in her eyes as she imagined how he must have suffered when it first happened.

'Only in winter and on rainy days. Then they ache. But mostly they're bearable.'

'How . . . how did it happen?' she asked a bit hesitantly, and stopped talking, just continued to stare at his ruined legs.

'My battalion was led into battle at the Somme by me. Their commander. We went across no-man's land right into the enemy's three lines of fire. They had a new and most deadly weapon, the machine gun. Hundreds of British soldiers fell into the trap, including me. It was a massacre, Georgiana.'

She was silent, tears trickling down her face.

Leaning towards her, James offered his hands. She took them, and he pulled her to her feet and held her close. She clung to him, then asked, 'Are you telling me the truth about them not hurting? I couldn't stand it if you were in pain.'

'I promise you they don't hurt when I'm warm. But I'm getting chilled, standing here naked with you.' He held her away, kissed her on the mouth, and then laughed. 'I think we'd better get dressed. At once. Otherwise, I'm going to take you back into that bed.'

She laughed with him, grabbed her silk robe and hurried to the bathroom.

James, watching her leave, understood yet again how much she meant to him, and he was touched by her reaction to his horribly scarred legs. As far as he was concerned, he was lucky. He had lived.

Fourteen

'It's been one helluva week,' James said. 'Thank goodness it's Friday!'

Chief Inspector Roger Crawford, one of James's closest friends, grinned at him. 'When is it not? Ever since I've known you, James, you've been hard at it. You never stop. But then I suppose that's why you're where you are today.'

James merely smiled. The two men lifted their glasses of Scotch and soda and clinked them. 'Cheers,' they said in unison.

The chief inspector went on, 'I'm glad we're having dinner here at your house. You've got the best cook in London and, like you, I find this room comfortable and welcoming. It's a pleasure to be here.'

'Thank you for your kind words, Roger. It's been such rotten weather, and it's nice to have a drink and chat in front of the fire. Anyway, how are things at the Yard?'

'Busier than ever, so much going on. You know, after the end of the war, a lot of foreigners stayed on, and some are a problem, especially the anarchists.'

'I read that in *The Times*. I think London is a dangerous city, but I guess all big cities are.' As he spoke, James looked keenly at the policeman, and raised a brow.

'They are. However, London, in particular, is a big attraction these days; people flock here. They think it's the centre of the universe. In a way, it is, so much to do. Pubs, bars, restaurants, gambling clubs, the variety shows, the theatres, and other less savoury spots,' Roger pointed out in a knowing voice.

James laughed. 'That's an interesting way to describe brothels.'

Roger laughed with him. 'I just want to add that you must be careful out there, my friend. You're too famous an icon. And criminals never sleep. You could be a target.'

'You've used that expression before, and I do take care. I've got the driver in the motorcar, plus a former bobby who gives me protection.'

'Glad to hear it.' After a long swallow of Scotch, Roger gave James a long look. 'You said you needed my help when you invited me to dinner. Got a problem?'

There was a moment of silence. Then James said, 'Not exactly, Roger . . . Not long ago, my daughter by Mrs Ward eloped with a man called Richard Rhodes. Do you know him?'

Roger shook his head. 'No. Heard of him, though. Good-looking chap, a bit of a dandy. Women seem drawn to him. Quite the socialite. His photograph is often in those society magazines women seem to enjoy.' Roger paused, then said in a low tone, 'Why are *you* interested in *him*?'

'There is something about him that makes me uneasy. Can't put my finger on it. Georgiana has had the same reaction, and he is now *Leonie's husband*.'

'I wish you could be more precise, James. You don't think he's a criminal in some way, do you?'

Falconer shook his head quickly and gave his friend a long, hard stare.

Roger found himself being held by those strikingly blue eyes which were, at this moment, icy cold. He felt a small shiver run down his back. Finally, the chief inspector said, 'So *what* then? *What's* troubling you really?'

'I suppose he's too bloody good to be true. Good family, Eton and Oxford. Good job in the City. Good-looking, Savile Row clothes. Mr Perfect, that's how I think of him. I believe he's an opportunist, although that doesn't bother me too much.'

'Are you suggesting that he's hiding something? Is he a philanderer?' Roger paused, then said slowly, 'Do you think he leads a double life? Might he prefer men?'

'Oh, I doubt the latter,' James asserted.

'One never knows about anybody. Lots of people have secret lives and are clever at hiding things,' Roger pointed out.

'You're correct. But, as I said, Rhodes just seems *too much*.'

'I understand. So you think Rhodes is a fake, is that it?' Roger frowned. 'In what way?' He gave James a quizzical look, although he trusted his judgement.

'In his character and personality,' James was quick to answer. 'The man he shows to the world at large is not who he really is. It's an act. Beneath the surface, I think something malignant lurks.'

The chief inspector was genuinely shocked. He exclaimed, 'Your daughter is married to him, James, so I'm not surprised you're worried.'

'I am. You're correct about that, Roger. On the other hand, she ran off with him and is madly in love, according to her mother. I doubt he will do her wrong, actually, because Georgiana says he's also besotted. And they're living with Georgiana Ward at the moment. He surely can't hurt Leonie while they're under her mother's roof.'

At that moment, Brompton came in and spoke to James. 'Dinner is served, Mr Falconer.'

'Thank you, Brompton,' James stood up. 'Let's go and eat, Roger. I, for one, am famished.'

'I'm looking forward to supper too. I missed lunch today,' Roger remarked.

'We're having our meal in the small dining room,' James told him as they walked out of the library. 'It's cosier, and there's a fire in there.'

The two men entered the room a moment later. The chief inspector smiled to himself. It had been a long time, and he'd forgotten how much he enjoyed his friend's company and this welcoming house. James had had this small room painted bright red, and it was dramatic but pleasing. On three walls hung three paintings, all Impressionists. Two Chagalls, which were colourful and full of life, and a Cézanne, which was darker in its tones, but equally as impressive. It balanced the other two. A Van Gogh was hanging over the fireplace. The room was illuminated by many candles. It had a special beauty.

James and Roger sat down in red-upholstered chairs, the velvet fabric matching the floor-length draperies at the window.

'Soup to start,' James announced, grinning at the inspector. 'Your favourite and mine, parsnip soup flavoured with ginger, then rib of beef with gravy, horseradish sauce, roast potatoes and green peas. '

'You spoil your guests marvellously, James. No one else gives suppers like you.'

FIFTEEN

When there was meat to carve, James always did it. And so, once he and the chief inspector had finished their parsnip-ginger soup, Brompton arrived with the beef. He put the carving board on a side table along with the carving utensils.

At once James stood up, and said to Crawford, 'I know you like your beef thinly sliced, as I do.'

'No other way to eat it,' Crawford answered. He picked up the glass of burgundy, swirled it for a second or two, and then took a sniff. 'Excellent wine, James,' he said, and put the glass down. He would not drink until his host sat down.

As he waited for his plate of food, the chief inspector thought about Richard Rhodes. Knowing James as well as he did – had done since he was a boy, in fact – he was quite certain Rhodes presented some sort of problem. So far, though, his friend had not been forthcoming. Crawford decided to wait to bring up that name again.

Over their meal, James talked about a new division he was thinking of starting at the Malvern Company: Travel. 'People are on the move these days,' he explained to the chief inspector. 'So I asked Peter to put a group of experts together and we're looking into doing arranged trips in England and abroad. We'll have guides and hotels booked. It's going to work well, I know that. We need to move into some new areas.'

'Clever chap, Keller, but I thought he ran your Wine Division, which I know has been quiet while you were both at war,' Crawford ventured.

'Oh yes, he does. He just gave me the idea and a sort of plan. The thing is, we can't stand still. The company just about survived us being away fighting, but I'm not going to deny that times are tough – for everyone in business,' James told him.

The chief inspector shook his head, chuckling. 'You never stop, James. You've always got something different bubbling on the hob.'

James chuckled with him and began to eat. The chief inspector did the same, and the two men fell silent, enjoying their food and the red wine. After apple crumble with custard was served and eaten, the chief inspector sat back in his chair and smiled at James.

'In my opinion, good old-fashioned English food can't be beaten when it's cooked properly. Thank you for the best supper I've had – since I was last here, James.'

'I agree with you, although I do like a few French dishes, and some Italian fare as well.'

Brompton came in with a tray of coffee and served it, and asked, 'Will you be taking cognac in the library later, sir?'

'Yes, we will. Thank you, Brompton.'

'I'm going to ask you a bit more about Richard Rhodes,' Chief Inspector Crawford said slowly.

He and James were ensconced in the library, sitting in front of the roaring fire, both nursing a balloon of Napoleon brandy.

James nodded. 'I knew you would, but there's not much more to tell. However, I can't get him out of my mind.'

'Do you feel he's a threat? Is that it?'

'Not sure. But as I told you, he's a fake in my opinion, not who he pretends to be.'

'Let me ask you this. Do you think he is a threat to Leonie? Is that where your worry lies?'

'I don't believe he would hurt her, as I've said. He's too smitten, adores her, according to Georgiana. Yet I still have that niggling worry.'

'I've not come across him, nor seen anything about him at the Yard, but I'll certainly do some digging tomorrow,' Roger asserted. 'Perhaps he's a bit crooked in business. It's banking, isn't it?'

'Yes,' James said. 'I've considered that too. There's a lot of hanky-panky going on in *that* world. Thievery, embezzlement, crooked deals, questionable transactions. You name it.'

Crawford nodded. 'I've heard all about that. The Fraud Division is run by a friend of mine. I'll go and see him tomorrow. Apparently, you haven't been able to win Leonie over, like you'd hoped?'

James shook his head, looking glum. 'No.' He peered into the brandy balloon, falling silent.

Crawford decided to let the matter drop. At least here and now. However, he made a decision. He would ask someone to quietly investigate Mr Richard Rhodes, and he wouldn't leave a stone unturned.

Sixteen

'It's not like Peter to be late,' William Venables said, looking across the table at James Falconer, raising a dark brow.

'I know,' James responded. 'He's a stickler about time, always prompt. I hope there's nothing wrong.'

The two old friends were sitting at James's favourite table at the restaurant in the Ritz Hotel. It was snowing outside, and it seemed to James that December was even colder than November. His legs were a good barometer when it came to assessing the weather. Both of them ached today, and he had been compelled to take his stick with him when he left Malvern House.

It had been a busy week, and he was looking forward to a restful Saturday and Sunday, and possibly a trip to Ascot.

'Shall we look at the menus?' William asked. 'And do you want a drink? A glass of their burgundy perhaps?'

'Menus, yes. Booze, no. I'm not up for it today. Anyway, you know I hardly drink at lunch, or during the day. But thanks for offering, old chap.'

William gazed at the menu, and said, 'The chef has some great winter dishes today, James. Lamb shanks in red wine, steak-and-kidney pie, and venison casserole. I think it's going to be the casserole for me . . .' William paused and looked up at the waiter, who had arrived at the table. 'What is it, Charles?'

'I have a note for Mr Falconer, sir, from the hotel receptionist.' As he spoke, he handed a small envelope to James.

Thanking the waiter, James opened it, took out the note and read it quickly. 'Problems!' he exclaimed. Then, leaning across the table, he said in a low voice, 'It's from Keller. Irina was attacked and is in King's Hospital with bad injuries. He's begging us to go there.'

James rose, and so did William. Striding towards the doorway, he said to the maître d', 'An emergency, Wallace. We have to leave. So sorry. Bill me for the bread and the wine Mr Venables had. I'll be in next week.'

'Of course, sir. And I'm sorry you have an emergency,' the maître d' replied.

James nodded, as did William. They left the hotel, walking swiftly. Within minutes, they were climbing into James's Daimler and on the way to King's Hospital.

Settled back in their seats, William said, 'How can Irina have been attacked? I mean, where? And who would do such a thing?'

'I've no idea,' James answered. 'The note was brief. But we must give Keller the support he needs.'

From the moment he had read the note, James Falconer had thought of that bulky man, the one who had been with Irina on Piccadilly. Arguing. But then he had helped her into a taxicab and got in with her. Several weeks ago. He suddenly wished he'd intervened; now he couldn't help wondering if it was that man who had attacked her today. And who was he?

He thought of mentioning the incident he had witnessed, but instantly changed his mind. The less said the better. He remembered the words his grandmother had always uttered: *A still tongue and a wise head.*

'You're correct,' James asserted. 'And I must admit this is

somewhat baffling. Who on earth would attack lovely Irina, a quiet woman who designs clothes? It's odd, to say the least.'

'London's not a very happy city these days,' William pointed out. 'Too many foreigners, and demobbed soldiers with no work, along with Russian anarchists setting off bombs. Then there are the vagrants, the homeless, beggars in the streets, vagabond kids, and all manner of pickpockets. I reckon anything can happen here these days. Nothing really surprises me.'

'Well said, my lad. Let us hope that Irina hasn't been too badly hurt. We must do all we can to help Peter cope with this sudden problem.'

When William and James alighted from the motorcar, they saw Keller immediately. He was hovering on the steps of the hospital, bundled up in a coat and scarf.

Walking over to greet him, James noticed at once the tautness of his face, which was the colour of bleached bone, and the stricken look in his eyes. Then, at the sight of his friends, relief flashed, and he stepped forward.

James gave Keller a bear hug, and so did William.

'Thanks for coming so quickly,' Keller said, leading them into the hospital entrance hall. 'We can go into the waiting room.'

'Lead the way,' James said. He and William followed Keller, who hurried to the far corner, which was empty. The three men sat down. Keller said, 'The police are with Irina now. Thankfully she has regained consciousness, and so has Mrs MacDonald, our house-keeper. Mrs Mac, as we call her, was also punched in the face.'

James grimaced. 'Start at the beginning, Keller, please. What exactly happened this morning?'

Keller nodded. 'I went to work around seven thirty, to Malvern House, of course. Around ten o'clock, our next-door neighbour, Mrs Copeland, heard loud noises, a ruckus, and went outside.

She saw a man running away down the street. Our front door was wide open, banging in the wind. When she went into the front hall of our house, she saw Irina sprawled in an armchair, with blood all over her face. Mrs Mac was on the floor, also with a bloody face. She felt their pulses. They were both alive. After that she sent another neighbour to find the copper on the beat where we live. Soon the police were there, investigating and calling for an ambulance. The police got a message to me at work, and I came here at once.'

'Your neighbour was a fast thinker,' William said. 'So she didn't see the man's face?'

'No, she didn't,' Keller answered, and then added, 'There's one thing that is odd. Drawers and cupboard doors in the parlour and the dining room were opened, as if the man had been looking for something.'

'Did you keep any valuables there?' James asked, his gaze resting on Keller, a quizzical expression on his face.

'Nothing. Only silver in the dining room,' Keller responded.

'Irina had nice jewellery,' James murmured. 'Where did she keep that?'

'Upstairs in a small safe, where no one could find it. I did run up and look, and the jewellery is there,' Keller said. 'Untouched.'

'So the man was looking for something, but we don't know what. Perhaps he beat up Irina because she wouldn't give him any information.' James raised a brow. 'Is that possible?'

'But there wasn't anything to find!' Keller protested, his voice rising. 'It's a mystery to me. I can tell you that.'

'Major Falconer!' a voice exclaimed, and to James it was a familiar voice. He swung around and a disbelieving smile spread across his face at the sight of his old comrade from the trenches. 'Good heavens! What are you doing here, Lieutenant Stead? I hope no one in your family is ill.'

'No, sir,' Jack Stead replied, walking over to join James and the other two men. 'No, no. I'm a copper now, Major. *Detective*

Stead, that's me. I'm investigating the attack on Mrs Keller. I'm with Scotland Yard.'

James nodded. 'Good choice, Stead. This is Mr Keller, and our friend Mr Venables.'

After they had all shaken hands, Keller said, 'The hospital staff says my wife is now conscious. When can I see her? Do you know, Detective Stead?'

'In a short while, I think,' Stead answered. 'Dr Mulroney will be coming out to see you, but I do know she will recover, if that helps you to feel less worried.'

'It does, thank you, Detective Stead,' Keller said, sounding slightly relieved.

'Has Mrs Keller been able to enlighten you about the attack on her this morning? And on the housekeeper.' James eyed Stead.

'Not really, Major Falconer. It was a shock, obviously, when this strange man suddenly burst through the front door. He attacked both women, beating them on their faces with his fists. She said he was a bulky man, well built, but wearing a hat pulled low on his brow, and a scarf. Neither woman saw his face, but Mrs Keller said she thought he was probably Russian.'

James gave Detective Stead an intense look. 'Did he ask her for anything? He must have spoken if she thought he was Russian.'

'Yes, he did say something in broken English, something that sounded to her like *heritage, our heritage*. But that is the only thing he said. Then he ransacked the drawers in two chests, went through the cupboards. From what the next-door neighbour said to me, he made quite a lot of noise, which brought her to the Kellers' door. The man was running hell for leather away from the house when she first saw him. She didn't see his face either.'

Looking at Keller, Falconer said again, 'Are you sure there was nothing *there*? Something this man wanted.'

'I am positive. But what now makes me worried is that Irina is half-Russian.'

'Yes, I know that,' Falconer said, and thought yet again about the man he'd seen Irina talking to on Piccadilly about two weeks ago. *He had been a bulky man.* Was it the same man? What was this all about, he wondered to himself. What did this man want? And where was it?

Detective Stead turned to Keller. 'Why are you worried, Mr Keller? Do you think this man might come back, attack your wife again for some unknown reason?'

'I don't know. I swear there is nothing in my home that is Russian, and no documents either. My wife hasn't been there for years, and our house is all in the modern style, with nothing from her parents or grandparents. As I just said, it's all a mystery to me.'

Detective Stead turned around at the sound of footsteps, and then nodded at Keller. 'Here comes Dr Mulroney. I'm sure he'll be taking you to see your wife.'

'Come and talk to me for a minute or two,' James said, taking hold of Jack Stead's arm. 'Will you excuse me, please, William?'

'Of course. I'm going outside to get a breath of fresh air.'

James nodded. He and Stead sat down in the corner of the waiting room.

'Not much chance of solving this, is there Stead?'

'I'm afraid not, Major. This city is full of foreigners, and unless he acts again, hits other women, then he's in the wind.' He sighed. 'However, I can't help thinking there's more to this than meets the eye.'

James sat up, alertly, staring at Stead. 'What do you mean? Explain.'

'That bulky Russian was looking for *something*, I'm absolutely certain, and you think the same, don't you, sir?'

'I do, Stead. Very much so. I also believe Keller. What the man was looking for is *not* in that house. It must be somewhere else.

However, I don't think Keller knows this, nor does he know where *it* is, obviously.' James nodded. 'I trust Keller.'

'Do you think his wife knows and wouldn't tell and was beaten up because of her silence?' Stead asked.

'It could be that. However, I'm wondering if she doesn't know what it is or where it is either. Perhaps there is another person involved, who took it and hid it, shall we say?' James shook his head. 'This is a damnable mystery, and it's not over yet.'

'I wish I knew what we were looking for,' Stead said.

'So do I. Let's stay in touch, Stead, and if you ever get tired of working at the Yard, come and see me at Malvern House.'

Jack Stead stared at his former commander in the Great War. 'I'm not misunderstanding you, I hope, Major, but have you just offered me a job?'

'I have indeed. In my Security Division. Top boss. Good pay. Perks.'

'I'll certainly consider it, sir, and thank you. I'm honoured that you'd ask me.'

James smiled and nodded. Then his face changed slightly, became solemn. 'I tried to find you, Stead, and never did. Nor did I find anything at all about Allan Lister.' There was a pause, and James said, 'He didn't make it, did he?'

Stead shook his head. A sad look settled in his eyes. 'I looked for his body, but never found it. I thought he'd made it out of Picardy. But he didn't. I'm afraid the Somme took him.'

'He's in some far corner of a foreign field,' James said quietly, filled with sorrow.

SEVENTEEN

Damn it! What a stupid fool I am! James Falconer thought with a flash of anger at himself. Why am I letting myself be manipulated by a resentful young woman? And my own flesh and blood at that.

He sat up straighter in his chair and dropped the document in his hand onto the desk. He'd read one paragraph three times because he wasn't concentrating and was so distracted. The events of the day had been horrific, and he wanted desperately to go to Georgiana's house to talk about them. A telephone call wouldn't be enough.

'So I'm going,' he muttered out loud to himself, and jumped up. As he went out of the library, he saw Brompton at the other end of the entrance foyer. 'I've got to run an errand,' he called to the butler and headed for the front door.

'But you need your topcoat, sir,' Brompton cried. 'It's cold.'

James was already outside and running down South Audley Street. Because it was an icy day, the street was almost empty. He flew across Curzon Street, dodging a bit of traffic. A few seconds later, he was dropping the brass lion's head knocker on her door.

It was opened almost immediately by her butler, Forrester. He looked startled to see James in a suit, no overcoat, and shivering.

'Mrs Ward is expecting me, Forrester,' James said, and stepped into the foyer, forcing the butler to open the door wider as he rushed in.

'I'll announce you, sir.' The butler closed the front door and turned around to see James hurrying towards the parlour, exclaiming over his shoulder, 'I'm late, Forrester. And you don't need to announce me.'

Georgiana heard his voice echoing and stood up, smiling to herself. Finally, he had had the guts to come and knock on her door because he needed her. This pleased her enormously.

The smile intact, she went out of the parlour, and nodded. Her eyes were sparkling as he came to a standstill in front of her.

Aware of the butler's presence nearby, she said, 'You're not *very* late, James. There's no problem.'

His back was to the butler, and he grinned at her and winked.

She wanted to laugh but kept tight control of herself. She addressed the butler, 'Would you ask Cook to prepare a fresh tea tray for Mr Falconer, please, Forrester? And no mad rush.'

'Certainly, madam,' the butler answered, and departed, heading to the kitchen.

Georgiana took hold of James's arm and pulled him into the parlour. As usual, he took her in his arms and closed the door with his foot. Leaning against the door, he held her close to him, breathing in her scent. He loved the smell of her skin, her hair. A mixture of lemon and roses.

'Just holding you like this is a joy,' he murmured against her hair. 'I'm sorry to burst in on you, but I just had to see you. *Now.*'

'I'm glad you came at last, of your own volition, James,' she responded, and moved slightly, drew him towards the fireplace. 'You're cold, darling. Why did you come without your overcoat?'

'I was in a hell of a hurry to get to you, Mrs Ward!' He smiled at her and went to stand with his back to the fire.

She followed, gazing up at him, thinking how very, very blue his eyes looked this afternoon. There was no doubt about it. He was a knockout of a man. The most handsome devil she had ever known. She smiled inwardly. And he could be devilish at times, especially when he teased her about things.

'What's going through that busy mind of yours, Mrs Ward?'

'I was thinking how thrilling it was to have you here, standing in front of my fireplace.'

'Listen, something really horrific happened today. Let's sit down here near the fire, and I'll tell you everything.'

'Of course.' Georgiana took one of the chairs in front of the fire, and James sat in the other one.

When he was silent, she stared at him. 'You look very solemn. It must be a serious matter.'

'Give me a moment to sort out my thoughts,' Falconer answered.

'It all began at lunchtime at the Ritz. I was with William. A waiter brought a note for me from the hotel telephonist. It was bad news.'

At this moment, Forrester knocked and came into the room.

'You can bring the tray over here,' Mrs Ward said, glancing at him. 'It will fit on this small table, and thank you, Forrester.'

'My pleasure, madam.' After putting the tray on the table, he left, closing the door behind him.

Looking at James, she said, 'Let me first pour you a cup of tea, and then you can continue telling me about the problem you had earlier.' She picked up the teapot and filled his cup.

'I'll grab a cucumber sandwich. I'm starved. Haven't eaten since breakfast. We had to abandon lunch.'

'Yes, do eat first, and the tea will help you to get warmer, James.'

Between bites of the cucumber sandwich, James asked, 'Where is Leonie? She must be at the gallery, I suppose, since you seem so relaxed.'

'She's in Paris.'

'Paris, France?' he asked, sounding surprised, staring at her.

'Is there another Paris somewhere else?' she asked, laughter in her tone.

James chuckled. 'Maybe. And is Richard Rhodes with her?'

'Yes, they were all packed and ready to go this morning, when I came down for breakfast. Leonie has a chance to pick up a couple of Chagall paintings and a Renoir, so she was excited to go.'

'How wonderful! We've got a few days alone together! Hey, sweetheart, can I stay for dinner and perhaps even breakfast?'

She laughed at his sudden eagerness, the happiness on his face. He looked very boyish, and she was flooded with such a complex mixture of emotions and feelings. Compassionate, kind, brilliant in business, and very loving with her. A man with many charms as well.

'You're not answering me, Mrs Ward.' He bit into another sandwich, enjoying it.

'Definitely dinner, and perhaps even breakfast if you're willing to throw caution to the wind.'

'I certainly am. I don't give a damn what the world thinks . . . but it's your decision, my love.'

A little sigh escaped, and she murmured, 'I'll think about it. I would like you to sleep here tonight. After all, you have such a long way to travel to get home.'

James threw back his head and roared with laughter. He had always loved her pithy sense of humour.

A moment later, he said, 'I'll buy the Renoir, sight unseen. Will she sell it to me?'

'I think someone else should buy it for you. Then you'll get it.'

'It's a deal.' Falconer leaned back in the chair, and said, 'Thank you for feeding me. I really was hungry.'

'I'm glad you feel better. So tell me what happened earlier, darling.'

'Someone was hurt,' he said, 'but let me assure you she will be all right.' He spoke in a steady, even voice, not wanting to alarm or upset her.

'*She*. Is it someone I know?' Georgiana asked with concern.

'I'm afraid so. Irina. But as I said, she is going to recover. She's in hospital at the moment and is now conscious.'

'Oh my God, whatever happened to her?' Georgiana's face had paled and there was a worried look in her violet-coloured eyes.

'She was attacked at her home by a stranger. At least, I believe he was a stranger. That man was obviously looking for something; drawers and cupboards were opened and ransacked—'

'A stranger did that?' Georgiana asked, sounding doubtful.

'The man did it, whoever he is,' Falconer replied. 'I find it all something of a mystery, to be honest. So, to continue.' James went on to tell her everything about the events of earlier, and finished, 'And guess who the detective was from Scotland Yard? My lieutenant, Jack Stead.'

'Oh, I'm so glad to hear that – after this terrible story about poor Irina – something good came out of it,' Georgiana said quietly. She obviously was still stunned by the attack on Irina and concerned for her.

'Stead will get to the bottom of it, have no fear. I am having lunch with Chief Inspector Crawford tomorrow, and I'll know more.'

She nodded. 'Thank you, James. Do you think I can go and visit Irina tomorrow, while you're lunching with the chief inspector?'

'Yes. We'll go together, and you can stay on with her for a while. It will be comforting for her to see you, and Keller will be pleased to see you too.'

'That poor man, how he must be suffering too,' Georgiana murmured, still unable to come to terms with the fact that Irina had been beaten up in her own home by a *stranger*.

This fact bothered her the most. All of a sudden, she thought that this man must know her and want something from her. Whether it was in the house or not. It certainly wasn't over, of that she was convinced.

About to confide this to Falconer, she stopped herself and remained silent.

James continuing to look at her, his expression loving, and finally he said, in puzzlement, 'What's going on in that fertile brain of yours? Come on. Out with it.'

'I was just looking forward to our weekend at Ascot,' she improvised swiftly.

'As am I,' he answered, and settled back in the chair, a smile on his face.

EIGHTEEN

The chief inspector liked this pleasant room at the Ritz, with its sense of luxury and good fare. Large and airy, it had tall windows that filled the space with light and allowed a lovely view of the park.

Glancing out of the window, Crawford saw a vast stretch of pure white snow, gleaming in the sunshine, and bare tree branches laden with icicles.

It had stopped snowing last night, and the wind had dropped, but it was an icy cold Saturday in December, the dead of winter.

Crawford looked around the restaurant and saw that it was filling up quickly now. Suddenly there was James Falconer, chatting to the maître d' at the entrance to the restaurant.

When he spotted Crawford, James raised a hand in greeting and started to move forward. Sunshine struck him, and he was bathed in light. Crawford saw him objectively at that precise moment, and thought he looked as if he had just stepped off a London stage. Matinée idol glamour, even with greying fair hair and a few lines on his chiselled face. The vivid eyes were as blue and as clear as ever. It was more than glamour. It was charisma.

It seemed to Crawford that James had become better looking as he had aged. He had known him since he was fourteen, and now he was forty-eight. But he looked much younger than that, and very handsome.

James limped towards the table, smiling now as he drew closer.

'Am I late? Or were you early, Chief?' James asked lightly, smiling again.

'The latter,' Crawford responded, and stood up.

The two old friends shook hands, and they sat down together; both looked pleased to see each other.

'What do we know?' James asked, staring at Crawford.

'Not much, I'm afraid. The Fingerprint Division has dusted the room where the two women were attacked and gathered a lot of prints. If the attacker is a criminal and has been arrested, the Yard will have his fingerprints on file. We might get a match and a name.'

'That's extraordinary!' James exclaimed. 'Drawers and cupboards *were* opened by the bulky man. So, let's have a drink. How about champagne, or do you prefer wine?'

'White wine, please, James.'

'I don't usually drink at lunchtime, but I'll join you.' He motioned to a waiter, gave the order, and turned to Crawford, laughing. 'How rude I am, Chief. I haven't even greeted you properly. *Good afternoon.*'

Crawford also laughed. 'You always have been an eager beaver; always need to get to the point at once.'

'Nobody knows me better than you.'

'How is Keller today? Have you seen him?'

'I have. I went to King's Hospital before coming here. Mrs Ward came too, and she's there now with Keller and Irina. Keller is calmer, and he's moved in with the Venables. William and Natalie invited him to stay with them because Detective Stead locked up Keller's house.'

'He had to do that, you know. We can't have a crime scene contaminated. I heard that Stead and other policemen from Scotland Yard are covering the entire house. Normal procedure. They'll be finished by Monday at the latest,' Crawford said. 'Then Stead will have to get Keller's fingerprints, and Irina's, so the Yard can match them to those they found in their house.'

When James was silent, looking odd, Crawford thought he might not have understood his explanation. He added, 'The police have to isolate the fingerprints of the attacker, you see.'

James nodded. 'I know what you were saying.' He shook his head. 'I have something to tell you, Chief.' James now hesitated. After a moment, he murmured in a low tone, 'I think Irina might have known her attacker. I saw her with a man of a similar description a few weeks ago.'

'Where?' the chief inspector asked, startled, staring at James. 'And why haven't you said anything to Stead about this? I presume you haven't.'

'I told no one. I suppose I was being discreet. However, I did see Irina talking, perhaps even arguing, with a bulky man. On Piccadilly.' Swiftly, but very accurately, Falconer told Chief Inspector Crawford what he had seen that particular day.

When he had finished, Crawford said, 'You say you were being discreet but you were being gallant, Falconer; in a sense, protecting Irina.'

'Oh, I don't know, Chief. Call it what you want, but if I'd spoken up that attack might not have happened.'

'That's speculation. Scotland Yard doesn't deal in that commodity. But I find it quite strange – the whole thing, I mean. A bit of a mystery.'

'I agree. And I do think the attacker *was* looking for something. It also occurred to me that *that something* had been in Keller's house and then removed. By a third party.' James took a sip of his wine and threw a questioning look at Crawford. 'What say you, Chief?'

'If you weren't so busy running a veritable business empire, I'd offer you a job at Scotland Yard,' Crawford said with a wry grin. 'I came to that idea too, earlier today. However, this case is not under my command. I run the Criminal Acts Division, as you know. I'm mostly dealing with murders. I'll pass this on to Stead, although he's probably thought of that already, all by himself.'

The maître d' had arrived at their table. 'Good afternoon, may I offer you the menu, Mr Falconer? Chief Inspector?'

'Yes, of course, thank you,' the chief inspector said, taking the menu.

James followed suit, glanced at the card and looked at Crawford. 'I know what I'm having; do you, Chief Inspector?'

'I do. Shall I order first?'

'Please do.'

Looking at the maître d', the chief said, 'I would like the vegetable soup to start and then the roast beef, please.'

The maître d' nodded, and wrote on the pad.

James said, 'Those are good choices on a winter's day like this. I'll have the same. Thank you.'

'Do you wish to order a red wine, sir?' the maître d' asked, looking at James.

Crawford said, 'Not for me, thank you.'

'Nor for me either.' James smiled at the maître d', who nodded and departed.

After a sip of white wine, Roger Crawford said, 'Going to King's Hospital must have brought back a few memories, didn't it?'

James half smiled. 'It did, and I thought of poor Denny, who died there. So long ago, Crawford . . . I was only fourteen when we both got beaten up by those thugs. Denny was a bit younger, but only in months. A sad time.' He glanced at the chief inspector, his face still grave. 'That's when I met you.'

'It is indeed. At first I thought it was going to be a cold case, but the Yard did finally solve it.'

'*You* solved it!' James exclaimed.

'Your legs were badly bashed in, I do remember that, and you had one enormous black eye. I think Denny got the worst of it, don't you?'

'He did. He wasn't as strong or as big as me, and one of those three bruisers seemed to focus on him. He couldn't fight back much. I did a little better.' James let out a heavy sigh. 'I don't know why, but my bloody legs always seem to get in the way when I'm in some kind of fight. Especially a world war.'

This was said with a hint of humour in his voice, and the chief inspector half smiled. James Falconer was an extraordinary man. Crawford had great affection for him, and was very proud of him too.

'Yes, you've been through the mill a bit, in different ways. Yet you've come out on top, Falconer. But then you have all the right assets.'

James stared at his old friend and asked, 'What assets are you referring to? I'm very curious. I didn't know I had *assets*.'

'Brains. Drive. Ambition. Fortitude. Gumption. And looks,' Crawford answered. 'Not to mention a lot of natural charm and a special charisma. How could you ever lose?'

That James was flabbergasted was obvious. He just sat there, absolutely silent, literally gawping at Crawford, wondering why he was saying this.

The policeman laughed. 'You seem to be astonished, but I'm telling you the truth, Jimmy lad. I saw it all when you were called that. I've watched you become the man you are today. But it wasn't just your assets that got you where you are. It was your ability to work hard, long hours, and you were never afraid. You also put work first. No woman ever distracted you.'

'Actually, I was truly afraid *once* – when I was worried my legs were going to be amputated. Thank God, they weren't, and thank you for all your kind words.' James lifted his glass. 'Here's to you, Chief, my good old friend. And to my late grandmother, who no doubt influenced you unduly.'

Roger Crawford chuckled and lifted his glass. 'To your grand-mother, Jimmy lad, who turned you into a true gentleman of the highest order.'

NINETEEN

The copper and the tycoon, friends for thirty-four years, sat together in the tycoon's library, at his house on South Audley Street.

They were enjoying coffee in front of the fire blazing in the hearth.

'Now that we're in the privacy of your home, I would like to speak to you about Richard Rhodes,' the chief inspector said, looking across at Falconer.

Instantly alert, James asked swiftly, 'What did you find out?' He sounded anxious.

'To be honest, not very much. But what my two detectives dug up from some old files at Scotland Yard might be of interest to you.

'I'm all ears, Chief. Tell me.'

'They came across a file with Rhodes's name on it. Inside was a copy of a report of assault, by a woman, naming him. Her name was Dorothy Miller. It gave her address. It was about five years ago.'

'Physical abuse?' James lifted a brow.

'I suspect it was, but the wording was different. The implication is there, don't you think?'

'I do. It suggests he could get rough with women. That does make me worried for Leonie.'

Acutely aware of James's sudden worry, the chief inspector said, 'I've discovered, over the years, that some men can be abusive with one woman, yet not like that with another. However, if you wanted to have him watched, I can direct you to the best private detective agency in London. It might ease your concern.'

James nodded. 'I'd better have that. What's the name of the agency?'

'Easy to remember. PDSW. That means Private Detective Service Worldwide. The man who owns and runs it worked for me at the Yard for many years. His name is John Scolding. And he sure can *scold* when necessary.' As the chief said this, he hoped it would make James smile, and it did.

'Give me all the details later, will you please. Georgiana and I both think there's something not quite right about Rhodes, and I trust my gut instinct. Can't put our fingers on it. I do believe he's an opportunist, though, which might work in my favour. Perhaps. I'd like to make friends with him, which might bring Leonie closer to me. That's the thing that really matters to me.' James took a swallow of the coffee. He glanced towards the window as frozen snowflakes bounced against the glass.

'Oh my God, it's snowing again! I can't believe this weather.'

The chief followed his gaze. 'You mentioned earlier you were going to Ascot tomorrow. That looks like a snowstorm, not your friend for a trip to the country, is it, Falconer?'

'You're correct.' Placing his coffee cup on the small table nearby, James rose and went to look out of the window. Swiftly turning around, he announced, 'You're staying here tonight, Chief. You can't set out to Hampstead in this.'

'Thank you, Falconer. It might be wise for me to stay put, as you suggest.'

'Damn right. If you'll excuse me, I'll go and speak to my butler. He can tell my driver to put the motorcar away and go to his quarters in the mews.'

Crawford nodded, watched him walk across the library and into the foyer, reminded afresh of the authority James had at certain moments. The chief inspector knew where it came from, at least some of it.

Although he had not been born an aristocrat, James Falconer *had* been born with aristocratic looks. He was a beautiful man. But it was his grandmother, Esther Falconer, housekeeper to a wealthy family in Regent's Park, who had instilled in James manners, proper behaviour, and a sense of elegance and style in his appearance.

She had constantly corrected his speech so that he had a lovely voice, sounded cultured, which he was. She had made sure of that as well. Esther had made sure he was going places and would be a big winner.

The chief inspector smiled inwardly, remembering that a young James Falconer had worked on a stall at the Malvern Market when he was eight years old. If only his grandmother could see him now and know what he had become. He looked and behaved like a true aristocrat. Whatever he did, he did with the self-assurance and confidence of one. It seemed bred in the bone, not acquired.

Within minutes, James returned, explaining as he walked into the library, 'You'll be happy to know that Cook has made your favourite dish for supper, Crawford. Haddock fried in batter, with chips and peas.' James chuckled. 'However, very shortly Brompton will serve us caviar on toast with glasses of champagne. A bit of an unusual mix, I must admit, but she wants to please you. She knows what you like to eat.'

The chief was smiling. 'Her son's a copper on the beat in the East End, as you are aware.'

'I am . . .' James sat down. 'No one else knows this, but I'm involved once again with Georgiana Ward. She's looked after me very well and it's developing into something more. I just hope Leonie doesn't create problems for us.'

'Is Leonie still being difficult about you?' the chief asked, frowning.

'She is, and I doubt she'll change. She resents me,' James murmured in a lowered voice. 'Dislikes me, in fact. She feels I abandoned her when she was thirteen.'

'Abandonment means someone has walked away from you and left you to defend yourself, and to fend for yourself. If I remember correctly, you have supported Leonie and Georgiana since you were twenty-one, when Henry Malvern made you managing director of Malvern's.' When James remained silent, Roger Crawford asked, 'I'm not wrong, surely?'

James was still silent, looked suddenly brooding. The blue eyes appeared to darken. At last he answered, 'I've supported them *always*, even when I was married to Alexis. Even afterwards. Even when I didn't see them.' He paused. 'I don't know if Georgiana has told Leonie this, or if she even told her I paid for her partnership in the art gallery either.' An unexpected look of sadness spread across his face; he shook his head.

'Perhaps you should ask Georgiana, James. After all, you've been an honourable man, and generously so. I think Leonie changing her attitude is actually something Georgiana needs to tackle.'

James stared at him, and nodded. 'To be honest, I've thought exactly that for ages. There are times when I think she's afraid of Leonie, or rather, of losing her because of me.'

Roger was so startled by this comment, he sat bolt upright in the chair. 'That's a peculiar thing to say. You don't actually believe *that*, do you?'

'Sometimes. Last week I told her she puts Leonie before me. She denied it, said there was the love a mother had for a child and the kind a woman had for a man.'

'Well, I do understand what she meant. Nonetheless, I think she has no *choice* but to make a decision. Is she going to marry you regardless of her daughter's opinion? Or is she going to be *ruled* by her daughter?' Crawford gave him a hard stare. 'Don't you think she owes you that, or rather the answer to that?'

'Yes, I do. I'm at the end of my tether if the truth be known,' Falconer answered. 'I want a relationship with my daughter, but she refuses to see me. And Georgiana won't make a date for our marriage until she sees Leonie well settled down with Rhodes, and, hopefully, pregnant.'

A long sigh escaped as Crawford stood, started to walk up and down the library. His face was grim. He was obviously rattled.

James stared at him, and said, 'You look angry, Crawford. I guess I'm a bit angry myself. I'm forty-eight now. I want to be married and settled down. I want to enjoy my life for a few years before I kick the bucket, enjoy the success I've earned. I've worked night and day for years to avoid loneliness; being on my own, living here by myself. Work was my comfort in a way, but now I must relax, do other things . . .' His voice trailed off and he leaned back in the chair.

The chief inspector was slightly choked up as he returned to the fireplace and sat down. He had always cared for James, felt more like an uncle than a friend, and he hurt inside for him. Oh, the strangeness of women.

He couldn't believe how foolishly Georgiana Ward was acting. James Falconer is a Bobby Dazzler of a man, he thought, remembering the phrase his mother had used. Brilliant, successful, staggeringly handsome, and one of the nicest, kindest men he'd ever known. And she was making him wait, even though her own daughter was now married.

'She's messing you around!' Crawford exclaimed. 'I can't tell you what to do, how to run your life, but I know what I'd do, Jimmy lad. I'd make a stand, tell her what *you* want, and forget about Leonie. She's her mother's project, not yours.'

'You've just said what I've been thinking myself lately, Chief. It's been a frustrating few weeks,' Falconer admitted.

'Perhaps I shouldn't interfer in your personal life, James, but you're like family to me. I just couldn't help giving you my opinion,' the chief explained. 'I want to help you.'

'And I'm glad you spoke your mind. Let's move on. If you find the bulky man and arrest him, what will he be charged with?' Falconer asked, now wanting to change the subject.

'Assault and battery, breaking and entering, invasion of private property. He broke the law in a few ways. However, we might not find him, you know. Although Detective Stead is brilliant.' Crawford glanced at James and smiled. 'What a funny coincidence you met again. I didn't know you'd tried to find him.'

'Yes, through the War Office. I knew he was alive. He'd been demobbed, but they didn't know his whereabouts.' James grimaced. 'It never occurred to me to ask you. I mean, to come to Scotland Yard for help.'

'I don't know Stead well. As you are aware, he's in a different division. But I could have asked around. Never mind, you got together in the end.'

'I'm having lunch or supper with him this coming week. It will be wonderful to catch up.'

TWENTY

James Falconer was busy on Sunday morning. After breakfast with Chief Inspector Crawford, he had sent him on his way home in a taxicab, and then had gone to work at his desk in the library.

His first task was to telephone Georgiana Ward to tell her they could not go to Ascot because of the bad weather. The snow had stopped overnight, and turned to rain, but it was slushy and freezing cold. After turning down her invitations to dinner or lunch, he agreed to tea that afternoon, explaining he had important work to do that was urgent. She sounded glad he was coming.

It was the truth when he spoke about work. Opening the ledger he had brought home on Friday, he stared at the line of figures, fairly current, for the shops in the Malvern Arcade. Oddly, sales in the shops were down. Most unusual.

His eyes remained on the page for a long time, as he tried to figure out what was going on. Sitting back in the chair, he realized he needed to look at the other ledgers to make comparisons.

Rising, picking up the ledger, he hurried out of the library and went looking for Brompton. He found him in the butler's pantry behind the main dining room.

'I've got to go to my office, Brompton,' Falconer explained. 'I won't be long, but don't have Cook make a heavy lunch. I don't feel hungry after that big breakfast I had with the chief inspector.'

Brompton nodded. 'I understand, sir.'

'What's it like outside? Very slushy, I suppose, after all the rain last night.'

'Not so bad, Mr Falconer, and every household has cleaned their pavements. Also, it's still raining, so the snow has almost disappeared. I think the rain is about to stop.'

'Righto. I'll get my overcoat.'

Brompton followed him, helped him into his warmest coat, and handed him a scarf. 'Best to take a taxicab,' Brompton told him. His staff never mentioned his leg but James knew why Brompton told him that.

'I will. See you later, Brompton. And thank you.'

'I am happy to be of service, sir.'

Falconer found a taxi immediately, and within a few minutes, he was alighting at his office on Piccadilly. He stood for a moment, staring up at Malvern House. Many years ago, when he'd first started working for Henry Malvern, it had been one building. Now it was three; the two others had been acquired when they became empty over the years. Not bad, he thought. I've grown this company well. I'm not going to let anything happen to it now. Over my dead body. I must protect it.

When he reached the front door of the oldest building from Henry's day, the watchman opened it for him.

'Good morning, sir,' he said, touching his cap.

'Morning, Atkinson,' James answered, stepping inside.

'Mr Keller is already here, sir,' Atkinson informed him.

Although taken by surprise, Falconer just nodded and proceeded to the lift.

As he walked down the corridor to his office, Peter Keller appeared in the doorway of his own office. 'Good morning,' Keller said.

'Why are you here, Keller? Shouldn't you be visiting Irina at the hospital?' James asked, puzzled by his presence.

'I've already been there. She's doing well, better than I expected, and I'll go again later.'

'I'm relieved to hear she's making good progress. Come into my office, Keller.' As he spoke, James went in, put the ledger on the desk, and took off his coat. 'Anyway, I'm glad you're here.'

'Let's sit near the window,' Keller said, choosing an armchair.

James sat next to him, and with a raised brow, he asked, 'Why *are* you at the office on a Sunday morning?'

'Because I noticed something a few weeks ago that bothered me. Then I forgot about it because of the attack on Irina. Suddenly, last night, it came back to me. I knew I needed to check my ledgers for the Wine Division. There might be a problem.'

Hearing this, Falconer's heart sank, and he stared at Keller, his face grave. 'How bad is the drop? Because that's what you're referring to, isn't it?'

'I am. And it's not all *that* bad, but there *has* been a drop in orders. Not only in our export of wine, but here in London as well. I'm not sure why this is happening, to be honest, James. I mean in London, of course. However, the wine merchants' orders are definitely less than usual. Somewhat worrying.'

Shaking his head, Falconer said, 'There has been a shift in the landscape—'

'What do you mean?' Keller cut in.

'London has changed. In fact, the whole country has. The war has created havoc. England's broke; very few men have returned from the war. Young men and middle-aged men went to fight and were killed on the battlefields of France. As I've said before, we're a country of *old men and women of all ages*. No men to work in the factories, the offices, the shops, down the coal mines, in the fields. No bloody men at all, in actuality. Except for a few like you and me.'

When Keller was silent, looking grim, Falconer said, 'Nobody's spending money. It's bad all around. Money is short. I hope we'll do well at Christmas, but I don't think that's going to happen.'

Keller, somewhat shaken, stood up and went to look out of a window. He believed every word his old friend and workmate had said. He knew no other businessman as clever as James Falconer. A sad thought entered his head. Everything *he* had built, which I helped him to do, is going to tumble . . .

James interrupted Keller's dour thoughts, when he said, 'Come back and sit, Peter. Let me figure out how to save Malvern's with your help.'

Hearing the steady voice, the cheerful tone, Keller rejoined his oldest and closest friend. He sat down, wondering what he had up his sleeve.

'Do you already have a solution?' Keller asked, a hopeful note now echoing in his voice.

'For the shops in the Malvern Arcade, I do. The retailers won't be able to pay their full rents next month. So, in the short-term, I'm going to lower their rents, make it possible for the shops to stay open.'

'You can't *do* that, Falconer! They'll never go back to the regular rent. They just won't want you to change their rents later, to go back to the proper amounts.'

'They will if they've signed a contract with me to do exactly that,' James shot back. 'They will sign because they're so invested in their shops in the Arcade. Also, I'm going to suggest they get rid of old merchandise by having some dramatic spring sales later on.' James gave him an intense look, and said, 'Let me explain something else. To keep all the accountants here happy and to protect the overall business, I will add up the difference, or rather they will, and I will give Malvern's a personal cheque from my own money. So the company does not lose anything and stays very stable.'

Keller was astonished and that expression stayed on his face. 'You'd do that?' he asked, his voice rising.

'I have no other choice. I can't lose what I've built, along with you and all my employees. This situation threatens the whole company. Anyway, luckily, I can afford to do it.'

'It's also a good thing you're not a public company,' Keller pointed out. 'So you can do what you want.'

'Malvern's will always be mine, to run as I please,' James assured him.

'You've a lot of arcades, or rather the company has,' Keller said, grimacing.

'I shall use the same method in all of them across the country, at least until I've worked out their future. I'll stabilize them all. Now, what about the Wine Division?' James sounded anxious to know.

'We're down in numbers because we've been in a world war. Obviously we couldn't export wine when everyone was fighting. We lost out in Europe, but we were not doing badly here. And we started exporting to America.' Keller pursed his lips. 'For some reason, in the last six months, the wine merchants have been ordering much less wine. I can't explain why.'

James sat back, dismayed by this news, but finally said, 'It seems clear that economic activity is in decline, along with this terrible epidemic.' He sighed. 'The country *is* indeed in a mess. But I believe in us English. We'll get back to normal. Now, how much do you need to bring the Wine Division back to its usual state? Let me know, and I will write you a check from my personal account.'

'I'll do the numbers and have them ready by tomorrow,' Keller answered.

'Don't look so troubled, my friend,' James said, suddenly

smiling. 'I thrive on challenge. I promise you, everything's going to be all right. We've won the war and now we need to hold our nerve.'

When Falconer left his office at four o'clock, he realized he didn't have time to go home and freshen up before going to Mrs Ward's for afternoon tea. Oh, to hell with it, he thought, as he hailed a taxicab and stepped in. I'll wash my hands and face when I get there.

It was Forrester who let him in. James immediately asked if he could go to the cloakroom. 'After I've taken off my overcoat, of course.'

'Let me help you,' the butler said, and did so. Then he showed James to the cloakroom door.

'Thank you, Forrester. Tell Mrs Ward I'll be with her in a moment.'

'Certainly, sir,' the butler answered and retreated.

Closing and locking the door, James took off his jacket, washed his hands, splashed water on his face and dried himself with a towel. He took a comb from his jacket and smoothed his hair. When he returned the comb to an inside pocket, he pushed his hand into an outer pocket and touched the small box containing a gift for Mrs Ward. He smiled. Naturally, it was there. He had taken it out of his safe at the house this morning.

After his conversations with Crawford, he had decided he needed to take action. Today was the day to give it to her.

Georgiana Ward rose to greet him when he strode into the room, smiling at him. He is always so self-assured, she thought, and somehow always filling the room with his charisma.

For a moment, she was transfixed, held by that unique, almost overpowering magnetism that seemed to define him.

Once he had kissed her cheek and greeted her warmly, he went over to the fire and stood with his back to it.

'Cold as usual,' he said with a grin.

'Do your legs hurt?' she asked.

'A bit. But I always remind myself that I got back alive. So many men did not get home at all.'

'I know.' She went and sat down in a chair near the fire, and said, 'Tea will be here shortly.'

He simply smiled, enjoying the heat from the fire, and thinking how lovely she looked this afternoon. Her hair was down, not all pushed up on top of her head. She had a girlish look about her. She wore an afternoon dress of greenish-blue silk. It was flattering to her colouring, clung to her, showing her shapely figure.

'Why did you have to work on Sunday?' she suddenly asked. 'Couldn't it have waited? The work, I mean.'

Pulled out of his thoughts about her, he was somewhat startled by her question. Oddly, slightly irritated by her tone. She sounded put out.

James had learned over the years to keep his emotions under control, and he had an iron will.

He said carefully, 'It was a necessity. I had a problem to solve *today*. Not tomorrow or next week. Instantly.'

'I don't remember you ever working on Sunday, though. Did you do that when you were married to Alexis?' she murmured, looking up at him.

A terrible flash of dismay and genuine annoyance went through his body. But again he remained in total control. He said, 'Sometimes. Now let the matter drop. I will never let anything get in the way of my business. As the chief inspector said last night, "I've never allowed a woman to distract me." So I certainly won't start that now.' James said this in a controlled but stern tone, meaning every word.

She caught the annoyance in his voice and wished she had kept her mouth shut. He was the kind of man who ruled the roost; he was cock of the heap in more ways than one. The whole world kowtowed to him. She was well aware that he did what he wanted to do and was accustomed to getting his way. He was a powerful man.

Noticing she was somewhat troubled, probably knowing she had irked him, he walked over to her. He pulled her to her feet. Wrapping his arms around her, he held her close. Against her face, he said, 'Let's not talk about my business life. Let's talk about us.'

She drew away, looked up at him, and asked, 'What exactly do you mean by that?'

He smiled. 'About us? Right *now*, at this moment, forget talking. Let's go upstairs and throw caution to the wind.'

She gaped at him. 'Tea will be here any moment!' she exclaimed.

'Cancel it,' he declared.

Aware of the obdurate look on his face, she stepped away from him and rang the bell. A moment later the butler appeared, carrying the tea tray, followed by a maid with two plates of food in her hands.

'Oh, here you are, Forrester,' Georgiana said quietly. 'Please bring everything close to the fire.'

'Of course, Mrs Ward.' He put the tray of cups and saucers and the teapot on a side table, and the maid placed the platters on the sideboard.

Twenty-One

O nce the two servants had left, James began to laugh. After a moment, he said, 'Oh dear, I've been thwarted in my attempt to take you to bed by a bloody teapot!'

Georgiana had to laugh and was thankful for his humour and good nature. But she knew she must tread lightly. He was never in a bad mood, yet strangely, this afternoon he seemed a bit different. Because it was so unusual, she was acutely aware of it and knew to be cautious.

Walking over to the sideboard, she brought a platter of sandwiches to the large table near the sofa, and said, 'Come along, darling. Cook has made new combinations of tea sandwiches today.'

He did as she had directed, took a seat next to her, and then picked up a sandwich. After eating it, he exclaimed, 'Excellent! It was crab, and that's certainly an innovation. I enjoyed it. I didn't have lunch today.'

In between eating and drinking a cup of tea, James decided not to confide in Georgiana about his business worries. Instead, he started to tell her about all the restorations his two building crews had done at her country house in Ascot. 'Every leak has been repaired, and they put a new roof along the front side. I had them polish all your wood floors, and they have washed all the rugs. All draperies have been brushed, ironed and rehung, and every piece of furniture is back in its rightful place.' He sat back, looking pleased. It had been a big job, and done well.

'Goodness, I didn't expect you to do all that,' she exclaimed, obviously surprised but also looking pleased. 'I don't know how to thank you, darling.'

'Oh, but I do,' Falconer was swift to reply. 'Let's go and throw caution to the wind.' He stood up and offered her his hand.

Georgiana also rose, took hold of his hand, and together they went upstairs without saying a word.

Once they entered her bedroom, he closed the door and locked it. He took off his jacket, waistcoat and tie, and then walked towards her, a small smile crossing his face. 'Don't stand there like a sucking duck, staring at me,' he said, laughter underscoring his words. 'Get undressed, for God's sake.'

She nodded and began to undo the buttons on her dress, saying, 'I've never heard *that* weird expression.'

'One of my grandmother's,' he answered, as he threw his shirt on a chair, to be followed by his other clothing. Naked now, he went over to the bed and got into it, saying, 'Hurry up, Mrs Ward, I'm dying to have you in my arms.'

A few minutes later, she joined him. He gently pulled her closer, wrapping his arms around her, murmuring how much he desired her.

His kisses were gentle, then grew stronger and more passionate, and she responded with the same ardour, clinging to him.

After a few moments, he threw back the bedclothes, surprising her for a second. Pushing himself up on one elbow, he looked down at her. Slowly, he began to smooth his right hand over her body, whispering, 'It's like silk, your skin, every part of you. I love touching you, especially here.'

With great expertise, his fingers flicked over the centre of her womanhood, and she began to tremble as he increased the pressure, arousing her fully. Within moments, he was lying on top of her, aching to be inside her, taking her to him as she began to spasm. For James that moment was thrilling, and he felt as though he was sinking into velvet.

A moment later he moved, and so did she, and they were tightly joined, floating towards a higher level of ecstasy, unable to let go of each other or to stop the rhythmic movement of their bodies.

Later, when they lay next to each other, sated and breathing heavily, James threw one of his legs over hers. Pulling her closer, he said in a low voice, 'Why is it always a little different when we make love? Why does it seem to get better every time?'

'I don't know, but that does happen with us, doesn't it, darling?'

'Yes,' he murmured, and realized then that the room had grown dusky. Through the window he could see a darkened sky, stars flickering, and a partial moon appearing. It occurred to him that they had been in the bed for almost two hours. He smiled to himself, feeling relaxed, fulfilled and happy, because she loved him as much as he loved her.

He decided to take a very big step. A big deal for him. Now was the time to move their relationship forward. He was resolved to seize the happiness he had denied himself for so many years, to build a life outside his business. Move on with her beside him.

Sliding away from her, he sat on the edge of the bed, then turned on the lamp that stood on the bedside table.

As he got up, Georgiana said, 'Don't leave me. I was so enjoying these quiet moments.'

'I'm coming right back. I have a present for you. Come on. Sit up, sweetheart.'

She did so.

He went to his jacket and took out a small red leather box, then returned to the bedside. Opening it, he took out a beautiful deep blue sapphire ring, surrounded by diamonds.

Taking her left hand, he slid it onto her third finger. Then looked at her attentively.

Her surprise was evident, and she exclaimed, 'Oh, James, darling, it's gorgeous. Thank you. How lovely of you to pick out something so special. Thank you.'

'I want us to be officially engaged at long last,' he said, smiling at her. 'Even if we can't marry yet.'

Georgiana smiled back, and then slid the ring off her finger and put it back in the red box.

Falconer frowned, and cried out, 'Why are you doing that? You have to wear your engagement ring all the time. And soon, if I have my way, you'll have a second ring next to it. A wedding ring.'

'Yes. Yes, I do understand, James, I really do, but you see I can't wear the ring right now. As I told you, I must prepare Leonie. She doesn't really know we're as involved as we are, though she knows I sometimes see you—'

'Why haven't you told her?' he snapped, a rush of anger running through his body. 'Told her the truth.' He was glaring at her, as the hurt and anger suddenly became genuine rage.

'If Leonie knows all about us, thinks I'm marrying you, I will lose her, James, and I can't do that . . .'

A terrible argument followed. Eventually, after realizing that nothing would change Georgiana's mind, James suddenly understood that he had had enough.

'Say no more.' James went over to his clothes, picked them up and rushed into the bathroom. Locking the door, he threw the clothes on the floor. Going to the sink, he wet a towel and held it to his face. He was shaking. The heartache was unbearable. He felt as if she had just ripped out part of his soul.

He knew one thing for sure. He had to get out of this house now, get away from her. Her words had stunned him beyond belief. Cruel, hurtful words, a knife in his heart.

Within minutes, he was fully dressed. He felt in his waistcoat pocket for the pocket watch his uncles had given him when he was twenty-one. It was there. After combing his hair, he left the bathroom.

Georgiana had pulled on a silk dressing gown, flimsy, almost see-through, and was standing near the bed, tearful and flushed. He paid no attention to her.

Full of a rage he had never experienced before, James walked to the small table where she had placed the red box. Picking it up, he put it in his pocket and then swung around to face her. His eyes were blue ice, his face grim.

'In God's name, why did you never try to bring Leonie and me together? All these years we've been estranged, since Alexis died, she resenting me, loathing me. *Why?*' he shouted. 'You could have done wonders if you'd tried.'

Georgiana was silent, almost afraid of him, having never seen him like this. His expression was glacial, his fury visible.

He cried, 'You never *bothered*, if the truth be known. Well, she's your bloody problem, not mine. Keep her.'

When he strode to the door, she called out, 'James, wait—'

Turning to look at her, he yelled, 'I've waited long enough! You've always put her before me, saying you couldn't lose her.' He opened the door and, in an icy voice, added, 'Well, now you've lost *me!*'

He slammed the door behind him and went down the staircase, filled with an all-consuming fury. But he would endeavour to control it until he got home.

Forrester, who had heard the raised voices, was waiting with his overcoat and scarf in the foyer.

'Thank you,' Falconer said as the butler helped him get into the coat, speaking in a low tone.

'Always *my* honour, Mr Falconer,' Forrester said. 'And I bid you good night, sir.'

'Good night,' James answered, as polite as always. He went down the steps and crossed Curzon Street. As he walked up South Audley Street to his home, his safe haven, he realized he was still shaking.

When James Falconer arrived at his front door, he couldn't be bothered to find his keys. He lifted the door knocker and let it drop once.

Within seconds, Brompton opened the door. 'Good evening, sir,' the butler said. Noting Falconer's pale face, he asked swiftly, 'Are you feeling ill, sir? You are very white.'

'I might be coming down with something, Brompton.'

'Let me help you out of your coat and get you up to bed.'

'Thank you.'

A moment later, the butler was helping him up the staircase, aware that all was not well with his employer.

Falconer had never wanted a valet, had always preferred to dress himself. But tonight, due to the state he was in, he allowed his butler to help him out of his clothes.

'You've been a great help, Brompton,' James said, in as steady a voice as he could muster. 'I can manage the rest.'

'Yes, sir, if you're sure.'

'I am. Thank you. However, would you throw more logs on the fire, please? Oh, and do I have water?'

'It is on your night table in a crystal decanter, with a glass, sir.'

'Good. You can leave the curtains open, and thanks again for your help.'

'My pleasure as always, sir.'

* * *

He lay very straight in his bed, on his back, amazed that he was still shaking inside. His legs ached, and he was almost afraid to move them. In fact, his whole body ached.

Is that what true rage does to you? he wondered, staring up at the ceiling, wide awake. In a certain sense, he was shocked that he had become so enraged with Mrs Ward.

He had never lost his temper with anyone ever before in his life. His fury, his intense reaction to her, when she took off the engagement ring, had surprised him as much as it had her.

It was also her words about Leonie not knowing the truth, and the fact that she would lose her daughter if she *did* know, which cut through him.

He felt she had made it quite clear their daughter came first, he second. He didn't like that. He wanted to be just as important in Georgiana's life as their daughter. He would be her husband, after all. Her soulmate for life. Leonie was not a small child any more. She was a grown woman with a husband, making a life of her own.

But Georgiana had reneged on her promise. They were no longer engaged. And so *he* had ended it. Their relationship was over. As far as he was concerned, it was a final decision.

The hurt he felt was enormous, and he knew it would take him some time to recover, if he ever did. Rejection was deadly, hard to overcome, but most especially for him. He had kept himself locked away for years after Alexis had died. And now that he'd tried to build a new kind of life, Georgiana Ward had done him in, and with a certain kind of brutality. He had hoped for something she would never give.

He moved his head slightly and asked himself why she had spoken so, been so cruel, and after all these years of knowing her.

Against his volition, a sob broke loose. He began to cry in the same way he had when Alexis had died. He could not stop sobbing. He buried his head in the pillow as the tears flowed.

Eventually, he had cried himself dry. He sat up, found a fresh pillow next to him and tried to sleep. But he couldn't. He suddenly wondered why she had asked if he had worked on Sundays when Alexis was alive. Now he thought it a strange question indeed.

A small smile flickered as he thought of his first wife. Of course, she hadn't minded. She knew he couldn't help it. That was who he was. He closed his eyes, needing to sleep, needing to put their hateful exchange behind him.

Suddenly, he stiffened. His chest had become tight, as if it was being stretched, and he was struck by a terrible pain. He brought his hands up to his chest and laid them there, wincing as the pain increased.

A memory of long ago came rushing back. He saw himself in his mind's eye, a fourteen-year-old boy, pushing a barrow up a steep hill in Camden Town. He had stopped because he had a pain in his chest like this.

Then he had seen a neighbour, Mrs Greenwood, coming towards him from the other direction, going to her work as Cook at a big house.

He heard himself calling out to her, asking her if a fourteen-year-old boy could have a heart attack. She had said that no, he couldn't.

But a forty-eight-year-old man could, no question about that. James Falconer lay very still, his hands on his chest, and hoped he was going to live.

PART FOUR

New Beginnings

Paris, France,
London and Kent, England

December 1918–January 1919

TWENTY-TWO

Leonie Ward, now Mrs Richard Rhodes, stood at the window of their suite at the Plaza Athénée Hotel in Paris. By stretching her neck, she could just get a glimpse of the Eiffel Tower. She knew this sitting room well. Her mother always had this particular suite when she came to the City of Light, as some called it.

She had always loved this beautiful city, with its chicly dressed women, wonderful shops, and those unique bistros where delicious food was served and gaiety filled the air.

A small sigh escaped, as she stared out at Avenue Montaigne, the bare trees, gloomy skies, and melting snow. For the first time in her life, this trip did not please her. Because of Richard. Her new husband was behaving in a most peculiar way, which disturbed her.

Firstly, he went out by himself, and quite a lot. And he had long lunches with two old Etonians, friends of his from their schooldays, who had shown up here. Unexpectedly, according to Richard. She believed Frobisher and Robinson were wild boys, who led Richard astray.

Secondly, he frequently came home very drunk after lunch, promptly went to bed and awakened in the early evening.

Thirdly, he was always in a dodgy mood and picked on her. He was beginning to get on her nerves.

Turning away from the window and the bleak, depressing view, Leonie sat down in front of the fire and glanced at the ornate French clock on the mantelpiece. It was just past two forty-five.

In fifteen minutes, her best friend, Anne Chalmers, would be arriving to have tea with her. Leonie treasured Anne's enduring friendship. They had grown close as children in Ascot and had attended the same finishing school in Switzerland. They had stayed in close contact.

Anne was married to Clarke Chalmers, Paris correspondent of the American News Bureau. She lived not too far away. They always met when Leonie visited Paris, for lunch, tea or supper. Leonie adored Clarke.

Gazing into the flames, Leonie wondered how to handle Richard in a better way. He seemed to find fault with her all the time.

Her hair looked awful, do something about it, was a recurring comment. Or he would criticize her clothes, hats, coats, and even her shoes.

The thing was, she was exactly the same as she had always been. Nothing had changed in her; *he* had changed since arriving in Paris.

The constant nagging and picking on her was not only annoying; it was demeaning. The heavy drinking alarmed her, because it brought out an ugly side of him.

Rising, Leonie went into the bedroom and put on the dark-blue woollen jacket that matched her tailored dress. Throwing a blue-and-white silk scarf around her neck, she picked up her handbag. Opening it, she dropped in the key to the suite and left.

* * *

Much to her pleasure, she saw Anne sitting in the comfortably furnished promenade, just alongside the restaurant, where tea was always served.

Anne waved and Leonie almost ran to her, enjoying the feeling of happiness that filled her. She was not often happy these days.

The two women embraced, smiled at each other and sat on the sofa together. Instantly, Anne exclaimed, 'Gosh, you do look beautiful, Leonie. The outfit you're wearing is so chic, and it emphasizes your very blue eyes.'

Leonie beamed. 'Thank you, Anne. And you don't look half bad yourself; rather dishy, in fact, in your red suit. But red's always been your colour.'

The waiter arrived, and they ordered tea and small tea sandwiches. They then sat back, regarding one another, obviously glad to be together.

'How is Clarke?' Leonie asked. 'Working as hard as ever, I've no doubt.'

'Of course. I'm just relieved the war finally ended in November. He was on the front line for the past year. It was so dangerous. My heart was in my mouth half the time. Naturally, he loved being out there in the trenches with the troops. He wrote some marvellous pieces, and the bureau is more than pleased. Next year, he will be made head of the bureau in Paris, a big promotion.'

'How wonderful! Give him my congratulations and my love.'

Anne stared at Leonie, her light brown eyes narrowing. 'But you can do that yourself, can't you, Leonie? I thought we'd made a date to have supper in the next few days. Has something changed?' She looked puzzled and frowned.

Leonie hesitated, and then said quietly, 'Yes. Richard.'

Anne gave her a hard stare. 'What do you mean?'

Taking a deep breath, Leonie told her everything. She then sat back and took a long drink of tea.

'Demeaning you in this way is abuse!' Anne exclaimed in a low voice, a concerned expression now on her face. 'Verbal abuse.' Anne leaned closer to Leonie, and asked, 'He hasn't physically abused you, has he?'

Leonie was silent, and then nodded her head. 'He did yesterday. When he woke up after another drunken lunch, he punched me in my lower back and shouted at me. He claimed it was because I didn't need him to come to view the Renoir and the two Chagalls I'm hoping to buy for the gallery.'

It was evident Anne was shocked. 'This is unacceptable. You mustn't allow a man to beat you up. If it continues, you will have to leave him, you know. Don't drag it out. He could *really* hurt you.'

'Yes, perhaps I *will* have to do that. And I am going to tell him this when he is sober.' Leonie shook her head. '*You* know how hard I fell for him when we first met. Head over heels, in fact, and I broke all of my rules about men. I slept with him three days after meeting him and kept on doing it until he insisted we elope. I didn't really want to do that. But he was adamant.'

'Yes, I know. You hurt your mother's feelings, I think. She had wanted you to have a lovely white wedding,' Anne reminded Leonie. She reached out and squeezed her hand.

'It certainly didn't please her, and anyway she was quite sure Richard wasn't right for me. There was something about him that bothered her. She couldn't pinpoint what, though. And seemingly, she was right.'

'He fitted the bill, I suppose: tall, dark and handsome, good family, good schools.' Anne pursed her lips. 'And very fine Savile Row suits, but clothes don't make a man. Never forget that *looks* don't, either.'

Leonie sighed. 'I want to see how he behaves in the next few days. And if he continues to be verbally abusive, and especially if he punches me again, I will return to London immediately. I promise.'

'I'm glad you're saying that,' Anne answered, feeling and looking relieved.

* * *

When Leonie returned to the suite an hour later, she was surprised to find Richard lounging on the sofa near the fire. He was awake. He sat up when he heard her come into the sitting room.

Staring at her, he said, 'And where the hell have *you* been? I told you to wait here for me.'

Aware he had been drinking as usual, Leonie said, 'I had tea with Anne Chalmers here in the hotel.'

'I didn't *see* you there when I came back. An hour ago. Sure you haven't been out screwing one of your old boyfriends? I know how much you like these bloody Frogs in your knickers.'

Leonie, startled by the heated tone and his words, did not move. She was frozen to the spot. And afraid.

Richard unexpectedly jumped up and strode over to her. He took hold of her arm, pulled her to the bedroom door. When she tried to get free of him, he laughed. 'Now I'm going to show you what a really *good* screwing is like, you bitch.'

'Richard, stop! Don't be like this, please!' Leonie cried, still struggling with him.

But he was tall and strongly built, and he held her firmly in his arms. He dragged her towards the bed and threw her on it, then joined her. He hissed, 'You're going to take all your clothes off and so am I. You're going to be a dutiful wife and do everything I want you to do. Understand? *Whatever it is I want.*'

Leonie, shaking inside, could not speak. She was filled with fear and a terrible dread.

He leaned over her and slapped her face. 'Wake up, Beauty. Get ready for me or I'll tear your clothes off you.' As he spoke, he grabbed the neck of her dress and pulled it so hard it ripped down the front.

Struggling to a sitting position, Leonie realized she had to do as he asked. Otherwise, she was positive he would really hurt her. Swiftly, she left the bed, stepped out of her shoes, shed her jacket, dress and underwear, and stood near the bathroom door.

Once he saw her naked, Richard got off the bed and shed his

suit, shirt and underclothes as quickly as she had disrobed. He walked towards her, laughing again in that insane way, and grabbed her breasts.

'You're hurting me,' she cried and managed to break free.

He caught one arm and pulled her to the bed, silent now. Once he had her prone on her back, he raped her, kissing her sloppily and then moaning loudly as he thrust himself inside her over and over again.

Leonie lay there, unable to move, because he was a heavy weight on top of her. Eventually, he rolled off her of his own accord, and she slid off the bed. As she went into the bathroom, he called, 'I'm not finished with you yet. There's more of me to come.'

In the bathroom, Leonie washed herself, patting her face dry and then washing every part of her body, wanting to get the smell of him off her.

She understood this ordeal was not yet over, and she was also aware that to protect herself she had to accede to his wishes. Otherwise, in his roughness, he might really injure her. Or kill her.

Taking a deep breath, she went back to the bedroom. He was propped up against the pillows, waiting. He smiled. 'Come here, Beauty, and let's make love a little slower. I want to savour you. I won't hurt you.'

Swallowing hard and steeling herself, Leonie went back to the bed and lay down next to him. He began to kiss her immediately, stroked her body, and didn't stop touching her until the jarring ring of the telephone on the night table brought him to a halt.

A flash of annoyance crossed his face, as he turned away to answer it.

Understanding this was her chance to get away, she made a move to get off the bed. He slammed the receiver on the table and grabbed her hard. He then told the caller he would ring back later.

'Not so fast,' he said. 'You are my legally wedded wife, Leonie. Don't forget that. And you will submit to me. Understand?'

Leonie nodded and let him do what he wanted with her.

Once Richard was asleep and snoring, Leonie moved slowly, gently, and left the bed. Dressing swiftly and then smoothing her hair in the bathroom, she covered it with the white silk scarf. In the sitting room of the suite, she found her handbag, and left, being careful to close the door gently.

In the lobby of the hotel, she sat down for a moment to think. If she went to get help from Anne, Richard might come there because he knew her too. He'll make a guess where I've gone, she thought.

She opened her handbag. In it were her money, train tickets and passport. She always kept these items together. She could leave her clothes behind. They didn't matter and she could return to London early tomorrow morning.

Making this decision, she went outside and asked the doorman to get her a cab. A taxi came by almost at once. She got in and told the driver to go to the Eiffel Tower. When they had left the front of the hotel, she spoke in perfect French, giving him Anne's address. Even if Richard guessed to whom she had run, he wouldn't come looking for her until tomorrow. If at all. He might be too afraid to face Anne and Clarke. Or even embarrassed to do so.

By then, she would have already left for London on the first boat train leaving Paris.

TWENTY-THREE

One hour after Leonie's feet stepped onto English soil, James Falconer knew about it.

The private investigator he'd hired, John Scolding, was sitting in his office at Malvern House, giving him all the details.

'I heard they had gone to Paris, but why did she return so quickly and alone?' James asked Scolding, a neutral expression on his face. He didn't want to reveal to Scolding that he'd broken things off with Georgiana Ward. Or that he'd decided to stop asking his daughter for a reconciliation. Nonetheless, he was interested in what was going on in her marriage. And he was concerned for her.

'Obviously something went wrong, or she had to return because of an emergency here,' John Scolding suggested. 'When you hired me to put tails on Mrs Rhodes and her husband, I did so immediately. Once they went to Paris, I put French agents on, along with part of my English team. We've watched them day and night.'

'I understand you did your job, and thank you. So give me

the details, please.' James leaned back in the chair, looking across his desk at Scolding, his vivid blue eyes fixed on the private detective he had hired.

'From the moment the couple arrived in Paris, Rhodes constantly left his wife alone. Apparently two of his old Etonian friends had shown up unexpectedly. He saw them every day for boozy lunches. I had put one of the Paris teams in a room next door to their suite in the Plaza Athénée Hotel. Yesterday afternoon there was a lot of shouting and noise in their suite,' he explained.

'Do you think Richard Rhodes was physically abusing her?' James asked, dreading the idea that Leonie was injured. 'Is she hurt?'

'Not too sure, sir. Around five fifty in the afternoon, that same day, Leonie entered the hotel lobby. She sat down, looked in her purse and then went outside. She asked the doorman to get her a cab to go to the Eiffel Tower. But instead the cab took her to the home of her old friend, Mrs Anne Chalmers—'

'So she didn't want the doorman to know where she was going,' Falconer cut in.

'Correct. We interviewed the doorman, of course. He gave us the first address. However, one of my team followed her in another cab.'

'So Richard Rhodes was still in the hotel?'

'Yes, he was, Mr Falconer. Leonie stayed overnight with Mr and Mrs Chalmers, who escorted her to the station to get the boat train to London very early this morning. She went straight to her mother's Curzon Street house.' Detective Scolding sat back, and added, 'I asked my team if she looked injured and they all said she did not, if that knowledge gives you some relief, sir.'

'To a certain extent, Scolding. But he could have hurt her body, you know, which is covered in clothing,' James said. 'Do you know where she is now?'

'At work, Mr Falconer, at her art gallery.'

James was taken aback for a moment, and then said swiftly, 'Then she must be all right if she went to work. What do you think, Scolding?'

'Actually, the same as you, sir. And this is what I think happened. They had some sort of row in Paris. We know that for sure. We also know he neglected her, going out with his Etonian pals for boozy lunches. I believe that she cut and ran, because of that row. Smart of her, in my opinion.'

'I agree. She wanted to save herself from possible trouble. I've always had my doubts about Rhodes, felt there was something off about him. Couldn't quite pinpoint it, though.' Falconer sighed. 'Well, we know she's safe now, thank God.'

'Indeed we do, Mr Falconer. I just want to mention one thing.' Scolding hesitated and cleared his throat. 'Rhodes has another addiction as well as booze. He likes to go to houses of ill-repute.'

For the first time that day, James laughed. 'Brothels, Detective Scolding. Let's call them by their correct name, shall we?'

The private detective also chuckled, and added, 'He likes prostitutes. Oh, and there's been another development. The woman you wanted me to find, Dorothy Miller, has been his mistress for some years. It took time to locate her, but we did. She lives in Stepney.'

This announcement startled Falconer for a moment, and then he asked, 'She's *still* his mistress, even though he's now a married man? Married to Leonie.'

'I'm afraid so, and she has a small daughter by him.' Scolding shook his head. 'Richard Rhodes is not nice; he is something of a ladies' man.'

Twenty-Four

After Detective Scolding left, James worked on the draft of the agreement his solicitors needed.

It was for the retailers to sign, as he would also. The rents would be lowered during these difficult economic times and go back to the higher rent when things normalized. He hoped this would help his retailers. The country was on its knees.

When the door opened, he glanced up and saw Peter Keller, and beckoned him into the room.

'Good news!' Keller exclaimed, and then stopped speaking, as he drew closer to the desk. Sitting down in the chair opposite James, he said, 'You look very white. Are you all right?' There was a hint of worry in his voice, concern in his dark eyes.

'I'm feeling a bit done in, if you want the truth. I've had a bit of a gruelling morning—'

'With that chap I saw earlier,' Keller interjected. 'Who was he?'

'A private detective I hired to tail Richard Rhodes and Leonie.'

Surprised though he was, Keller said, 'I know you and she are estranged, but why put a tail on her? On them?'

'Because there is something I don't like about Rhodes, and I want *him watched*. As for Leonie, we are indeed estranged. She hates me. However, nonetheless, she is my daughter, and I wanted to make sure she was safe.'

'I understand,' Keller said. 'You've always been one of the good guys, Falconer. But I think Rhodes is rotten, a snake in the grass. So, what did the private detective find out?'

Falconer told him everything he knew, finishing, 'At this moment she is at her gallery, around the corner from here.'

Keller exclaimed, 'Thank God she was smart enough to cut and run. I think she saved herself from serious injury.' Keller grimaced, looked at his dearest friend, and added, 'And naturally she's smart. She's your daughter and has your eyes.'

Falconer smiled, and said, 'You were about to tell me some good news, so go ahead.'

'Orders for wine in London have suddenly increased. However, that's because it's nearly Christmas, only a few days away,' Keller remarked in a more cheerful voice. 'Not so great on imports.'

'Glad to hear about the London wine merchants bucking up. Sorry we don't have the European orders,' James replied. 'But we'll manage. Somehow.'

'I hope you're not thinking of putting more of your own money into Malvern's.' Keller's eyes were keen and riveted on him.

'No, and you've put some of your money into the company, too,' James pointed out. 'And thank you for that.'

'I'm your best friend, remember?' Keller smiled suddenly, when he saw the icon shining in the sunlight on Falconer's desk.

'You've still got that!' Keller sounded surprised.

'Yes, it was in my library at home, but I spotted it the other day and thought I'd bring it here, liven up the place. Do you recall when you and I were at Aunt Cheska's house and we first set eyes on them?' Falconer asked, touching the past as he so often did.

'I do! There were about forty of them on Irina's aunt's table.

A magnificent collection. They had belonged to their mother, who was Russian . . .'

Keller stopped short and shook his head. 'Good God, I've just had an odd thought, Falconer. Do you think that man who burst into Irina's house, weeks ago now, was looking for the icon collection?'

'It did cross my mind last week, but then all this trouble with Leonie began, and I forgot until today. I suppose we'll never know who that chap was. Detective Stead couldn't find a thing on him, or match his fingerprints to those in the files at Scotland Yard. Out of curiosity, where is the collection?'

'In a bank vault – where else?' Keller answered. 'And very safe. Irina says it's their umbrella. For a rainy day. They'll only sell the icon collection when they need money.'

'Then it will never be sold. We are both successful men. I'm certain next year we'll see an improvement in this country. Malvern's is safe, Keller.'

'After all the ravages of the war, and the epidemic. If only the economy would take a turn for the better.' Keller stood up, and said, 'Come on. I'm going home and so are you.'

Falconer sighed and started to protest, but instantly changed his mind. Locking the centre drawer of his desk, he also rose. 'Let's go then. I can't walk it, old chap. My legs are killing me today.'

'I hope you're not coming down with something.' Keller sounded worried again. 'You're awfully pale today.'

'It's the weather that affects my legs,' Falconer muttered. 'And I've told you that before. As for being pale, we don't live in a sunny climate. This ain't Africa.'

Keller merely laughed, and changed the subject, but his worries about Falconer's health stayed at the back of his mind.

* * *

It was with great relief that James limped into the library at his house on South Audley Street. Immediately, he went and stood in front of the blazing fire, warming his legs.

Peter Keller followed him in, exclaiming, 'I do love this room, Falconer, and especially the art. You've got a good eye.'

'And an empty stomach. I've not had lunch and neither have you.' James forced a smile. 'You'll find Brompton in the butler's pantry, Keller. Could you please go and ask him for some snacks and hot tea?'

'I will,' Keller replied, and left the library, deciding to include two glasses of wine. He had recognized that Falconer was taut, very tense, not well. The wine might help to make him relax. He hoped so. He didn't like his friend to be out of sorts and suffering.

Eventually James sat down on the Chesterfield, stretching out his long legs. Blowing out air, he leaned back and closed his eyes, running the events of the last few weeks through his mind.

He detested problems of a personal nature; he was also still a bit shocked about the way he had lost his temper with Mrs Ward. It was not like him at all.

When Keller returned and sat next to him, James sat up, and said, 'I want to ask you something.'

'Yes, go ahead. What is it?'

'Have you ever seen me lose my temper, go into a rage?'

Keller began to laugh. '*You?* Never, ever. And we've known each other for thirty years. You're always in total control of yourself. Did you go into a rage recently? If so, it's most unusual.'

'I did, yes. It was . . .' James paused when Brompton knocked and entered the room. He wheeled in a tea trolley which he placed near the sofa.

'Cook has prepared these small snacks, sir, and a pot of tea, as well as two glasses of wine. Shall I pour the tea for you and Mr Keller?'

'Thank you, Brompton, you can do so.'

A few seconds later, the butler left, and Keller said, 'Nice snacks, too. Caviar, toast, terrine and slices of cheese. Fits the bill very well. I am a bit famished now.' Keller reached for the wine glass and took a sip.

'So am I.' James spread caviar on a small triangle of toast, ate it, and then sat holding the tea, warming his hands. He finally drank some of it. 'I do think this is the coldest winter we've had in years. Icy weather most days. I can't wait for summer.'

'Bloody awful, I agree.' Keller decided to remain quiet so James could get some food inside him. He had already begun to look a little better since being in the warmth of the library.

Keller loved this room with its green velvet curtains, walls of books, the burgundy Chesterfield, the Impressionist paintings. It was elegant yet comfortable, masculine, without being overbearingly so. But then Falconer had always had good taste when it came to the finer things in life.

Once he was satisfied and had warmed up after two cups of tea, James said, 'I lost my temper recently. With Georgiana Ward.'

Momentarily surprised, Keller stared at him. 'I knew you'd been seeing her again. And I wasn't sure it was the right idea, if I'm honest. But I'm surprised you flew off the handle. It's not like you.' Keller pursed his lips, eyeing Falconer. 'Want to tell me more, James? It might help to unburden yourself. You seem uptight today.'

'So it shows?'

'It does, old chap. Come on, let me hear it all.'

After drinking some of the wine, James Falconer confided everything to his old friend and felt better as he talked, leaving nothing out, making sure to include all the details.

'I actually flew into a rage when, after saying she wanted us to marry, she reneged yet again, took off the sapphire ring and put it back in the box. I was furious because she said she couldn't wear it; Leonie would see it and wouldn't approve of our serious involvement. She then explained she would lose Leonie if our daughter knew about us, and she just couldn't lose Leonie.' James shook his head. 'She's never really given me a proper date, or she changes it, playing games with me. I told her in no uncertain terms that Leonie was a grown woman, a married woman. That she couldn't let her dictate her life – or mine. Leonie chose to marry Rhodes. And then I told her she could keep her. And that she had just *lost* me. I ended our relationship.'

'I know you've been frustrated. And why should you play second fiddle? I've never understood why Mrs Ward didn't try to close the gap between you and Leonie. Or stand up for her own right to have a relationship with you. It seems odd – to me, anyway.'

Falconer exclaimed, 'I said that to Georgiana myself, but she had no answer.'

'So you walked out?'

'I did. It's ended. Over and done.'

'And Leonie?'

'God knows. Maybe if she's left that man there might be a possibility for me to rebuild our relationship.'

Peter nodded, then looked up at James.

'Where's the sapphire ring?'

'Here in my safe upstairs.' James half smiled. 'I picked up the red Cartier box and put it in my pocket before I left.'

'You should take it back to the jeweller's where you bought it. Get your money back, which could be invested in Malvern's.'

James couldn't help smiling broadly. 'You do have some good ideas at times, old chap. I'll take your advice.'

Keller nodded. 'The food and the warmth seem to have perked you up. You're looking much better. Now, onto other things. Are you going to Kent tomorrow as planned, for Christmas?'

'I am indeed. Lady Jane and Lord Reggie are expecting me in time for tea. I shall stay through Christmas Eve, Christmas Day and Boxing Day. I will have to come back to London for two days, but they want me there for New Year's Eve. I'm looking forward to being with them in Kent. With friends.' For a moment, the famous businessman's face had a shadow of great sadness across it.

TWENTY-FIVE

Long ago, James Falconer had come to understand that memories of his past were important in his life today. They always would be. In a certain sense, he couldn't live without them. They gave him great comfort.

On this cold but sunny day, visions of his darling Alexis came rushing back to him as he walked along the terrace of Lord Reggie's house, Tower Lodge, in Kent.

When he paused and stood gazing out across the snowy garden, and the land beyond, he knew that tonight, if he went down to the edge of Romney Marsh, he would be able to see, in the distance, the twinkling lights on the French coast.

How often they had done that together. Alexis had loved the Romney Marsh, as he did himself. It was mystical and thrilling at certain times of the day, mostly in the early evening when mist floated everywhere, and later when the moon rose and cast its silver glow across the land.

He loved Kent. He also associated it with Lord Reggie, Lady Jane and the Glendennings. He had also recuperated from his war wounds at a military hospital in Kent.

For James, it was a positive place to be, reminding him of that happiness that felt so long ago. Another life almost. His spirits always lifted when he was here. Walking back along the terrace, he went into the drawing room through the French doors.

At this moment, Lady Jane was hurrying into the room, and a huge smile spread across her face when she saw James.

They came together and embraced, and Jane said, 'I'm so sorry I wasn't here to greet you, but Cook needed to speak to me. Reggie is on the telephone, talking to the editor of *The Chronicle*. Always a problem about something or other when you own a newspaper.'

'I remember that from my Uncle George. And I was fine out on the terrace, enjoying the view.'

'Reggie won't be long. He'll join us for tea. Let's sit down, James. Near the fire. I know you like to be warm.'

He smiled. 'I think you know a lot about me after all these years, Jane. However, I do have something to tell you. When Reggie comes down.'

Settling in one of the chairs in front of the fireplace, Jane raised a brow. 'You sound serious. Do tell us more. It must be important since you're announcing it when you've just arrived.' She gazed at him intently, thinking how well he looked.

'It is, and I want to get it out of the way. One thing you should know is that it has given me great relief.'

'There you are, old chap!' Lord Reginald Carpenter cried as he rushed towards them, as usual full of smiles and exuberance.

James stood up, and the two men embraced. They looked at each other, their happiness at being together apparent. 'It's good to see you, Carpenter.'

'Welcome home, James,' Lord Reggie exclaimed. 'We've missed you.'

'I've missed you and Jane, but here I am now. And thank you for inviting me for Christmas.'

'You've been coming for so many years it wouldn't be the same without you.' As he spoke, Lord Carpenter pulled up another chair and joined them.

Lady Jane said, 'James has something to tell us, darling. Something *important*.'

Reggie glanced at his old friend, whom he cherished, and eyed him acutely. 'I hope it's good news . . .' He let his sentence trail off.

Falconer said, 'It is, actually. As I just told Jane, it's given me a lot of relief.' He sat up straighter in the chair, looked from Jane to Reggie, taking a deep breath, and said, 'I have ended my relationship with Mrs Georgiana Ward. A short while ago. It is final. I can explain it if you wish.'

Jane appeared to be surprised, but Reggie's expression was neutral. However, there was a knowing look in his dark eyes as he focused them on Falconer.

It was Lord Reggie who spoke first. 'Jane seems startled, but I'm not, Falconer. I know it's been such an on-and-off situation for as long as I can remember. I often wondered why you never married and decided that perhaps she was the one who was . . . *uncertain*, shall we say?'

'You are correct. I'd propose and she'd accept, and then find a reason to renege, put it off. There have been long gaps, years, when we didn't see one another. She just retreated to Ascot, and we lost touch. Then I fell in love with Alexis, and we married. And you know all about that and how much we cared for each other.'

Jane nodded. 'After Alexis died, I believe part of you died, darling. You were perhaps . . . catatonic. What I mean is, you were in catatonic shock. You just plunged into your work, and that's all you did. Night and day. Around the clock. Work and no play. That was not good.'

'I know, and I know you were worried about me. As I look back now, I believe I needed help from a doctor, perhaps one like Sigmund Freud. Alexis so believed in him. She saw him herself after Sebastian Trevalian died. I certainly was . . . a *goner* for some years. I did need a mind doctor.'

Lord Reggie said slowly, 'You blame yourself because you stopped seeing Leonie at that time. You've told me on many occasions that she resents you because of that. I believe you have said she *detests* you.'

'That's true,' Falconer replied. 'It was my fault. I stopped seeing her when she was thirteen because I had plunged into a terrible grief. Yes, I'm to blame.'

'I understand what you're saying,' Lord Reggie responded. 'On the other hand, in my considered opinion, Mrs Ward is also to blame. I don't understand *why* she did not intervene and bring you and your daughter together. She also seems to have vacillated about marrying you, long after Leonie was grown up. I think she cannot be excused.'

'And now she is gone from my life.'

'What finally brought it to a head, James?' Jane asked.

James explained that he had become frustrated with her, how his growing impatience was concerning to him, and how the final straw had been her taking off the sapphire engagement ring.

Lord Reginald, looking across at James, knowing what a kind man he was, exclaimed, 'I'm glad you're free of her. A new beginning, Falconer. The world is at your feet.'

After tea, James went upstairs to his bedroom, the one Jane had announced was his and his alone, years ago. No one else could use it, she had told him.

A fire glowed in the grate, and he undressed, put on a dressing gown and went over to the fire.

As he sat there, relaxing and daydreaming, he thought about

the last year and how it had panned out. After a while, he decided he had managed to come through it reasonably well. *Unscathed.*

He was still worried about Malvern's, though. These economic difficulties were bound to linger on into 1919. The retail side had suffered terribly from the impact of the epidemic. And trade internationally had been hit by the war.

Oh, let it all go, he told himself suddenly. Enjoy yourself for a change. He was able to swerve away from his worries and focus on these few days here in Kent.

Tonight the Glendennings would come over for dinner. The only other house guest would arrive tomorrow sometime. Jane's niece, whom he knew nothing about except that she had lived in America for some years, was coming.

He was looking forward to seeing his great friends, Claudia Trevalian Glendenning and her husband Cornelius, Connie to his friends. Claudia, in particular, was special to him, because she had been Alexis's best friend. And she cared for him.

The warmth of the fire, the sense of peace that pervaded the room, the comfort lulled him to sleep.

He awakened some time later and, for a moment, was disoriented, wondering where he was. He was startled to hear the grandfather clock in the corridor outside striking six times.

Falconer pulled out his pocket watch and looked at it. It was indeed six o'clock. He had to be downstairs in an hour. Thank God he didn't have to wear a dinner jacket tonight.

The dinner party was off to a good start. Claudia and Jane sat on each side of Falconer, each radiant in their different ways. It was a relaxed dinner, not a formal one, but the women had dressed in soft, jewel-coloured dresses, Claudia in a fashionably cut pale-green silk, with lace panels, and Jane in her favourite deep burgundy velveteen.

Lord Reggie was next to Claudia, and Connie was Jane's dinner partner. No other guests had been invited. It was a small, very close group of devoted old friends.

After James had caught up with the Glendennings, it was Lord Reginald who changed the subject. He went straight into politics, when he said, 'Well, Falconer, what are your thoughts about the country at the moment?'

James was not an expert on the politicians and politics of the day, but he did understand some of its goings-on. After a moment, he said, 'I never liked Asquith much, and I'm waiting to see what happens with Lloyd George. Personally, I've got my eyes on Winston. Winston Churchill, that is. I think he's going places.'

Connie exclaimed, 'Some people think Churchill should just go away, but I agree with you. He'll be a force in this country, you'll see.'

'But he's not even in the Cabinet,' Lord Reggie pointed out. He then lifted his glass of white wine, and declared, 'Here's to the New Year – to 1919. Let's hope it's a better year. To Peace, at last.'

Everyone joined in the toast and then fell silent as they tasted the hot ginger-and-potato soup. The main course was roast turbot.

Portman, the butler, moved around the table, filling the water goblets, and then disappeared. He returned almost instantly with a bottle of red wine which he placed on the sideboard in a wine coaster.

Connie drank his white wine and sat back in his chair, looking at Reggie. 'What are your thoughts, old chap? You're the owner of a newspaper. You're really in the know, if anyone is.'

'I tend to go along with Falconer, actually, in that I do think Winston is brilliant. He's about forty-three now and still MP for Dundee. But he will be a force to be reckoned with in the next few years.'

'So you think he has lived Gallipoli down?' Jane asked, surprising her husband that she had spoken out.

Lord Reggie nodded. 'Good question, darling, and I do. The public love Winston Churchill. I've watched their faith in him grow. He's that wonderful mixture – a genuine aristocrat with a marvellous talent no one can buy. He has the common touch.'

TWENTY-SIX

The Christmas tree looked beautiful, magnificent, in fact, and James felt his heart fill as he stood gazing at it. When he'd been in the trenches, he'd been unsure if he'd ever stand on English soil again, if peace would come, or if he and his friends would celebrate together ever again.

The tree was in the conservatory, which was full of windows, and the sunshine was pouring in.

It was the morning of Christmas Eve, and he had stopped to view the handiwork of the staff who had started to trim the tree late yesterday afternoon and had continued until it was finished.

He himself had helped Lady Jane in picking out the colours – silver, blue and gold – and the mixture of ornaments, round glass balls and crystal icicles in those same colours. Simplicity did work sometimes. The tree actually glowed brightly, just the way he had hoped.

Smiling inwardly, he left the conservatory, relieved to see the heating units, which the butler had placed around the space. They threw out good heat, thank God. This end of the house was often cold for him.

Walking into the breakfast room a few seconds later, he paused in the doorway. He was surprised to see a little boy sitting there, all dressed up in a suit and tie, waiting patiently.

James walked over and looked down at him. The boy looked up, and a wide smile spread across his face, as he stood up, and said, 'Hello, sir. Oh no, that's wrong. *Good morning, sir,*' and then he saluted James.

Biting back a smile, Falconer saluted him in return, and said, 'Good morning to you. May I join you?'

'Yes, please,' the boy answered, and pushed himself back onto his chair, managing to do this quite well.

Falconer couldn't take his eyes off this child, who looked to be about five years old. He was beautiful, with blond hair and blue eyes, and had a lovely little face. He's just adorable, James thought. Sitting down next to him, he said, 'May I know your name?'

The boy nodded. 'Adrian Paul Kelsey Longden Evans.'

'My goodness, *that* is a very long name indeed. I am James Lionel Falconer.' Stretching out his hand, James added, 'I'm very pleased to meet you, Adrian.'

The boy put his small hand in James's much larger one, and responded, in a solemn voice, 'How do you do, sir?'

A moment later, Portman, the butler, arrived in the breakfast room, carrying a silver dish.

'Good morning, Mr Falconer,' he said, and placed the dish on a hotplate. He turned and smiled at the child. 'Good morning, Master Adrian.'

James greeted the butler, and so did the child. Then James addressed the butler, asking, 'What do you have over there, Portman? Lots of good food, I'm certain of that.'

'A wide selection, sir. Fried bacon, ham, sautéed potatoes, fried tomatoes, fried kidneys, sautéed mushrooms, pork sausages and beef sausages. And Cook will make any kind of egg dish you prefer. She doesn't like eggs to stand around too long. Boiled, scrambled, fried or poached.'

'Yes. I do know that, Portman. Thank you.' Falconer turned to Adrian. 'What would you like to eat today?'

'I can't order yet, sir. I have to wait for Mummy.'

'I understand. What is Mummy's name?'

Looking somewhat perplexed, the child said, 'Mummy. That's her name.'

Falconer nodded and glanced across at Portman, who said carefully, 'I am sure Lady Annabel will be joining you moment-arily, sir. Lady Jane and Lord Reginald won't be far behind. In the meantime, Master Adrian can have his milk. Would you care for a coffee, Mr Falconer?'

'Thank you, I would.'

Adrian said, 'I think Mummy is coming now.'

Falconer frowned. 'How do you know?'

'I can hear her heels clicking on the marble floor.'

And sure enough, moments later, a young woman appeared in the hallway just outside the breakfast room. As she moved forward, a blaze of sunshine surrounded her.

James Falconer caught his breath and froze in his chair as she walked in.

The young woman was tall and willowy. She had shining auburn hair and, as she drew closer to them, Falconer realized her eyes were bright green. Alexis's colouring. His chest tightened.

Stunned though he was, Falconer remembered his manners and jumped up to greet her. Thrusting out his right hand, he started to introduce himself.

She interrupted him, and exclaimed, 'Goodness, Mr Falconer, I know who you are! According to Jane, you're probably the most famous man in England after the King.'

She took his hand anyway. Her smile filled her face with radiance. She said, 'I'm Annabel Kelsey. I do hope my child hasn't been pestering you, been a nuisance.' She raised an auburn brow, her green eyes fastened on his with great intensity.

'Not at all, Lady Annabel,' Falconer said, relieved that his voice sounded normal. 'In fact, I think he's charming. He wouldn't order breakfast until Mummy came.'

'Oh dear, you must be hungry.'

'I was happy to wait, I assure you.'

Portman cleared his throat, and Falconer realized their hands were still clasped together. So did she; a pink flush filled her face as she let go of his right hand at last.

'Oh dear, here I am clinging onto your hand like this!' she exclaimed. 'I'm so sorry. How silly I am!'

He simply smiled, unable to think of a reasonable answer, and trying to remember what Jane had told him about her niece. She certainly didn't tell me Annabel was beautiful, he thought, as he followed her around the child and pulled out the chair next to her son so she could sit down.

Returning to his own seat, he said, 'When did you arrive, Lady Annabel?'

'Late last night,' she answered, and then kissed the top of Adrian's head.

'What would you like?' she asked him, still smiling.

'A boiled egg, please, Mummy, and toast, so we can make soldiers.'

'What a grand idea,' she said and looked at the butler. 'I'm sorry, Portman – I haven't even greeted you yet. Good morning. And Master Adrian will have a boiled egg, as usual, and so will I, thank you. What about you, Mr Falconer?'

Suddenly, James didn't feel hungry. 'I will have a fried tomato and toast, but I'll help myself Portman,' he said, addressing the butler. He then smiled at Adrian, who smiled back.

Before James could turn his attention to Annabel, which he badly wanted to, there was sudden noise and bustle in the hallway.

Lady Jane and Lord Reggie came rushing into the breakfast room, apologizing profusely for being late.

Greetings. Explanations, chatter. Food being served onto plates as they all stood to choose their breakfast. A lot of noise. So many thoughts were swimming around in James's head, he decided to eat his breakfast and remain quiet. He looked at Adrian several times and realized he was doing exactly the same.

As he cut the tomato in half, and then into quarters, James spread the pieces on the toast. He did so without looking up, eating slowly.

In a peculiar way, he was reluctant to see anyone. Annabel's vivid colouring, so much like Alexis's, had truly startled him. But she didn't look like Alexis, whose face had been clearly chiselled, even sharply angled.

Lady Jane's niece had a softer, rounder, more girlish face. She was much younger too. Finally, he raised his head, gave her a small smile and began to eat again.

Not long after this, Lady Jane and Lord Reggie, explaining they had things to finish for the dinner, departed.

Once they were alone, Annabel exclaimed, 'I was so pleased to hear you would be visiting for Christmas. You see, I've long admired you, Mr Falconer.'

Although her comment took him by surprise, James smiled. 'Thank you for your kind words, but may I ask why?' He looked slightly perplexed.

Annabel gazed at him, and answered swiftly, 'Because of your success, of course. You're one of the greatest businessmen in England. A genuine tycoon of the first order. There's no one like you. I read about you in the newspapers.'

James simply gazed back at her. Her face was soft and young, her complexion perfect, and she had high cheekbones and a full, rather sensual mouth. There was enormous energy there, and a freshness that was most appealing to him, not to mention an enthusiasm that was infectious.

He wondered how old she was. Thirty? Certainly not much older than that.

It was Annabel who broke the silence, when she announced in her high, clear voice, 'I'm thirty-two, Mr Falconer. But going

on forty, as Aunt Jane says, because she thinks I'm very smart.'
She laughed, her dimples showing.

'Did you just read my mind?' James said, still staring at her,
enjoying being here with her. All his worries were forgotten, at
least for now.

'No. But I knew you'd be wondering about my age. You're
forty-eight, I know that.'

'Yes, I am. Forty-nine next year, and then I'll be fifty. An old
man.'

'Oh bosh to that! *You'll* never be an old man. And at forty-
eight, you're in the prime of your life.' Annabel stopped speaking
when the nanny arrived at the table. She quickly glanced at
Adrian, who fortunately was dozing.

Jumping up, Annabel exclaimed, 'Oh, here you are, Nan! I
think Adrian seems a bit sleepy. Perhaps a little stroll would
help. He needs exercise.'

'Yes, m'lady. I'll wrap him up well, don't you worry.'

Adrian, now wide awake, slid out of his chair, and exclaimed,
'Can I go and see the Christmas tree, Nan? I want to see it.
Please, please.'

'Of course you can, Adrian.' The nanny took hold of his hand.
She smiled at his mother, and said, 'Have a nice morning, Your
Ladyship.'

Annabel smiled as the two of them walked off. 'And you too.'

'I'd forgotten he was here,' James said, and then added quickly,
'Well, obviously, I could see him, but we weren't watching our
words, were we?'

Annabel raised an eyebrow. 'It's all right. I don't think we said
anything unusual, and he was half dozing. He's happy with his
Nan.'

'He's the most adorable child I've ever met,' James told her.

'And you were adorable, the way you were treating him,
talking to him before. Thank you for that. So, how about a walk
through the gardens?'

Having been momentarily nonplussed a few seconds ago, he was caught off-guard. He had only just met this woman.

Taking a deep breath, Annabel said, 'I know Aunt Jane told you I'm talkative but honest, and sometimes too blunt. I'm a bit of a free spirit. But I do have a serious side. Did she say all that?'

A faint smile flickered on Falconer's mouth, and he said, 'Only part of that, but I like honesty. We all have different aspects in us, and our own personalities.'

Enthusiastic, joyous, and full of high spirits, Annabel had insisted that they go for a walk right out to the edge of the gardens.

Falconer, carried along by her light-heartedness, agreed. By the time they had reached the small wood near Goldenhurst, he understood it had been a big mistake. It was still icy weather, and his legs had begun to ache so badly he thought they might give way. His back ached as well.

He struggled on but Annabel, who never missed a thing with anyone, soon noticed that his limp was worse and there was a sheen of sweat on his brow. She brought him to a stop.

'Come and lean against this tree,' she cried, leading him to a grand old oak. 'You need a rest. You're limping badly.'

Falconer simply nodded and let her guide him. Once he had the tree trunk against his body, he experienced a bit of relief. He took a deep breath.

'This is all my fault,' she exclaimed, her voice rising. 'I'm so thoughtless. But you're so tall and strong, I forgot about your wounded legs. I'm so sorry.' She was staring up at him, looking stricken. 'You must think I'm a silly, thoughtless girl.'

Looking down at her, more aware than ever of her fresh, youthful face, his chest tightened. He touched her cheeks with his fingertips, flicking away the tears. 'It's not your fault, Lady Annabel, but I think we must turn back. My legs react badly to the cold.'

'Yes, yes, we must. I will help you. Lean on me, I'm strong.'

Moving away from the tree, Falconer began to laugh. 'You're as strong as an ox,' he said, and started to laugh again. 'So you think.'

She was puzzled, and taking hold of his arm, she asked, 'Why are you laughing? Are you laughing at me?' A hint of indignation echoed.

Calming himself, James said, 'No, not at all, but at *us*. Look at us . . . I've got bad legs and you must weigh about half a pound of fairy dust. And off we go for a walk in the woods, and I get tired and you believe you can carry me home. Daft, that's what we are.'

'I said you could *lean* on me,' she corrected him, and then asked quietly, 'How did you come up with *half a pound of fairy dust?*'

'Because fairy dust enchants mortals, and you've managed to enchant me from the first moment we met – when you were spreading your fairy dust.'

Annabel was thrilled, but speechless. Before she could respond to this extraordinary statement, he was limping off down the path.

'Wait for me!' she shouted, and ran after him.

TWENTY-SEVEN

Annabel managed to help James to walk, and she got him back to the house in record time.

Once they had shed their overcoats, gloves and scarves, she insisted they retreat to the small parlour rather than his room.

'It has a bigger fireplace, and I'm going to fetch lots of shawls. I'm going to get you really warm,' she explained.

Falconer didn't have the energy to argue, and let her take charge, which she was determined to do anyway. He wondered if she was bossy because she was in her thirties, or was that her nature? Right now, he didn't care.

The small parlour was lovely, decorated in the pale colours he liked, and looked very comfortable. She walked him over to a chair in front of a roaring fire, and said, 'I'm going to get some of my cashmere shawls. They'll keep you warm.'

Sitting down, feeling relieved, he said, 'I know all about cashmere. I deal in luxury goods.'

Annabel started laughing, and said in her light-hearted voice, 'Oh, I know what you deal in, Mr Falconer. I know a lot about you.'

Before he could question her, she had rushed off to her bedroom. He wondered what she was implying.

Falconer sat back, relaxing, thinking Lady Annabel was a firecracker. Yet caring and kind. And probably a handful. He sighed to himself. If he was honest, he had been drawn to her the moment they met – sexually attracted to her, in fact.

But was he up to embarking on a romantic liaison? After all, he was sixteen years older than her—

Her voice interrupted his thoughts, as she came into the parlour, saying, 'I'm going to ring down to the kitchen and get us a pot of hot tea, once I've wrapped you up.'

'I think you might have already done that,' he said, dryly.

Annabel merely stared hard at him, and then stepped towards the chair. She laid a beige cashmere shawl over his legs.

'Thank you,' he said.

'Do you want one around your shoulders?'

'Not for the moment, thanks.'

She said, 'I'll be back in three shakes of a lamb's tail. Off to get the tea.'

He looked at her, and smiled. 'You'd make a good nurse, I'm sure of that.'

'Oh, I know. I'm good at everything I do.' She laughed and winked at him. 'And I do mean *everything.*'

Left alone, Falconer sat thinking about tomorrow. Christmas Day. Gifts would be opened. He had brought lovely velvet scarves for the ladies, selected from Rossi's fine collection, and Cuban cigars for the men. Nothing for the little boy. *Adrian.* Who he'd not known would be here. He pondered on that. Perhaps Lady Annabel would be able to help out, have some ideas.

James smiled inwardly. Ideas she did have, at least about them being together. Of that he was certain. Too many innuendos and frequent references to the difference in their ages for him to think otherwise.

Lady Annabel was soon hurrying back, carrying a tea tray. She was followed by a young maid with another tray.

'I've brought afternoon tea so you don't have to move again. You'll get a bit of extra rest before dinner.'

Placing the tea tray on a nearby table, she took the second tray from the maid, who left.

Lady Annabel put the tray of sandwiches next to him on a side table. 'I'm sure you're hungry, so here's the usual selection. And I shall pour you a cup of tea.'

This she did promptly, and said, 'I made it myself. It's a little different. Try it.'

After glancing at her, puzzled, he did so, and then grinned. 'You put some Scotch in it, and honey!'

'Oh, you guessed too quickly!' she cried.

'My mother sometimes made this tea when we had colds.'

He watched her moving about the room, thinking how graceful she was, and finally said, 'Won't you come and have a cup of tea with me, Lady Annabel?'

'Where else would I have tea but with you?' she answered, her smile intact. A second later, she was sitting in the other chair.

She sipped the tea and then looked at him. She then asked carefully, 'Aunt Jane said you're only staying for Boxing Day, that you're leaving the day after.'

'That's correct.'

'But why?' she asked, her voice high and clear again, a perplexed look in her eyes.

'Duty calls, Your Ladyship. I have a business to run,' he replied in a cool tone.

'I understand, but what about New Year's Eve? Are you really coming back? She said you were.'

'I hope so.' The crestfallen look on her face made him add, 'I'm sure. I will definitely come back.'

She eyed him for a long moment. 'That makes me very happy. It wouldn't be the same without you.'

'But you've only just met me, Lady Annabel.' He removed the shawl and pushed himself up to his feet, with his back to the fire.

She looked up at him, a knowing expression on her face. She smiled to herself. Standing up, she went and stood in front of him. He was six feet two, and she was five feet eight. They were not exactly eyeball to eyeball, but their faces were close enough.

Annabel stared into the most strikingly blue eyes she had ever seen, and said, 'You want *me* to say it, Falconer, don't you?'

James stared back at her, a flicker of a smile on his face. 'What do I want you to say, my lady?'

'That I am smitten, that I fell for you when I first saw you.'

'You did that?' He reached out and took her in his arms; he held her close to him. 'If the truth be known, I'm smitten with you. But I'm far too old for you, darling.'

'No, no, you aren't!' she said emphatically, drawing away. She stared at him, mesmerized by those vivid blue eyes, his handsome looks, his strong body. 'Please, let's be together.'

'What does that mean?' he asked, looking into her lovely face, fully aware of what she meant.

'It means I want you to make love to me. I want to make love to you . . .'

She did not finish her sentence.

James cleared his throat, and hesitated, then said, 'I didn't expect anything like this to happen at Lord Reggie's over Christmas. Nor did I expect to meet a vibrant thirty-two-year-old potent, very sensual *young* woman, who wanted to . . .'

James did not finish his sentence. There was a knock on the door. After he had called, 'Come in,' the butler did so.

'I'm so sorry to interrupt you, Lady Annabel, but Lord Reggie wishes to speak to Mr Falconer in the library,' Portman announced.

'Right now?' she asked, trying to speak calmly.

'Yes, Your Ladyship.'

James patted her arm, and said, in a steady voice, 'If you'll excuse me, m'lady. I had better go to the library. I'll try to make it short.'

TWENTY-EIGHT

Lord Reginald Carpenter looked at the door when it opened to admit Falconer and smiled at him.

'Sorry to interrupt your rest, but I thought you would want to know the bad news I've just received,' Reggie announced.

Limping badly, as he had earlier, James reached the desk, exclaiming, 'My God, what's happened?' He sat down opposite his old friend, staring at him.

'An avalanche of reports from my journalists out in the field. All across England. Things have grown really serious. Factories are closing, offices closing. Naturally unemployment is rife, able-bodied men – the few of them who are left – are on the dole. Empty bellies tonight and for nights to come. Chaos in the government, if there actually is one. No real leadership. I couldn't tell you who is in charge of the country if I tried. Catastrophe rules the day.' Lord Reggie shook his head, and then asked, 'How is Malvern's? Is it safe, Falconer?'

'It was, Reggie, at least when I left on the twenty-third. Retail is down in all my arcades, but I poured in my own money to cover the deficit. Wine has been hit hard. Trading generally hasn't recovered from all the restrictions of the war, let alone the flu epidemic closing shops.' James sighed. 'What you're saying is that 1919 is going to be worse than this.'

'I am. However, I want to offer a little advice, if you don't mind. I know you're a brilliant businessman and won't lose your nerve, but hold still. Don't sell any buildings, especially in the docklands.'

'I've ridden through a few rough patches before, but why are you pinpointing the docklands?' James asked, his eyes riveted on Lord Reggie.

'Because things *will* normalize eventually, and in 1920 they'll pick up. England will start exporting again. We're a country of merchants, and our goods will be in demand. In America especially. The Americans love British products and you just need them to forget this Wartime Prohibition nonsense.' His Lordship said. 'I have all this on good authority.'

James Falconer nodded. 'Sit tight. Sell nothing. Plug holes. Don't get nervous. Hang in there. That will be my mantra. And thanks for underscoring my own perceptions of the problems in the country,' he finished, with a smile.

'I'm always here for you, Falconer. Have been, ever since you were a lad of twenty.'

James laughed. 'So long ago. Oh, to be young again!'

'You're not old at forty-eight, James,' Lord Reggie said, giving him an odd look. 'You're in the prime of your life. Go and look in a mirror.' Lord Reggie laughed, and said as an aside, 'You've always been catnip to women. They fall at your feet.'

James exclaimed, 'Never in my entire life has any woman ever fallen at my feet. Or perhaps I've never noticed them,' he finished with a grin.

'My niece has fallen for you, Falconer. She couldn't take her eyes off you at breakfast. Fallen hard, I would say. Well, you don't look surprised one bit, so I suppose you know.'

James stood up and went over to the fireplace, needing to warm his legs. After a second or two, he said, 'She told me she had, but I am sixteen years older than her. *Too old.*'

'Age only matters on a bottle of wine,' Lord Reggie pronounced in a droll voice. 'And as I tried to point out, you don't look your age anyway. Or act it. You'll be good for Annabel. She needs an honourable and kind man like you to love and cherish her, which I'm sure you would. Jane will be thrilled you've bonded. She hoped that might happen.'

Taken aback, James gave Reggie a questioning look. 'Are you saying Jane set me up, that she was matchmaking?' Disbelief flashed across his face.

'But of course, Falconer. She's so very fond of you, and believes you are a lonely man. And she loves Annabel, who she *knows* is lonely and somewhat adrift. She believes you are well suited.' Reggie paused, frowning. 'Don't you agree with my last statement?'

James simply nodded and took a deep breath. He then said, 'It just so happens we are. I think she's beautiful, so young, fresh and outgoing. But the age difference has to be considered.'

Reggie ignored this comment, being more interested in their feelings. 'I can read Annabel like a book. I've known her since she was a child. She's fallen for you, hook, line and sinker. From that moment she appeared for breakfast, you've had your eyes glued on her. Your behaviour is very telling. So forget about the age thing, you are one hell of a handsome man. But I'm now repeating myself.'

'I have fallen for her, as I said earlier.'

'She's standing next to you with the same emotions, I do believe,' Reggie assured him.

'But I don't know about her life, whether she's married, divorced, widowed.'

'Well, you know she's thirty-two, with a lovely outgoing personality. Annabel is optimistic. Tomorrow will always be a better day. But she's not had it easy with men. Two sods she's been with – really rotten buggers.'

These comments surprised Falconer, who exclaimed, 'How could any man treat Annabel badly?'

'Those two did – a fiancé who stole her jewellery, tried to dominate her, and finally ditched her. And there was a husband who was blatantly unfaithful. He embarrassed her, humiliated her, and even his own upper-crust New York family disowned him,' Reggie confided. 'They were certainly on her side.'

'Is she still married to him?' Falconer asked in a low, dismayed tone, shocked by what he was hearing.

'No. She left America just before the war started in Europe. She brought Adrian with her, of course. He was just one year old. She started divorce proceedings. Nick Evans, her American husband, joined the Army when America entered the war. He was killed in France. So she was both divorced and widowed, in a sense,' Lord Reggie finished. 'He was Adrian's father.'

'Thank you for filling me in,' Falconer said. 'It's hard for me to think of any man mistreating a woman as lovely as Annabel.'

'Believe you me, Falconer, the world is overflowing with men who are real bastards.' He suddenly smiled at James, and said, '*You* can repair any damage that might have been done to her. You know what loss is – and you have a loving heart.'

When James returned to Annabel's suite, she was sitting by the fire, reading a book. She put it down, and asked, 'What did Uncle Reggie want to see you about?'

'To warn me bad times are coming economically in 1919, and that although the war is over, I must watch Malvern's very closely, be very careful what I do in business.'

'Oh! I thought he might have wanted to warn you off me,' Annabel murmured, looking at him intently, obviously curious.

James sat down next to her on the sofa, and said, 'He did talk about you, and about us. He said your aunt Jane would be happy we were drawn to each other, and that he was, too.'

'Oh, that's so nice to hear!' A bright smile filled her face.

'And although I *do* think the age gap is large, he doesn't think it's an issue. Told me I could be just what you need.'

Annabel drew close, leaning against him, and she said softly, 'I can solve the problem with your bad left leg.'

He peered at her in the firelight. 'I don't think you can, darling. It's a war wound that acts up in the bitter weather. It's healed in a certain sense.'

'I know, but I have an ointment that's very potent, and I could massage your leg. I'm sure it would help,' Annabel persisted. 'We could try now.'

Falconer smiled to himself, and said, 'Perhaps later, but right now I do believe I have to go and get dressed. And you have to do the same. We have a dinner to attend shortly.'

'Oh gosh, yes. I have to do my hair and make myself beautiful.'

'You are already. You could help me with one thing, though.'

'Tell me,' she replied eagerly.

'I haven't got a Christmas present to give Adrian.' James pursed his lips, looking at her.

'Oh, that's easy enough!' Annabel exclaimed, laughing and standing up. 'Do you have half a crown to spare?'

'Yes, I do,' he answered, also rising and putting his hand in his trouser pocket.

Annabel went to the small writing table, picked up a Christmas card from a box, and said, 'You can write something on this card, saying he can go and buy himself a new toy soldier. He'll be thrilled. We will just pop the half a crown inside the envelope with the card.'

'I see you are very good at solving problems,' James said, going to join her at the desk, smiling.

TWENTY-NINE

There was no doubt in Falconer's mind that his left leg was damaged again in some way. Once he was in his bedroom, he took off his day suit and pushed himself onto the bed.

Leaning against the pile of pillows, he looked down at the left leg and touched it. It felt sore, and yet it was not inflamed. It looked exactly like his right leg.

He shook his head and lay back on the pillows, wondering why it was so tender. Overworked perhaps. It had always been the weaker leg, after his many operations. Anyway, there was nothing he could do about it over the Christmas holidays, and while he was in Kent. He would go to his doctor when he was back in London. Perhaps Dr Miles would have a solution.

In the meantime, he had to get ready for Christmas Eve dinner. He still felt cold, despite the warmth of the bedroom. It seemed as if a chill had settled in his bones. But he would throw more logs on the fire and dress as fast as he could.

James went into his dressing room, which opened off the bedroom, and took his evening dress trousers off the hanger.

After attaching the braces, he sat down and pulled them on. He then reached for black socks. Standing up, he put his feet in his black evening shoes and went over to the chest in the bedroom. Taking out a white dress shirt, he unfolded it and shook it. He then turned back the cuffs. He spotted his cufflinks and the studs for the front of his shirt already laid out on a table nearby.

Walking over to the table, he looked at the studs. They were made of gold, inset with deep blue sapphires. Alexis had given them to him years ago, along with the gold-and-sapphire cufflinks. To match his eyes. He smiled to himself, remembering the moment.

Unexpectedly, there was a tap on the door, and a light-hearted voice said, 'It's only me,' as Annabel whirled into his bedroom, stopped and stared at him.

James was thunderstruck and could not move for a moment. He was wearing only his trousers, with the braces hanging down. He was bare-chested.

A surge of embarrassment made him exclaim, 'Please leave, Lady Annabel, at once. As you can see, I am getting dressed.'

Flushing bright pink, stammering in her haste to apologize, she backed out and closed the door quickly.

Falconer let out a long sigh and went to look at the shirt. It was very heavily starched, so much so that – as he went to pull it on – he realized he could not wear it. He rang for Portman. He sat down in front of the fire and wondered why Annabel had barged into his bedroom in that way.

A second later, Portman knocked and came in. 'Can I be of help, sir?'

'Yes, you can, Portman. Could you ask Lord Reginald if his valet is available? I think Vincent could help me with the studs and cufflinks, and maybe find a better shirt. The one I took out is heavily starched.'

'I will fetch Vincent, Mr Falconer, and then he can look at the other shirts in the chest.'

'Thank you,' James said, and leaned forward to warm his hands as the butler hurried out.

Within moments, Vincent arrived with Portman, who said, 'Lady Jane wishes the guests to assemble in the blue-and-white drawing room, sir, instead of the conservatory. For the champagne toast.'

James nodded. 'Thank you,' he responded, and Portman inclined his head and departed.

Turning his attention to Lord Reggie's valet, he said, 'I'm afraid all the shirts might be over-starched, Vincent.'

Vincent, already standing in front of the chest, turned around as Falconer walked over to join him. 'I've found one, sir, that's not too bad. But I will have the other washed and only lightly starched. It'll be ready tomorrow.'

'Thank you, Vincent. I really appreciate that.'

Within fifteen minutes, James was wearing the shirt, and the studs and cufflinks were in place, along with the black bowtie. Vincent helped him into the evening jacket, stood in front of him, making sure it was hanging well, adjusting the satin lapels.

'Impeccably tailored, Mr Falconer,' the valet said. 'A great piece of Savile Row engineering.'

James chuckled. 'I've never heard it called engineering before. But you're correct. It is a good way of describing this particular suit.'

'It fits like a glove, sir,' the valet remarked admiringly.

Although he knew he looked good in the new evening dress suit, James Falconer was not a vain man. He had no idea what an imposing figure he cut when he arrived at the doorway of the blue-and-white drawing room.

There was a sudden silence as all eyes were on him when he walked in to join the others. For a moment, everyone was struck by his stature and good looks. But for the first time in a long while, there was also an indefinable spring in his step.

James said, 'Good evening, and my apologies for being late. I had a problem with a very starched shirt.'

The women, knowing what he meant immediately, laughed. Lord Reggie said, 'Better than a problem with a stuffed shirt.'

This comment also drew laughter, and James chuckled, as he took a crystal flute of champagne from one of the junior footmen. Lifting his glass, he said, 'Happy Christmas!'

Everyone said the same. Peter and Irina Keller walked over to join him. The old friends greeted each other and started chatting at once, James questioning Irina on how she was after the attack and her discharge from hospital. She looked a little thinner than usual, but as striking as ever in a very fashionable pale gold silk gown, her dark hair piled up on her head, glittering topaz at her neck. Keller explained they had arrived only a few hours earlier.

Almost immediately, Lady Jane glided towards them, wanting to get Falconer to the other side of the room.

Annabel was standing in the bay window area, and Lady Jane was hellbent on promoting a relationship between her niece and Falconer.

She genuinely believed they were ideal for one another. Lady Jane also trusted Falconer implicitly. She knew he had integrity and was a kind man. Just what Annabel needed. This aside, he was handsome and highly successful.

After a welcoming chat with the Kellers, Lady Jane took hold of Falconer's arm, and said, 'Come and say hello to Annabel before all of you men cluster together in a group, as you usually do. She'd love to see you.'

'Of course,' James answered, smiling at Lady Jane, and walking across the room with her.

From a distance, James saw that Annabel looked solemn, not her usual light-hearted self. Drawing closer, he noticed sadness in her deep green eyes, a change in her.

Was that his fault? he wondered, recalling at once how sharp he had been when she had barged into his bedroom an hour ago. He must make amends, if that was the case. He knew deep down it was.

'Annabel, Mr Falconer just arrived and was asking where you were. And here you are, darling, hiding near the bay window.' Lady Jane smiled and hurried away, leaving them alone together.

It was James who spoke first, wanting to apologize, to placate her. 'I'm so sorry,' he said swiftly, looking at her with some intensity. 'I didn't mean to be so sharp with you earlier. I was just taken by surprise. That's all it was, Annabel. Nothing more than that.'

'No, it was my fault!' she answered. 'I shouldn't have come to your bedroom. But Aunt Jane had asked me to tell you we were meeting here, not in the conservatory. When I caught you dressing, I was so embarrassed. I just fled. Please forgive me, Mr Falconer.'

'There's nothing to forgive,' he replied. 'And what's all this *Mr Falconer* about? We agreed to use our first names this afternoon. I thought we were friends.'

'I know, but I made you—'

'Not another word. I'm not angry, and by the way, I can't take my eyes off you. You must always wear purple. It makes your eyes look greener than ever.'

She smiled at last, her lovely young face filling with radiance. 'Thank you. Do you like my gown?'

'I do indeed,' he said, gazing at her soft white shoulders and the top of her breasts. The dress had a shawl collar, off the shoulders, and a deep cleavage that was most revealing. Her skin was pearly white. He longed to touch her.

'I think your emerald earrings are lovely too,' he said at last.

Her hand went to touch the large square-cut emerald on her right ear. 'They are unique. None like them anywhere.'

'A family heirloom, I've no doubt,' he said, his knowledge of jewellery kicking in. They were very valuable, he knew that.

'No, they were a gift,' she announced, her eyes sparkling. 'From a friend,' she added, still smiling.

He simply nodded, suddenly feeling a spark of jealousy. Another man must have given them to her. Why the sudden jealousy? Because he wanted her, for himself.

Breaking the silence that had fallen between them, Annabel said, 'We are neighbours in London, James. Will you come to tea one day? Or dinner perhaps?'

He stared at her, and exclaimed, 'I would like that! Where do you live?'

'In Grosvenor Square, and you are on South Audley Street. You can be in my flat in less than five minutes.'

'That's nice to know,' he began, and then stopped when Portman announced that dinner was served.

The dining room was large and airy, with a high ceiling from which hung a glittering chandelier. The walls were covered in rose-coloured brocade, with matching draperies and chair upholstery.

The table was large and round. James was happy he was seated next to Annabel, rather than facing her. Otherwise, he would have gazed at her only throughout the meal.

Lady Jane had planned a traditional Christmas Eve dinner. The first course was oyster patties, the second chestnut soup, to be followed by roast goose, with all the trimmings, and ratafia trifle for dessert.

As James helped Annabel into her seat, he glanced around the table. Irina was on his left side, and all around the table were good friends of long-standing.

Claudia and Connie Glendenning, Peter Keller. Their hosts, Lady Jane and Lord Reggie, and Paul and Kate Talbot, who were neighbours and close friends of the Glendennings.

A lovely group, he thought. He glanced in shock at Annabel, who had put her hand on his right leg and was stroking it. Her green eyes were full of sparkle and her laughter light as she gazed at him.

He stared at her, shook his head, and whispered, 'You're incorrigible!'

'Isn't it exciting?' she whispered back. But to his relief, she removed her hand.

The food was delicious, the various wines superb, and the conversation entertaining, touching on everything from politics, the state of the country, the theatre, and finally gossip.

A lovely evening was had by all. James, in particular, felt much better. Although his left leg was still aching, he managed to control his limp when he went upstairs to bed.

Unable to sleep, James put on the bedside lamp and looked at the clock. It was almost two, and he was wide awake. Pushing himself up, he got out of bed, put on his dressing gown, and went over to the fireplace.

Removing the fireguard, he threw on more logs and sat down in the chair, as usual enjoying the warmth from the flames.

His thoughts turned to Annabel. She had looked so beautiful at dinner, and he was as drawn to her as he had been at breakfast. Yet he knew she was too young for him. Or rather, he was too old for her. It would not work, perhaps because she also seemed younger than her age in certain ways.

He smiled to himself, thinking of her lovely laughter, her free spirit, and her cheeky comments. Some of the sudden things she did – like stroking his leg at dinner. He chuckled quietly, thinking she had a few tricks up her sleeves, this spirited girl.

Closing his eyes, he dozed, still thinking about her. Then he was unexpectedly sitting up straight. Someone was knocking on his door.

He got to it as it was opening. There she stood. Annabel. He pulled her inside. He looked up and down the corridor, dimly lit but thankfully empty.

Closing the door, James looked down at her. 'What are you doing up at this hour and knocking on my bedroom door?' he asked in a low voice. 'Anyone could have seen you'.

'I brought you the cream,' she responded, smiling up at him. 'I forgot to give it to you earlier.'

'Thank you. It's kind of you. But you must leave. Right now.'

'Oh, don't be mean to me, James. Let me sit by the fire with you for a few minutes. I can't sleep.' She sounded woeful, her expression pleading.

A deep sigh escaped, and he nodded. 'Five minutes, okay?'

'Oh yes, five minutes only.'

When she sat down, he realized she was wearing a lovely robe of soft green silk, similar to a dressing gown yet fuller. Of course, she looked stunningly beautiful. His chest tightened, and he knew he should send her away. At once. But he couldn't.

She leaned forward, and he glimpsed her breasts as she handed him the cream. 'It's a very good ointment for aches and pains. I can massage your leg with it, if you want.'

'I'll manage to do it myself,' he said in a clipped tone. He looked at the label. 'Is this Chinese on the label?' he asked, looking across at her. She had pulled the robe tight across her chest.

'Yes. I get it in Chinatown, or at least a friend gets it for me. You can keep this jar.'

'Thank you. You're still wearing your earrings,' he remarked, having just noticed them.

'Oh, I forgot to take them off,' she murmured, and smiled at him. 'It was such a lovely evening being with you, sitting so close.'

He was silent, then asked, 'Who gave you the emeralds? Your fiancé? Your husband?'

Annabel laughed lightly. 'Of course not. They were both rather cheap with a buck, as the Americans say.'

'So who? It must have been a man. You said they weren't family heirlooms.'

'It was a man. Of course, it was a man.'

'Who?'

'James, why are you questioning me like this? It doesn't matter.' She gazed at him, suppressing a smile.

'I'm sorry. It's none of my business. But I'm a bit jealous, I think.' He began to laugh. 'Oh dear, what a fool I am.'

'No, you're not. And I was trying to make you feel a bit jealous, if you want the truth.'

'Why?'

'I like you. And so I didn't want to tell you that my father gave them to me on my twenty-first birthday.'

'I'm not sure I believe you. I can't abide the idea of another man.'

'It's not important.' She stood up, came across to his chair and sat down on his lap before he could stop her.

Leaning into him, she kissed him lightly on his mouth, then took hold of his right hand, pulled it into her robe, and put it on her breast. 'I want you to touch me,' she said softly.

For a split second he was taken off guard. He hesitated for a moment. Then he began to kiss her passionately; she returned his kisses with great ardour. Eventually, they drew apart and gazed at each other lovingly.

She spoke first. 'A long time ago, at least so it seems now, we met for the first time. At breakfast. And we have admitted, quietly to each other, that we were smitten. Are you still smitten?'

'I'm afraid so. Are you, Annabel?'

'More than ever.' She opened her robe and put his hand on her breast again. 'Kiss me. Kiss my breast. Oh James, I want you all over me . . .'

He did as she asked for a moment or two, stroking her breast, kissing it, and then quite suddenly she stopped him. She got off his lap, went to the door and locked it.

Walking back to the fireplace, she unfastened the robe and took it off and came back to him, naked.

Slightly startled though he was, James stood up and unfastened his dressing gown. He took it off to reveal he was only wearing pyjama bottoms but no top.

She said, 'Take them off,' and pointed to the pyjamas.

He did so and then drew her into his arms. They held each other tightly for a moment. Then she said, 'Take me to bed, James Falconer. Take me to bed and let me love you as you've never been loved before.'

Against her hair, he said, 'We must be very careful. I've no protection. You know that.'

'I do. I promise I will be careful, and I'll make sure you're careful too.' She laughed lightly, her eyes full of happiness. Lifting her up, he carried her in his arms to the bed and laid her down.

He lay next to her, pushed himself up on one elbow, looking at her lithe young body, stroking it, touching her where she asked to be touched. He marvelled at her beautiful skin, unlined, pure pearly white, and was thrilled by her eagerness to touch him all over, to arouse him with her hands and her mouth.

She was correct. She made love to him as he'd never been loved before. In return, he brought her to new heights of ecstasy and pleasure that she had never experienced in her life.

THIRTY

Adrian was sitting alone at the breakfast room table, waiting patiently.

'Well, here we are together again,' James said, smiling at the child when he arrived at the table. 'Good morning. And Merry Christmas!'

'Good morning, sir,' Adrian answered, his face lighting up as he looked up at James, who winked back. 'Merry Christmas.'

'May I join you?' James then asked solemnly.

'Oh, yes, please. Mummy won't be too long. She's doing her hair. She wants it to be nice for Christmas Day.'

'Does she now?' James pulled out a chair and sat down. 'Mummy is quite beautiful, Adrian. She always looks nice. I'm sure today will be very special.'

Adrian nodded. 'Will you stay with us, sir? Oh please say yes. Please.'

'Yes, I am staying until Boxing Day, and then I must go to London. But I will come back for New Year's Eve,' James said.

'Oh no, no! I mean will you stay *always*?' Adrian explained quickly, looking anxious. 'I meant for ever.'

'We'll see what we can manage,' James answered somewhat evasively, not really knowing how to respond. But he was touched by this child and had immediately liked him when they'd met yesterday. 'Anyway, your mummy told me that we are going to open the Christmas presents after breakfast. That will be fun, won't it, Adrian?'

'Oh yes! I can't wait. But Mummy said I must have breakfast first.'

Portman had just arrived and was peering in the many silver dishes on the sideboard. Looking across the room, he said, 'Good morning, Mr Falconer, and Happy Christmas.'

'Good morning, and the same to you, Portman.'

Adrian said, 'Happy Christmas Day, Mr Portman.'

'Happy Christmas, Master Adrian, and I do believe Father Christmas came down the chimney last night and left you some presents.'

'Oh, did you *see* him?' Adrian asked, his eyes wide with wonder and excitement.

'I caught a glimpse of him as he was emptying his sack,' Portman said, smiling at the child. Then, addressing James, he explained, 'We have all the usual breakfast dishes, Mr Falconer, but Cook always adds a few extras on Christmas Day. We have fried liver, fried black pudding, kippers and sautéed sweetbreads. Don't get up sir, let me serve you something.'

'What a delicious selection,' James said. 'I will have a fried tomato plus a slice or two of the black pudding. I've not had that for years.'

'Very good choices, sir. What can I serve you, Master Adrian?'

'Mummy said I can have anything I want today, so I will have some tomato and black pudding, like Mr Falconer.'

'Certainly,' Portman said, and picked up a plate, going to the silver dishes.

James looked at Adrian, frowning slightly. 'Are you sure you'll like black pudding?'

Adrian nodded vehemently. 'I've eaten it before,' he confided. 'Many, many, many times,' he added with childlike enthusiasm and some exaggeration.

At this moment, James saw Annabel coming into the breakfast room.

She looked stunning. Her auburn hair fell around her face in curls, and she wore a red velvet jacket that was short and ended at her waist. Underneath the jacket was a white silk blouse with a frilly lace jabot down the front. The matching red velvet skirt was narrow and ended just above her ankles. It showed off her figure to perfection.

James, always the gentleman, stood up at once. After sharing greetings, he said, 'Where do you want to be seated?'

'Somewhere I can't be right now. So . . . *avec toi*,' she finished in French.

Swallowing a smile, James pulled out the chair next to him and helped her to sit down, smoothing his hand down her back as he did so.

'Oh that was delicious,' she murmured in a low tone. 'You can do that all over later,' she whispered in his ear once he was seated.

'I will,' he said quietly.

Portman, who had gone to ask Cook to prepare more black pudding, returned to the breakfast room with a platter of it. Greeting Lady Annabel and accepting her Christmas wishes, he told her which dishes were on the sideboard, and she served herself bacon and kidneys, plus half a tomato and toast.

Settling back in her chair, she slid her hand onto James's leg and stroked it. She stopped when she saw the surprise in his brilliant blue eyes. 'Just wanted you to be aware that everything is always available whenever you wish, Falconer,' she murmured enigmatically, eyeing him flirtatiously.

'That is wonderful to hear,' he responded, unable to hide his laughter. 'Availability is my motto in a sense – I mean in my arcades. Availability and very fast delivery. And, of course, every request is met.'

'Is it really?' she asked, assuming a surprised voice. 'And do you have a delivery person?'

'For small items. The really big stuff, the important jewellery, for instance, I deliver myself.' He grinned at her, and she laughed. 'I can't leave anything *big* to chance,' he finished, his expression suddenly serious.

'Regarding your help last night, I do want to thank you again for being so kind and understanding,' Annabel said softly. 'It's always satisfying when someone really understands one's needs.'

'My pleasure. I am always at your service whenever you wish,' James answered. He then stopped as Lady Jane and Lord Reggie came into breakfast, bringing Christmas greetings to all.

'And so ends our discussion,' James whispered, squeezing her arm. 'I enjoyed our bit of banter.'

'I hope you visualized it all,' Annabel said softly.

'*Too vividly* at times,' he answered.

It was obvious that young Adrian could hardly wait to open the gifts under the tree in the conservatory. It was Lady Jane who suggested James and Annabel go ahead while they finished breakfast with Claudia and Connie Glendenning, who had yet to come down.

'Christmas is for children anyway,' Lord Reggie said, 'so let's tell him to go and enjoy himself.'

James and Annabel immediately stood, and Annabel offered her hand to her little boy. 'Aunt Jane says *we* can go *now* to open some of your gifts, Adrian.'

The child was on his feet at once, his beaming face and sparkling eyes denoting his excitement. Looking up at James, he said, 'I'm glad you're coming too, sir.'

'I wouldn't miss it for the world,' James replied, taking hold of Adrian's other hand, walking along with him.

Once in the conservatory, Adrian stood gazing at the tree and then at the piles of presents arranged underneath.

'I don't know where to begin,' he said, looking at his mother.

'Mr Falconer will help you, and so will I, sweetheart,' Annabel said. Bending down, she saw the envelope James had added yesterday and reached for it.

'Now, just look at this,' she murmured, handing it to her son. 'Something special inside, I know that for sure.'

Adrian opened the envelope carefully and saw the half a crown wrapped in a piece of paper. 'Oh, some money,' he cried, sounding very pleased.

'You must read the card,' Annabel said. 'Come here. I'll help you.' Kneeling next to him, she pointed to the words, saying them slowly, '*Wishing you a Happy Christmas. You can buy a new soldier with this half a crown. With love, from James Falconer.*'

'Oh, oh, thank you, sir! I need a new lead soldier for my brigade.'

James smiled, thinking how easy it was to make a child happy. 'My pleasure, Adrian, and perhaps later you'll show me your brigade.'

'Now we'll open a couple more presents, Adrian, and then stop. Aunt Jane plans to open the others just before lunch, so you must leave a few of yours for then.'

'Yes, Mummy. Can I open two more, please?'

'You can.' She started by handing him one from her, and James saw the love in her face as she watched her son. She had given him a toy train.

Falconer drew Lady Annabel to one side, and said in a low voice, 'Would you mind if I went back to my room. I need to rest my left leg. It's quite painful.'

Alarm flooded her face. 'Oh my God, I hope the ointment didn't do you harm!' She stared at him, worry in her eyes.

'I'm sure not. It's been a bit sore for several days. I won't miss Christmas Day lunch, I promise. Lady Jane told me it will be at two o'clock.'

'That's right. Let me come upstairs with you to help.'

'I can manage on my own.'

'No, you can't, and I want to look at the leg.'

He tried to argue, but she was stubborn and, leaving Adrian playing happily, she accompanied him to his room.

Once inside his bedroom, James headed for his dressing room. He shed his jacket and trousers, and then put on a dressing gown.

Getting onto the bed, he covered his right leg with the robe and revealed only the lower left leg.

Annabel rushed to his side. She was shocked when she saw the many scarred patches. 'Oh my God, these must hurt.' She looked up at him propped against the pillows. 'Why didn't I notice them . . . last night?' she asked in a tremulous voice.

'I'd dimmed the lights, and we were somewhat preoccupied, weren't we?'

'What can I do to help you?' she asked, and reached for his hand.

'Not much. I'll rest for an hour or two, and see you at lunch. So scoot, let me doze for a bit.'

Reluctantly, she did as he asked.

There was no question in Falconer's mind that he must go to the doctor's surgery immediately upon his return to London. His left leg was now permanently in pain. He prayed it was nothing that would mean more operations. Yet it didn't look any different from his right leg, oddly enough.

For a moment, he wondered about the Chinese ointment

Annabel had given him, but the leg had been aching before, for days. Hopefully, Dr Miles would have the answer and a solution.

He couldn't allow the leg to slow him down. Bad times were coming, and he would have to pay close attention to Malvern's. It had been his life's work. He must keep it safe at all costs. Fifteen to eighteen hours a day, seven days a week he had worked, for much of his life. No wonder he hadn't had much of a personal life.

Settling back against the pillows, his thoughts went to Annabel and her child, Adrian. They were so adoring of each other, and it touched him. Once he had been like that with Leonie.

This sudden thought of his daughter made him wince. Despite the row with Georgiana Ward, he knew it was his fault he and his daughter were estranged. The guilt about that hovered at the back of his mind always; he was to blame.

But this estrangement had happened long, long ago. It was in the past; the past could not be replayed or altered. On the other hand, the future was his for the making. Even though she detested him, and even though he had severed his ties with Mrs Ward, so that was no longer a route to reconciliation, could *he* reach out? Without going through her mother?

Why not? What did he have to lose? Nothing. She would reject his advances; that he knew only too well. Yet he also suddenly knew it was imperative that he give it a try. Leonie was twenty-nine now. Perhaps she might see the sense of healing that old wound at this time in her life.

James pursed his lips. His daughter was almost the same age as Annabel, who was thirty-two. My God, was he cradle-snatching? He was startled at this thought.

In the past, he had been involved with two other women. His wife Alexis, who had been eight years older than him, and Mrs Ward, ten years older.

Now he saw Annabel in his mind's eye – her peaches-and-cream complexion, so smooth and soft. She was like that all over. Her lithe, shapely body was silk under his hands, and there wasn't a line on her face. She was eager and excited to be with him – compliant, wishing to please him, and sometimes sexually aggressive, which had aroused him at once. They pleased each other.

But he was still forty-eight and she thirty-two. Perhaps this didn't matter *now*. However, as he got older, the difference would more than likely become acute and very visible.

A deep sigh slid out of him, and he felt a sudden chill in his bones. *He was too old for her.* And there was no way to change *that.*

Thirty-One

Lady Jane was highly impressed by James Falconer's behaviour. A few minutes ago, he had arrived in the conservatory, as usual filling the room with his presence. His charisma and self-assurance never left him, even when he was leaning on a stick.

Standing in the doorway, glancing around, he offered them all a huge smile, and came forward to greet her warmly.

'So sorry, I'm a few minutes late, Your Ladyship. My leg is acting up, so please excuse the stick.'

'My dear Falconer, you don't have to apologize. The Kellers are not down yet. As for the stick, I'm happy you are making use of it,' she replied, sounding sympathetic.

Within seconds, Lord Reggie came over. The two men greeted each other with their usual affection. 'You've got to give me the name of your tailor in Savile Row, Falconer. That's another impeccable suit you're wearing. I like the grey check.'

'No problem, Reggie. And I'll go with you—'

'Hello, everyone,' Annabel interrupted, hurrying to join them, her eyes fixed on Falconer.

Lady Jane noticed at once how keen her niece was to be close to Falconer. He, in turn, had a bland expression on his face, and his strikingly blue eyes did not waver. His self-control was amazing. He revealed nothing. The perfect gentleman.

'How lovely you look, Lady Annabel,' James said, inclining his head. 'Red suits you so well.'

'Thank you,' Annabel answered in her light-hearted voice, her green eyes sparkling.

Turning to Jane, Annabel said, 'I think James ought to give out his gifts first, don't you, Aunt?'

'Well, why not? Would you like to start off by giving the ladies their presents first, James? *Yours*, I mean. I can hear Irina's voice, so the Kellers will be here in a moment.'

'As you wish, Your Ladyship, I am always at your service,' he answered with a smile, and walked towards the tree.

He bent down to say hello to Adrian, who was engaged in examining the presents he had opened earlier: several toy soldiers, a white lamb and a train.

As James selected several packages wrapped in silver paper, Lady Jane glanced at Annabel, who was gazing at Falconer, her emotions somewhat visible, at least to her aunt.

Walking across the room, Jane took hold of Annabel's hand and led her to a corner. 'Stop gazing at Falconer, Annabel. People are growing aware of your interest.'

'I don't care,' Annabel murmured.

'But he does, and so do I and Uncle Reggie. Maybe we don't matter, but Falconer seems to matter to you. Hide it. If you are flagrant, you'll never get near him again. He's an extremely private man. I should know. I met him when he was twenty, and his attitude has never changed. He doesn't want people to know his business. Would hate people talking.'

'Oh, all right,' Annabel mumbled, and started to say something else, when Falconer's voice closed her off.

'Welcome, Irina and Peter, you're just in time. I've been asked to give the ladies their gifts.' He smiled at them warmly. 'This is for you, Claudia,' Falconer said, walking over to her, handing her the gift. 'It's from me, and with much affection.'

Claudia thanked him, and unwrapped the present. 'Oh, James, how wonderful, a gorgeous velvet scarf from Rossi's collection. Thank you so much.'

Falconer handed a silver package to Lady Jane, then Irina, and finally to Annabel. 'All from Rossi's collection, I'm afraid,' he said.

Annabel smiled at him tentatively and thanked him, not daring to say anything else. She saw the warning look in his vivid blue eyes, the taut set of his mouth.

Jane smiled inwardly, thinking how skilled Falconer was. Not a flicker of intimacy shown towards Annabel. She knew what had happened last night. Yes, indeed, a true gentleman protecting a woman's reputation and honour.

It was Lady Jane who now took over, distributing boxes of Cuban cigars to the men, also from James. She then passed around all the other beautifully wrapped gifts from herself and Reggie, the Glendennings and the Kellers. Everyone was busy for a while.

'What a haul, and what a mass of paper,' James exclaimed, standing up to stretch his leg. 'But worth it. Now, we're ready for a glass of bubbly, I think.'

Adrian came to him, and said, 'Can I see your presents, sir?'

'Why, of course you can. This lovely grey cashmere muffler is from you and Mummy.' He felt a warm sense of happiness; some of the loneliness had ebbed away.

'I know. She said she wants to keep you warm and that's why she chose it,' the child informed him solemnly.

'It will keep me cosy,' James replied and, one by one, he picked an item and told Adrian who it was from, until Lord Reggie came across and told James he needed him to open the bottle of champagne.

'Sorry about that, old chap,' Lord Reggie said, as he walked over to the other end of the conservatory with James. 'You've been awfully kind to that child, but enough's enough.'

Falconer laughed. 'He's such a darling, but my haunches were beginning to ache, bending down like that.'

Balancing himself carefully, using the stick as they traversed the terracotta-flagged floor, James frowned with pain. But he pushed the discomfort away and made up his mind to enjoy Christmas Day.

THIRTY-TWO

Doctor Harry Miles had known James Falconer for fifteen years, and had been his doctor for most of them. They had become friends, often met socially, and had many shared interests. Falconer appreciated Harry's skill and insight as a doctor, and Harry admired his famous patient, and his work ethic.

Now, on this Monday morning, 13 January to be exact, Dr Miles was examining Falconer's left leg, frowning as he ran his hands over the many scarred parts.

'Do you feel a lot of pain, when I touch you?' the doctor asked, looking down at Falconer stretched out on the examination table, naked under a cotton medical robe.

'No real pain, Harry. I do feel a dull ache when I walk these days. But not much when you touch me.'

The doctor nodded. 'You said you hardly felt anything when I ran my hands over your right leg. So it seems both legs are identical, when it comes to touching. And they look the same. The left leg shows no signs of wear and tear. However, it has always been the weaker leg. That's why I want you to use the stick much more than you do. It will ease the left leg.'

'I will,' Falconer promised. 'By the way, I did use some of that Chinese ointment on the left leg. Do you think it might have had a bad effect on me?'

The doctor shook his head. 'No, it hasn't harmed you. But it's not helped you either, as far as I can see.' Harry Miles frowned, and asked, 'How did you come by it?'

'A friend gave it to me, a lady friend.'

Harry smiled broadly. 'Not that lovely young woman I saw you with at Lady Jane's?' he asked, still smiling somewhat knowingly.

'Actually, yes, it was Annabel.'

'Throw it away. Better still, I will ditch it for you. Now, let's get you dressed, Falconer. You're shivering.'

Once he was fully dressed, James sat with the doctor in his office.

Harry Miles studied him across the desk, and said, 'You're fine, Falconer, and your health is good. I'm glad we did a full check-up.'

'So am I, and I do feel fine, Harry. Fit as a fiddle. What about this troublesome leg?'

Dr Miles nodded. 'It's weak, and it's flared up, but I can't find anything else obviously wrong with it. I think you've been over-doing things.' He then added, with a frown, 'You're nearly fifty now. Any chance you can slow down, find yourself a wife to take care of you and cosset you a little? That leg won't ever recover properly as long as you keep working such long hours and driving yourself so hard.'

James looked away and unconsciously rubbed his calf. He knew Dr Miles was right.

Then the doctor added, with a smile, 'Just try not to put too much weight on it when you're having intimate relations, Falconer, especially with a much younger woman. They do tend to get a bit carried away.'

Falconer burst out laughing, and then said in an amused voice, 'Thanks for the tip, Harry.'

He left the doctor's office relieved. His leg was always a worry in the back of his mind. But a part of him still dwelled on Harry's warning. The leg might never fully recover if he kept working so hard. If he didn't change something.

PART FIVE

Fantastical Situations

London and Hull, England

January–March 1919

THIRTY-THREE

January grew colder. Lady Jane made a decision; she and Lord Reggie were going to spend a month or two in warmer climes.

She had chosen Madeira, and sat explaining this to James in the library of his London house late on a freezing cold Friday afternoon. Lady Jane had arrived swathed in an elegant sable fur, her fitted blue wool suit cut in the latest fashion. She told James she was tired of being cold. She yearned for warmth and sunshine.

'I couldn't agree with you more,' he said. He knew Dr Miles would agree too, and remind him of his advice. He could hear the doctor's voice in his head, telling him to take things easier. But Malvern's needed him – all the time. 'But unfortunately, I cannot get away, or even join you later. Several problems have developed in my business, and I've got to solve them. I'm so sorry.'

Lady Jane, looking crestfallen, nodded. 'I do understand. You've devoted your life to your business. But can't you come for a couple of weeks perhaps? It would do your leg the world of good.'

'It's not next door,' James answered, smiling. 'And I just can't. This is a serious matter, I'm afraid. On top of everything else, the Americans have approved an amendment to their Constitution, banning the sale of alcohol.'

'All I can say is you will be missed, especially by Annabel.'

James was glad she had mentioned her niece. He had been hoping to speak to Jane about her. Taking a deep breath, James said, 'I'm happy she and Adrian are going with you on this trip, getting some sun. The child, in particular, will certainly benefit from the weather. Since you brought up Annabel's name, I need to talk to you about her.'

Not really knowing what he had to say, Jane simply nodded. She studied Falconer's face, and it told her nothing. It was bland.

He said, 'Annabel is lovely, in every way, but I want you to know that I have made a decision about her and our budding relationship. I must bring it to an end. Now. Before she becomes more involved with me. And—'

'But you've been so close!' Jane interjected, shocked by his words. 'At Christmas, you spent the night with her . . .' She stopped, seeing the odd look on his face. Was he affronted? His blue eyes were cold.

Clearing her throat, Jane said swiftly, 'I don't mean that the way it sounded, James. I am aware she is a very modern girl – or woman, I should say – because she's been married and engaged and has a child. I know she was quite uninhibited with you. That's her way – she's outgoing. And refreshing.'

'All that is true,' he said in a steady voice. 'However, it takes two to tango, you know.' He smiled, and went on, 'I don't want to let her go, if the truth be known. But I have no choice. I'm far too old for her, Jane.'

'Oh, James, don't let age get in the way of something I think could be so special. You need a woman in your life, and Annabel certainly needs a man. *You.* She's been so unlucky in the past and has never found happiness with the men she was involved with.'

'Yes, I know about the fiancé and the husband. Reggie told

me. Buggers, they were. However, my decision is made. It's final. Besides, my leg isn't getting any better. I don't want her pushing me around in a wheelchair.'

Jane was shattered by his words and didn't know how to respond. She dreaded the thought of Annabel's reaction. She knew her niece was head over heels in love with Falconer. And James admitting his leg was bad worried her also.

Finally, finding her voice, she said, 'When will you tell her all this?'

'When you return from your holiday. I don't want to ruin it for you all. Then I will be travelling, not in London, so she won't be running into me all the time.'

'I see. Well, that's thoughtful of you, James. Anyway, nobody ever runs into you.' She smiled at him. 'You're always in your office until ten at night. Maybe you should change *that*.'

James had the good grace to laugh, and explained, 'When I'm fifty, in two years, she will only be thirty-four, and when I grow older, the difference will be telling.'

Letting out a long sigh, Jane said quietly, 'I see you are determined to go ahead with your plan, but I do wish you would think it over – you're letting something special go.'

Falconer stared at her and raised a brow. 'What is that? What do you mean?'

Jane said, 'You're throwing away a chance of great happiness, a wonderful life with a woman who adores and admires you. Please rethink this, James.'

Falconer nodded. 'I will think on what you've said, since you are so insistent, so sure,' he replied. But he knew he wouldn't. His mind was made up. What he had chosen to do was the right thing for him. He would remain unmarried. Malvern's would be his mistress, loneliness his way of life.

* * *

Later that week, James Falconer had Brompton pack two large suitcases. The morning he left his house on South Audley Street, he warned the butler not to say he had gone away. 'Tell no one,' were his last words, before bidding Brompton goodbye.

Having made the decision to end his relationship with Annabel, he acted swiftly. His destination was Hull, the city where he had opened his very first shop, and where his shipping experience had been gained in his uncle's company. His cousin and friend William Venables, who had inherited the business from his father, still spent much of his time there. In the taxicab going to King's Cross Railway Station, he was sure no one would think of looking for him there.

Later, as he sat on the train, speeding north to Yorkshire, he began to relax. Soon he realized he was looking forward to visiting the City of Gaiety, as it had always been called. His favourite arcade was there. Suddenly, the future looked a bit brighter, the problems with Malvern's less worrying. He was in control of his life again.

THIRTY-FOUR

Ten years ago, James Lionel Falconer had bought the Bettrage Hotel in London. He had grabbed it the same day it had come on the market. The deal was made overnight, much to his delight. The hotel had a special meaning for him.

Once the hotel had been renovated and redecorated to his taste in design, he opened one in Hull, another in Leeds, and the fourth in Bradford. He was fully aware that these last two big industrial cities could use well-designed hotels. All of them had been successful thus far.

His favourite was the one in Hull, and, as the manager, Douglas Langford, showed him into his suite, he was filled with a sense of homecoming.

'Everything looks wonderful, Langford,' James remarked, as his eyes roamed around the sitting room. A fire blazed in the grate, vases of flowers were everywhere, and a pile of magazines, local newspapers and the nationals were laid out on a side table.

'I'm glad everything is to your satisfaction, sir,' Langford responded. 'Will you be dining in the suite tonight, Mr Falconer? Or shall I make a reservation in the hotel dining room?'

'I'll eat in the suite, thanks, Langford. I'm a bit done in after the train trip from London.'

'I understand, sir. The dinner menus are on the desk. Shall I send Morgan up to unpack for you?'

'That's a great idea. Thank you, Langford, and I'll give you a ring if I need anything else.'

The manager nodded, and thought to add, 'The suite for Mr Keller has also been prepared, sir.'

James thanked him again.

Once he was alone, he took off his overcoat, hung it in the foyer cupboard, and strolled over to the windows, wincing a little from tiredness. There were two which faced the North Sea.

He stood, looking out, gazing at the port, one of the biggest in England. His grandmother, Esther Falconer, had brought him to Hull many years ago to stay with her sister. His great-aunt Marina was a well-known artist and had painted this view. She had given the finished painting to him. It still hung in his house in South Audley Street and was a treasured piece.

A rush of nostalgia took hold. He remembered how much he had enjoyed his year here and the friends he had made. Everything he had learned about the Wine Division and shipping from his great-uncle Clarence Venables. And how a warm friendship had been formed with his cousin William, with whom he had worked, as well as enjoying many entertaining evenings out as a young lad.

Of course, it was here in Hull that he had opened his first little shop, filled with Rossi's capes and scarves, Irina's hand-made dresses, and some of the accessories Natalie had found for him.

Yes, Malvern's, as it was today, had actually started here, where he had vowed to become a great merchant prince. He had achieved his ambition; his boyhood plan had worked. Dreams can come true sometimes, he thought, gazing out over

Hull's rooftops towards the horizon, if you work hard enough. And he had. But, increasingly, it seemed to him, his reward had been loneliness at times.

Because he did everything above board and by the book, James Falconer had personally bought the top floor of this hotel, paying the Malvern Company for it with his own money.

He had then embarked on the design and building of three suites, next to each other, all overlooking the North Sea. Again, he paid for the work.

The one he occupied was the largest, with a dining room, this sitting room, and three bedrooms. One bedroom was his; the other two were for his siblings, Rossi and Eddie. The suite next door was for Peter and Irina Keller, and the third for any guests James might have from time to time.

Falconer liked his privacy, and also a fire for his aching leg. But the fire now burning in the hearth was the only one in the entire hotel. Falconer was cautious about everything. He had modernized the hotel, installing steam heating, and now did not allow fireplaces in any other rooms. Too dangerous. He was a stickler about safety.

A moment later, there was a knock on the door, and as Falconer called out, 'Come in,' the valet he preferred, Morgan, entered.

'Good afternoon, sir,' Morgan said, smiling. 'Is it convenient for me to unpack your suitcases now, Mr Falconer?'

'It is, Morgan, thank you. They're in the bedroom.' He flashed a smile at the valet, and said, 'It's nice to see you again.'

The following day, James was speaking into the hotel telephone and ordering tea for three for later that afternoon, when his siblings burst into the sitting room.

Within seconds, Rossi and Eddie were embracing Falconer and telling him how well he looked.

'I feel pretty good, and it's sort of nice to be back in Hull. I haven't been up here in almost a year,' he said.

'Why *are* we having a family meeting in Hull and not in London?' Eddie asked, in his usual blunt manner. His younger brother was smartly dressed in a tweed suit, which was beautifully cut, as were all his clothes these days.

'Because I'm in hiding,' James answered.

Eddie peered at his brother, thinking he was joking, but there was no merriment in those strikingly blue eyes. James was serious.

'Who from?' Rossi asked, also looking perplexed.

'A woman,' Falconer murmured.

'Surely not the Lady Annabel?' Rossi exclaimed. 'She's a beauty and very charming.'

'Very beautiful, very charming, and very distracting,' James was quick to say. 'I need to focus on Malvern's and only on Malvern's. I've come away to think: I've a few rather serious problems to solve.'

'Why am I here?' Eddie asked. 'Do you have legal problems? Are you in trouble?'

Rossi exclaimed, 'Don't be daft, Eddie! James would never be in trouble; he's not made that way.'

'Rossi's correct, Eddie. However, you have the smartest legal mind I know, and I will need your advice, I think. I also trust you implicitly.'

'Anything you want, Jimmy. I've got your back.'

'As do I,' Rossi interjected. 'So tell us, what is this meeting all about?' She deposited her warm wool shawl on one of the chairs and sank down into it, stretching her hands out towards the fire. 'Gosh, the train was chilly.'

'First, I need *your* take on the arcades, Rossi, especially the Malvern in Piccadilly,' her brother answered.

'None of the stores are doing well; even I'm down in business. We all thought we'd pick up at Christmas, but we didn't.

As for Kensington, it's as flat as a pancake.' She shook her head. 'But surely you know retailing is off, James?' Rossi raised a brow. 'It's been so damaged by no one having any spare money, by the influenza shutting shops, and customers being terrified to go out, let alone the problems we've all had obtaining stock during the war years.'

'I do. I can't keep pouring my own money in . . .' He broke off as there was a knock, and the waiter came in, pushing a tea trolley.

Once the waiter had left the suite, he continued.

'I don't want to close the Malvern arcade. I did lower the rents some time ago, and I can do that again. *If* I can raise the money to meet the deficit. I don't care about the Kensington arcade. I need to close that,' James explained.

'I hope you have a contract with the shopkeepers regarding the lowering of the rents?' Eddie said, somewhat worriedly. 'You do, don't you?'

'Of course, and I would need a new contract if I lowered the rents again.'

Eddie said, 'What if some people want to break their leases? Would you do that?'

'I suppose I wouldn't have a choice . . .' James got up and brought the tray of teacups to the fireplace. Once he was seated again, he continued, 'If people who rent from me have no money, they will *need* to break the lease. So, I'd have to agree, wouldn't I?' James asked.

'Yes, and you could sue them. However, I know you, and that's not your style,' Eddie answered. 'If you want to keep the Malvern arcade open, yet with some stores closed, the arcade won't look so nice. Any ideas about that? Can it be concealed, or dolled up?'

Rossi cut in. 'I think I can do that. We could ask those retailers to leave their goods in the windows and put up a notice saying the shops were closed for a holiday. If the shopkeepers want to take their goods, we could cover the empty windows with blinds. We could add a notice which says the shops were being renovated. How about that?'

'Very clever,' James said. 'Thank you, Rossi.'

THIRTY-FIVE

'There are three ways to raise money quickly,' Eddie announced, between bites of a cucumber sandwich. 'Raise it, borrow it, or steal it.'

'Two ways,' James exclaimed swiftly, staring hard at his brother. 'Raise or borrow.'

Eddie chuckled. 'I knew I'd get you on that one!' he said. 'I was just kidding you, big brother.'

Rossi threw Eddie a warning look and immediately jumped into the conversation. She said in a confident voice, 'I think we should raise money, James. Malvern's is fully extended, by the sound of things, and this is no time to be trying to sell property or hotels. I think you should raise it by selling certain things, or auctioning some of your possessions, I should say.'

James sat up straight in the chair and focused all his attention on her. 'I suppose you're referring to my paintings, the Impressionist paintings I own.'

'I am. They are *valuable*,' Rossi murmured.

'I realize that, but is this the right time to sell valuable paintings?' James wondered aloud. 'Who would buy them? As you have just said, times are hard right now, and people are struggling.'

'The rich aren't struggling, though, only the people in the streets, the everyday folk. There are plenty of wealthy people who have money for art – great art, like paintings by Monet, Cézanne and Van Gogh,' she announced. 'But if you prefer, you could auction the jewels.' As she said this, she was filled with sudden regret, but there was no way she could retract her words.

Eddie looked at her, puzzlement on his face. 'What jewels?'

'Yes, what jewels do you mean, Rossi?' James asked, sounding surprised. 'I only have sets of studs, cufflinks, and the watch that the uncles gave me years ago.'

Knowing she had no alternative but to explain, Rossi said, in as steady a voice as she could summon, 'The jewels that belonged to Alexis, which you gave to her, as well as those from her father and a number of pieces from Sebastian Trevalian. Don't you remember them, James? They were a fabulous collection.'

There was a silence, and James closed his eyes for a moment. He pictured Alexis, with her auburn hair and her lovely green eyes, and emeralds around her neck, on her wrists and her ears. And diamonds, and coronets, and so much else.

He remembered how she had enjoyed wearing the pieces he had given her, remembered how he had put everything in a vault at the bank after her death, not wanting to see them ever again. Because the jewellery had been hers and he had so loved her, and for a long time his life had been unbearable.

Rossi cleared her throat, got up to get another cup of tea. James also stood and went to stand next to his sister.

He said in a slightly strained voice, 'The collection is safe in a vault at my bank. I put it there because I didn't want anyone else to ever wear the collection. Nor did I want to ever see it again. Too painful.'

'And you forgot about it, didn't you?' Rossi murmured, touching his arm. 'I do understand why.'

'It just slipped my mind, that's all. And then I did forget about it actually, until you mentioned it just now.'

'Perhaps you don't want to auction it,' Eddie said, now fully understanding the significance of the jewellery collection. 'But it would solve your problems, I do believe.'

'I must think about it,' James replied, returning to the fireside with another cup of tea. Changing the subject, he said, 'I must close some of the smaller arcades. The one in Harrogate and the one in Leeds. But I'll definitely keep the one here, and the London one, as well.' He looked at Eddie. 'Can I just close the other arcades?'

'I think you might have to negotiate deals, if people don't want to break their leases. On the other hand, the way things are in the country, with retailers suffering, you might be able to slide out of most of the leases at little cost to you.' Eddie then added, 'I need to see the leases and other documents, so I can give you the proper legal advice. Do you have them with you?'

'Enough to give you the whole picture, Eddie. And just so you both understand, it's mostly the arcades that are a problem. Other divisions are still working well at Malvern's.'

'What about the Wine Division?' Rossi asked. 'How's Keller doing?'

'Keller is good. He and Irina will arrive later. He's very chuffed at the moment, because a South American entrepreneur, by the name of Jorge Royce, is coming next week to sign up with Malvern's. He has a British father and wants to import European wine, so that could really change things for the better.'

James really smiled for the first time that afternoon, and added, 'Prices may be rocketing and denting our shoppers' confidence, but with a new export market we could benefit.'

'Bravo!' Eddie cried, and Rossi smiled too on hearing this news.

* * *

After tea was over, James excused himself and went into his bedroom. He felt tired, and yet there was also a sense of relief. This was because Rossi had reminded him of the jewels which had belonged to his late wife, his darling Alexis.

Many years ago, she had once said to him a few words he had never forgotten, 'I will always be here for you whenever you need me.'

And she was here for him now; in his heart, as she always was, and in his head. Even in his mind's eye. He knew without a question of doubt that she would want him to auction her jewels to save Malvern's.

After all, the company had been hers, after her father's death. She had left it to *him* in her Will. It was theirs. He ran it now the way they had run it together, and he would protect Malvern's at all costs. He owed her that.

Thirty-Six

'Any reason we're having breakfast at the Bettrage Hotel in Hull, and not in London?' Peter Keller asked, his face filled with curiosity.

'Because I am in hiding,' James Falconer answered.

Peter stared at his best friend and business associate, somewhat startled by this answer. He knew from the expression on Falconer's face that he was not joking.

'From whom are you hiding?' Keller asked, after a moment's silence.

'A woman.'

'Aha, the lovely Lady Annabel, I've no doubt about that!' Keller exclaimed. 'And why on earth would you want to hide from her? She's gorgeous, and obviously taken with you.'

'That's the point, Keller. She is, and she wants to be with me all the time. And I'm just too old for her. In addition, I have to work long hours at the moment to resolve the issues I have with Malvern's. She's not a nuisance – don't misunderstand me – but she's bloody insistent. I need this time alone if I'm going to keep the business above water. Europe is too busy trying to import food to feed itself to need anything from us, and America is bringing in Prohibition.'

'I've got it, and I suppose not being in London for a little bit is the only way to deal with the situation.'

James nodded, changing the subject. It was all too painful to dwell on. 'By the way, congratulations on the deal you made with Jorge Royce. How did that come about?'

'Sheer luck!' Keller admitted, grinning. 'I'm very friendly with Jacques Foch, the head sommelier at the Ritz Hotel. He buys most of our good wines, and Royce, a guest at the hotel, complimented him on the wine list in the Ritz Hotel restaurant. That was a few months ago. When Royce came back to London, Jacques brought us together at Royce's request. He really boosted our Wine Division, I can tell you that.'

'A whole new export possibility, eh? Quite a coup.' James looked pleased, which made Keller feel better than ever.

After perusing their menus, the two men ordered breakfast. Both asked for coffee rather than tea. After the waiter disappeared to fill their order, Keller said, 'She's not a flibbertigibbet, you know. But rather a clever young woman. An art historian, and she writes pieces, too.'

'I assume you are referring to Annabel,' James said, adding, 'and I'd no idea she wrote. I hardly know her, in fact.'

'She hardly knows you, Falconer,' Keller responded, laughter echoing in his voice. 'But you both fell for each other.'

James looked at him and smiled, but made no comment. Instead he drank the coffee that the waiter had just brought to the table. Finally, he asked, 'Who does she work for? What newspaper, I mean?'

'*The Chronicle,* and Lord Reggie holds her in high regard. She writes a column twice a week. It's called "Annie's List", and it's all about art.'

'Good God! *She* writes *that*? Why, it's brilliant. I read that column religiously. How amazing! She knows a lot about art then.'

'Indeed. And she is very clever, your girl.'

'She's not my girl,' James protested strongly.

'But she could be, you know.'

'First, Lady Jane was matchmaking, and now you, Peter. I'm facing huge problems, and I can't get entangled with a lovely young woman at this moment.' He hadn't told a soul about the doctor's warning about his leg. Or how painful it was now.

'Of course you can. All you have to do is leave that bloody office of yours at six o'clock rather than ten or eleven,' Keller pointed out. 'Sometimes even midnight,' he thought to add.

James sighed. 'I suppose you're right. I'll try to do that a few nights a week.'

'Changing the subject, Irina has offered to sell her half of the icons she owns, at auction, of course. She will give the money to me for Malvern's.'

This comment so surprised Falconer that he couldn't speak for a moment. In fact, he was so touched, he choked up. Finally, he managed to say, 'What a wonderful offer, so generous of Irina. I will thank her later. But I think I'll be all right, once I've sold the jewels at auction. It will give me ready cash to pump into the company.'

'I've been going over all our divisions, and I don't believe the problems are quite as bad as you think,' Keller said. 'Our Bettrage Hotel group is steady, as are most of our property holdings, such as those in the docklands, in central London, as well as Mayfair. It's basically the retail side, the arcades, isn't it?'

'Yes.' James took a sheet of paper from the inside pocket of his jacket and looked at it. 'They're draining cash at a terrible rate. I can pull out of my problems if I get rid of the Kensington arcade and those in Harrogate and Leeds. I went over everything with Eddie earlier. He's advising me on any legalities we might face.'

'So we would be left with the arcade in Piccadilly and the one here in Hull. Two are enough, I'm certain. But, what about those problems in the Malvern in London? Some people can't pay their rent. That's the root of the problem.'

'I know. I'll deal with it easily enough by lowering the rents again, or letting my renters break their leases. It's a case of trimming down. And make do and mend as far as the Malvern is concerned.'

'Explain that, could you, Falconer?'

'I will. We have to make the arcade look as if it's normal, that's all. We can't have empty shops. So we fake the windows.'

'We could have discussed all this in London, you know.'

Falconer smiled. 'I know, but I did want to escape from Annabel, until she goes away, and—'

'That's foolish of you,' Keller interrupted. 'She's a very special girl.'

'Listen, it's not going to happen.' James said. 'And anyway, I wanted to come up to Hull to check on the Bettrage. Also, don't forget, I opened my first shop here, when we were both working for Henry Malvern in London. I felt nostalgic, I guess.'

'Why of course! Now I remember. It was Natalie who found it for you, and you rented it immediately.'

'It was the beginning of it all,' James said.

That night, before he went to bed, Falconer went through his list again, making notes and calculations on a pad. His talk with Keller, who had agreed with his decisions, had been useful; it had increased his confidence in what he planned to do. The economy might be booming now but he didn't trust it. He and Lord Reggie both felt that bad times were coming. Europe was on its knees from a brutal war, buying food from America. It was no time to take risks.

Cash was king. The cash from the jewellery auction, plus the sale of his paintings, would pull him out. With money to spare.

He could save Malvern's and, with a little luck, make it bigger and better.

Ten days later, James Falconer returned to London. He was totally at ease when he walked into his house on South Audley Street.

Brompton welcomed him home and gave him his messages, adding that his mail was on his desk. There was nothing of any importance, and that was a relief.

However, among the messages Brompton gave him was one from Lady Annabel, explaining she would be returning from Madeira in four weeks. She had stopped by to say goodbye two days after he had gone to Hull.

He smiled to himself. She was nothing if not persistent.

THIRTY-SEVEN

'You're not going to like what I have to report,' Detective John Scolding said, looking across the desk at James Falconer, bracing himself for a bad reaction.

James gazed back at Scolding, his bland face revealing nothing. 'I don't get surprised easily these days,' he replied. 'And I always expect the worst, Scolding. So give it to me straight, don't mince words. I need the truth.'

'Leonie has left her mother's house and gone back to live with Richard Rhodes in his Chelsea flat. Not a good move on her part.'

'It certainly isn't! After she ran away from him in Paris, I thought she had made a very smart move then. So, do you think this is a reconciliation?' James raised a brow and sat back in his chair. Inside he was suddenly worried and a bit shaken up.

The detective nodded. 'What else can it be? Also, the reports coming in from my agents, tailing them in the field, show that he's been wining and dining her, shall we say? And taking her shopping. For clothes, mostly.'

James Falconer let out a long sigh. 'I do hope he doesn't get up to his old tricks. The unfortunate thing is that my hands are tied. I can't intervene, and obviously I wish I could. Just keep your agents tailing them and telephone me, or come and see me anytime you wish.' James gave him a penetrating look. 'I have a need to know.'

'I will, sir, and try not to worry. It's hard not to, I know. But rest assured, if we spot any scratch on her, or think something bad is going on, we'll let you know at once.'

'Thank you, Detective . . . By the way, is she going to work at the art gallery?' Falconer asked, internally praying that Leonie was, in fact, doing that.

'Yes, she is. She's there right now.' Detective Scolding stood up. 'I'll call you every day to fill you in.'

Just a few minutes after the detective had left, Brompton was showing Rossi into the library. She had travelled back down from Hull with him.

His sister was smiling as she came to greet him. After they embraced, she exclaimed, 'Are you going to be in for a surprise, James! The jewellery collection is extraordinary.'

'So you had no problems with the bank manager?'

'No, not at all. With your letter giving me permission to view the boxes, and holding the keys for the vault and the boxes, Mr Coleman was most obliging. So come on, get up. We must go back to the bank immediately.'

'But why? I take your word for it,' James answered. 'I'm loaded up with work today.'

'You have to come *now* with me. We may even have to return tomorrow, there's so much beautiful stuff. It's mind-boggling. The collection will save you, I guarantee that,' Rossi said, still smiling at him.

James appeared puzzled, and frowned. 'Funny, though. I don't remember the collection; at least not that it was so many pieces.'

'It's *enormous*,' Rossi said. 'Maybe a lot of it was from Sebastian Trevalian, and Alexis didn't wear those pieces. She wore only those you gave her, or those from her father. Out of respect for you,' Rossi suggested. 'But there're piles more.'

'Let me get my overcoat, and I'll go with you to the bank,' James replied. 'And have you found the right auction house?'

'Yes, I have. I think we should use Bonhams. It's a long-established house, going back to the seventeen hundreds, actually. I know one of the directors, and he says they're very interested in holding the auction. Later this summer. They're thrilled, in fact.'

James pursed his lips and gave her a knowing look. 'And will anyone attend? The economy is in a poor state,' he said glumly.

'Oh yes, plenty of people will come. Bonhams has a list of clients; also, there are a lot of rich people in London. Many of them foreigners, Russians, in particular, who fled here after the Revolution. They've loads of money to spend.'

'So, let's go,' James said, taking hold of Rossi's arm. He loved and admired her, and she had always been his confidante. He certainly trusted her judgement.

The room at the bank was large, and bright lights shone down on the series of tables which stretched across the floor.

Falconer could see they were covered with jewellery boxes. These were mostly black, although there were a few red boxes which he knew were from Cartier.

'Alexis did have quite a collection,' he said to Rossi.

'Oh, these are just the gifts you gave to her.'

Falconer's steps faltered for a moment, and he frowned at Rossi. 'I gave her gifts, I know that, but surely not all of these! There must be about fifty boxes here . . .' He let his voice trail off.

'Forty boxes from Garrard, the royal jewellers, and the rings from Cartier.'

James was silent for a moment, and hurried forward. Rossi realized that he was walking better, and using the stick religiously. This pleased her.

Opening one of the Garrard black boxes, he saw at once the small white envelope with Alexis's name on it in his handwriting. Inside the box was an emerald necklace made entirely of square-cut emeralds. The stones were large, square, and intersected with small diamonds. He smiled inwardly, remembering how thrilled she had been. It was one of her favourites.

Rossi admired it, and then opened her handbag. She took out a folded cotton bag with handles. Opening it, she picked up the card and dropped it inside the cotton bag, put it on her arm.

James glanced at her, an eyebrow raised quizzically.

'I am collecting all these cards, James. They are your very personal words to Alexis. You must take all of them, since these boxes will soon be unavailable to you.'

'Oh, yes, yes, of course.' He nodded and moved on, opening more boxes. Rossi followed, picking up envelopes. There was one in every box, except the red ring boxes from Cartier. The envelopes were too big, Rossi decided. Maybe they are somewhere in his house, she thought.

For a moment, Rossi thought her brother was reluctant to leave the bank, and she looked at him swiftly, puzzlement in her eyes. Finally, she said, 'Are you all right, James? We should go now.'

He jumped slightly, as if she had startled him. 'Sorry, I was just wondering about all the jewellery from her father and Trevalian. I mean, how much is there of that?'

'About another forty boxes, maybe a few more. All very lovely things. You probably never saw them, because she was always discreet in everything she did. She only wore your gifts to her once you were married. I'm positive of that.'

'It seems we're going to have a big auction, doesn't it?' James murmured quickly.

'We are indeed. I must get started this week, having pieces photographed, contacting a few newspapers. We need to have publicity, James. People have to know about it.'

For a moment, he looked surprised, then said, 'Will they want to interview me?'

'I'm sure they will. They will want to know why you are selling all this stuff, this extraordinary collection. You can handle it.'

'Oh my God, no! What am I going to say? Will it look as if I'm broke?' he added in a worried tone.

'No, not if we come up with the proper story – the truth, actually. *The truth is the best.* Because we never forget it.' Rossi smiled at him.

'And what *is* the truth, Rossi?'

'That you realized this extraordinary collection was sitting in a bank vault where no one else could see it. You decided to auction the Alexis Malvern Falconer Jewellery Collection so other people could buy it and enjoy it. And you plan to give a percentage of the money to your favourite charity and the balance will be invested financially, to benefit Alexis's heirs. How does that sound?'

'Very clever of you,' her brother said. 'I don't have a favourite charity, though. I give cheques to a number of them once a year.' James lifted his hands in the French way.

'I know a charity that would love your support. And it's the one Alexis was involved with for years. She supported The Safe House for Battered Women. That's the one you should use. I'll introduce you to the woman who runs it . . .' Rossi laughed, and added, 'Actually, you know her. It's Lady Jane.'

'Oh, goodness me! Thanks for this help, Rossi. I was a bit

flustered about it all. I think Lady Jane and Reggie will be back in about a month or so.'

'Actually, they will be coming back early, James. It's been very hot in Madeira, and Lord Reggie didn't enjoy it so much. I had a letter from Lady Jane. It arrived yesterday. They'll be on our doorsteps before we know it.'

Falconer nodded. 'How much money will this collection bring in?'

Rossi shrugged. 'It's hard for me to estimate because it's all in the bidding. One piece everybody wants can go up and up and up. Really high. But with about eighty-odd pieces, it will be hundreds of thousands of pounds, I can assure you of that. You see, two other things help. The names of the jewellers and the provenance – the origin, in other words, the owner selling. Alexis was a socialite of some prominence, and you are one of the best-known men in England, after the king.'

'Oh, come on!' he exclaimed, and couldn't help laughing.

'It's true. You are the most famous business tycoon in the country.'

'Come on, let's go.' James took hold of Rossi's arm and led her out of the building.

'Where are we going?' she asked, endeavouring to keep up with his long strides.

'To the Bettrage Hotel. I'm taking you to lunch.'

'Why there and not the Ritz?' she asked.

'Because I own it.'

Rossi smiled to herself. She loved teasing him. He was so serious most of the time. As they had looked through Alexis's jewellery, she had remembered how much more joyful he'd been while Alexis was alive. She couldn't help feeling her brother needed to find love again. All he did was work, often until late at night. She must try and intervene, set him straight, and encourage him to seek out Annabel.

Thirty-Eight

The first week of March had been almost spring-like, with warmer weather and, thankfully, no rain. He had loved the walk to his office.

Now, tonight, there was a thunderstorm brewing, James was certain. Rising, he left his desk and went to look out of the library windows. Oh yes, dark clouds had gathered and were about to burst. It would be a humdinger.

When he sat down again and continued to sign some contracts, he glanced at the date on his desk calendar. It was Tuesday 18 March 1919. And winter's come back, he thought miserably.

He sighed. For the first few weeks of the month, his leg had been better. Most likely because he was using a new balm that Dr Miles had sent him, and walking with the stick, most of the time. Plus the warmer climes, of course. He hated the stick, wished he could rid himself of it.

Thunder, followed by flashes of lightning, told him that they *were* in for a bad one tonight.

Sitting back in the chair, he thought about his meeting with Rossi a few days ago and the enormous amount of jewellery he owned, now up for auction. His sister was right. It would bring in big money. Malvern's would be safe. This was a great relief to him. His life's work had not been in vain.

Rising again, James went and put more logs on the fire, and poked them around. He sat down on the Chesterfield, enjoying the fire. Unexpectedly, he felt like having a drink, and wished Rossi were here so he could toast her. It was not usual for him to drink alone, but he rang for Brompton anyway.

Within seconds, the butler appeared in the doorway. 'Do you need me, sir?'

'Yes, I do, Brompton,' James said, turning around to look at him. 'Do we still have any of that Italian wine that Mr Keller sent a few weeks ago?'

'We do indeed, Mr Falconer. Would you care for a glass?'

'I would, please, Brompton.'

'Certainly, sir.'

Left alone, James suddenly thought of Lady Jane, and how she and Alexis had started that women's charity. He would be glad to tell her he was going to give them money for it.

Within a few minutes, Brompton returned with the bottle and a glass, which he filled and brought to James.

'Thank you,' he said. 'I need to relax for a short while before supper. Brompton, tell Cook not to rush.'

'I will, sir.'

James sat nursing his wine, sipping it slowly and thinking about Lady Jane again, or rather about Lady Jane returning from Madeira. And bringing back Lady Annabel with her. *Annabel. Annabel. Annabel.*

He hadn't forgotten that lovely young woman. In fact, quite to the contrary, he couldn't stop thinking about her. And wanting her near him, if he was honest. There was something about her

presence that was soothing. She put him at ease, made him feel
. . . *whole*. Not alone, as he had felt before meeting her. He
longed to be with her, loving her, holding her in his arms, and
taking possession of her. Certainly, she had truly possessed him
at Christmas, made love to him with great ardour.

There was a knock on the door, and Brompton came into
the library. He closed the door quickly and hurried over to the
fireplace.

'I'm sorry to disturb you, Mr Falconer. But I – we – have a
problem, sir. There's a young lady out in our foyer, asking for you.'

Falconer put down the glass of wine and stood up. At once he
noted the alarm on the butler's face and gave Brompton a penetrating stare. 'A young woman? Who is it? Didn't she give you a
name? Come on, Brompton. Why are you looking so worried?'

'She's dripping wet from the storm, sir. She said she knows
you, that she is Leonie Rhodes. I think you have to come—'

'Right away, Brompton!' James exclaimed, cutting his butler
off, rushing into the foyer, his chest tightening.

When he saw Leonie, soaking wet, with blood on her face,
running down onto her neck, his heart seemed to stop for a
moment. Her face was black and blue, and there was a cut on
her forehead. She was hurt. Water was running off her coat and
pooling on the floor.

He went over to her, looking at her intently now, his thoughts
only for her, and helping her. Not able to speak for a moment,
he swallowed hard.

She stared up at him, tears still in her eyes, and asked in a
small voice, 'Can you help me? Can you help me, Father?'

James thought his heart was breaking as she said those words.
She hadn't seen him properly for years, didn't know if he would
still stand as her father. And she seemed so meek and afraid.

At last he spoke. 'Yes, Leonie, I am your father. Now let me
help you to take off this very wet coat. Then my housekeeper
will take you upstairs and find something else for you to wear.'

She simply nodded. 'I'm sorry, but I had nowhere else to go. I thought he would kill me.'

'Richard, your husband? Did he do this to you?' James asked in a tight voice, his fury rising inside him, bubbling up. He was taut.

'Yes, he did,' she whispered.

Turning to Brompton, James discovered he wasn't there. Then, a second later, the butler arrived with Mrs Thorpe, the housekeeper, whom he had brought up from the servants' quarters downstairs.

James looked at Brompton and nodded. He said to the house-keeper, 'Mrs Thorpe, please take Miss Leonie up to the blue guestroom and help her out of these soaking wet clothes. Will you please?'

'Immediately, sir, and what about a hot bath to warm her?'

'Of course. Once Miss Leonie has washed and dressed in something dry, she can come down to the breakfast room. We'll both have a bowl of hot soup.'

Brompton and James Falconer stood in the foyer, staring at each other. The butler saw that his employer was as white as bleached bone and genuinely upset. In fact, he'd never seen him like this before.

Clearing his throat, the butler said, 'Come with me, sir. Let us go into the library. Maybe a brandy will help.'

James shook his head. 'I'll have a drop of the wine, thank you, Brompton, and wait for Miss Leonie. She seemed afraid, don't you think? As well as being hurt.'

'Yes, sir, I agree. Very upsetting for you, Mr Falconer, but Mrs Thorpe is very motherly and kind.' Ushering Falconer into the library, he added, 'Once you and Miss Leonie are having supper, I'll ask Mrs Thorpe to prepare the blue bedroom. Miss Leonie isn't leaving, I hope.'

'Not on your life, Brompton. I'm not letting her out of my

sight. I'm glad she had the good sense to come here, where she's protected, safe.'

'Quite right, sir. I doubt her husband would dare to come knocking on this door.'

'So you heard what she said, did you?'

'Yes, Mr Falconer. I was just going downstairs to find Mrs Thorpe. I think there are some clothes in one of the guestrooms. Miss Rossi keeps things here if she has a busy week. I can look, sir.'

James suddenly remembered that Rossi did exactly that. But he could send Rossi out shopping tomorrow anyway. Leonie wasn't going to go back to Richard Rhodes; that was a certainty. He would call Eddie tomorrow, and Eddie would put Leonie in the hands of the best divorce lawyer in London.

Looking at the butler, he felt obliged to say, 'Miss Leonie is my daughter, Brompton.'

'Yes, I know that, Mr Falconer.' He hesitated before adding, 'I've always known that, sir. Anyway, she looks like you.'

A half-smile flickered on Falconer's face, and he said, 'So everyone says, Brompton.' Now, having regained some of his composure and being in full control of himself and the situation, he continued, 'Once Miss Leonie comes down, I'll talk to her for a few minutes in the library. I need to know the full story.'

'I understand, sir. Just let me know when you wish to have supper served.'

'I will, Brompton.'

'If you don't need me, sir, I'll find one of the maids to mop the foyer floor. We don't want anyone to slip, Mr Falconer.'

'I agree. Do what you need to do, Brompton. And thank you for your understanding. I appreciate your discretion.'

'You always have it, sir.'

* * *

James sat at his desk, staring at nothing. He let out a sigh and thought about Annabel, realizing that after only half a glass of wine he had forgotten about his resolution not to get involved with her. Oh God, she was barely older than Leonie, his daughter. Cradle-snatching, he thought again, his heart sinking. She was *verboten*.

There was a knock on the door, and Brompton's face appeared. 'Excuse me, sir, could Mrs Thorpe have a word with you?'

'Of course.' Falconer stood up and walked around the desk, and asked, 'Is everything all right now? What I mean: is everything all right with Miss Leonie? Come in, Mrs Thorpe. Don't stand at the door.'

'Yes, sir, it is. I coaxed her into having a hot bath, and she's getting dressed in some of Miss Rossi's clothes.'

Mrs Thorpe, still standing near the door, waited until Brompton had closed it behind him then spoke again, hesitation echoing in her voice as she said, 'Her body is quite bruised, Mr Falconer. Her back and thighs . . .'

'Oh my God,' he exclaimed, feeling an icy chill running through him. 'Old? New? Did you get a good look?'

'Not really, sir. She tried to hide them. Mostly old bruises, turned yellowish, I saw. But there were a couple that looked recent.' Mrs Thorpe cleared her throat, then added, 'I just thought you should know, sir.'

'Thank you, Mrs Thorpe; you did the right thing giving me this information. Is Miss Leonie going to come down for supper?'

'Yes. Although she does have to dry her hair. If it's all right with you, Mr Falconer, I should go back to help her.'

'Of course. Do that, Mrs Thorpe, and thank you again.'

'No trouble, sir. That's why I'm here – to help you any way I can.' She smiled and slipped out of the room.

James walked back to his desk, seething inside. That bastard

Richard Rhodes had obviously been beating her for months. *Old bruises,* Mrs Thorpe had said. Now *this*, tonight. A very visible attack. On the face, for God's sake. What a brute!

Could the police be brought in? Was it assault and battery if it was your own wife? He would get in touch with Jack Stead tomorrow. Maybe Rhodes could be arrested and thrown into jail. That's where he deserved to be. He would definitely get to Eddie first thing in the morning. Leonie needed legal help, and who better than his brother to provide it?

THIRTY-NINE

Leonie gazed around the guest bedroom of her father's house and saw how well it had been decorated. Lots of green, her favourite colour, and well balanced by crisp white sheets and pillows on the bed, under a rich eiderdown with beautiful embroidery. She couldn't help but be curious about James Falconer. She could feel how welcoming and comfortable his home was, not too formal or too masculine.

She sat in front of the fire, drying her hair with a towel, and then brushing it with a Mason Pearson she had found in the bathroom cupboard. Her hands had finally stopped shaking. Only desperation and having nowhere else to turn had brought her here.

The kindly housekeeper had lit the fire while Leonie had been taking a hot bath. She was glad she had, because she had been chilled to the bone. It had warmed her up. She realized Mrs Thorpe had seen her bruised body, but she hadn't been able to hide the bruises. She sighed and let the worry go.

Once her hair was dry, Leonie dressed in the undergarments that Mrs Thorpe had laid on the bed. After pulling on a pair of light beige stockings and fastening them to the garter belt, she went over to the wardrobe. She was already feeling a little better about her troubles.

Inside, she discovered a dark blue skirt and put it on. It was a little big, but fitted her and dropped to her ankles. There was a pale blue silk blouse hanging there, and Leonie knew they belonged together.

As she was putting the blouse on, there was a knock on the door. When she called, 'Come in,' Mrs Thorpe did so.

Leonie turned to face the housekeeper and gave her a small smile. 'I thank you for helping me, Mrs Thorpe. I look a bit more normal, don't I?'

'I'd say you look beautiful, Miss Leonie. Blue is your colour, especially with those blue eyes of yours. Just like his.'

'You mean Mr Falconer, don't you?'

'I do. Such a lovely man, miss. Wonderful to work for. Do you know, in the twenty years Brompton and I have worked for him, he's never raised his voice to us, or anyone else for that matter? Even when we've made mistakes. Bad ones, at times. He's like that with everyone. Always a gentleman.'

'He seems very . . . nice,' Leonie volunteered, and stopped. Then she added, 'A little overwhelming though.'

Mrs Thorpe said, 'Oh yes, that's his personality. Brompton says it's his great charm, his height and his good looks that combine to make him so outstanding.' She nodded her head. 'He's a true gentleman.'

'I suppose I must go downstairs. I think we're having supper,' Leonie now said.

'You are. But are you going to put your hair up? I think it should be pulled back. Somehow. Maybe a twist?'

'Oh yes, of course. Let me just pop into the bathroom to look in the mirror and fix it.'

* * *

The moment Leonie walked into the library, James Falconer saw the female version of himself. The same chiselled face, arched blonde brows and blonde hair, softly pinned up. Her eyes were blue, but not quite as vivid as his, and she held herself the way he did, had his stance.

There was no doubt who she was: his daughter. Even a stranger would spot that at once.

Her step faltered as she came forward, and she stopped. He was staring so intently at her she lost her confidence, felt nervous suddenly.

'Do I look . . . appropriate . . . for supper?' she asked in that hesitant, timid voice he'd heard earlier.

'Of course you do – you look beautiful, Leonie, and elegant. I'm so glad you found something nice to wear,' James assured her, trying to smooth over the awkwardness between them.

'It's your sister's, I assume,' she murmured.

Taking hold of her elbow, he guided her to the fireplace, and said, 'Let's sit together on the Chesterfield where it's warm. And have a little chat before supper.'

James had a glass in his hand, and he asked, 'Would you like to try this Italian wine, Leonie?'

Not sure what to do, she automatically said she would, not wanting to offend him in any way. She was not a big drinker.

A moment later they were seated on the sofa, sipping from their glasses. After another moment, he said, 'Would you mind if I asked you a couple of questions? You see, I'm really puzzled by some of this evening's events.'

'Yes, I'll tell you anything,' she murmured.

He again detected that strange timidity, almost fear, in her voice, and he wondered if she was afraid of *him*. Or was it her normal way of speaking? Or was it fear of Rhodes?

'I realize you ran away from your home and from Rhodes tonight, because he obviously attacked you. But why did you come to me?' James asked, sounding baffled.

'Because I knew you would take me in and protect me. I had nowhere else to go.'

'But your mother lives here in Mayfair, just a few streets away. Why didn't you run to her?' James gave her a searching glance.

'Perhaps you don't know this, but Mother is in hospital. She collapsed and fell down the stairs a few days ago,' Leonie informed him, her voice breaking a little.

'Oh my God. I'm sorry to hear this. Which hospital? And how bad is it?'

'King's Hospital. You see, she hit her head on the marble floor in the foyer. Bad injuries, I'm afraid, on the back of her head.' Leonie hesitated, clearly upset. 'She's drifting in and out of consciousness, asleep most of the time. I do go and see her every day, but she doesn't know I'm there.'

'I'm so sorry to hear this. I truly am. I will go with you tomorrow, if you wish,' James said in a sympathetic tone. Whatever their differences, he was shocked to the core by the news that Georgiana Ward was so unwell.

Leonie nodded and took a sip of the wine. She was beginning to understand that James Falconer was a very kind, very nice man. Not the monster Richard Rhodes had claimed he was. After a second or two, she said, 'What are the other questions, sir?'

James glanced at her swiftly, and said, 'Call me James, Leonie. I certainly don't think *sir* is appropriate – or Mr Falconer.' He smiled at her.

Leonie found herself smiling back, enjoying being here with him. She felt welcome – and for the first time in a long while, she felt safe.

James now asked the most difficult question. 'I know you left your husband in France. What made you go back into your marriage? Why in God's name did you return to Rhodes and his Chelsea flat?'

'He started to send notes and flowers, and stopped by the gallery sometimes. I began to go to supper with him, and he was so pleasant. And sober. I sort of fell into a trap. That's the only way I can explain it. And I was lonely.'

'And once you had moved in with him, he reverted to his old self, is that it?' James raised a brow.

'I'm afraid so. I've come to understand that he's an alcoholic, and he's easily influenced by his old Etonian friends. I was growing restless and wanted to get out, leave him, even though he hadn't become abusive. But then he *did* start to hit me, called me names. He was good at psychological torture.' Leonie shook her head. 'He started drinking early today, and when I got home, he accused me of having an affair with one of his friends—'

'I'm quite sure you weren't,' James interjected, filled with sadness for his daughter, coupled with his anxiety about her safety.

'No, I wasn't. He beat me up, knocked me down, and kicked me. Then one of his friends showed up. I ran into another room, grabbed my coat and bag, and fled. I hope you don't mind but . . .' She hesitated. 'I knew you would take me in.'

'I'm glad you had enough faith in me to come here. And here you can stay, as long as you want.'

'As long as I'm not in your way,' she said in a steadier tone. 'I couldn't stay at my mother's house, as he could find me there. And I'm suddenly worried about going to the art gallery to work . . .' She paused, left her sentence unfinished, and gave James an odd look.

'Perhaps it's better you lay low, stay home from work,' James said, his face serious. 'Not that I think Rhodes would do anything in public. Look, if you need to go, Leonie, I will take you there and bring you back here. How's that?' He smiled at her, his striking blue eyes holding hers.

She felt the tears rising, so touched was she by this unusual man, a man she had grown up determined to dislike. Yet he was not only kind and considerate, but a truly gentle person. His charm was natural, captivating.

Brompton arrived and announced that supper was ready. Together she and James went into the small breakfast parlour, a welcoming room with warm red walls. 'Cosier in here than that big dining room,' James explained, as he pulled out a chair for her.

'Thank you,' she said, as he sat down opposite her.

Brompton arrived with a basket of bread, and said, 'We have choices tonight, from Cook. Would you like duck terrine first, Miss Leonie, or artichoke salad? And what about you, sir?'

Leonie said, 'Oh, the terrine, please, Brompton.'

James half smiled. 'The same for me, Brompton, thank you.'

'The second course is a choice of fish. Cook has sautéed sole, with mixed vegetables. Or haddock dipped in batter with chips.' Brompton looked at James and added, 'She knows how much you occasionally enjoy fish and chips, sir.'

'So do I!' Leonie said, smiling. She looked at James. 'Is that what you're having?'

'I am indeed, and it's quite obvious we seem to like the same food. So fish and chips for two it is, Brompton. And thank Cook for such delicious choices.'

James Falconer found it hard to fall asleep. In fact, he was so restless he finally got out of bed, put on a dressing gown and stoked the fire with more logs.

He found himself relaxing in his favourite chair in front of a fire. The arrival of his daughter so unexpectedly in his life tonight had brought with it countless problems. Obviously, it was something he had hoped for, dreamed of, for so long. Yet it was not straightforward. Of course he could help her, and he would. She had to get a divorce and start a new life. He would let her live at his house for as long as she wished. That was not a problem. She would need support while Georgiana Ward was so unwell too.

However, once she was a free woman, he would buy her a flat or a house, whichever she preferred. She could then lead the life she wished to have. And be properly independent, not living with her mother. He frowned. Assuming that Georgiana recovered from these injuries. Something about her collapse worried him.

This evening, talking, laughing, and enjoying Leonie's company, he had felt alive again. He was lonely, living here by himself. No matter how hard he worked, he realized he actually liked the company of other people, had needed it since his experiences in the war.

His thoughts jumped suddenly to Annabel, and he wondered if he had been too hasty in dismissing her in his mind. Was he being silly thinking he was too old for her? He suddenly wished Jane and Reggie were here in London. He could unburden himself to them. Because he needed their advice.

In the past, his lover, Mrs Ward, and his wife, Alexis, had been older than him. Peter Keller had always teased him about that. He had suggested James liked to be 'mothered', as Keller put it. That was not the case. However, Peter wouldn't believe him, if he denied it.

James knew, deep down, he would be a fool not to pursue Annabel. He had not met anyone else like her. He pushed himself to his feet and shook himself. Leonie must be his focus now.

FORTY

When he had a big project, James Falconer moved with great speed, efficiency and focus.

The following morning, he was up early as usual, and downstairs and ready to start the day by seven thirty. After his breakfast of two soft-boiled eggs, toast and tea, he went to the library. He had telephone calls to make that were urgent.

His first was to Detective Jack Stead at Scotland Yard. Stead had been his lieutenant in the Army, and ever since they had been reacquainted after Irina Keller's attack, they had stayed in touch with each other.

Once James had explained the situation he was in, and how Leonie had run to him beaten up and afraid, Stead said he would arrive in an hour. James then called Rossi and told her. He asked his sister to bring some more clothes Leonie could wear. She agreed, and said she was available to help him in any way she could.

Someone knocking on the front door now brought Falconer to his feet. As he walked across the library, he heard Brompton saying good morning to Mr Scolding.

James greeted the older man in the corridor and then ushered him into the library. 'Oddly enough, I was just about to call you,' James said, leading the tall, thin private detective over to the fireplace.

The two men sat down, and Mr Scolding said, 'I'm here to tell you that your instincts about Richard Rhodes are correct. He's a criminal, a thief, in fact, and actually a fence. He sells stolen goods to others, and God only knows what else he's up to. He's a bloody crook.'

'He abused my daughter,' James replied. 'Physically abused her. I've called Detective Jack Stead, and he is on the way here. So, what else have your men in the field found out? Anything else?'

'Yes. He's been let go from the bank in the City where he worked. I haven't heard whether they're prosecuting him for anything, but that doesn't mean a damn thing. He's obviously done something they don't like. But banks often prefer misdemeanours to be hushed up. They hate bad publicity.'

'Rhodes can be arrested for assault and battery, can't he?' James asked, his anxiety apparent.

'Oh yes, absolutely. But I think there's a lot happening in his life, as well as that. I'm awfully sorry your daughter was hurt, Falconer. I've been advised that the Miller woman, who lives in Stepney, was in hospital for a night last week. She was treated for wounds to her head, and is now recovering at home. She apparently claimed she'd fallen down her cellar steps, but nobody believed her.'

'Oh, so she's still with Rhodes? Still his mistress?' James threw a questioning look at Scolding.

'Obviously. Don't you worry, Mr Falconer – once you've talked to Detective Stead, Rhodes will be in cuffs and on his way to jail.'

A few minutes later, Brompton showed Detective Jack Stead into the library, announcing his name.

James was on his feet again and going over to greet him immediately. 'Nice to see you, Stead. Just wish it were under better circumstances. Come and join us, won't you?'

'I feel the same way, Major. What's all this about? Rhodes is a dangerous man, in my opinion.'

'I'll explain, but first let me introduce my private detective, Mr Scolding, whom I hired a while ago. He'll also give you some facts.'

Scolding was precise and told Detective Stead everything he had just heard from Falconer. He did so swiftly yet without missing any details.

Jack Stead listened attentively and then looked across at Falconer, and asked, 'Is this the first time Rhodes has physically abused your daughter?'

'I would have said yes, to my knowledge, but the housekeeper helped her to get out of her wet clothes and noticed some faded bruises on her body. She reported this to me.' Falconer grimaced. 'But I've never seen anything wrong with her face until last night.'

'I will go and arrest him now, sir. Assault and battery, plus other charges perhaps. What's his address?'

Before James could answer, Scolding said, 'He has a flat in Chelsea, but I doubt he's there. He spends a lot of time at a place in Gloucestershire, in Cirencester. It belongs to his best friend, Patrick Campbell, another old Etonian. Campbell inherited his father's business in India and travels there frequently. Rhodes keeps an eye on Campbell's house. I don't know the address, but the Campbells have lived in that old manor house for a century at least. You'll have no trouble finding the house. He may well be on his way there now.'

'Thank you for this information. And for being so detailed.' Looking at Falconer, Jack Stead said, 'Clever of you to put a tail on Rhodes and your daughter, Major. It's given us some useful information. Saved us a lot of time.'

'Yes, I'm in agreement. Now, do you need to speak to my daughter?'

'I'm afraid so, sir,' Detective Stead replied, looking apologetic. 'But I'll make it quick and easy. Actually, I only need to see her bruised face and ask a few questions, Major.'

'Excuse me for a moment, Stead. I'll go and fetch her.'

James found Leonie in the yellow sitting room, looking at ease with Rossi, who had arrived a short while ago.

After greeting his sister affectionately, he smiled at Leonie, and explained, 'Detective Stead needs to see you, Leonie, and ask a couple of questions. It won't be difficult and we'll keep it short. He's a friend. We were in the Army together.'

'All right,' she replied softly, and got up. Smiling at Rossi, she murmured, 'Please excuse me for a moment or two.'

Rossi said, 'I'll be waiting here, Leonie.'

As they crossed the foyer, Falconer looked down at his daughter, and flinched inside. The bruises looked worse than they had last night. 'Is your face hurting?' he asked gently, half smiling at her.

'It's sore, and I know it looks awful. Rossi brought me this nice dress and jacket. Lovely clothes help me to feel better, though.' She stopped, looked up at him. 'Thank you for letting me stay here.'

'I want you with me, where you are safe and comfortable. Now, here we are. Let's go into the library. It won't be difficult.'

Ushering her inside, he announced to Scolding and Stead, 'This is my daughter, Leonie, and as you can see, her face is badly bruised. She will answer any questions you have about last night.'

It was Jack Stead who walked over first and shook her hand, greeted her kindly. Scolding followed, his manner also nice.

Both men, individually, sympathized about her bruised face, and she said, 'Richard was drunk. As soon as his friend arrived, I was able to run here. When he drinks, he becomes nasty, with me at any rate. He loses control.'

'Has he beaten you up like this before, Miss Leonie?' Detective Stead asked. 'Or was last night the first time?'

'Not really. When we were in Paris, he got drunk one lunch time. That afternoon we quarrelled; he beat me on my body . . .' She paused and tears came into her eyes, as she finished. 'He threw me on the bed and raped me.'

Falconer stiffened, shocked to hear this. But he kept tight control of himself, although a rush of rage gripped him internally.

Detective Scolding said, 'I'm sorry you've had to endure this horrendous behaviour on Rhodes's part. Very sorry indeed, Miss Leonie.'

Falconer glanced at the library door and stepped out into the foyer, just as Brompton was opening the front door. He was astonished to see Chief Inspector Roger Crawford entering his house.

'Chief Inspector! Why are you here?' James said, going to greet one of his oldest friends.

After the two men had embraced affectionately, Crawford said, 'I know Detective Jack Stead is here about Miss Leonie being assaulted by Richard Rhodes. I'm here about Rhodes regarding another matter. I've never stopped digging, you know. Two days ago, I found an old file on him, buried in the oldest section of information at Scotland Yard. A fluke that I happened to find it. I'm glad I did.'

'Did he rape somebody, or bust them up like he beat my daughter?' James raised a brow. 'He's a truly rotten bugger.'

'No, Falconer, nothing like that. Much worse. I think I can charge him with attempted murder, as well as murder. Two women involved.'

Astonishment settled in Falconer's vivid blue eyes. 'I hadn't expected anything like that!' he exclaimed. 'Not at all.'

'Oh yes, James. I believe I've got Mr Rhodes on murder most foul.'

FORTY-ONE

James grabbed hold of Chief Inspector Crawford's arm, and said in a low tone, 'Five seconds in the dining room here, please, Chief Inspector.'

Crawford saw the mixture of shock and anxiety on Falconer's face, and nodded, needing to fill him in anyway.

Once inside the dining room with the door closed, James said, 'Who did Rhodes murder?'

'Heather Miller, the older sister of Dorothy Miller, years ago. As I told you, I just dug it up. Then it seems he recently attacked Dorothy, his mistress. She didn't fall down her cellar steps. She was probably pushed by Rhodes, or bashed up earlier and then dragged down the stairs by him. He's as guilty as sin.'

'How can you be *sure*, Chief Inspector?' James asked. 'And you do seem positive.'

'Witnesses, James. A couple, Tim and Coleen Brown, were coming home that night when they saw Rhodes leaving Dorothy Miller's house. They thought he looked furtive, in a great hurry. When there was no sign of Dorothy Miller the next day, they eventually went into her house. The door wasn't locked. They found her in the cellar and got her to hospital,' Crawford finished. 'And, by the way, she will recover and can be a witness against him,' the chief added.

'I can't bear the thought that Leonie is married to him,' James exclaimed, sounding anxious again.

'I understand, but she has grounds for divorce. She can start proceedings straight away, get rid of him,' Crawford pointed out.

'My brother Eddie will be here soon. He'll take that on at once. I'm sure you remember that he's a lawyer with a well-known firm of solicitors. He's brilliant.'

'His reputation precedes him. Now, I think we should go into the library, and I'll have a word with Stead. He has to find Richard Rhodes and arrest him for assault and battery.'

'Let's go and talk to him, Chief, but just one question. Why wasn't Rhodes arrested and prosecuted years ago? You did say he murdered Heather Miller, didn't you?' James asked, filled with curiosity.

'According to those old files I just dug up, there was insufficient evidence, and he was bloody clever. No fingerprints were found at all in Heather Miller's house, and no way of proving he was there. But again, a neighbour of the victim saw him go into her house earlier and reported this when the body was discovered. However, Rhodes also had an alibi.' Chief Inspector Crawford grimaced. 'Dorothy Miller, the victim's sister, swore he was with her on the night of the murder. And I do mean *all* night. She's been his mistress for donkey's years.'

'I can't believe she'd defend Rhodes when he'd killed her sister,' James muttered, throwing the chief a questioning look, a perplexed expression on his face.

'Yet she did. What people can do, and actually *do* do, boggles the mind. I tell myself I've seen it all, every rotten thing in the world there is to see. But I'm constantly taken by surprise,' Crawford said.

'And so am I. The main thing is that my daughter Leonie escaped from Rhodes and had the sense to come to me. I am keeping her at my home until Rhodes is caught and in jail,' James explained. 'I want her to be safe at all times.'

'I heard Mrs Ward had an accident and is in King's Hospital,' Crawford said. 'How is she doing?'

'Mrs Ward is in a coma, Chief Inspector. That's all I can tell you. Leonie is living with me until I can find her a nice flat in one of the buildings I own. Once Rhodes is under lock and key, of course.'

'So, shall we go in and talk to Stead? He's one of the best. But then you know that, since you were in the Army together.'

'Indeed I do.' James and the chief inspector went into the library. Once greetings had been exchanged, James went over to Leonie and murmured, 'I think the detectives need a chance to talk all this through, Leonie. So why don't you and I go and find Rossi? Come along, my dear.'

Leonie nodded and walked out with James, still a little stunned by his ability to make things happen, but mostly touched by his kindness.

When Leonie finally went to bed that night, she discovered she was wide awake. Unable to fall asleep, she finally got up out of bed and went to sit in front of the fire.

James had kindly helped her to telephone the hospital to ask about her mother, but there was no change. Her mind was focused on him. *Her father.* For some reason Leonie had believed for a long time that he was difficult, bad-tempered, selfish and domineering. But this could not be further from the truth. In fact, he was just the opposite.

What impressed her most were his impeccable manners, the way he spoke to everyone in the same tone with that lovely voice of his. An actor's voice; and his charm, of course, was undeniable.

Certain things he did reminded her of herself, and she was the spitting image of him. Blonde, blue-eyed and slender. A smile flickered around her mouth as she stared into the flames. They even enjoyed the same food.

Why had she spent so many years hating him? Her mother had always seemed scared to write to him again once he broke off contact, saying only that he was grieving terribly about Alexis, and wanted nothing more to do with them.

In the meantime, she was going to get to know him as best she could, spend this time with him in a fruitful way. She would ask him a few questions too, about the past. Instinctively, she knew he would tell her the truth.

One thing her mother had told her was that he had proposed to her many times, but that she had not wanted to marry him, and that he had supported them financially for years. James Falconer was obviously a man who shouldered his responsibilities, was reliable and caring. His actions proved that to her.

Across the corridor, in his own bedroom, James Falconer was also restless. He, too, sat in front of the fire, pondering. Naturally, he was reviewing the day and what had happened, as he usually did at night.

Chief Inspector Crawford and Detective Jack Stead had matters under control, and he knew they would be successful.

They would track Rhodes down, cuff him, arrest him, and bring him to trial for his physical and psychological abuse of Leonie, and his attack on Dorothy Miller. They were two of the best detectives from Scotland Yard. And Rhodes's past would be dealt with as well. He wouldn't be allowed to get away with murder.

His thoughts skipped to Leonie, and he focused on her. How different she was to what he had expected. He had only seen her intermittently as a child, for short visits to the Ascot house, and had never got to know her properly. And since his return from the war, Mrs Ward had warned him that Leonie could never know they still saw each other from time to time, because she detested him and resented him. Mrs Ward had added that she would lose Leonie if the girl ever knew they were growing close.

Yet, this sweet girl he had just met, who had run to him in the pouring rain, looking for help and safety, was lovely in every way. Any resentment or bitterness she had harboured seemed to have vanished.

She was rather quiet in her demeanour, timid even, which was something he didn't quite understand, but suspected Rhodes might be responsible for. She was built in his image. Anyone who saw them together would know they were father and daughter, so alike were they.

She was approachable and easy to be with. He would find a way to make her understand who he really was as a man. And as her father. She had to know the truth.

The following day, Leonie arrived a little early at the Bettrage Hotel. Falconer had left a note before leaving the house very early for his office at Malvern House. Would she please join him for lunch at one? Mrs Thorpe would escort her. The venue: the restaurant in this elegant hotel on Davies Street where she now sat.

As she glanced around, she noticed the other women there *were* wearing hats. She was glad she had listened to Mrs Thorpe. Falconer's housekeeper had insisted she wear this stylish felt hat on top of her head. It was a fresh green and matched the soft green dress and coat she wore. Borrowed from Rossi, of course.

Picking up the menu, she studied it carefully, wanting to select the right dishes. Unexpectedly, the room seemed to become still, silent. As she looked up, she saw James Falconer walking in with his usual self-assurance. Every woman in the room was staring at him, and some of the men as well. His sudden presence dominated. Many people knew he owned the hotel.

What panache, what good looks, Leonie thought, as if seeing him more objectively than ever before. He appeared to fill the entire space.

Suddenly, he was there, towering over her, a smile on his face. 'Of course I knew you'd be punctual,' he exclaimed, as he sat down opposite her. 'Just like I am. I hate being late.'

'So do I,' she said. She settled back, looked at him and offered a small smile, somewhat tentative.

'I'm going to order champagne. Rosé champagne, to celebrate,' Falconer announced, beckoning to a waiter.

'What are we celebrating?' Leonie asked, curious.

'Seeing you again, being with each other. I last saw you when you were thirteen, you know.' He proffered her a wide smile, his blue eyes strikingly vivid, full of sparkle as he gazed at her lovingly.

'I do know,' she murmured, her own gaze focused on him intently. 'And I've often wondered why you stopped coming. I've struggled with why you rejected me. . .' Her sentence was left unfinished, and she shook her head helplessly.

Leonie saw at once that there was now a stricken look on Falconer's face, and he appeared to be upset. 'Oh, no, no, you didn't do anything wrong, Leonie! And you were a *good* girl, very good.' A deep sigh escaped, and he said in a tense voice, 'I became ill at that time, mentally ill. I went into a deep and overwhelming depression. My wife, Alexis, had died after three miscarriages, our baby son too, and I blamed myself. I felt guilty. I buried myself in my work and cut off my social life. It took years for me to get myself well. I should have gone to see Dr Sigmund Freud; my late wife knew him. But I didn't. However,

I did need a mental doctor, and I eventually got help from a good friend.'

'Oh, I'm so sorry you suffered like that. I knew only a little about that.' Leonie's expression was full of sympathy for James.

James nodded. 'Your mother was probably trying to protect you, as you were a child, but it seems it left you confused about why I vanished from your life.' He paused while the waiter poured their champagne, his face serious. 'I do owe you an apology for cutting off contact. But I hope you know I was a responsible man. Once I knew of your existence, I did support you both financially.' His eyes remained on her. 'I still do.'

'Mother did tell me, but only recently, and thank you for that.' Leonie paused, then asked, 'When did you first know of my existence? I've often wondered about that as well.'

'I was twenty-one, and your mother sent me a birthday card. She congratulated me on becoming managing director of Malvern's. She asked me to come and see her in Ascot . . .' James paused again when the waiter came to take their order.

James selected smoked salmon and lamb chops, and Leonie ordered the same.

Picking up his glass of champagne, he said, 'I toast you, Leonie, and your arrival in my life is the best thing that's happened to me ever.'

She clinked her flute against his and, knowing he was being honest, she said, 'And I can say the same about you.'

This comment obviously pleased him. After another swallow of champagne, he continued from where he had left off.

'So I went to Ascot to see your mother, with whom I'd had an on-and-off relationship since I was seventeen. We talked in the drawing room for a few minutes, and then she took me out on the terrace. Suddenly, a little girl appeared outside the summer-house. It was you.'

'I must have been two years old,' Leonie volunteered.

'You were. And you came running down the path as fast as

your little legs would carry you. I thought you were going to fall, and I rushed onto the path. And on you came, running right into my outstretched arms. You clung to me, put your arms around my neck, and nestled against me. I said to Georgiana, "She's mine, isn't she?" Your mother said, "Yes," and you sat on my lap all through lunch. You wouldn't let go.'

Leonie's eyes were moist with tears, and she said, 'And I won't let go now, not ever again.' She plucked up her courage. 'I want to live with you, at your house. Where I'm safe. I can, can't I, Father?' There, she had said it, knowing he wanted that verbal acknowledgment from her, and needing to please him.

'I want you to live at the South Audley Street house with me. I *am* your father, and that is where you should be – safe and protected. And I will enjoy having you under my roof . . .' His sudden laughter broke through and interrupted his conversation.

Recovering, he said, 'Sorry about that, but I just remembered that when you fell into my arms, all of two years old, you spoke. You said, "Pa . . . Pa . . ." Mrs Ward had taught you to say, "Papa" obviously, but it came out as two words when you said it. It's probably the first word you ever said.'

Leonie smiled, happiness on her face, and pleased to see this very nice man was also happy. Understanding his pain and depression after the death of Alexis Falconer had helped salve the pain of his disappearance from her life. And it seemed that her mother was fearful of pushing either of them to reconcile, either James in the years he was so distant, or Leonie herself since his return from the war.

For now she would concentrate on James Falconer, hoping she could make up for some of those lost years, give him some happiness as his daughter.

FORTY-TWO

Detective Jack Stead walked slowly up South Audley Street, heading in the direction of James Falconer's house.

As he walked, he pondered his dilemma. He had only bad news to give, yet he felt he needed a remedy for that, before he arrived. Something to balance the problem, make it seem possible to solve. But nothing halfway decent came to him by the time he reached the major's front door.

He always thought of Falconer as his major because he had been under his command in the Army. In a certain sense, he revered Falconer, had great faith in him and his many talents. He trusted him implicitly.

Brompton opened the door and led him into the library where Falconer was waiting for him.

After greetings were exchanged, James said, 'I've just asked Brompton for a pot of coffee. Will you join me, Stead?'

'Thanks, Major, I will.'

The two men sat down on the Chesterfield in front of the fire, which as usual was blazing up the chimney. Stead knew

Falconer felt the cold in his horribly wounded legs, healed but still bothersome in bad weather.

'I don't think you have good news by the look on your face, Stead,' Falconer remarked.

'I don't. Rhodes was not in Cirencester when we got there yesterday. Patrick Campbell's house was unoccupied. His cleaning lady said Campbell was in India and Rhodes hadn't been there recently. We searched the town. No one had seen him there for months, sir. It was very disappointing for me and my team.'

'So he's in the wind?' Falconer stared off into space, looking thoughtful, his mind working overtime.

'He is, Major. My team and I are bloody stumped! He's obviously in hiding, but *where*?' Stead was glad to take the cup of coffee from Brompton.

'Most likely he's still in London,' Falconer murmured. 'He must have other friends. We have to find them.'

James took the cup of coffee from his butler, thanked him, and placed the cup on a side table. 'He is a member of my club. I can look at the members list and see if a name strikes me. The bank where he worked might be able to pinpoint a few names, men he mixed with.'

'That's certainly worth trying,' Stead said, and then looked at the door as it opened.

Leonie stood in the doorway, hesitating. 'Oh I'm sorry, I didn't realize you were busy,' she said, addressing Falconer. She was now wearing her own clothes, James having sent two servants round to her mother's in Curzon Street – and to Rhodes's flat – to collect her belongings.

'You're not interrupting, Leonie. Come in, darling. You might be able to help us,' Falconer responded.

'I'll try,' she replied, closing the door behind her. 'Hello, Detective Stead,' she murmured as she joined them and sat down in a chair near the fireplace. She looked at James expectantly.

Falconer told her that Detective Stead could not find Rhodes in

Cirencester. He continued, 'Nobody's seen him. So he's in the wind, so to speak. What good friends does he have? Do you have any idea who he might go to, men who were working at the bank, perhaps?'

'He didn't have a lot of close friends, to my knowledge,' Leonie said softly. 'In a sense, I think he was a bit of a loner. You've ruled out Patrick Campbell, who was his *best friend*. They were close from their days at Eton. But I can't think of anyone else.'

'Any old Etonians he hung around with?' Detective Stead asked. 'Those he got drunk with in Paris?'

She shook her head. 'I can't remember their names. I'm so sorry.'

Leonie sat back in the chair, racking her brains, but could not put a name to those raucous men who had surrounded him at the Plaza Athénée Hotel.

Then all of a sudden she sat up, as a thought flew into her mind. She exclaimed, 'Perhaps he went to hide out with his mistress, Dorothy Miller. They've been an item for years and years, long before he married me. He's never actually given her up.'

Falconer gaped at his daughter, taken aback by her suggestion, and then he laughed. 'By God, Leonie, I think you've just hit the nail on the head. The most unlikely place to look for him, and yet the easiest place for him to go. Because who would ever think of her, under the circumstances, given her sister's murder, and the fact she's also complained about assault at his hands?'

Leonie said, 'From what Chief Inspector Crawford said, it was my understanding that Dorothy Miller remained his mistress even after he had killed her sister Heather. Am I correct?' Leonie stared at Stead.

'You are *very* correct,' Stead answered. 'And you are brilliant for thinking of the mistress, Miss Leonie. Thank you.' Stead rose. 'I shall call in my team and head there now. The chief inspector has her address in Stepney. Anyway, it's on file at Scotland Yard, I'm sure. I'm confident we will see this man stand trial.'

* * *

After Detective Stead had left to go back to the Yard, Falconer sat alone with Leonie, smiling at her. 'That was clever of you, my darling girl. Whatever made you think of the mistress?'

Leonie studied him, pleased whenever he used endearments when he spoke to her. Finally, she said, 'I suppose I thought of his mistress because I'm a woman. I know that men in trouble often go to the important woman in their lives when they need help, Father. And that some women take them in, whatever the circumstances.'

'I understand what you mean. I only hope that Rhodes is indeed with his mistress. I won't rest until he's got handcuffs on and is under lock and key. I'm so sorry you've had to suffer at his hands.' Falconer drank his coffee, and then said, 'Would you come and sit next to me here, Leonie, please? I have a question to ask you.'

She nodded and went to join him on the Chesterfield. 'You sound serious. What is this about?'

Taking hold of her hand, smiling at her, he said, 'It's about you and me. Are you afraid of me in some way?'

'No, I'm not.' She sounded puzzled by the question. 'What makes you think I am?'

'You sound so timid at times, hesitating, not showing the self-assurance I know you have, that you had as a child. I thought perhaps I might intimidate you. I hope I don't, Leonie.' He was sincere, half smiled as he gazed at his daughter.

'No, I'm not afraid. But my husband sort of . . . brainwashed me. I think that's the best way to say it. And my mother always told me how important you were, what a large business empire you ran, and so I suppose I had the impression that you weren't to be bothered, once you stopped visiting. I think I've been hesitant because of both of these things. I really thought I'd lost you.'

Falconer pushed down on the bubble of anger rising inside him and said, 'I am so sorry you got that impression, Leonie.

I've always wanted you in my life, since the day I met you. I feel very sad that you thought otherwise.'

Leonie leaned forward and kissed him on the cheek. 'And now I am here, of my own free will. I want you to know that I love you, Father, and I always have.'

'You will never know how happy that makes me feel. Thank you for expressing yourself so well, darling. Will you live here with me? At least until Rhodes is under lock and key?'

'If you don't think I'll be in the way.'

This comment made him laugh. 'You're my only child, my daughter. How could you possibly be in the way? Let me keep you safe here until Rhodes is in prison.'

There was a pause between them before James spoke again. He judged that Leonie had dwelled on her marriage for long enough this evening.

'And now, let's move on to another question . . . no, not a question, a point I want to make.'

She nodded. 'What is it?'

'You are my heir. My only heir. I have a great business empire . . .' He broke off, got up, poked the fire and threw on two logs, gaining time to find the right words.

Sitting down next to her, he took hold of her hand again, and asked, 'Would you ever consider coming to work with me at the Malvern Company? To learn how to run it yourself one day?'

There was a silence.

Falconer gazed at her, loving this beautiful young woman who had come back to him, the daughter he had thought was lost to him for ever.

'Yes,' she said at last. 'If you think I can do it?'

A broad smile spread across Falconer's face. 'You're *my* daughter, and we're very much alike. Of course, you can do it. But you must put your heart and soul into it, Leonie, and love Malvern's as I do. If you can do *that*, all will be fine.'

'I want to learn from you, Father. I know you'll teach me properly. I am honoured you've asked me to be part of your business life.'

'And you won't miss the art world?' he asked, leaving this important question until now, fearful of her answer.

'No, I won't miss it. And I prefer to work with you.' She gave him a long, intense look. 'After all, I am your heir, and I should be by your side, shouldn't I?'

Falconer, thrilled in a way he had never been before, put his arms around her and hugged her to him. 'Instinctively, I feel you'll be a great businesswoman, and we'll make a great team.'

She nodded, and then said, 'Will it be possible to change my name . . . to Falconer?'

Startled though he was, James Falconer was happy to hear these words. 'Of course, you can. We'll put that in the works at once. After all, you are my daughter, my heir, and Malvern's is your future. You must bear my name since you were born a Falconer. You are my flesh and blood.'

PART SIX

Relative
Values

Kent and London, England
May–July 1919

FORTY-THREE

Lord Reginald Carpenter turned from the window of his library, with its view over the sweep of formal gardens, and said, 'I'm happy to be alone with you, James. I need to talk to you without the ladies around.'

Falconer nodded. 'I thought you were itching to have a private chat. But I must take something up with you first. I don't—'

'I know. I know. I didn't tell you Annabel would be here at this house party. I knew you wouldn't come to Kent if she was present.'

'So you tricked me!'

Lord Reggie laughed. 'It's not the first time! I tricked you and Alexis, years ago now, and got the two of you back together.' Smiling at Falconer, he added, 'How about a glass of sherry?'

'Thank you, but I don't like to imbibe in the morning, Reggie. A plain soda is fine.'

After pouring the drinks from a silver tray at the side of the room, Reggie handed James a heavy crystal glass and said, 'I wanted to talk to you about the opening of the trial of Richard Rhodes. I understand you were there with Leonie.'

'I needed to be. I couldn't let her face such a terrible ordeal alone.'

'And how did Rhodes behave? Protesting his innocence, I've no doubt,' Reggie said. He sipped his sherry, and then continued, 'He's always been a sod in my book.'

Falconer smiled faintly. 'And a murderer. With the information Chief Inspector Crawford discovered in those old files at Scotland Yard, that cold case is now open and will become a closed case in short order. He is now in irons and will obviously be found guilty of the murder of Heather Miller.'

'Are you certain the jury will bring in a guilty verdict? After all, the evidence in that case seemed to be somewhat scant.' Reggie stared at Falconer, a questioning expression on his face. 'At least, that's what I've read in *The Chronicle*, my own paper.'

'His former mistress, Dorothy Miller, has finally seen the light, after he forced her to give him refuge when he went on the run, and has agreed to give evidence against him. He pushed her down the stairs only the week before, just as he had pushed her sister Heather. Dorothy luckily survived.'

'What did he have against Heather?'

Falconer grimaced. 'She was about to kiss and tell, so to speak. He was sleeping with her and getting rough, and she threatened to tell Dorothy, whom he was two-timing.'

'They both were, in my opinion. So he'll swing at the end of a rope. Get the death penalty.'

'Oh yes, indeed he will, thank God. It's been a terrible experience for Leonie. Thank you for keeping her name out of the stories as much as possible.' James sat forward in the leather armchair that faced a bowl of early summer flowers on a low polished table between him and Reggie. In a low voice, he asked, 'Why didn't you tell me that Annabel was here?'

'Obviously because I knew you wouldn't come. I wanted you here together in Kent, under the same roof, relaxing for the weekend. I want to make the two of you see sense, get together again.'

'That's not possible because I'm—'

'Don't say it, Falconer,' Reggie cut in. 'You're *not* too old for her. That's bloody nonsense.'

'*She* doesn't want to come back to *me*, because I hurt her feelings, shut the door in her face. She is also angry with me because I never responded to several notes she left me, before and after you all went to Madeira.' Falconer sighed. 'That was rude of me,' he admitted.

'Bloody crazy, if you ask me.' Reggie shook his head. 'Do you want to end up a lonely old man, Falconer? No life in that. You're going to be forty-nine later this month. Now is the time to grab hold of Annabel and run with her. Marry her. She's in love with you. And you're in love with her.'

When James remained silent, Reggie said, 'I don't want you to lie to me and say you're not.'

'Yes, I am,' Falconer finally said softly. 'I haven't attempted to make amends because I'm not sure how to go about it now. It's been too long, you know. I think I might have lost my nerve. Women can be very touchy . . .'

Reggie burst out laughing, and exclaimed, 'You don't have to tell me! And talk about emotional. Wow!' Calming himself, Reggie said, 'Did you read today's *Chronicle*?'

'No, not yet. And thanks for sending one up to my room.'

'Read "Annie's List" as soon as possible. Annabel has done an interview with a man called Professor Andrew Harcourt. He's a very famous art historian and could value your collection again for you, given you were talking about raising capital, to keep Malvern's safe. He can also spot a fake painting better than anyone.'

'A fake painting? Do you mean a fake of a *famous* painting? And one by a *master painter*?' James was gaping at his friend.

'Yes. Apparently there are quite a few hanging on walls, paintings people have paid huge sums for, mostly Impressionist and Post-Impressionist works.'

'Like mine? Those I own?' James asked, sounding aghast.

'Yes. That's also why I'm telling you this.'

'What should I do?' James seemed suddenly worried.

'Get them checked out to make sure they are the real thing. Authentic.'

'So I need an expert.'

'You have one in your backyard,' Reggie answered.

'I don't have a backyard.'

'Then in your pocket. The Lady Annabel Kelsey, the woman you're in love with, can take you to meet Professor Harcourt. Or, better still, she can bring him to your house, and he can examine them there.'

'You make it seem so simple.'

'It is, Falconer.'

'But Annabel, while being polite this weekend, is angry with me.'

'I don't blame her,' Reggie responded. 'But I think I have a solution for you. Can I talk to Jane, sort of on your behalf? She can intervene, perhaps, bring Annabel around. Mind you, my Jane might insist on talking to you first.'

Falconer did not answer. Myriad thoughts were whirling around in his head, and he felt that for the first time in his life, he was floundering. And not in charge of himself or his future. An unusual position for him to be in. Control of himself was a given.

Finally, after a few minutes, he nodded. 'I'd better have Jane's help,' he said. Oddly enough, as he uttered these words, he felt a great sense of relief flowing through him.

James felt the need to get outside to take a walk in the beautiful Kent countryside. He was used to walking quite a lot in London, and he knew it helped his legs. They had been better in the last few days, mainly because the weather was warmer.

It was 6 May 1919, a Tuesday, and he had arrived on Sunday to spend a few days with Lady Jane and Lord Reggie in Kent.

What he had not been told, or anticipated, was the presence of Lady Annabel and her child, Adrian. Seeing her again, being around her, had suffused him with all manner of emotions. Reggie had just revealed that Jane hoped to bring them back together.

A deep sigh escaped. Jane meant well, but the road to hell was paved with good intentions. On the other hand, she was a positive woman, and wise, and he had listened to her for years. Since his early twenties, in fact, when he had delivered a letter to Alexis Malvern from Henry Malvern, her father and his boss.

Lady Jane and Lord Reggie had been staying with Alexis at Goldenhurst, and they had been very kind to him.

Alexis. He walked down through the gardens of Reggie and Jane's house towards that beautiful house in the distance, designed, built and decorated by Sebastian Trevalian. His mind settled on his first wife. Actually, his only wife. He had loved her deeply, and her death had devastated him. It had taken him years to come to grips with himself. His only solace had been his work, building the Malvern Company into the huge business empire it was today.

And lately, he had been blessed with the arrival of his daughter in his life. Leonie, who was the spitting image of him.

Leonie was a lovely young woman, intelligent, with a good business head, charming and very pretty. The thought of her married to that monster Richard Rhodes horrified him. He tried hard not to dwell on that unholy union. Yet she had done this to herself. She had elected to elope with him. Her mother, Georgiana Ward, had been unable to prevent it, and he had had no say in the matter at that time.

James calmed his riotous thoughts by reminding himself that his younger brother Eddie had brought in the best law firm in London. Leonie was in the middle of a divorce, but Rhodes might well be swinging at the end of a noose before the divorce came through.

Pushing these thoughts away, he paused for a moment, gazing towards Goldenhurst. So many memories rushed through him. Alexis's best friend Claudia Trevalian Glendenning lived there now. She had inherited it from her father, Sebastian Trevalian. It was entailed and must always be passed on to a Trevalian.

As he turned, he heard a little voice calling, 'Sir! Sir! Wait for me!'

Much to his surprise, he saw Adrian running down the long stretch of lawn, waving his hand. He was alone.

Falconer hurried forward, waving back as he did, and then suddenly ran towards the child. He was moving so fast, he might easily fall. But James was there to catch him in his arms as Adrian hurtled the last few feet and fell against him.

For a moment or two, James held the boy close, smoothing his hand down his back. Adrian was out of breath and panting.

Soon his breathing was more normal, and James released him and stood up. 'My goodness, you were going fast, Adrian. A bit too fast, I think.'

Adrian looked up at Falconer and smiled. 'I wanted to talk to you. I saw you through the window. I sneaked out.'

'And where is your nanny?'

Adrian sighed. 'She fell asleep in her chair when she was knitting.'

Falconer swallowed a smile, and continued, 'And where is Mummy?'

'Oh, she's with Leonie. They're planning something . . .' He broke off. 'I'm not supposed to speak about it. You see, it's a big secret. So don't ask her anything.'

'I won't, don't worry. Now shall we walk back to the house?'

'Can we rest a bit, please, sir? I'm a bit puffed.'

'Well, I'm not surprised about that. You were running hell for leather.' Still staring at this beautiful little boy, James could see he was worn out. He said, 'I know you wouldn't want me to carry you, a grown-up boy like you. But how about a piggyback ride?'

'I've never had that!' Adrian exclaimed, his face lighting up.

'Then you're in for a treat. I am going to kneel down, and you will climb on my back and put your arms around my neck. Then I'll stand up and off we'll go. But you must hold on tight.'

'I can do it, sir. I know I can.'

Within minutes, James was upright, walking up the lawn to the terrace, with Adrian comfortably settled on his back, his bad leg only causing him the odd grimace.

It was just before they reached the terrace that Annabel appeared and came down the steps onto the lawn. She was carrying his stick.

'Was that a nice piggyback? she asked, looking at Adrian.

'It was wonderful, Mummy.'

James knelt down so the boy could alight, and then straightened up.

Looking at Annabel, he said, 'Good afternoon.'

She replied, 'That was kind of you to do that. It's a first. Thank you.'

'He's a lovely child. Annabel, I wonder if we might have a talk—'

'I think there's nothing to say,' she murmured.

'It's not personal. It's about my Impressionist paintings. Lord Reggie thought you might be able to have your art expert authenticate them.'

'Oh, I see. Well, yes, I suppose I could. When will you be back in London?'

'I shall be leaving here on Thursday. I have a board meeting on Friday. After that, I will be available. Nor am I going away in the near future.'

Annabel handed him his stick. 'You should use this, you know. I will speak to Professor Harcourt and be in touch.'

'Thank you, I appreciate this.'

'Come on, Adrian,' she said, and again with a faint smile, she led her son up the steps.

James Falconer never took his eyes off her. He knew he *was* in love with her. He was convinced she had the same feelings for him. But he was not going to act on it.

FORTY-FOUR

Rossi felt like jumping for joy. The photographs of the jewellery from the Alexis Collection, as she thought of it, were sensational. So very well arranged on different fabrics, by the best photographer in the business.

She was positive every shot of the forty-eight pieces would be grabbed by the top magazines and newspapers.

She stood looking at them laid out on the boardroom table, a smile on her face. James would be thrilled; he was already impressed with the publicity campaign she had put in place in April. Today it was Tuesday 13 May, and she had had lots of stories published about the auction, now set for July.

When the door opened, she turned around and said, 'Peter! Come on in. I'm thrilled with the photographs. You've done such a great job. The pieces are so well displayed. Thank you for all your hard work.'

Peter Keller beamed with pleasure, hearing her praise. 'I know I took rather a long time arranging everything, but it paid off, I think.'

'It did indeed. I love the way you used black velvet and navy silk for the diamonds, cream velvet for all the ruby pieces, and white velvet for the sapphires and emeralds. They show up so well against the fabric backdrops.'

'Chuck Langly is the best photographer for what I call "still lifes". He knows how to drape the fabrics on small wooden busts and stands. He's a perfectionist. He places the jewellery just right.'

'I want to finish up the captions today, even if I have to work tonight, and then I'm going to messenger the pictures to the top magazines that have a month's lead time. I know they'll get used at once.'

Peter nodded. 'I can help with that, Rossi. My secretary can certainly address envelopes and help in any way she can.'

'Thank you. I'd appreciate that, Peter. Now help me to put this tablecloth over the photographs, and then let's invite James in here. I think he'll be surprised.

Keller grinned. After helping put the tablecloth on the board-room table, he left.

James Falconer was startled when his sister removed the cloth to reveal the extraordinary photographs of the jewels he had given his late wife, Alexis, many years ago.

He simply stood there in silence, gaping at them, drawing closer to the table and then peering at them all. He took his time, studying each one. At times a special piece would bring back a flash of memories, and occasionally he choked up.

Falconer was digesting the display, and then he looked from Rossi to Peter, and finally spoke. 'You've both done a magnificent job of showing off the jewels to perfection.' He smiled faintly. 'I can only add that I can't remember giving her all this . . .' His voice trembled slightly with emotion and he paused. He took hold of himself.

'Well, you certainly did, James.' Rossi murmured. 'Don't forget, this is the First Lot, as Bonhams calls it. There are still those other jewels from Henry Malvern and Sebastian Trevalian. About another forty pieces, although some items are not as valuable as yours.'

'I hadn't forgotten, sweetheart,' he responded. 'I know how generous both men were. Just one question, Rossi: if I want to keep a few pieces from this selection, when do I have to let you know?' James gave her a quick glance.

'By the end of May, early June. We can pull anything out until then. After that, it becomes a bit difficult. Just let me know,' she finished, smiling at him.

He thanked Peter and Rossi, and swung around, walking to the door.

Rossi exclaimed, 'Can you spare five minutes, James?'

'Of course.'

'Then I'll come with you to your office.' Smiling at Keller, she followed her brother.

Once they had entered his office, Rossi closed the door, and said, 'I've had to deal with a slight problem, and I hope you don't mind.'

Gazing at her as he sat down behind his desk, James asked, 'Oh really, who with?'

'Actually, Annabel, oh, and Leonie.'

Falconer frowned. 'Why? What did they do?'

Rossi spoke carefully when she said, 'Leonie and Annabel announced to me yesterday that they were going to give a birthday party for you. A surprise party. They came to me because they didn't know who to invite, other than Lady Jane and Reggie, Charlie and me, and Eddie.'

James chuckled and shook his head, then said, 'Knowing you, Rossi, my love, you'd already planned a party and put everything in motion.' He looked amused as he sat back in his chair, his eyes on his sister, to whom he was close.

She had the good grace to laugh, and said, 'All true, and now the surprise is spoiled.'

'I guessed you'd be doing something, Rossi. You've been throwing parties for me since you were ten. So you invited Leonie and Annabel, I suppose.'

'Naturally, and they accepted at once. I did explain to them that I'd sent out invitations in the post, booked the private room at the Bettrage Hotel, and done the menu . . .' Rossi laughed. 'They were a bit taken aback.'

'So am I. You've been busy. So is the entire Falconer clan coming? By that, I mean my nieces and nephews as well as my siblings?'

'Oh yes, they're all old enough now. I can hardly believe that my Lavinia is twenty. Where does time go?'

'It seems to just fly away,' James answered. 'You've no doubt included Lord Reggie and Lady Jane, haven't you? And Crawford?'

'Yes, and I'd never forget the chief inspector. He's like your Dutch uncle since you were very young. Fourteen. I also invited Jack Stead, since you're such good friends and you were in the war together.'

'Well done, darling. Oh, and I do hope you put *no gifts* on the invitation.'

'I did, but nobody pays attention to that.'

Rossi got up and went over to the window, looking down at Piccadilly below and seeing that it was as busy as always. Her mind was racing. Eventually she returned to the chair opposite her brother's desk and looked at him intently, reaching inside herself for her courage.

'Is something suddenly upsetting you, Rossi?' He frowned, well aware of the change in her mood and the expression in her blue eyes. Her body was unexpectedly tense. Worry surrounded her.

After a few seconds, she said, 'I would like to talk to you

about Annabel, which I think you might resent . . . say it is none of my business.'

James was somewhat startled by her words, because there was a family rule: relationships were private, and no family member could question or interfere in a sibling's personal life.

Leaning forward, his elbows on the desk, Falconer answered in a calm, steady voice. 'Of course, you can speak to me about her. But I don't really have much to say.'

Relieved that he was being pleasant and not dismissing her question, she said quietly, 'I was under the impression that you'd been drawn to each other when you first met. Somewhat smitten, actually, and that you became involved. Am I correct?'

'You are indeed, Rossi. She's lovely, and we did get . . . entangled. However, I came to the conclusion I am too old for her. So I decided to end the relationship in its early stages.'

Rossi let out a long sigh and gazed at him, disbelief etched on her face. 'You're daft, Jimmy lad, just silly. No, I'd go as far as to say, "You're stupid." She's beautiful, kind, and extremely clever. And *she* is in love with *you*.'

'Everything you say about her talent and beauty is true,' James acknowledged, half smiling at his sister. 'However, I made up my mind to end it, and I did.' He sounded adamant.

Rossi shook her head. 'Sometimes I think I don't know you at all. Certainly I never quite understood that strange on-and-off relationship with Mrs Ward and—'

'Neither did I eventually,' he cut in. 'I ended that. And you know that Georgiana Ward is still at that nursing home near Ascot. She may never leave it, I'm afraid.'

'I'm sorry to hear that. But getting back to Annabel, I want you to at least *think* about the two of you being together. She's young and lovely, and only thirty-two. She could give you children.' Rossi stopped abruptly. She saw the sudden change in his demeanour and realized she was now treading on very dangerous ground. She should have never brought up children. It was *verboten* as far as her brother was concerned. Too many awful memories for him.

There was a long silence, and James was looking off into the distance, as if he saw something only visible to him. He looked sorrowful, lost for a moment or two.

He's remembering the past, Rossi thought, and wished she'd kept her mouth shut. But they had always been open and honest with each other. Confidantes.

At last, Falconer spoke. 'I've thought of having children with Annabel, because knowing her the way I do, I think she would want them. Unfortunately, it's genuinely hard for me to forget the miscarriages Alexis had, and that childbirth killed her and my son. I suppose it's imprinted on my brain. Though it was a long time ago, I know.'

'I'm so very sorry I brought it up, James,' Rossi murmured, her chagrin and sympathy apparent. 'You didn't need to hear that.'

He gave her a faint smile. 'It's all right, darling. I know you didn't mean any harm. And I know Alexis was eight years older than me, and perhaps too old, in her late thirties, to be getting pregnant. But things happen in life that we don't expect, and we have no control over them. And often they change us, stay with us, and even change our lives.'

'I understand.'

James pulled a drawer in his desk open and glanced away. 'Let's change the subject, shall we?'

Rossi nodded then exclaimed, 'Oh, while we are on the subject of Annabel, when I saw her yesterday, she asked me to let you know she will bring Professor Harcourt to your home tomorrow afternoon to look at your paintings. About two thirty.'

'Oh, that's great. Thank you, Rossi.'

'Why is he coming? You're not thinking of selling the paintings as well as the jewellery, are you?' Rossi sounded upset, and stared at her brother, scowling.

'No, not now that I've seen all the jewellery photographs. I had considered it, though. The fact is, Annabel wrote a column in *The Chronicle* about forgeries, which I read the other day, when we were at Reggie's in Kent. So I asked her to arrange a meeting with Professor Harcourt to authenticate my paintings, in case I ever do want to sell. I am glad that she has arranged the meeting so soon.'

'Well, she's a real expert on Impressionist and Post-Impressionist paintings. I know she studied in Paris. I suppose this professor is just back-up for her. But she really knows art and is especially talented about spotting fakes.' Rossi smiled, and added, 'She's quite well known in the art world and highly respected. So listen to her.'

'I will,' James promised, suddenly intrigued by this different side to Lady Annabel.

Rossi returned to her own office in Malvern House. Now that they had closed some of the arcades, she was helping James in other matters, and no longer went to her shop in the Malvern Arcade.

She had promoted Alice, made her the manager and taken on an assistant to serve. Her name was Petula, and she had turned out to be a hard worker. The shop was holding its own.

After looking at different papers on her desk, Rossi sat back, her thoughts on James. How could she get him back together with Annabel?

One thing was important. They were actually meeting to-morrow about the art. At two thirty.

Between now and then, she had to talk to Annabel, explain that she must take this opportunity to make all the moves. She must captivate him again.

FORTY-FIVE

James Falconer was in fine fettle as he walked from his house in South Audley Street to the Bettrage Hotel on Davies Street.

Everything had improved no end. Malvern's was steady. The loss-making arcades had been shut, with only two still running. The Wine Division was making a profit, and the hotels were in the black. And there was the auction ahead.

In particular, he loved the Bettrage Hotel here in London. It held fond memories for him, and especially of his grandparents, Philip and Esther Falconer. Often his grandfather had taken him there for lunch, and his eighteenth birthday party had been held there. By God, thirty-one years ago, he thought, and smiled to himself. The years had flown; so much had happened in his life.

He was feeling very proud of his sister today. Rossi had done a wonderful job with the publicity campaign for the jewellery auction, and those photographs she had shown him yesterday were quite extraordinary.

He knew the auction would go well, and the money he made would keep Malvern's afloat. For many years the company had grown; now that times were difficult, he was content to put some of his own funds in to keep his life's work going.

Now Rossi was about to present him with another idea, a real moneymaker, she had said last night. But she wouldn't tell him what that was. He was burning with curiosity.

As he went into the hotel lobby, he saw her there, standing with Keller. He knew he was about to find out what she had been keeping up her sleeve.

Once they had all greeted each other, Rossi said, 'Come along, James. Let me show you something.' As she spoke, she led James and Keller over to the door of the private room used for dinners, luncheons and events.

Once they were inside, James noticed at once that much of the furniture, mostly a dining table and chairs, had been moved to one end of the room. Turning to his sister, he asked, 'So, what's the moneymaker you envision here?'

Rossi gave him a huge smile, and said, 'A shop.'

James burst out laughing, and then managed to say, 'I guess being a shopkeeper is in our blood! Taking after our great-grandfather in Kent.'

Rossi also laughed, and Keller said, 'But one thing is for certain. You have captive shoppers right here in the hotel. Brilliant.'

'Of course we do,' Rossi asserted. 'And before you ask me, James, there are several really nice suites on other floors of the hotel that can become rooms for private dinners and events. I can show them to you later.'

'What kind of shop do you plan on having in here?' James asked, glancing around, trying to visualize it, aware there was a lot of space.

'Two sides, with a counter in the middle, and a cash register there. One side for ladies and one side for men. But mostly small things – gloves, scarves, socks, ties and cravats, cufflinks, some good costume jewellery. All the items people forget to bring, or suddenly need, which don't take up a lot of room. Because I will need storage space.'

'I get it, and no clothes like suits and dresses?' James said. 'Too bulky.'

'Correct,' she answered.

'Clever idea indeed,' Keller told Rossi. 'You might want to include ladies' hats as well. Many a time Irina has told me she wished she'd brought a hat with her when we've been out and about.'

'Thank you, Peter. That's a good idea. I want to add small bags, evening purses, and possibly some shoes. I think I'll do well.' As she finished, she gazed at her brother, and asked, 'Can I do it? Do I have your approval?'

'Naturally you do, and I think, once again, you've had a brainwave that can become a great asset to Malvern's. I believe we should consider a shop in the other Bettrage hotels as well, Rossi. And bravo, darling.'

When James arrived home, Brompton gave him a letter, which had been pushed through the letterbox. After thanking the butler, he went into the library and sat down at his desk. Opening the envelope, he found a note from Annabel explaining she would arrive a little earlier and Professor Harcourt would be about fifteen minutes late.

Smiling to himself, he put the note in his desk drawer and rang for Brompton, who arrived within moments.

Glancing at the clock on the mantelpiece, James said, 'Ask Cook to give me lunch at twelve fifteen, please. Something simple like a fish cake or an omelette, Brompton. I want to be finished by one o'clock.'

'Right away, sir,' the butler replied, and hurried off.

Falconer sat back in his chair, staring up at the ceiling, thinking about Lady Annabel. She hadn't been her normal self lately, somewhat quiet, subdued; even rather sad. And in Kent she had been polite but distant.

Her note told him she would arrive half an hour earlier than the art historian, in order to be alone with him. She had something on her mind. And so did he, in point of fact.

Rossi had made him think again about a proper relationship with Annabel. His sister had no doubts about his feelings – and Annabel's too, for that matter. She believed they were in love. He knew he would never convince her otherwise.

What Annabel's emotional state was, he did not really know any more. They had not seen much of each other.

Could he risk telling her how he felt? Was it fair to risk their feelings again when he was so much older?

He wished he knew the answer.

After his early lunch, James Falconer went upstairs and changed into his new grey checked suit and refreshed himself in general. He was back at his desk at one o'clock, signing letters, several contracts, and reading the morning's mail.

Finally, at one forty-five, he put the papers and contracts in their folders. He glanced again at the clock. Between now and two o'clock, Lady Annabel would arrive. Of that he was absolutely positive.

FORTY-SIX

As James had anticipated, Lady Annabel Kelsey arrived at exactly two o'clock. The grandfather clock in the corridor was striking as she knocked on the front door.

The moment Brompton showed her into the library, he knew from her expression that she was going to be all business today. She was here to work, certainly not to flirt.

Jumping up from his desk, James went to greet her, taking the hand she had proffered. She gave him a small smile, and said, in a slightly clipped tone, 'I've got a list of things I'm going to need, James, please.' She took a piece of paper out of her bag and read aloud from it. 'A ladder, a strong flashlight and a sharp knife.'

'Well, these things are not a problem, Annabel,' James replied, ringing for Brompton. He gave him the list and asked for them to be brought up to the library immediately.

Turning to Annabel, he went on, 'Won't you sit down for a moment? Can I offer you tea or coffee, perhaps?'

'Oh no, but thanks, James. I will sit until Professor Harcourt arrives.'

Seating herself on the Chesterfield sofa, she said, 'I forgot to ask you from which galleries you bought your paintings. I'm presuming in Paris.' Looking at him intently, she raised an auburn brow.

James Falconer sat down at the other end of the sofa. 'Yes, they *were* bought in Paris. I went to three galleries: Talleyrand, Paradiso and Lejeune. They were all bought before the war, naturally, and in a certain way they're my pride and joy.'

'That's the way I feel about a couple of paintings I own,' Annabel told him. 'You explained that you had them hung throughout the house, so I think I should do a walk around with you before the experts get here.

'Of course, I'll show them to you. But you spoke in the plural. Is someone else coming with Professor Harcourt?'

'I hope so. I asked him to get in touch with a Frenchman I'm acquainted with, as he is, too. Jean-Louis Roboutin, who has spotted more fakes than anyone I know of. He lives in London.'

James nodded. 'Just to set the record straight, Annabel, I've never thought any of my artworks were fake – forgeries. It was only because I was considering selling, and reading your column last week made me think of having them authenticated. You'd written about forgeries suddenly turning up, as no doubt you recall.'

'Yes, that has been happening. Professor Harcourt drew my attention to it. A couple of paintings were bought at Talleyrand and another at Paradiso in Paris. Which is why I'd like to see the art you bought from these two galleries first,' Annabel explained, sounding anxious.

Rising, James walked to a painting on one side of the fireplace, and said, 'This is a lovely Monet, and hanging on the other side is a Cézanne. In the cream sitting room and the small dining room, there are others.'

Annabel got up and went to look at the paintings. 'I can't see anything wrong with these two paintings here,' she said, after staring at them for a good few minutes.

James had joined her, and asked, 'But how can you tell? What are you looking for? Some sort of . . . flaw?'

'It's hard to explain. An art expert like me, the professor and Jean-Louis see something in the paintings, and know it . . . *looks wrong*. That means to us that it's *not right*. This leads us to believe it's a forgery.'

'So only the very experienced art expert can spot this? Not the average buyer?' James asked.

'Exactly,' she answered.

'But I don't understand. What tells you it's *wrong*?' James sounded puzzled and stared at her. 'Can't you explain this *fault* in a better way?'

'No, I can't!' she exclaimed, and then gave him a small, apologetic smile. 'Let's wait and see what the professor and Roboutin have to say.'

When they entered the cream sitting room, Annabel let out a cry that startled James so much he swung around.

'Oh my God!' she said in a joyous voice. 'I can't believe it! You've got a Cassatt and a Morisot!'

She had rushed forward into the room, and was gazing at the two paintings, which hung together on a side wall. When she turned around, he saw her face was flooded with happiness. 'Oh James, these are wonderful Impressionist paintings.'

He came to join her, and said, 'I liked them the moment I saw them. But not together – separately, of course. I bought them at different galleries.'

'Clever of you to hang them together.' She beamed at him. 'Do you know much about the artists?'

'Not really. But obviously you do,' he replied. Wanting to please her, he continued, 'Please tell me about them.' He sounded eager.

'Mary Cassatt and Berthe Morisot knew each other. By 1881

they were good friends. Degas, one of my own special favourites, introduced them. The two women and Degas were part of the Impressionist movement in Paris. So many great artists were at work in those years. Today their paintings are hugely valuable, some even priceless.'

'That I do know and, as you can see, all of my art is Impressionist.' He glanced at her and saw the approving expression on her face. 'You must be an expert, Annabel. So why do we need the two men who will be arriving shortly?'

'I just explained, and you read it in my column, that there have been some great fakes floating around. I am sure your paintings are the genuine thing, but I want authentication for you from other experts.'

'Actually, I meant to ask you earlier, who paints the fakes?' James asked.

'Obviously very talented painters. Brilliant artists. Why do they do it? For the money, of course. Those clever rotters probably make more for a fake painting by a Master than for one of their own works.' Annabel shook her head. 'I loathe forgers.'

There was a moment of silence, and then she confided, 'Art has been the joy of my life, and has helped me to heal when bad things happened to me. I've studied art all my life. I think Rossi probably told you something about that. Anyway, art became my profession. I have my own company, Kelsey Fine Art, which my brother Christian has helped to fund. He's sort of my partner, but I do the art work.'

'I didn't know any of this,' James murmured. 'Although I did know your brother inherited your father's earldom when he died. Are you close? Silly question, since he's involved in your business.'

'Yes, we are good friends. We've seen each other through troubles and problems – life can be sickening.' Annabel stepped towards James and gave him a big bear hug. 'Shall I tell you the secret of life?'

'I would love to know it,' Falconer answered, holding her

away, staring down at her. He had forgotten how spontaneous she was, how unstuffy.

'Never give in, never give up, just keep on going.'

'I want to show you some other paintings,' James said, taking hold of Annabel's arm, leading her out of the cream sitting room.

A look of surprise slid onto her face. 'You have more?' She gazed up at him, and added, 'Are they Impressionists as well?'

'Yes, they are,' he replied, and walked her across the foyer and into the blue-and-white sitting room. 'Come and look at them. Tell me what you think.'

Three framed paintings were lined up together on the long sofa. Annabel knew at once that two were by Cézanne and the third was a Van Gogh.

They stood together, looking at the paintings. Finally, Annabel exclaimed, 'So beautiful! You have great taste in art. Did someone help you to select these?'

James Falconer shook his head. 'These three were a gift to me. A friend left them to me in his Will some months ago. Naturally, I treasure them, because it was such a generous gesture.'

'He liked Cézanne, your friend. That's obvious. Cézanne is a favourite of mine, because I love all the greens and blues he used, and the darker colours. And I like his brushstrokes.' As she moved away, Annabel suddenly thought to ask, 'You did receive the provenance of each painting when you accepted them, didn't you, James?'

'Actually, I didn't, and we couldn't find any documentation. But it's most likely that they were bought at one of the Paris galleries I mentioned earlier.'

A look of dismay crossed Annabel's face. Swiftly, she asked, 'Do you have the provenance of the other Impressionists, the ones you bought? Oh, I do hope so!'

James smiled at her. 'I do. They are in a folder upstairs in my safe. I'm not that daft, you know.'

She threw him a smile. 'You're the cleverest man I know, Mr

Falconer. Anyway, our experts can help us with these three paintings.'

As she followed James into the small dining room, she went on, 'I do pray they're not forgeries.'

'So do I. What does one do if a painting is a fake?' James asked, filled with curiosity.

'In France, it has to be destroyed immediately. Because it could get passed on or sold as the real thing,' she told him. 'The French are very tough about fakes.'

'I see. And how is the painting destroyed?' James wondered out loud, also sitting down.

'It has to be slashed to shreds.' Annabel shook her head. 'I once had to do that, and it was an awful experience.'

'I can imagine it would be. Just one more question: how is it possible for a painter to copy another's work? I don't quite get that.'

'Forgers have lots of tricks. Obviously, they have to have a *copy* of the painting they are about to create. Usually it comes from an art book or a magazine. Then they set to work. First, they have to make the canvas *look* old. Sometimes they soak it in tea, or they buy an old picture and clean it several times until the paint becomes faint. They then work over the old paint. If they dye it with tea, they have to find old nails to attach the canvas to an old stretcher. Endless preparation.'

'My God, it sounds like it!' James shook his head. 'I suppose the forger thinks it's worth all that effort. Oh, and just one other thing: what happens to forgeries in England? Do we have a law like in France?'

'No, we don't,' Annabel answered, and grimaced. 'I for one believe we should have one, though.'

She walked over to the fireplace and looked up at the Van Gogh hanging there. She then glanced at the other walls. Two Chagalls were beautiful additions to the room, and she complimented him for his great taste in art yet again.

Watching her, James said suddenly, 'Can you have supper with me tonight?'

There was a moment's hesitation and, because she missed nothing, Annabel saw disappointment suddenly flicker in those stunning blue eyes.

'I did have another invitation. But I shall cancel it, and so I accept.' She knew from the smile on his face that she had made him happy, and she was glad.

There was a knock on the door, and Brompton came in. 'Mr Roboutin and another gentleman have arrived, sir.'

'Show them in, Brompton,' James replied. As the door closed, he glanced at Annabel. 'I hope you have all your questions ready.'

'I do.'

FORTY-SEVEN

'I think we should meet them in the hall,' Annabel exclaimed, hurrying to the door. 'So that we can give them a proper tour of the rooms.'

James nodded and followed her out. Once introductions had been made, she took charge.

'I think it's a good idea to start our viewing of the paintings in Mr Falconer's library, and move from room to room, Professor Harcourt, Mr Roboutin.' She looked at the two art experts, and added, 'But before we start, I want you to know that Mr Falconer has the provenance for the paintings we are about to look at, showing the lines of ownership before he bought them.'

Roboutin said, 'You told us you felt sure that he would have, Lady Annabel, and that's why we agreed to come to view the collection.' His English was perfect, and he had only the slightest accent. He gave her a warm smile.

The professor interjected, 'Provenance is vitally important, as you're aware, Your Ladyship. We also pay particular attention to the galleries where the art is purchased.'

'Mr Falconer bought all his paintings at three galleries in Paris: the Talleyrand, Paradiso and Lejeune.'

Roboutin said, 'Those galleries have sold fakes, unfortunately – albeit unknowingly.'

'Only too true,' James remarked. 'But let's not forget that other galleries have also been fooled, not to mention numerous museums, including the Louvre. What about the many experts who have not recognized forgeries, as well as well-known curators in London and Paris? I've come to the conclusion that the art world is a dangerous place.' These last few words were said with laughter. 'But I'm in it now, and not too worried about my safety.' James chuckled again.

The professor said, 'You've hit the nail on the head, Falconer, and yet we all love art, enjoy what we do.'

'We certainly do!' Annabel said swiftly, taking control. 'Let's go to the library first.' She led the way across the hall, walking quickly, her heels clicking against the marble floor. It was a sound James loved to hear.

In the library, she pointed out the Monet and the Cézanne. She then moved on to the cream sitting room, where once more she could not help voicing her admiration for the Mary Cassatt and Berthe Morisot. The professor and Roboutin were in agreement, and were also impressed with another Cézanne, gazing at it for several minutes.

All in all, the walk around was a success. When they returned to the library, Annabel asked if they would like to view any of the paintings more closely.

'If it's not too difficult, I think we should take several paintings down. Not that I see any problems,' Roboutin said.

'May we have a look at the provenances, please, Lady Annabel?' the professor asked.

'Of course.' She looked at Falconer. 'I believe you have the provenances in your safe, James.'

'I do, and the bills of sale. I'll go and get them.'

She smiled at him as he rose and left the room.

Turning to the two experts, she remarked, 'It's very hard to explain about fakes, how these forgeries are created. The average person doesn't know about the feeling *we* get when we look at a painting, and how we think almost immediately that it's *wrong*, and therefore *not right*.'

'It's instinctive,' Roboutin murmured. 'Coupled with our knowledge, our education in art, and our understanding of a famous painter's methods – brushstrokes, the angle of a human body, use of colour, and so much more. Like you, Your Ladyship, I have such a loathing for these forgers. *Thieves*. That's the only word to describe them – stealing a Master's work, his talent, his inspiration.

Roboutin shook his head. 'I become angry, feel murderous, I must admit, when I think about it.'

Annabel said, 'I understand. I share the same feelings. But fakes have been around for hundreds of years, you know . . .' She broke off when James entered the library with a bunch of folders. He handed them to the professor and went and stood in front of the fire.

As the two experts read the contents of the folders, Annabel moved closer to the fireplace and sat down on the Chesterfield. She said quietly, 'I shall ask which paintings they would like to examine. Perhaps Brompton can help to get them down.'

Falconer gave her a smile. 'I can do that easily enough. Don't worry about that. I'm not that ancient!'

By four thirty the professor and Roboutin had finished examining the paintings. They were satisfied that all were genuine, and Roboutin said that the provenances were proof anyway that they were the real thing. He added that he would send a letter to that effect tomorrow.

James thanked them profusely, and Annabel also expressed her gratitude to both men before Brompton showed them out.

Turning to James, she said, 'I think they were efficient and did a thorough job.'

Falconer nodded. 'Shall we have a bit of bubbly to celebrate?'

'What are we celebrating?'

'The fact that I wasn't duped, and that all my paintings are the genuine thing.'

'Well, why not?'

'Going for the champagne,' he called out over his shoulder.

As Falconer hurried out of the library, she sat down on the Chesterfield and let out a sigh of relief.

Annabel leaned back and closed her eyes, recalling the moment when Roboutin had let his eyes linger on several paintings for what seemed like ages.

She suddenly felt tired, and the old, familiar sadness flooded through her. She didn't understand why. She didn't understand why James had more or less shut her out.

He was oddly remote these days, and even though he had asked her to supper tonight, she was convinced his detached attitude wouldn't change. She sighed again. She had always been unlucky with the men she fell for.

Quite suddenly, she made a decision. She had helped him out today, and that was that. From now on, she would concentrate on her art company, build it up. She had learned long ago that she must rely on herself. So be it. She would move on, be more ambitious, and take comfort in her child. After all, James Falconer was a grown man and could look after himself.

The sound of James coming back into the library made Annabel sit up straighter. Glancing across at her, he remarked, 'I can ask Brompton to bring us tea sandwiches if you wish.'

'I'm not hungry, but thank you anyway.' Rising, she joined him at the table where he had put the ice bucket containing the champagne bottle.

As he opened it, he said, 'This is Dom Pérignon. I thought it the best one to toast the best with.'

'Oh, are we toasting the two experts then?'

'No, no, don't be silly. We're toasting you, Annabel.'

'Now you're being silly.'

'I am very grateful to you, and you know that.'

Once the bottle was opened, he half smiled at her. 'I believe I need two glasses,' he muttered, and left the room.

She smiled inwardly, knowing he was embarrassed. He was such a proud man, hated to make mistakes, even if they were small and unimportant.

He came striding back in, holding two flutes. He immediately filled them with the most expensive champagne there was.

Clicking his flute of champagne against hers, he said, 'To you, Annabel, the best art historian in the business.'

'And to you, James, and your wonderful talent for picking great art.'

He laughed. 'I didn't do so badly, and I'm excited about the newest Impressionist paintings in my collection. It was so generous of my friend to leave them to me.'

'Damn!' Annabel exclaimed, staring at him.

'What is it?'

'I should have asked Roboutin and the professor to look at those paintings you inherited. How could I have forgotten? I'm stupid.'

'No, you're not. You were very engaged with them, and I forgot about those paintings, too.'

'Who left them to you? Oh, sorry, is that too personal a question?'

'Not at all. It was an old friend and business associate, Richard Marsden. We bonded over our love of art and also did a lot of business together. He was a bachelor, with no siblings, but there is a cousin, I believe. His solicitor said Richard's art collection was mostly left to the cousin. But that Richard had chosen three of his favourites to leave to me because he knew I would treasure them.'

'What a lovely gesture, James. Come, let's go and have a look at them. I know they're in the blue-and-white sitting room.'

'Yes, they are. I'll bring the flashlight.'

The two of them left the library, holding their glasses of champagne, and crossed the foyer.

In the blue-and-white sitting room, Annabel made a beeline for the paintings lined up on a sofa.

The last of the sunlight filled the room, but James turned on the electric lights anyway. They needed the flashlight to examine the backs of the paintings and the stretchers, which Annabel had explained were important and told their own story.

After staring at the three paintings for a few minutes, Annabel placed her glass of champagne on a nearby side table. Then she went to the sofa, took one of the paintings and put it in a chair. She did the same with a second one.

Left with the single painting, she stared at it for a long time. She examined the back, using the flashlight. After gazing at the painting for another few minutes, she let out a groan.

'What's the matter?' James asked, sounding worried, noticing the look of surprise on her face.

'It's *wrong*,' she said quietly.

FORTY-EIGHT

James Falconer knew at once why Annabel looked chalk-white and worried. The painting was a forgery.

Taking hold of her arm, he led her to a chair and sat down next to her. She leaned back, then stared at him. 'I'm so sorry, but your friend, Richard Marsden, was sold a forgery. A good one, yes, but still not the real thing.'

'I agree, obviously, but he was such an expert and a big collector . . . I hope his other paintings are not fakes . . .' James broke off and pursed his lips. 'I also hope his cousin hasn't inherited a lot of phony paintings. Oh, do you think we should inform the cousin about these?'

'Let's do a bit of research first,' Annabel said. 'I'll make a few tests on all three, and I think we should get Roboutin to come back – tomorrow, if he possibly can. I need another opinion to prove I'm right.'

'Let's do that. And what do you mean by *tests*?'

'I'll do them shortly. I need a few moments to recover. I must say I am shocked about this, mostly because your friend was so knowledgeable about art, and especially Impressionists and Post-Impressionists.'

'I suppose we're dealing with paintings by an extremely talented painter who is a forger.'

'Absolutely, and one who knows all the tricks of the trade.' As she spoke, she took the frame off the painting, and went on, 'This is a Cézanne; he has always been relatively easy to copy. Come and see it close up.'

Falconer moved nearer to the painting on the sofa and looked at it. 'Why do you say he's easy to copy?'

'Because he has done many paintings of woods and trees, nude women bathing outdoors, and woodland scenes in general. But I just spotted something at once. The dark colours that Cézanne uses are not all that *deep* in tone in this painting. I'm going to do a test. If you'll ask Brompton to bring me a glass of water, a white table napkin and a pair of pliers, please.'

'Right away.' James hurried out and was back in a few minutes. He placed the items on a small table. 'Now what?'

'I'm going to wet one corner of this Cézanne. Then we wait for a while. If the paint runs, then the paint is definitely *new*. If it doesn't run, then it's the real thing, because *old* paint won't run. Another thing we'll do is bring one of your real Cézannes from the room next door and compare them. By that I mean, we'll put them side by side and look for the differences between your Cézanne with a provenance and this one here on the sofa, which I think is not real.'

'You certainly are a great art expert,' Falconer said, throwing Annabel an admiring glance. 'I'm most impressed by what you know.'

Annabel merely smiled and got to work. Once she had finished, they left the room.

An hour later, the two of them returned to examine the probable forgery. Annabel looked at the corner she had dabbed with water, and exclaimed, 'The paint has run, so it *is* new paint. No doubt about that. Now, stand back, James, and regard the two Cézannes. Can you see the differences?'

'I can. The real one that I took off the wall in the other room is altogether much darker – the blacks, greens and blues in particular. The shapes of the trees are different, and *bold*. The forgery is not as . . . *strong*. That's the best word I can use. So, Richard left me a fake,' he finished, shrugged and shook his head.

'*Three fakes*,' Annabel corrected him. 'Because I'm sure the other two are fakes as well, created by the same forger. The work is the same quality.'

'Aren't you going to test them?'

'Not now, maybe later. But I bet they are *wrong*.'

The following morning, Roboutin arrived on time at eleven o'clock, half an hour after Annabel had returned to Falconer's house.

The Frenchman was very dismayed when Annabel showed him the Cézanne she had tested with water. He examined it at length and agreed with her. It was indeed a forgery.

'Let us now take apart the other two paintings that Mr Falconer inherited,' Roboutin said. 'Although they are so similar in many ways, I think they have been painted by the same artist. A clever forger at that.'

'So do I,' Annabel agreed. 'I also feel sure that Mr Marsden, who gave them to Mr Falconer – gifted them in his Will – had no idea they were not genuine. I think he, too, was fooled, don't you?'

Roboutin nodded. '*Ah oui*.' He began to remove the frame, and Annabel tackled the third painting. They then shared the pliers to remove the canvasses from the stretchers. 'Old nails!'

Roboutin exclaimed, glancing at Annabel when he handed her the pliers. After working on the nails for a few seconds, she nodded. 'These are old, too. So now let's test the paintings with the water.'

As she looked again at the Van Gogh, she couldn't help thinking what a clever fellow had painted this work. Or perhaps a woman? Whoever it was, the person knew Van Gogh's brush-strokes and methods. It was an extraordinary copy.

While the two art experts worked in the blue-and-white sitting room, James Falconer had been standing in front of the fireplace, warming his legs, observing them.

Finally, he spoke. 'So I've got three fakes. What shall I do with them? Put them back in the attic?'

'No! No!' Annabel cried. 'They should be *destroyed*. We don't have the same law as they do in France, but they have to be shredded.'

'By shredding, do you mean slashed?' James asked, gaping at Annabel, looking shocked.

'I do. They must be rendered unusable. Forgeries can't be left hanging on walls or hidden in attics. Because someone, one day, who doesn't know they're forgeries, might sell them.' She threw a warning look at Falconer. 'Like an heir, for instance. *They must be destroyed.*'

'We should commence,' Roboutin murmured. He glanced around, and said, 'I don't see a knife.'

Falconer walked across the room, explaining, 'I think we need three carving knives from the kitchen. We shall each slash a painting.'

A few minutes later, when James returned, each of them picked up a canvas and began to slash a painting.

Both Falconer and Lady Annabel looked at one another and flinched as their knives ripped into the canvasses. But in the end they had done a good job. They slashed their canvasses until they were in ribbons.

Only Roboutin looked unconcerned, but then he had obviously dealt with forgeries before. Slashing a piece of art was more than likely a common occurrence for him. For Falconer and Annabel, it was a difficult task, despite knowing the truth. James felt more glad than ever that it was jewellery he was selling to help Malvern's.

FORTY-NINE

They are all here, James Falconer thought, glancing around the room at the Bettrage Hotel. All my Falconers. My clan.

A broad smile settled on his face. He caught Rossi's eye and winked at her.

A moment later they were hugging each other. He then held her away and said, 'Thank you for giving me a birthday party, yet again. You always spoil me.'

'You deserve it. Look what you've done for all of us over the years. You've stepped into the breach whenever one of us has needed you, needed help.'

'You're of my ilk,' he murmured, and squeezed her arm. 'I see a few more familiar faces, the chief inspector, Jack Stead, and—'

'The Lady Annabel,' Rossi cut across him. 'Be nice to her, James. She's so sweet and caring.' Rossi then added swiftly, 'And I am right that she's in love with you.'

James was silent for a moment, before he said, 'I'm not sure about that. She's been somewhat cold lately – remote, distant, not so friendly.'

'Don't take my word for it. Go and ask Lady Jane and Lord Reggie, standing over there with Eddie. They are *positive* about her emotional involvement with you, Jimmy lad.'

He laughed, as he always did when she called him that. 'I'm not your Jimmy lad any more. I'm James Lionel Falconer, and I'm forty-nine today. I'm too old for her.'

'Not true. Here comes your daughter, James, so ask her what *she* thinks,' Rossi suggested.

When his eyes rested on Leonie, now drawing closer, his face filled with love for her. What a blessing she was. He was thrilled she was part of his life now.

A moment later, she was in his arms, and he was hugging her tightly.

'Happy Birthday, Father,' she said, smiling up at him. 'And many more to come.' Leonie looked beautiful now, much less strained. Her hair was newly cut by one of the top coiffeurs in London, and her dress the new, shorter length, made from a coral-coloured chiffon.

'Thank you, sweetheart.'

Rossi said in a low voice, 'Tell him what *you* think about Annabel, please. Convince him.'

Leonie whispered to James, 'The Lady Annabel is crazy about you, Father, and you should marry her.'

James stared at his daughter. 'This is a plot. You're all plotting my marriage—'

'And why not?' Rossi interjected. 'Stop wasting time, James. Bring Annabel back into your life. *Now.*'

He sighed. 'If only I knew how, Rossi. I did push her away, distanced myself, because I thought I was too old for her. Are you suggesting I was wrong?' There was a puzzled look on his face.

'Yes, you *were* wrong. It doesn't matter.'

'But when I age, then the gap will matter. I'll be an old man.'

Leonie burst out laughing, stepped back and stood staring at James Falconer.

After a moment studying him, she said, 'What I see is a tall, slender, impossibly handsome man in the prime of his life. A man who won't grow old in the usual way. You'll always be a handsome devil, Father. Anyway, Annabel *is* head over heels in love with you. But you've made her sad lately. *She* told me that. All she wants is to be with you for the rest of her life. She is convinced you are as smitten with her now as on the day you first met.' Leonie paused. 'So she is puzzled by your behaviour, and so am I, to tell you the truth.'

James was silent.

Rossi said, 'James, you are the most truthful person I know, and you always have been. So, are you still smitten with Annabel or not?'

A long sigh escaped James as he nodded.

'That's not enough. A nod won't do,' Rossi exclaimed. 'I want a proper answer.'

After a moment, Falconer said, 'Yes, I am still smitten with Annabel. I feel the same as she does.'

'Then make your move,' Leonie said impatiently. 'As soon as possible.'

'I'm not sure how to go about it,' James murmured. 'It's been months.'

Both women looked at each other and began to laugh. Finally, Rossi spoke first, laughter still echoing in her voice.

'Be your old self. You have loads of natural charm. You exude the kind of magnetism that pulls people to you. That's who you are. And always have been. You dominate a room when you're in it.'

'Mostly, push that age idiocy away from you, Father. Go and look in a mirror, and then come back here and do your stuff.' Leonie eyed him objectively for a second time that night.

'There you stand, drop-dead gorgeous in your impeccable dinner jacket. You could have any woman in this room if you merely smiled at them. They'd fall at your feet.'

'You're exaggerating!' he exclaimed, although he did laugh.

'No, I am not.' His daughter grinned at him. '*I* notice how women look at you all the time, wherever we are, and especially this evening. You're the kind of man that women will do anything to be with. They'd commit all kinds of indiscretions to be in *your* arms. Even cheat on their husbands.'

'My God, that's one hell of a statement!' Falconer exclaimed, obviously startled by this comment.

'It's true,' Rossi said. 'So go on, go out there into the crowd and work your magic.'

'And also look for Annabel,' Leonie instructed him. 'Seek her out.'

'I will,' he said, and paused suddenly.

Walking towards him was a posse of his men friends, led by Eddie, his brother.

'Here come your gang,' Rossi remarked, sounding annoyed. 'Don't let them deter you. Find Annabel.'

The women disappeared as his male pals were about to surround him.

Alongside Eddie were William Venables, Peter Keller, Jack Stead, Chief Inspector Roger Crawford, and Lord Reggie. Lord Reggie handed James a flute of champagne, and said, 'Here's to you, James. Happy birthday!'

As he spoke, the others joined in, and they all clinked glasses. They were full of merriment and good cheer.

'I'm so glad you could all make it.' James grinned at them. 'As usual, my sister has pulled out all the stops. Aside from supper, there'll be dancing later to a quartet. She thinks of everything.'

'We've all got our dancing shoes on,' Lord Reggie said. 'And so I hope you have too. First dance, as the birthday boy, is no doubt with the beautiful Lady Annabel.'

'But of course,' James answered, noting they were probably all in on it – a conspiracy, no doubt. But he was amused.

FIFTY

After chatting together for a while, James explained he ought to mingle with the other guests. And so he excused himself, and limped into the crowd, scanning the room, happy to see so many familiar faces.

He finally spotted Annabel talking to Lady Jane and Irina Keller. She was dressed as fashionably as ever, in a modern silk gown that was a steel colour, pearls at her neck. He slipped past Rossi and Natalie to reach her.

After greeting them all, he focused on Annabel, smiling at her. 'Can I steal you away for a few minutes?' he asked, his vivid blue eyes focused entirely on her.

If she was surprised, she did not show it. 'Of course,' she murmured, and raised her glass. 'Happy birthday, James.'

The other women did the same. He thanked them, then took hold of Annabel's arm and gently guided her away.

'Where are we going?' she asked quietly.

'I don't know, but I need a few moments alone,' he told her. 'I have to speak to you privately.'

'Oh, I see.' She glanced at him and added, 'This room is full, but we could pop out into the hotel lobby.'

'Grand idea,' he answered, and led her towards the door.

Outside the party room, James noticed an empty corner in the lobby and, taking hold of her arm again, he guided her over there.

Looking down at her, James said, 'I'm sorry. So very sorry, Annabel.' Sincerity underlined his words.

Gazing up at him, as usual mesmerized by his overwhelming presence, losing herself in those incredibly blue eyes, she could not answer for a moment. Eventually, she murmured, 'Why are you sorry?'

'For making you sad, so unhappy . . .' His sentence was left unfinished when, out of the corner of his eye, he caught sight of the lift. 'Come on. Come with me.' He took her hand and rushed her over to the lift. When they were inside, he pressed the top button. The lift went up.

Annabel, startled now, asked, 'Where are you taking me?'

'To a place where we can have total privacy for a few minutes. Only a few minutes, sweetheart, I promise. I need to say something important to you.'

Annabel was further taken aback when they stepped out of the lift, and she realized they were in a corridor of the hotel. A second later, James took a key out of his pocket and unlocked a door. She found herself being led into a well-decorated suite at the top of the Bettrage Hotel.

Turning to look at him, she asked, 'Is this your suite, James?'

He nodded. 'You know I own the Bettrage?'

Annabel gazed at him. 'You're full of surprises—'

He stopped her words by kissing her on the mouth. She kissed him back, and then he held her away from him, staring into her face.

He said, 'I am sorry I turned away from you, let you go. I'm sorry I made you sad and unhappy. I was being a stupid fool. Please forgive me.'

'Why did you do it? Drop me?' Annabel asked in a cold tone.

'Because I thought I was too old for you. That, when I was an old man, you'd still be so young. I thought it wouldn't work.'

'Age doesn't mean a thing to me!' she cried.

'Are you saying it *will* work? You and me is what I mean. The two of us together?'

'Do you love me, Mr Falconer?'

'Yes, I do. From the first moment I set eyes on you, I loved you with all my heart.'

'And I felt the same way.'

'And now?'

'I am in love with you, James. I will never love any other man as long as I live. You made me yours when we slept together, and I was happier than I'd ever been in my life. No other man has affected me the way you do.'

Against her own volition, tears filled her eyes. She flicked them away with her fingertips. 'You made me understand what true love really meant. You were so kind and loving, so tender with me when we made love. So yes, I do forgive you for letting me go.' She gave him a small smile. 'And we'd better *go*, or they'll send out the cavalry.'

He laughed and drew her close. Against her luxuriant auburn hair, he whispered, 'Can we start all over? Be together again, my darling love?'

There was a moment of silence. Slowly she said, 'Yes, that's what *I* want. *You*. But there are a few conditions. The first one is about tonight. After the party is over, will you bring me up here so I can give you my present?'

'But of course. Though you can give it to me now.'

'No, I can't. It's a unique gift.'

'So what is it?'

'*Myself*. I want us to make love up here on your birthday night and do the same every year on your birthday.'

He smiled. '*Done*. What's the second condition?'

'That you'll not leave me when I'm an old lady and need pushing in a wheelchair.'

'*Done*,' he said, swallowing his laughter. 'What's the third?'

'That you'll be mine and mine alone. You can never be with another woman for the rest of your life. Unless I die, of course.'

'Don't be silly. You're not going to die. You're only thirty-two. And yes, I will be faithful to you. So it's a *done deal*!'

She smiled and kissed him. 'Just so you know, I forgive you absolutely.'

'I've a question for you, Lady Annabel.'

'So ask it and then we must go back to your birthday party, or people will talk.' She started to cross the room.

'Oh, let them talk. Who cares?'

As she walked across the floor, he caught up with her and swung her around to face him. His gaze was intense and serious, as he said softly, 'Will you marry me, Annabel?'

Her heart leaped and she gasped. She paused for a moment, then looked up with a smile. 'Yes, I will, Mr Falconer. The sooner the better, but you know I come with a little bundle.'

'I do. And I love Adrian, too. We'll be a happy family, the three of us. Just you wait and see.'

In the lift going down to the birthday party, James drew Annabel closer, and said, 'I meant it when I said I would be faithful to you. I've never been a philanderer, or played around with two or three women – at the same time, I mean.'

She looked up into those striking eyes, bluer than ever it seemed to her. 'I know that,' she murmured. 'You have a good reputation in every way.'

James smiled at her. 'So we have made a deal. You're stuck with me, you know. I'm not going anywhere. Ever.'

'You'd better not,' she shot back. Touching his cheek, she

whispered, 'I can't wait to go back to your suite after dinner, to be with you.'

'Likewise,' he answered. As the lift door opened, they stepped out into the lobby.

FIFTY-ONE

Rossi, who had been watching the door, wondering where they had gone, was relieved when her brother and Annabel returned.

She saw at once a huge smile on Annabel's face, and that light-hearted sparkle was again in her eyes.

As for James, he looked elated, somewhat like the cat that had swallowed the cream. Very pleased with himself, she decided.

Smiling inwardly, she glided across the floor to greet them. 'I thought you'd got lost,' she exclaimed. 'Wherever did you go?'

'Sorry to disappear for a moment,' James said smoothly. 'We needed a private word together. But all is good between us, Rossi darling. I apologized to Annabel for shutting her out. I was a fool. But she's forgiven me, and we are together again.'

'I'm glad to hear this. You two are ideal for each other. Now, come and sit down. Dinner is about to be served.'

James nodded and, laughing, he took hold of Annabel's hand, crossing the room to the table. He found his place card. He was happy to see that Annabel was to sit on one side of him and Lady Jane on the other. After pulling out the chairs for Annabel and Lady Jane, he stood waiting until all the other guests were seated. Only then did he sit down himself.

Glancing around the table, he was filled with happiness to see all those familiar, well-loved faces of the Falconer clan: Eddie, his beloved brother, as well as his closest male friends and their wives. Rossi had missed no one out.

After the first course of crab salad was served, it was Rossi who tapped her wine glass with a knife. Everyone stopped talking and looked at her as she stood up.

'I want to welcome you all. You are present tonight because my brother James truly wanted you with him on his birthday. And in this particular room in the Bettrage Hotel. Thirty-one years ago, he celebrated his eighteenth birthday in this very room at a party given for him by our grandparents, Philip and Esther Falconer. He's never forgotten that special celebration, and he wants tonight to be just as joyous. Will you all please raise your glasses and wish James the happiest of birthdays?'

Rossi smiled at her brother as she lifted her flute of champagne, as did everyone else. In unison, they all cried, 'Happy Birthday, James!'

He beamed at his family and friends, thanked them profusely for coming, and mildly chastised them for bringing gifts. He then thanked them for doing so, laughter in his voice.

He turned to look down the table at Eddie, and then at Rossi and blew her a kiss, raised his glass. 'Here's to you, darling sister, for being who you are.'

Everyone was chatting and enjoying themselves, as different courses were served. After the crab came roast leg of lamb with mint sauce, thinly sliced, with fresh peas, roasted potatoes and carrots. Following that, a green salad with slices of Brie cheese was served. Then a pause before the birthday cake was to be brought in later.

It was during this period that each one of James's male friends got up to toast him. Some praised him, others boldly teased him, but it was touching, funny, hilarious at times, and he enjoyed every second, knowing so much of it was in jest, as well as born of loving friendship.

Eventually, the birthday cake was wheeled in on a trolley. It was large, two-tiered, and covered in white icing sugar with touches of blue.

Much to his amazement, the chef had managed to get forty-nine small white candles on the top layer.

'Goodness me!' James exclaimed. 'What a marvellous cake!'

'And you've got to cut it, Jimmy lad,' his brother Eddie exclaimed. 'Glancing at the waiter, he asked, 'Could you give the knife to Mr Falconer, please, Gervais?'

Gervais, swallowing a smile, nodded. He wheeled the trolley down the room, and said, 'Happy Birthday, sir. I suggest you blow out the candles first before you cut it.'

The entire gathering laughed, and especially so when James kept blowing at the candles until eventually they were all dead. Still standing, he stared at the cake, worriedly.

'I'm not quite sure how to cut this cake,' James muttered, looking at Lady Jane, who obviously wanted to help.

She smiled and nodded, then stood up next to him. 'It's not so hard, James,' she said. Taking hold of his hand holding the knife, she guided it to the top layer and pushed the knife into it. 'Now, cut the other side and you'll have a piece to go on a plate.'

During the entire meal, Annabel had stroked his leg, something she had often done. James liked the feel of her hand running up from his knee along his thigh. In a sense, it was comforting, and no one else could see what she was doing. He enjoyed it.

Tonight it was slightly different for him; his reaction was sexual. She was arousing him, but obviously unaware of this.

It all had to do with him, and the acknowledgement he had made to himself earlier. And then to her. He wanted her in his life for the rest of the days he had left on this planet.

He was in love with her, and constantly filled with a desire to make love to her.

At times, it was overpowering, and when that happened, he had plunged into his work. Lost himself in his business. Malvern's was his life blood and always would be.

Suddenly, he thought of the auction. It was in July. Today it was 27 May. A Tuesday.

He had only until the end of the month to pull out jewellery he wanted to keep. He did need to select some of the pieces for Rossi, for Eddie's wife Christina, and, of course, for Annabel. He would speak to Rossi later and visit the bank tomorrow.

He had bought that jewellery for Alexis and he understood which jewels would best suit each of the three women he had chosen.

Alexis: she had been his great love, the love of his life. He had mourned her for years. But he had now fallen in love again. It was not quite the same, but, nonetheless, it was real.

Lady Annabel Kelsey was just that, a true lady, which pleased him. He loathed loud, pushy, abrasive women. She was perfect for him.

He smiled suddenly. Annabel could be forward sexually, easily displayed what she wanted from him, yet that was different, part of her vivacious charm. He was always willing to please her. What man wouldn't be? She was lovely.

Which was why, in a few minutes, when the dinner came to an end, he would bid goodnight to everyone. Then he would take her up to the suite he owned at the top of the hotel. She had asked again for this rendezvous when he had danced with her a few moments ago. No, she had begged for it, leaving nothing to his imagination.

He had agreed that she would stand next to him as he bade his guests farewell. She apparently did not care what people made of this – though he did, to a certain extent, wishing to protect her reputation.

Her answer to that had been that he was escorting her to her home in Grosvenor Square, and he could make that known quite easily to all those leaving.

James Falconer stood in the middle of the sitting room in the suite on the top floor of the Bettrage Hotel.

Annabel was facing him, unable to speak or move. She was totally transfixed by him at this moment – hypnotized, almost.

He was the most elegant man she had ever seen. Because he was so tall and slender, the black evening dress suit hung on him perfectly. Savile Row, no doubt, she thought, her gaze unwavering. His pristine white shirt was finely pleated, fastened with sapphire studs. She noticed his cufflinks matched and were made of sapphires and gold.

Falconer was looking at her quizzically. She felt weak in the knees, totally enthralled by his potent masculinity. He was his own man, and this showed in his powerful presence and self-assurance. He knew exactly who he was.

Finally, he spoke. 'You said you wanted to come up to my suite. So here we are. Just staring at each other. What's this about?'

'I'm admiring you,' she murmured, at a loss as to what to say.

He smiled. 'I can say the same thing, sweetheart.'

Taking charge of the situation, James stepped forward and drew her into his arms, held her close, stroking her hair. When he released her, he gave her a serious look, and said, 'Listen, I didn't anticipate this, being alone with you, Annabel. So I'm not prepared. I don't have any protection with me. We're treading on dangerous ground without that.'

'We can be careful, James.'

He sighed. 'What you mean is that *I* must be careful. That's tough when I'm with you.' He half smiled, and added, 'You know I get carried away – how passionate I become.'

'Please, James, I want you so much.' She stared at him. 'Or don't I look bed-worthy tonight?'

He burst out laughing. 'I've never heard that word before. Of course you do. You're beautiful and very desirable, my Annabel.'

'Am I *yours*?' she asked.

'You betcha! And don't ever forget it.'

Taking hold of her hand, he led her into the bedroom, as beautifully decorated as the sitting room. As she glanced around, she said, 'Why do you have this suite?'

'For out-of-town business associates to use,' he answered, turning to look at her, frowning, obviously surprised by her question.

'Have you ever brought a—'

'No,' he said interrupting her in a somewhat stern voice. 'I've never brought another woman up here.' He swung around, took off his jacket, and laid it neatly on a chair, ignoring her.

Annabel knew she had annoyed him. How stupid she was to ask those questions. The past didn't matter. Unsure of what to say now, she sat down in a chair and took off her shoes, continuing to watch him undress.

He stepped out of his shoes, dropped his braces to the side and took off his evening tie. Very carefully, he pulled out the sapphire studs on the front of his shirt and laid them on a nearby table. He then placed the cufflinks next to them.

Now wearing only his shirt, he smiled at her, and said, 'Here

I am, all yours, darling. So don't you think you should get undressed?'

'Yes, yes, of course. I'm sorry, I just got carried away, watching you,' she answered, realizing he was in a good mood now.

He smiled again and sat on the bed, turning down the lamp as Annabel went into the bathroom.

Within seconds, she returned. He had taken off his shirt and now lay on the bed, where she joined him. Putting his arms around her, he said, 'I proposed to you tonight, and you accepted. We're going to be married.' That endearing smile slipped onto his face once more. 'I think we should get a little practice in, don't you, sweetheart?'

She laughed and drew closer to him. Within moments, they were entwined. Their passion for each other soaring. He was a sensual, virile man, and a caring, experienced lover. He took possession of her with confidence and skill. She clung to him, as aroused and ardent as he was.

FIFTY-TWO

O nce again, James was impressed with the photographs
of the jewellery he had put up for auction. Rossi and
he had picked out ten photographs, and he would decide
to whom he would gift some of the pieces this week.

Aside from Rossi and Eddie's wife Christina, he wanted to
give Annabel something special as well. He had also added
Natalie, once his assistant, to the list, along with Irina and Peter
Keller. Irina was a devoted and loyal friend, and Peter had been
his business partner for years.

He had a good eye for jewels, and swiftly knew which
particular item would work well for each of the recipients.

Opening the top drawer of his desk, he placed the folder
inside. He then began to look at the many papers on his desk.

Suddenly, the door flew open, and Keller hurried in, a frantic
look on his face. 'You've got to come now, Falconer! At once.
Annabel and Irina have been in an accident—'

'My God, what happened to them?' James asked, jumping to
his feet, crossing the room, a rush of anxiety flowing through
his body.

'They got knocked down by a motorcar in Piccadilly. Come on, let's go!'

The two men were outside in seconds. Peter Keller hailed a cab. As James got in after him, he said, 'Which hospital?'

'King's,' Keller replied, and repeated this to the cab driver.

'Oh God, no! That means head injuries!' James exclaimed, his chest tightening. Fear for Annabel and Irina ran through him, and he filled up with tension and anxiety.

Annabel, my darling, Annabel, Falconer thought. I hope to God she's not badly hurt. His mind filled with myriad thoughts once again, as he tried to imagine her injuries. Suddenly, nothing was clearer than how much she meant to him. He couldn't lose her now. Calming himself at last, he said to Keller, 'How did you find out about Irina and Annabel?'

'The hospital called me here at the office, and I came to get you at once.'

'Didn't they give you any details?'

'Not really. But they're both stable. The hospital doctor said that. I was so stunned; I just hung up and came to get you. I should have asked more questions. I'm sorry.'

'You were in shock,' Falconer said. He leaned back against the seat, endeavouring not to imagine the worst.

The hospital's receptionist directed them to the waiting room, explaining she would send the doctor in to see them at once. They thanked her.

Keller and Falconer went into the waiting room and sat down in silence. They both were lost in their own thoughts and obviously worried, brimming with concern for the two women in their lives.

Within a few minutes, a white-coated doctor, with a stethoscope around his neck, walked in and closed the door.

Keller and Falconer stood up.

'I'm Doctor Alvin Mattison, gentleman.'

'James Falconer.' James offered his hand.

'Peter Keller,' Peter murmured and did the same.

Once the introductions were over, Doctor Mattison said, 'Both patients are stable and can be released tomorrow. Fortunately, neither of them is as badly injured as we thought at first. Mrs Keller has some severe cuts on her forehead, and her left arm and leg are very bruised, but not broken. Those are her only injuries.'

Keller nodded. 'Thank you, Doctor Mattison.'

The doctor looked at Falconer, who was shaking inside. The doctor explained, 'Lady Annabel fell on her face and on one side; the right side is grazed and bruised. However, there are no cuts. Her right hip is bruised, and quite badly, but not broken. To be honest, they have both been extremely lucky. Their injuries could have been much worse.'

'Does Lady Annabel have any head injuries?' James asked.

'She does not,' the doctor replied. He glanced at Keller, and added, 'And neither does Mrs Keller. Only her forehead is damaged. However, I think it is important that they both remain in hospital until tomorrow, under observation, gentlemen. We need to be sure there are no internal injuries.'

'Do you know what happened, Doctor?' James asked.

'Apparently, Mrs Keller and Lady Annabel were leaving the Ritz Hotel after lunch today. As they crossed Piccadilly, a motorcar, out of control, hit them both. I was told that the driver slewed across that main road, unable to bring the motorcar to a stop. Within ten minutes, the police and an ambulance were on the scene, thank goodness.'

The doctor paused. 'When I said they were lucky, I mean it. The motorcar was a Daimler, a heavy piece of machinery. They could have been killed.'

James Falconer nodded, and asked, 'Can we see them for a few minutes? Are they up to it?'

Keller said, 'Once they return home, they will have to stay in bed, won't they?'

'Absolutely, and for the next couple of weeks they will have to take it easy. So, come with me. I'll take you to your ladies.'

Annabel and Irina were in the emergency ward of King's Hospital, in beds next to each other. They were both conscious and looked pleased to see James and Peter.

Both women were swathed in bandages around their heads. Annabel had a large wad of cotton wool and bandages on the right side of her face. Irina had her forehead covered in a similar way because of the severe cuts. Both women had their arms bandaged as well.

Each man went and sat down next to their loved one. Falconer gently touched Annabel's face, and said, 'I'm so sorry this happened, sweetheart, but thank God you're alive. Are you in great pain?'

'No, just feel sore. James, can you go to my house, please, to see the nanny? Tell her I had to go and see Aunt Mary, whom she knows is not well. Explain I'll be home tomorrow.'

'I will, but you'll arrive home in bandages, won't you?'

'Yes. But I just want to keep things calm today. I don't want Adrian to know anything yet.'

'I understand. Who's living in? The staff, I mean. Nanny obviously, but anyone else?'

'The housekeeper and Cook. He's safe.'

'I shall make a point of seeing him. Adrian's such a lovely little boy. I'll invite him for tea.'

Annabel attempted to smile. 'Thank you, James. You're so good to me.'

He seized both her hands, surprising her. 'I love you, Annabel.'

'And I love you too. But James . . .'

He turned, a question on his face.

'There is something I need to tell you. Not today. But soon.'

FIFTY-THREE

Because James Falconer was an imposing and powerful man, many people were in awe of him. Yet his affability and easy-going manner drew others into his orbit. Once they really knew him, they became his friends for life, and cared about him and his well-being. He was known for being even tempered, rarely displaying anger or raising his voice.

The man who knew him best and genuinely understood him was Peter Keller. They had met when they both worked for Henry Malvern, thirty-odd years ago. The company had been small then. Together they had grown it, made it into the business empire it was today. They still worked side by side and were best friends. They rarely disagreed, and they both knew they had each other's back, would take a bullet if necessary. This gave them a sense of security in the dangerous world beyond their office walls.

On this warm July morning, Keller sat in his office at the Malvern Company, pondering something his wife had said. At once, he had warned her not to repeat this piece of information to anyone. To forget it. She had promised him it was forgotten.

What Irina had said had startled Keller, and he absolutely knew, without a doubt, that if Falconer heard it, he would be upset, angry even. This thought worried him, and so he pushed it to one side for the moment. Later he would try to work out a plan. To bury the information. At least for now. It would come out later, he was certain of that. He cringed at the thought.

This was the wrong week for trouble. Tomorrow the auction was taking place at Bonhams, and expectations were very high.

Rossi had done a fabulous job, and had run a successful publicity campaign. Photographs of the Alexis Malvern Falconer Jewellery Collection had been in every magazine and newspaper, and the auction house was sure of a big turnout.

Keller knew that Falconer was excited by the event and looking forward to it. He had asked Keller to reserve the front row of seats for the Falconer clan, Irina and himself. This he had just done.

A moment later, James Falconer pushed open the door and limped into his office. Keller said, 'You should be using your stick.'

'Oh, it's a bloody nuisance. I'm okay, Keller. It's the humidity today. My legs act up in this weather and when it rains. Anyway, I'd like to give a small supper after the auction tomorrow evening. What do you think?'

'It's a great idea. Are you thinking about having it at the Bettrage? Or somewhere else?'

'The Bettrage. I know Rossi turned that nice private room into a shop, but there are other spaces in the hotel that would work well.'

James sat down in the chair opposite Keller, and continued, 'Let's keep it fairly small. I'll invite Eddie and Christina, and there's you and Irina. I'll ask Annabel if she'll join us. And there's Rossi and Charles.'

'What about William and Natalie? That makes ten. Just right, I'd say. Do you want me to book it?' Keller added.

'Thanks, but I have to go to the Bettrage tonight, so I'll do it then.' He paused. 'How's Irina now? Do you feel comfortable that the accident really was that – an accident?'

'Yes,' Keller replied, nodding. 'Your friend Roger was helpful but the driver was a fool, a young lad back from France last year who had been drinking.'

'Good,' said James. 'I was terribly worried it was linked to the robbery, or even to Rhodes. Thank God our luck is turning at last. I just spoke to Rossi, and expectations about the auction are still on the rise. I hope it's the success we think it will be. The proceeds will ensure the safety of Malvern's for years.'

Lady Annabel Kelsey sat in the lounge area of the Bettrage Hotel, waiting for Falconer to arrive. He had sent his motorcar and driver to pick her up, because he had a late business meeting and couldn't come for her himself.

She felt oddly nervous about seeing him tonight. She pushed those thoughts to one side for the moment, touching her face briefly where her injuries had healed well but left a faint mark.

It had taken her ages to get ready, not liking anything she tried on. In the end, she had chosen a dropped-waist cream satin dress with a flowing jacket. Despite its simplicity, it was glamorous. James would like it, she knew that. Her only jewellery was her emerald ear clips and a Cartier evening watch. She loved the clean lines and shorter styles of the new fashions.

Looking at the watch now, she realized he was late, which was not like him at all. He was the most practical person she knew.

Then suddenly, there he was, standing in the entrance to the lounge area, smiling at her.

She stood up, smiling back, and they met in the middle of the room. He kissed her on the cheek and took hold of her hand.

'Sorry I'm late. Couldn't be helped. I had to sort out a problem. Come on, sweetheart, let's go up to the suite.'

Taken aback, she said, 'I thought we were having supper in the Grill here.'

'It's jam-packed, so I've arranged for dinner to be brought up a little later. We'll have a drink first to celebrate.'

'What are we celebrating?' she asked as he walked her across the foyer to the lift.

'Us. Our engagement.' He threw her his endearing smile, his eyes sparkling. 'And the fact that you're alive and as beautiful as ever; all of those bruises have gone away.'

'That's true, and thank goodness Irina is also back to normal. We were lucky.'

'I'll say!' he murmured, and led her into the lift.

A few seconds later, when they went into the suite, Annabel gasped and stared at him. 'How beautiful the sitting room looks. The flowers, the candles. Oh, James, did you do this for me?'

Falconer laughed. 'No one else, that's for sure. I told the manager to brighten it up, and he did so.' Glancing around, he saw the silver bucket on a table. 'And over there is the champagne.'

After opening the bottle, he filled two flutes and carried them over to the sofa where Annabel was sitting. When he had given her one, he sat opposite her in a chair. He lifted his glass. 'To you, Annabel.'

She smiled. 'And to you, James.'

After a sip or two of the champagne, Annabel said, 'Now that we are engaged, I would like you to meet my brother. Because I've met most of your family, now you should meet mine.'

He stared at her, and then chuckled. 'And what will the earl think? I'm sure he won't like the idea of you messing around with Jimmy, the working-class lad from Camden Town, now will he?'

'First of all, you're no longer Jimmy the lad. You're James

Lionel Falconer, the biggest business tycoon in England. Successful, wealthy, and living in a townhouse in Mayfair. Secondly, I don't care what he thinks. I'm thirty-two years old and a grown woman who can do what she wants. And thirdly, we're not messing around, as you call it.'

'Certainly that's true. What we do in there . . .' He glanced at the bedroom, and finished, 'is magic.'

She smiled at him then adjusted her watch, distracted. 'I'll arrange for him to come for lunch.'

'Yes, do that. Listen, I've something to ask you. I've been thinking a lot about having a house in Kent. Either buying one, if I can find a suitable abode, or building one. Would you like that? Enjoy being with me in the country?'

'I'd go to the ends of the earth with you.'

She said this so seriously, looked pained. He glanced at her swiftly. 'Is there something the matter?'

She shook her head. 'No. But, well, sometimes I worry that you might tire of me, find another woman. After all, there are so many who are after you, none would turn *you* down.'

James was somewhat startled by this statement. He knew she meant every word, and it baffled him. 'I'm not so sure you're right about that. But, in any case, I'm only interested in you. I love you. We're engaged, remember? I'm a one-woman man, Annabel.'

'I think I have to go home.' She stared at him, tears filling her eyes. She half rose then sat down again, tears trickling down her cheeks.

James jumped up and went to sit next to her. 'Whatever is it, sweetheart? Why are you crying?' He had no idea what was going on with her.

Annabel took a deep breath and attempted to steady herself. Finally, she said, 'There's something I must tell you before I leave. Do you remember, I mentioned it after the accident?'

'Why do you keep saying you're leaving?' he demanded.

'Because you won't like what I've got to say.'

'You can say anything you want to me, darling. *I love you.*'

'I-I'm . . . I'm pregnant, James. I'm carrying your child. The doctors at the hospital confirmed it.'

Her eyes were riveted on him as she told him. She saw the sudden paleness of his face, the tension in him. Knowing he had an iron will and was capable of controlling his emotions, she had expected nothing less. He revealed nothing.

Falconer let out a deep sigh and leaned back against the sofa, still silent, but she knew he was trembling.

She said, 'I'm sorry, so very sorry.'

These words made him stiffen, and he sat up straighter. 'Why are you saying *you're* sorry? I'm the one who made you pregnant.' He gazed at her. 'I guess I wasn't careful enough, but then I get carried away with you. I become very passionate in a way I never have before.'

'It's the same with me. I said I was sorry because of Alexis—'

James turned away abruptly and said in a sombre voice, 'That is something I cannot bear to think about. Can you understand?'

'I will never mention it again,' she replied quietly, angry with herself, knowing she had said the wrong thing. The miscarriages had been too much for him to bear, and Alexis had died during childbirth, as had the child.

'Excuse me for a moment,' James said. He suddenly stood and left the room. She watched him go into the bedroom, now worried about their relationship and where it was going after this stupidity on her part.

James went into the bathroom, closed the door and leaned against it, shocked that a few simple words had torn him apart. She hadn't meant any harm. Annabel was innocent of any wrongdoing. He stepped up to the washbasin, took a small towel and wet it. He then placed it on his face. He liked the cold water.

He wet his face again and dried it. He gazed in the mirror. He looked like himself, but somehow he felt different.

It's time to move on, he thought. I must bury the past if I am to have a future. That is an imperative.

Taking a few deep breaths, he turned away from the mirror and straightened up to his full height. He walked back into the sitting room of the suite, completely in control of himself and the situation.

Annabel was sitting on the sofa. He realized she had been crying while he was in the bathroom. Her eyes were red.

He seated himself next to her and put his right arm around her. He drew her close into a tight embrace. 'I'm sorry darling. Since we are going to be married, I think it's time you had this.' As he said those words in a low voice, he took hold of her left hand, put his own in his pocket and pulled out a ring. When he slipped it on her engagement ring finger, he murmured, 'Now it's official.'

Annabel looked down at her hand and drew in her breath when she saw the modern, square-cut emerald ring on her finger. She stared at him, her surprise most apparent. 'It's beautiful, James. Thank you, thank you so much. I didn't expect this.'

'It matches the colour of your eyes, you know. I chose it most carefully. Now, stand up.'

She did so. He also rose, went around her, put a necklace on her and fastened it. 'And if you go to a mirror, you'll see something I also chose for you – only *you* should wear this. It belonged to Alexis. I bought it for her years ago and now it's yours.'

Turning, Annabel gazed at him, and swallowed hard, pushing back her tears.

There was such a warm and loving expression on his face. She was moved beyond all measure. That this man truly loved her was evident.

They sat down again, and he was silent for a few minutes, and so was she.

It was James who spoke first. He said, 'About your pregnancy – how many weeks along are you?'

'About seven.' She paused. 'I understand your fears. But remember, I've already had one child. I'm healthy and I feel very well.' She looked up at him. 'Actually, James, I think you made me pregnant when we first came to this suite. The night of your birthday, the twenty-seventh of May. After everyone else had left.'

He gazed at her, realizing how much he loved this unique young woman. 'I'll be damned,' he exclaimed. 'I made you pregnant on my birthday. What a present!'

The following morning James Falconer got up early. He was bathed, shaved and dressed in less than an hour.

At seven, he was sitting at the table in his breakfast room having scrambled eggs on toast. Once he was finished, he left his house on South Audley Street and walked to his office.

It was another warm day, but there was no humidity. His legs felt better as he strode down Piccadilly. He thought about the news Annabel had given him.

When she had announced she was pregnant last night, he had been taken by surprise, because he had been careful. But not as careful as I thought I was, obviously, he now decided.

Lady Annabel was thrilled. He was a little troubled by this development. Memories of those three miscarriages were still embedded in the back of his mind.

On the other hand, Annabel was only thirty-two, and he had heard Doctor Mattison say on the day of the accident that she had a strong constitution and was a good healer. And, as she had pointed out, she had had one healthy pregnancy already.

Everything would be all right. He had to believe that for his peace of mind. He would be by her side and take care of her when she needed him.

Arriving at the Malvern buildings, he went up to his office, dropped his briefcase on a chair, and went in search of Rossi.

FIFTY-FOUR

Rossi looked up when the door of her office opened and her brother walked in.

Unexpectedly, she saw him objectively for once, realized how imposing he was and how handsome, felt that magnetism he exuded at the same time.

'Don't you look smart!' Rossi exclaimed, smiling at him, a sense of pride in him rising inside. 'Ready for the auction later, I suspect.' He wore a dark-blue suit and a pale-blue tie with a white shirt.

'And good morning to you, my sweetie. Yes, I won't have time to go home to change.' He sat down in a chair in front of her desk, and went on, 'Were the women happy with their necklaces?'

'They were, very much so. Irina loves the rubies, Christina the aquamarines, and Natalie was almost disbelieving when I gave her the sapphires. I'll be wearing the diamond necklace and ear clips tonight. Thank you again, James, for being so generous to us all.'

'I especially wanted you to have the diamond necklace. You must insure it, as well as the ear clips.' He put his hand in his pocket and took out a ring. He leaned over the desk and handed it to her. 'I hope this fits you, Rossi, darling. It's part of the suite. So insure it, too.'

Astonished, Rossi took the large baguette diamond ring and put it on her finger. 'It does fit!' she exclaimed. 'It's beautiful.' She stared down at her hand, admiring the ring she knew he had bought for Alexis long ago. 'I'll treasure it always. Thank you, darling.'

Falconer smiled at her. 'It's because I took your advice and apologized to Annabel that we're together again. All is peaceful.'

'I'm so pleased, especially now she's pregnant.'

Taken aback, Falconer stared at Rossi intently, frowning. 'How do you know that?'

'Irina told me. Oh dear, you look perplexed. Is it supposed to be a secret?' Rossi herself now appeared worried, knowing what a private man he was. He loathed the idea of gossip about him, tittle-tattle, and the like. 'She heard her ask about it at the hospital, after the accident. Annabel was terribly anxious.'

'Let's just say I'd like to keep it in the family. I'll talk to Keller later,' he said evenly.

'Are you thinking of an August wedding?'

'No, September. Annabel wants to plan a *nice* ceremony, as she calls it, and she thinks August is too hot.' He suddenly began to laugh.

Rossi stared at him. 'Why are you laughing now? Do you want to share the reason with me?'

'I will. Annabel told me last night that it's usual in her family to put an announcement in *The Times*. For births, marriages and deaths. So, she is going to ask her brother, the earl, to announce our engagement in *The Times*.'

Rossi smiled. 'And why not? I like that idea.'

The laughter lingered in Falconer's voice, when he answered, 'Just imagine, Jimmy, the working-class lad from Camden Town, marrying into the British aristocracy. It's beyond belief.'

'I don't think it is, James Lionel Falconer,' Rossi replied in a serious tone. 'You are one of the most successful tycoons in Britain, smart, talented and hard working. Not to mention a very nice man.'

'Don't overdo it, darling.'

'I'm not. It's nice to remember your roots, but you moved on and up years ago.' Rossi gazed at him lovingly. 'What time shall we leave for the auction?'

'I thought about two o'clock. I know it doesn't start until four, but I think we ought to check everything. I don't want any slip-ups.'

'I agree. I did what you asked and hired a protection company. They're sending ten men who'll mingle with the attendees. I know Bonhams has guards, because of all the jewellery being *there*, but I want as much security as possible. And I know you do.'

'Good girl; you did the right thing, as always. I don't know what I'd do without you.'

'You will always have me, James.'

'Likewise, Rossi-Prossi.'

She grinned. 'You haven't called me that for years, since I was a child.'

When they arrived at Bonhams, the large auction room was filled with small gold chairs. The podium had been placed on a raised platform at the front of the room. Bright lights were already on.

Rossi nodded as she took in everything, and then said to Falconer, 'The manager is over there, talking to the auctioneer. Shall we go and see them?'

'Absolutely.' His eyes went around the large space. As he assessed the number of chairs, he couldn't help wondering aloud if they would be filled.

'They certainly will,' Rossi reassured him. 'I did a good campaign. I had a lot of press coverage. Also, don't forget there are many foreigners in London – rich Russians, to be precise. We'll sell out, you'll see.'

James Falconer nodded, then smiled at her. 'From your mouth to God's ears, Rossi.'

Together Rossi and James edged through the chairs, walking over to the other side of the room to speak to the manager and auctioneer.

Frank Thomas, the manager, knew Rossi, and hurried over to greet her and meet Falconer. Once introductions were finished, he took them to meet Aubrey Andrews – according to Rossi, the greatest auctioneer in England.

Aubrey was a man of great charm, particularly when he was up at the podium. Falconer noted his clear, polished voice, and knew very quickly that they were in good hands.

'I'm looking forward to selling your beautiful jewels,' Andrews said to Falconer. 'A unique collection. I understand you bought it all, sir. You have great taste.'

'Thank you, Andrews,' James answered, liking this man. 'I know you will do an excellent job.'

FIFTY-FIVE

rank Thomas led Rossi and James to the front row, where
large cards marked *Reserved* had been placed. They sat
down. Thomas left, assuring them he would personally
accompany their guests to their seats.

Within half an hour, Peter and Irina Keller arrived with
Annabel, who immediately went to James, her eyes sparkling
and his ring on her finger. He kissed her cheek and indicated
her seat next to him. Falconer's brother Eddie soon joined them
with his wife Christina. They were followed by William and
Natalie Venables, with James's daughter Leonie.

Turning to Annabel, Falconer was rendered speechless for a
moment. She had never looked more beautiful to him. Her auburn
hair, parted down the middle, fell in waves around her face, and
her eyes were greener than ever. Perhaps because of the emerald
necklace he had given her.

She wore cream again, a colour that emphasized her creamy
complexion. The dress had a square collar, edged with lace, a
dropped hem and long sleeves. The emerald necklace was very
visible around her slender neck.

'You're staring at me,' she whispered, gazing at Falconer, her eyes dancing.

'Only because you look positively gorgeous. I love you in these cream outfits, my lady.'

'Why thank you, kind sir.' She slipped her arm through his and drew close. 'I missed you all night. Wished you were in bed next to me,' she whispered.

'I know what you mean. But we'll be together later,' he replied, keeping his voice low.

The room had quickly filled up. Not one chair was empty. The doors had been closed and locked.

Aubrey Andrews was up on the platform in front of the podium with an assistant on each side of him. One would hand him a piece of jewellery, which he would hold up and describe. Then he would give it to the assistant on his right, who would place it back in its box. Great care was taken to keep the valuable jewels safe. Bonhams was responsible for them and was very aware of that.

Everyone seated had a catalogue and a paddle, which was raised when a bid was made. Falconer was glancing at the catalogue, which he had approved the other day, when the auction suddenly began, surprising him.

Aubrey Andrews had a cultured, mellifluous voice, which he raised to announce the first piece. It was a diamond and ruby necklace that resembled a lace bib.

'Burmese rubies, very rare, interspersed with flawless diamonds. Handmade, a bib in its design.' He went on describing it, then announced, 'I will now take the first bid, not below twenty thousand pounds.'

Startled at the high price, Falconer now sat very still. Annabel took hold of his hand tightly, understanding how important this auction was for the future of his company.

Paddles were going up rapidly. Competing bidders raising the price until someone outbid everyone else, and the hammer came down. Aubrey Andrews announced, 'Sold to the last bidder!'

It went on like this for an hour. Pieces were shown, described and sold, all at exceptional prices. Necklaces, ear clips, brooches, bracelets, rings, coronets, and a collection of beautiful pearl necklaces. Diamonds, rubies, sapphires – every gemstone under the sun on view.

Paddles up. Hammer down.

All sold within two hours.

Falconer felt slightly befuddled. Looking at Keller, who sat on the other side of him, he said, 'It went so fast. I could hardly keep up.'

'I know what you mean. But it's been a sensational success, old chap. You've made a lot of money.'

Falconer nodded, flooded with relief. 'I'm glad.' He closed his eyes briefly. 'Malvern's is safe for Leonie and my heirs.' He stood up when Leonie walked over, smiling broadly.

'Congratulations, Father,' she said.

He pulled his daughter into his arms. 'Thank you, darling. Will you join us for supper? At the Bettrage.'

'I'd love to, Father. Thank you.'

'See you there, darling. Better still, you must come with me in my car.'

James Falconer, Lady Annabel and Leonie were the first to arrive at the Bettrage Hotel.

It was far too early for dinner as far as Falconer was concerned. After speaking to the maître d' of the Grill Room and changing the number of his party to eleven, he ordered champagne and canapés to be sent up to his private suite, as well as three waiters to serve his guests.

It was there that everyone assembled, following on from the auction house. Within fifteen minutes, Falconer's immediate family and friends were present. He cared about his family and his friends, loved to be in the middle of his clan. They gave him comfort, as did Lady Annabel, who had been so supportive.

Once everyone had a glass of champagne and was settled down, enjoying themselves and talking about the fantastic auction, Falconer drew Annabel to one side.

'Thank you for coming,' he said softly. 'Could you stay on a bit after supper? Or would it be too late?'

She pursed her lips and nodded. 'I think it might be.'

When she noticed the flicker of disappointment in his vivid blue eyes, she swallowed hard, and said, 'But perhaps not. I do want to be with you, James. We can be quick.'

James couldn't help laughing. Annabel was one of the cleverest women he had ever known. An art expert with great talent, intelligent, and beautiful. Modern and irreverent and full of *joie de vivre*. Yet there was a kind of innocence about her at times, as if she were a young girl, inexperienced, unworldly.

'Don't laugh at me,' she murmured, her face clouding up.

'I'm not,' he protested. 'I'm laughing at us. We'd better get married as soon as possible, sweetheart. It breaks my heart that we're not together all the time.'

'Have you ever had your heart *really* broken, Falconer?' she asked. 'At some time in your life?'

He frowned, thought it was a strange question. After a moment, he said, 'Yes, I have.' As always he was being truthful. He knew no other way to be.

'It's painful, isn't it?' she murmured, her eyes still on him.

'Yes. When Alexis died—' He broke off, adding in a low voice, 'I don't want to talk about it, Annabel.'

'I understand,' she said, and put her hand on his arm. 'You know what I think, Falconer. You have to break a heart and have your heart broken before you can really appreciate love. Don't you agree?'

'I do indeed. But you and I are not going to break each other's hearts. We're going to be happy together. We are perfect for each other.'

'I know. My brother is putting the announcement in *The Times* next week. Is that all right with you?'

He smiled at her and led her down the room so that they stood alone near the window. 'Of course it is. You can do anything you want.'

'To a certain extent. I'll never do anything to upset you or hurt you. I'll always have your back.'

'I know *that*, my Annabel. I know you through and through. And I will always have yours.'

Leaning closer to him, she said, 'Put your hand on my belly, please.'

Startled though he was, he did so, looking into her deep green eyes, noticing at once that tears were welling. 'Are you all right?'

'Yes, I am. But there's part of *you* inside *me* now, and I love knowing that, knowing that we are creating a child. I love you so much. My life wouldn't be worth living without you.'

'Please don't be sad. I'm never going to leave you, sweetheart. I love you too, with all my heart and soul.'

She put her glass down and then took his and put it on the same table.

'What are you doing?' he asked.

'I am going to kiss you and go for a glass of water.'

'I'll get it for you, Annabel.'

'No, no. I don't want you to move. Just stand here, waiting for me, so that I can see you when I walk back, knowing that I belong to you and you belong to me. For ever.'

'I won't move,' he said, unable to keep the smile off his face.

She kissed him on his mouth, clinging to him tightly, and then she walked away.

He watched her go and watched her coming back to him. He knew she was the most beautiful woman in the room. She was his for the rest of his life. What a life it was going to be. She was carrying his child, and she loved him passionately, as he did her.

For a split second, the past rushed through his mind. The pain, the grief, the losses, the failures. And the successes, the achievements, the good stuff, too. His life in a fast flash.

What a lucky blighter he was. And oh, the wonder of it all.

ACKNOWLEDGEMENTS

I want to thank my long-time editor Lynne Drew, publisher of general fiction at HarperCollins UK. Lynne is a wonderful sounding board for me and devotes much thought to my books. Editor Lucy Stewart is also invaluable in helping me to sort out many details. Head of publicity Elizabeth Dawson is a gem when it comes to getting my books out to the public and I am grateful to Liz for accompanying me on many trips on the road. We always manage to have lots of laughs and fun which makes the work so easy. Lucy Vanderbilt does a great job selling foreign rights so that my books are sold all over the world.

In the US I am published by St. Martin's Press. Jennifer Enderlin, president and publisher of the company, does a splendid job promoting and selling my work throughout America. She is a special sounding board like Lynne and comes up with lots of suggestions and ideas that add extra dynamics. Altogether I have two very special teams at my disposal which I appreciate very much.

Finally, but by no means least, I must give very special thanks to Linda Sullivan. For years, Linda has typed my manuscripts, and sometimes has also pointed out an error or made suggestions. I am appreciative of this dedication she shows. And my editors, like me, love her beautifully typed manuscripts.

Barbara Taylor Bradford is proud to support the National Literacy Trust, a charity dedicated to improving literacy across the UK. Barbara is passionate about improving life chances, particularly among women, to ensure everyone reaches their full potential. To find out more, please go to: www.literacytrust.org.uk.